WITHDRAWN

They force-marched Hannah into the asylum side of the building. By now her anger was giving way to fear mingled with disbelief. This couldn't be happening to her, it couldn't!

Another woman met them there and Hannah was taken into a small room, then the two men left.

Matron pulled a bundle of clothing from a shelf. Inmate's clothing. 'Will you take your clothes off yourself, Hannah, or do we have to undress you?'

'I don't understand what I'm doing here or why I should take my clothes off. Please tell me what's happening? I'm sure it's all a dreadful mistake.'

'Your daughter-in-law has committed you to our care as being unrestrained and dangerous. You'll be held here until the doctor decides what is best for you.'

The last of the anger vanished, leaving behind it a cold fear. 'Patty's lying.'

The other woman took a step forward. 'Well, she's out there and you're in here, so if you have any sense left, you'll do as you're told. Take off your clothes and put these on.'

D0685729

WITHDRAWN

Also by Anna Jacobs

Salem Street
High Street
Ridge Hill
Hallam Square
Spinners Lake
Jessie
Like No Other
Lancashire Lass
Lancashire Legacy
Down Weavers Lane
Our Lizzie
Our Polly
Our Eva
Our Mary Ann
A Pennyworth of Sunshine
Twopenny Rainbows

About the author

Anna Jacobs grew up in Lancashire and emigrated to Australia in 1973, but loves to return to England regularly to visit her family and soak up the history. She has two grown-up daughters and now lives with her husband in a spacious waterfront home. Often as she writes, dolphins frolic outside the window of her study. Inside, the house is crammed with thousands of books.

ANNA JACOBS

Threepenny Dreams

HODDER

Copyright © 2004 by Anna Jacobs

First published in Great Britain in 2004 by Hodder and Stoughton
First published in paperback in Great Britain in 2005 by
Hodder and Stoughton
A division of Hodder Headline

The right of Anna Jacobs to be identified as the Author of
the Work has been asserted by her in accordance with the Copyright,
Designs and Patents Act 1988.

10

All rights reserved. No part of this publication may be reproduced,
stored in a retrieval system, or transmitted, in any form or by any
means without the prior written permission of the publisher, nor be
otherwise circulated in any form of binding or cover other than that in
which it is published and without a similar condition being imposed on
the subsequent purchaser.

All characters in this publication are fictitious and any resemblance
to real persons, living or dead, is purely coincidental.

A CIP catalogue record for this title is available
from the British Library

ISBN 978-0-340-82140-4

Typeset in Plantin Light by
Phoenix Typesetting, Auldgirth, Dumfriesshire

Printed and bound in Great Britain by
Clays Ltd, St Ives plc

Hodder Headline's policy is to use papers that are natural, renewable
and recyclable products and made from wood grown in sustainable
forests. The logging and manufacturing processes are expected to
conform to the environmental regulations of the country of origin.

Hodder and Stoughton
A division of Hodder Headline
338 Euston Road
London NW1 3BH

This book is dedicated to my editor, Carolyn Mays, to celebrate ten years of working happily and constructively together.

CHAPTER ONE

Lancashire: July – August 1863

Hannah Firth watched from behind the parlour curtains as her younger son Malachi jolted off down the street on the carrier's cart. She held back a sob only with a huge effort. Australia was so far away and who knew what might go wrong there? He was only nineteen. A man in appearance and more sensible than most – but a boy still in her heart.

Hearing footsteps behind her, she swung round.

'He's gone, then?' Her older son Lemuel stared at her from the doorway.

She nodded, not trusting her voice. She had dreaded this since her husband's death: living in a house which now belonged to her son and his shrew of a wife, being dependent on them for her daily existence, with no one to take her side if there were disagreements – especially with a daughter-in-law like hers.

Patty pushed her husband aside and came into the room, looking round with the proprietorial air which had already begun to irritate Hannah. 'Well, maybe now you'll notice that you have another son, Mother Firth, one who's worth ten times as much as your precious Malachi.'

'I love both my sons,' Hannah said, keeping her voice

steady only with a huge effort, 'but I can surely be allowed to grieve for the one I've lost.'

Lemuel moved across to pat her awkwardly on the shoulder, a tall young man of twenty-three already well on the way to being as heavy as his father. She'd been eighteen when she'd borne him, a child herself still in many ways with only strangers to help her through this terrifying and painful experience. Her husband had been forty-two, the same age as she was now. Strange that he had seemed so old then when she still felt young.

John had been a steady, dependable man and Lemuel was just the same. He would run the cooperage exactly as his father had. They were both dull, so very dull, with minds that ticked along slowly and an old-fashioned approach to life. She wished, as she had many times, that her parents hadn't pushed her into marriage at seventeen with a man so much older than herself. John had been kind enough, treating her more like a pet than a wife at first, but always expecting her life to revolve round his needs as master of the house.

'I'd better go and open up the workshop. Those barrels won't make themselves.'

She watched Lemuel leave. He didn't look back, his mind already set on the day's tasks.

'Well, no use moping, Mother Firth,' Patty said briskly. 'We have plenty to do. First I want you to clear up the kitchen while I feed little John, then we'll think about today's meals. And, of course, there's Malachi's room to clear out. It'll make a fine nursery.'

'I'll do that,' Hannah said quickly.

'No, I'll do it later. I want to rearrange the furniture.'

Patty looked at her challengingly, as if she would relish an argument, so Hannah bit her tongue and got on with clearing up the kitchen. She paused for a moment to stare round before she started work. It was only two days since her son and his wife had moved in and already Patty had set her mark on what had been Hannah's domain for over twenty years, rearranging everything, whether it needed it or not.

Why could her husband not have left her some money of her own, just a little, so that she could have rented a cottage and lived in peace? She wasn't greedy, wouldn't have needed much, but all she had now was what she'd saved over the years from the housekeeping money, and she'd dipped deeply into that to help Malachi buy some trading goods to take with him to Australia.

She sighed and closed her eyes for a moment. Perhaps she should have kept more of the money for herself, but she'd wanted him to get a good start. He'd had such dreams of making a new life for himself in a land full of sunshine. She smiled at the thought. The two of them had a name for big, important dreams like that: threepenny dreams. She and Malachi were alike in so many ways, interested in the wider world, needing to feed their brains as well as their bodies.

Who would she share her dreams with now? It suddenly occurred to her that she had none left for herself anyway, not even a halfpenny one. She still felt numb, because John's death had been so unexpected. As she looked out of the window at the grey skies she shivered, though it was warm enough in the kitchen. No wonder Malachi hankered for sunshine. It seemed to have been raining for weeks, even though it was high summer.

She sighed as she began to gather the dirty dishes together. How was she to face years of being subservient to Patty? Other women coped with this situation when they were widowed, but . . . she froze as she realised suddenly that *she* simply couldn't endure it. Those other women didn't have Patty for a daughter-in-law.

She'd have to work out what to do instead. She would put up with things for a while until she saw her way clear to making a new life for herself. After all, she was young for her years, still strong and energetic like all the women of her family. There were only a few grey threads in her dark hair and she was as slender as any girl in the village. Surely she would have no difficulty in finding employment?

Another thought slipped into Hannah's mind unbidden: or even a new husband. No, she was too old for that. And she could never marry for mere convenience, not again.

A wry smile twisted her face. Getting away from Patty was only a penny dream, because there was no joy in it, but it'd do for a start. Taking a deep breath, Hannah carried hot water through to the scullery and poured it into the tin bowl in the slopstone, tossing in some soda crystals.

When Patty didn't join her, she guessed that her daughter-in-law was delaying, waiting for her to finish. Patty was lazy about housework. Hannah had suspected it for years but it hadn't mattered when the other woman lived in her own house. It would matter now, though, if her daughter-in-law tried to treat her as an unpaid servant.

She'd have to find a way to escape or she'd go mad.

The following day was fine and when Patty started complaining and scolding, Hannah suddenly couldn't stand it a minute longer. She was still grieving for Malachi, still trying to get used to her new status. Holding her head high, she walked into the kitchen, slipped her old shawl off the hook by the door and went out through the rear garden. Ignoring the shrieks of 'Where are you going?' then 'Come back at once!' from behind her, she walked past the cooper's workshop where her son was moving about purposefully and left by the back gate.

Following the narrow laneway behind it, Hannah slowed down as she passed the last building in the village: the workhouse built for the six neighbouring parishes on a patch of sour land. It was an ugly place, widely detested by those living hereabouts, and Hannah remembered when she was a girl how strong resistance had been in the area to complying with the new Poor Law Act, and how it had taken nearly ten years for the Assistant Commissioners appointed by London to bring her own Hetton-le-Hill and the nearby parishes into line with the law.

As she walked past the high stone wall, topped by broken glass, she shivered. It was such a dreary, hopeless place, looked unwelcoming and was, apparently, even worse inside. It housed not only paupers but idiots, lunatics and unmarried mothers, the least fortunate of the six parishes. And everyone knew how strictly its inmates were treated.

'Poor souls!' she muttered, as she always did when she passed this place. Things were even worse there now since the new parson had become Chairman of the Board of Guardians. She didn't like Parson Barnish, who seemed to her to act scornfully towards his poorer parishioners.

As she strode up towards the moors that overlooked her village, she took deep breaths of the clean air, enjoying the wind and the shifting shadows of the clouds rolling across the tops. Her thoughts were not so pleasant. She'd known it would be difficult to live with her daughter-in-law, but already it was proving far harder than she'd expected. To be ordered around like a half-witted drudge outraged her – and was in no way necessary because she had always prided herself on being a good housekeeper, and indeed, was more used to being asked for advice than told what to do.

Breathless, she stopped at an outcrop of rocks and sank down, brushing the tears away from her eyes with her fingertips. What good did it do to weep? She'd learned that when first married. She leaned back, closing her eyes, enjoying the quiet sounds of nature. The breeze whispered around her and somewhere above a bird was calling, its voice full of fluting silver joy. Sunlight warmed her face intermittently as clouds shaded then revealed the sun. Relaxing, she let herself drift into a doze.

'You all right, missus?'

'What? Oh!' She jerked awake to find a man staring down at her anxiously, one of the local shepherds whom she knew by sight. 'Yes, I'm fine. Just tired.'

'It'll be coming on to rain soon. You'd better get yoursen home, Mrs Firth.'

She tried desperately to remember his name.

He smiled as if he could read her thoughts. 'I'm Tad Mosely. I've dealt with your husband a time or two. Do you need a hand to get up?'

She shook her head. 'No, thank you, Tad. I'll just sit here a little longer, then I'll go back.'

'Don't leave it too long. Look at them rain clouds gathering.' He hesitated then added, 'I'm sorry about your husband. He were a decent fellow. You're allus welcome to stop off at our hut if you're out walking on the tops. We can usually find a cup of tea for a friend.' He waved in the direction of a small grey-stone building higher up the moor, a shepherd's shelter, gave her a nod of farewell then whistled to his dogs and strode off.

She pulled the shawl more tightly around her shoulders, shivering in the cold, moist air as more clouds gathered in the sky, dark ones this time.

Not until rain began falling did she start back, not caring whether she got soaked or not, her steps slow and reluctant.

Life could be cruel. This was the second time fate had been unkind to her. She had remembered the first every time she'd looked at Malachi whose face was so like his father's – and so unlike her husband's.

That night in bed Patty said, 'I'm worried about your mother, Lemuel. She's getting very vague. And she stayed out today even though she must have seen it was going to rain. She was absolutely soaked when she got

back. Why did she want to go walking on the moors
anyway? I need her help here. She forgets how much
extra work a baby makes.'

He let the words flow past him, as he'd learned to do.
He wished she didn't always see the worst in people,
wished she'd be kinder to his mother. But if he said that,
it'd only make her worse.

When she stopped talking he reached for her. They'd
agreed to try for another baby. Well, he'd said he
wanted more children and she'd said she'd have one
more and then see how things went. She put up with his
fumblings, so that he finished feeling slightly ashamed,
as usual, but at least he'd got his relief.

In the village of Marton, on the other side of Preston,
Nathaniel King looked up at the sky. Past noon. Time
to go back to the house and get his wife something to
eat. Not that she'd eat much. She had little appetite
these days and was almost skeletal in appearance. Poor
Sarah had never been strong, but now the doctor said
her heart was failing and the end couldn't be far away.

Inside the small stone farmhouse he went into the
room which served as both kitchen and parlour,
because they rarely used the small, chilly front room on
the north side of the house. He found Sarah lying on the
daybed gazing dreamily out of the window. She didn't
notice him come in and when he laid one hand on her
arm, she jumped in shock.

'Time for dinner, love. I'll just wash my hands.'

'I don't want anything, Nathaniel.'

'You have to eat, Sarah.'

'Why?'

'You can't just – give up.'

'I can. I have. I've been thinking about it all week and if I don't want to eat, I shan't from now on. Please don't try to make me because I won't do it, even for you.'

'But, Sarah, love . . .'

'Nathaniel, I'm just a burden to you, and as for poor Gregory – well, a lad of ten shouldn't have to watch his mother die inch by inch, should he? And I'm finding life – difficult. So the quicker I can go the better.'

'Oh, Sarah.' He sat down beside her and took her hand in his. Once they had been very much in love but after several years of her being ill, that bright feeling had faded to a mere fondness on his part and he didn't know what on hers. She had an air of otherworldliness now, as if she were not really part of this life, as if she were seeing things no one else could. And she was right: Gregory was suffering. Watching his mother die was bound to upset a lad. How long was it since Nathaniel had heard his son laugh?

'How are the strawberries coming on?' she asked after a while.

'Well enough. I shall have another load to send to market by the end of the week.'

She nodded and her gaze slid back to the view from the window: neat rows of vegetables and a border of flowers close to the house, which her husband had planted specially because he knew how much she loved them.

Nathaniel stood for a minute surveying his small kingdom, as he liked to call it, making a play on his surname. He'd never thought to become a market gardener, having grown up on what he still thought of as a 'proper farm'. But his father had died when he was only sixteen, so he'd lost the chance to carry on the lease. He and his mother had moved to Preston for a while, but he'd hated living in a town so he'd worked hard, saved his pennies and found a way to return to the country after his mother died.

Growing vegetables and fruit paid quite well nowadays because here in Marton they were within easy reach of industrial Preston. There seemed to be an insatiable demand for food in the expanding textile centres of Lancashire, plus a ready supply of fertiliser coming back to the country from the dairy animals which were still kept in the town so that the richer folk could have fresh milk. He himself thought it a shame to keep the poor cows penned up all the time and would never keep a living creature away from the sunlight like that.

But even though he brought in good money, at the moment most of it went to pay for help with the household tasks like washing and care of his wife, so he never managed to get much ahead or afford the improvements he yearned to make, the things he read about in newspapers or heard spoken of on his occasional visits to Preston. And even if he did propose such improvements, he wasn't sure his landlord would let him change anything.

Richard Dewhurst was a decent man, who had made a fortune in cotton and then married a lady-wife and bought the estate which included Marton Hall, but he hadn't spent a lot of time there. His wife had only given him two sons and had died years before, after which the nanny had brought up the younger boy and the older son had run wild. Nathaniel had heard recently that Dewhurst had come home to stay this time. Well, he was nearing seventy, time to leave others to manage his cotton mills surely? He'd recently been appointed a local magistrate, but it remained to be seen how well he'd fulfil that role.

The two sons lived permanently at Marton Hall. Walter, the elder, had only grown nastier as he grew into manhood and like the other tenants, Nathaniel avoided him as much as possible. Apart from making a nuisance of himself with young women, whether they were willing or not, he'd recently developed one of his sudden passions – this time for hunting what he called 'ground game'. This entailed barging through people's fences and crops to kill rabbits, hares and the very occasional fox, leaving a trail of destruction behind him. People hadn't dared complain to the father, sure it'd only bring more trouble down on them, because Walter was known for getting his own back on those who'd offended him. And after all, the land agent always paid compensation for the damage, didn't he?

Nathaniel wasn't sure he could stand by and let Walter Dewhurst damage his land and crops, but luckily the fellow had never come near his smallholding.

The younger Dewhurst son, Oliver, was as unlike his brother as a primrose to a pig. He had been ill a lot when younger and you could see the lines of suffering on his face, though he had grown into quite a good-looking fellow and seemed in much better health nowadays. Pity *he* wouldn't be the one to inherit because he had a kindly nature, sending help to folk in trouble and speaking to the tenants politely.

After another futile attempt to persuade Sarah to eat something Nathaniel spent the afternoon digging and watching old Tom Ringley exhaust himself trying to weed the strawberries. He made no comment on this. Tom was past working, really, with little strength left in him, but all he asked was a bed in the barn, food for his bent old body and the odd screw of tobacco, so Nathaniel continued to employ him. Like many old people, Tom's main concern was not to be put in the poorhouse.

Well, you were a poor sort if you couldn't offer that much, at least, to a man who had taught you how to grow fruit and vegetables, a man who'd once been as tall and strong as Nathaniel himself and who had shared his knowledge so generously all those years ago. And there were times, even now, when Tom Ringley knew the answer to a problem or how to deal with a pest that was attacking a crop when no one else did. Nathaniel loved to see the old fellow's delight when this happened.

Hannah found that it grew harder, not easier, living with Patty. Her daughter-in-law was openly hostile when no one was around, snapping orders and doing as little as possible herself because she said the baby took up her time. But John was the quietest baby Hannah had ever seen and little trouble to anyone.

One day she went into her bedroom to fetch a clean handkerchief and found Patty there, going through her top drawer.

'What are you doing?'

Patty turned to stare at her, not seeming in the least embarrassed to be caught ferreting through someone else's things. 'Seeing what you've got. I like to know everything that goes on in my own house.'

Hannah watched her saunter out then sank down on the bed, shocked to her core to think of someone doing such a thing.

She waited until they were all eating their evening meal that night before saying quietly but clearly, 'If I'm not to have the privacy of my own room, then I'm not staying here.'

There was a pregnant silence. Patty threw her an angry glance. Lemuel looked from one woman to the other then said quietly, 'Of course that room is your own, Mam, yours to do with as you wish. How do you lack privacy?'

'I caught your wife going through my drawers.'

He turned to stare in shock at Patty, who sniffed and repeated, 'I have a right to know what goes on in my own house.'

'Nay, love, that's a bit much. I'd never think of going through my mother's things and you shouldn't neither.'

She stared at him through narrowed eyes, shoved her chair back and jumped to her feet, shouting in a shrill voice, 'Either this is my house or it's not! Make up your mind, Lemuel! But if it's not, then don't expect me to do a hand's turn here.' Then she burst into tears and stormed upstairs to their bedroom.

He got to his feet, looking unhappily at his mother. 'I know she's being unreasonable, but I don't want to upset her at the moment. We're trying for another baby and, well, you know what it's like.'

He followed his wife upstairs and angry voices floated down. Hannah tried not to listen, but was shocked at the way Patty berated her husband, shocked too at the things her daughter-in-law said about her, hinting that she was trying to evade her share of household duties and growing absent-minded.

When Lemuel came down again, he avoided his mother's eyes and went on with his now cold meal.

'It'll get better,' he offered as he went across to sit in the big armchair by the fire. 'We'll all shake down together if we give it a chance.'

Automatically Hannah started clearing up the tea things and getting ready to wash the dishes. 'She still has no right to go through my things.'

He sighed. 'I doubt you'll stop her. She allus has to *know*. It's how she's made. You'll get used to it. After all, you've got nothing to hide, have you, so it doesn't really matter.'

Hannah went to bed early that night, as she usually did now, trying to read one of her few treasured books by the light of a single candle, but putting it down with a sigh when the words refused to register. If she hadn't come into the room just then, Patty would have found her savings and no doubt tried to claim them for the family's use. Hannah would take the money round to her friend Louisa's the very next day and leave it there for safety. They'd known one another since they were girls and she trusted her friend completely.

She blew out the candle and slid down in bed, but her mind wouldn't be still. She couldn't continue like this, would have to find a job to take her away from here. She'd ask in the village, see if anyone knew of a housekeeping job going, and she wouldn't say anything to Lemuel until she'd found herself something.

*   *   *

The following day Patty was even more waspish than usual, banging pots around, snapping out orders, criticising anything and everything.

After they'd cleared up the midday meal, Hannah took off her apron. 'I'm going out for a while.'

'I need you here, Mother Firth.'

'Then you'll have to do without me. I'm not a slave, Patty, not to anyone, and I work hard enough to deserve the odd hour or two off.'

'You should be glad to repay us for all we spend on you.'

'And you should remember that I'm not and never shall be your servant.' She took her good shawl from her bedroom, put on her bonnet and came out again with her savings in her pocket, certain that Patty would finish going through her things once she was out.

'Where are you going?'

'That's my business.' She blinked in shock as her daughter-in-law thrust herself in front of the door.

'I *will* know what you're doing. I'm mistress of this house and—'

Taller and stronger, Hannah set her aside quite easily and opened the door, holding it against the hand that tried to shut it in her face.

'You'll be sorry for this!' Patty panted. 'He listens to *me* not you now. You have to learn your place in my house and not try to boss me around.'

Hannah bit back hasty words about who was trying to boss whom and strode out, heading towards the south end of the village. At the corner she glanced back and saw her daughter-in-law standing at the gate, watching her to see where she went. In a spirit of sheer devilment she walked right to the other end of the main street, then turned up the lane that led to the moors, but doubled back once she was out of sight to take the rear pathway to her friend Louisa's house. When she got there, she rapped on the kitchen window, sure enough of her welcome to slip through the door without waiting to be invited inside.

'Hannah, love. Eh! I thought you'd forgotten us.' Louisa studied her friend's face. 'What's wrong?'

'I'm finding things – difficult at home. Today I just had to get away for a while.'

Louisa snorted. 'You mean you're finding Patty difficult to live with. I told you not even to think of staying there with them.'

'I didn't want to upset Lemuel, but you were right. I should have found myself a job straight off.' Louisa had offered her a temporary home, but it had gone against the grain with Hannah to accept what felt like charity, even from her best friend.

Louisa bustled around, brewing a pot of tea and sitting across from her at the table to drink it. 'That Patty's just like her mother: takes umbrage if you speak and gets annoyed if you stay silent. You can never please folk like that. Mind you, I shouldn't speak ill of poor Susan Riggs. They say she's getting more forgetful every day.' She tapped one finger to her forehead. 'I hope I never lose my senses, I do indeed. It can be difficult for the family.'

'Patty hasn't said anything about her mother having problems.' But then, Patty rarely spoke about her family.

'Well, she wouldn't, would she? The whole family's trying to pretend it's not happening. They'll end up having to put Susan in the asylum, though, you mark my words. Softening of the brain, they call it. I've seen it afore. Some folk manage to look after them at home, but that sister of Patty's is getting wed soon an' she'll be leaving the district so what's to happen to Susan then?'

'That sort of thing makes my own troubles seem less important.'

Louisa shook her head. 'I don't think so. You look fair worn down and it takes a lot to get you in that state, my lass. The question is, what are you going to do about it?'

'Well, first I'm going to ask you to look after my savings. She's started going through my drawers now and I'm sure she'd try to take the money if she found it.' Hannah blinked away a tear of shame at this admission.

'Oh, love, surely even she wouldn't do that?'

Hannah had to swallow hard and dig her fingernails into her hands to prevent herself from weeping. There was nothing like a bit of sympathy for making you lose control of yourself. She fumbled in her pocket and held out the worn purse, trying to make a joke of it. 'Here it is: all my worldly wealth.'

Louisa took the purse. 'I'll put it in my bottom drawer and only George will know it's there. He won't say a word, you can be sure.' She reached out to clasp her friend's hand for a moment. 'What else?'

'I was wondering if you knew of anyone looking for a housekeeper. You have such a lot of relatives and you're always first with any news.'

'Good idea. Anyone would be lucky to get you. I'll ask around.'

'Do it quietly. I don't want to upset *her* before I have to.'

Three days later, Patty came home from visiting a friend and stormed into her husband's workshop, cheeks flaring red. 'Do you know what your mother is doing? Shaming us, that's what. I've never been so embarrassed in my whole life as I was this afternoon when I found out.'

He blinked at her in shock, put down the long knife he was using to hollow out the barrel staves and jerked his head to the lad he'd taken on as an apprentice in a silent command to make himself scarce. 'What are you talking about, love? My mother would never do anything to shame us. Eh, you've got a right down on her lately.'

'That's because you never really know someone until you have to live with them,' she said ominously, scowling at him.

When he put his arm round her shoulders, she shook it off and began to pace up and down.

'Tell me, then.'

'Your mother's looking for a job as a housekeeper and if that's not shaming us, I don't know what is.'

Lemuel stared at her in dismay. 'She'd never do that. This is her home.'

'Come and ask her then.'

'I'll see her tonight.'

'You'll see her now! This needs sorting out. And I warn you, I'm *not* having it!'

Sighing, he followed his wife into the house, wishing she were just a bit less sharp with the world.

Patty burst into the kitchen, finding Hannah with little John on her knee, the two of them laughing at one another. She snatched her baby from his grandmother's arms, holding him so tightly he began to cry, and said dramatically, 'Go on! Ask her, Lemuel!'

Hannah stared in shock from one to the other, her heart sinking at the expression on the younger woman's face. 'What's wrong?'

Lemuel cleared his throat. 'Patty's heard – I'm sure it's not true, Mam – but she's heard that you're looking for a job as a housekeeper.'

Hannah sighed as she looked at her earnest, rather sheep-like son. She'd rather have presented them with a *fait accompli*. 'It is true.'

His face crumpled. 'But Mam, why? You have a home here, you know you do. There's no *need* for you to seek employment. Tell her, Patty!'

'No need at all, Mother Firth. I'm upset you'd even think of leaving . . . shaming us in front of our neighbours like that!'

Hannah tried for diplomacy. 'I think it's better for a young couple to be together, without other relatives, especially if you're trying for another baby.'

'But Mam—'

She held up one hand and Lemuel fell silent. 'And there's my side to consider. I think I'd like to do something –' she hesitated, searching for a phrase that wouldn't give offence, but not finding one '– more interesting with my life than stay here in the back room until I die. I don't feel old, Lemuel. I don't feel old at all.'

Patty burst into loud tears and cast herself and her son into her husband's arms. 'I shall die of shame.'

He looked at his mother severely across the tops of their heads. 'I won't have it, Mam! Patty's right. It *is* shaming for you to do such a thing.'

She sighed, realising she had to say it bluntly. 'Lemuel, Patty has her own way of doing things and I find I don't take to being ordered around. It'll be better for us all if I leave before we start quarrelling. Besides, I shall *enjoy* doing something different. You know I've always wanted to travel a bit.'

'Housekeepers don't travel!' Patty said scornfully. 'They stay at home – and in someone else's home, too – and do just the same sorts of things as you do here.'

'But they get paid for their labours and are treated with respect. No one goes through their drawers, as you've been doing again.'

Patty gasped and turned bright red. 'You see what I have to put up with, how she talks to me? She's setting people against me, I know she is. How shall I ever hold my head up in the village again?'

Lemuel looked at Hannah with the eyes of a puppy which had been kicked. 'I'm not having it, Mam. I'm not having you upsetting Patty and I'm not having you going to work for strangers. You have a home here and you'll stay in it.'

'How will you prevent me from leaving if I choose to do so?' Hannah asked quietly, then spun round and went into her bedroom, slamming the door behind her because she didn't want to make matters worse by speaking out about exactly why she was leaving.

As she leaned against it, she prayed she would find a

job quickly. The quicker the better. Otherwise she might have to take up Louisa's offer of a bed, even at the cost of offending her son.

When Lemuel had gone back to the workshop, Patty sat down, her expression thoughtful. If her mother-in-law left, all the work would fall on her shoulders, and why should it, when she had someone else to share the burden?

'How will you prevent me?' Mother Firth had asked.

Well, there had to be a way, there just had to. Patty usually did get what she wanted if she bent her mind to it.

CHAPTER TWO

Late August 1863

Nathaniel watched Walter Dewhurst and his two cronies rampage across a nearby field of oats, already too drunk to hit the rabbits they were there to shoot, though it was only mid-afternoon. Their horses looked tired and lathered, and there was much use of riding crops on the poor creatures.

He sometimes thought it was the destruction this notorious trio enjoyed most, especially when he saw the expression on Walter's face as he trampled down the neat rows of oats. Nathaniel only hoped he'd be able to find another piece of land to lease before this bully inherited this estate.

The trio hadn't entered Nathaniel's smallholding yet, but he had no doubt they would one day. They'd not find him opening the gate for them, though, or even pretending to smile at what they were doing. Every man has his sticking point.

In fact, his was reached a few days later. He heard some dogs barking furiously, saw something tawny running down the lane, and realised with a sinking feeling that they were enjoying the rare treat of chasing a fox. Like the nearby farmers Nathaniel took care to dispose of foxes quietly whenever he could, because he wanted to give Walter Dewhurst no excuse for coming on to his land.

What were these fools playing at anyway? This part of Lancashire wasn't good hunting territory, nor did they have a pack of hounds, let alone the approval of the true gentry who controlled the hunting in the county. To his mind, these sons of prosperous cotton masters were just pretending to be gentry – and they were fooling no one.

When the fox, thin and limping, slipped through the bars of his gate, Nathaniel groaned, wishing it had gone anywhere else. The poor creature was panting and in distress. It was vermin, he agreed it should be got rid of, but why kill it in such a cruel way?

Before he could turn and go indoors, Walter rode along the lane and yelled, 'Open up, King! I saw the fox go through your place.'

'Sorry, sir, I've got a dying wife here and I'd prefer to keep things quiet.'

'Damn you, do as you're told!'

But Nathaniel couldn't. He just couldn't do it. A chill settled in his stomach to think of poor gentle Sarah witnessing a bloody killing or these brutes rampaging across their few precious acres at such an important growing season.

With a curse, Dewhurst leaned from his horse to fumble with the gate catch while his two companions yelled and harooed behind him.

The stupid fools would have frightened away the fox by now, Nathaniel was sure, but even as he took a step forward to protect his property, Tom came up behind him and grasped his arm, shaking it urgently.

'Don't do it, lad! They'll claim you attacked them and haul you before the magistrate, like they did to Bill Dooney, then you'll lose this holding.'

So Nathaniel stood rigid and grim-faced as three half-drunk young wastrels galloped up and down his precious rows of plants, destroying them underfoot and slashing at the fruit bushes with their riding crops for no reason he could see. But from the way Walter looked at him before doing it all over again, he knew they were enjoying upsetting him. It seemed a long time before they galloped off down the lane again.

'Send the bill to Pa!' his landlord's son yelled as he left the gate swinging open behind him.

Only then did Nathaniel let out a long groaning breath.

'Eh, the wicked waste of it!' Tom muttered. 'They should be took out and hanged, that they should.'

'Let's start counting the cost,' Nathaniel said in a voice which sounded to have been forced through rusty wire. 'I intend to make sure old Mr Dewhurst pays for every pennyworth of damage.'

'Perhaps you'd better go and take a look at your missus first,' Tom suggested. 'She can't help but have seen what they were doing an' she'll be upset about it. There's not one of her flowers left standing, not a single one. You're not telling me they didn't do that on purpose.'

Nathaniel found Sarah stretched out on the floor, as if she'd risen from her couch and tried to get to the door.

She was dead, still warm but with that waxy look on her face. She must have seen what was happening, which meant her last few minutes on earth had been filled with anguish. Kneeling beside her, Nathaniel suddenly found himself weeping, great racking sobs that seemed to tear him apart, weeping for both his wife and his crops. It wasn't fair that some men had such power over others, could make their fellow creatures' lives a misery at a whim.

The doctor came, goggled at the waste where formerly there had been a thriving market garden, and examined Sarah's body gently. 'What happened?'

'Walter Dewhurst,' Nathaniel said, not needing to make any further explanation. 'She was killed by the shock of what she saw him doing and you'll not persuade me different.'

'The shock probably did hasten her death.' The doctor sighed as he looked down at the thin face, still wearing an expression of anguish, then turned to lay one hand on Nathaniel's shoulder. 'I wish there was something I could do, but Dewhurst won't listen to reason about his son, says he wants him to behave like gentry.'

'It'd make me feel better to black that young lout's eye for him, that it would,' Nathaniel muttered. And he might have done when he was younger, but he'd learned a bit of sense now.

'They're going way beyond what's right and I shall make sure it's known that the shock of their rampage contributed to your wife's death.' The doctor sighed then said in a quieter tone, 'I'll send Mrs Bostill to lay her out for you.'

The doctor was a kind fellow, Nathaniel thought as he watched him drive away in his shiny new gig. But he doubted Dewhurst would care about what had happened. The old man might be a local magistrate now, but he didn't really understand Marton and the folk who lived here.

When Gregory came home from school he stared in shock at the devastation, then came running inside to stop short at the sight of his father and stare at his mother's empty couch.

'I'm afraid your mother passed away this afternoon, son.'

Gregory stood with clenched fists, not weeping at his mother's death but keeping his pain locked up inside himself, as he'd begun to do. The tight, old man's expression of endurance on his face upset Nathaniel greatly.

'Why did they do it?' the boy kept asking as the evening passed. 'Why did those men destroy our crops, Dad?'

'Because they're selfish brutes with no thought for others.'

'How shall we eat if we've no stuff to sell?'

Nathaniel sighed. 'Old Mr Dewhurst will pay for the damage. But I'd rather have my plants than money.'

A little later his son said quietly, 'We shan't have any flowers to lay on her grave now, shall we?'

'We'll find some, son. Not only to lay there, but to plant. She'd like that.'

Richard Dewhurst frowned down the dinner table and couldn't hold back a growl of anger as he stared at his older son. 'You went beyond what was reasonable yesterday, Walter.'

'Eh?'

'Destroying King's crops like that.'

'A few pounds will soon shut him up.'

'Will it bring his wife back, though?'

'What do you mean?'

'The shock of seeing what you were doing killed her.'

Walter gave a snort of disgust. 'He's lying! The woman's been ill for years. And we found a fox this time. Would have had it, too, if King had opened the gate for us, as I told him to.'

'Why should he open the gate when he knew you'd destroy his crops?' Oliver snapped.

'Because *we* own the land, not him, and he'd better learn his place. If he behaves like that after I inherit, he'll be thrown out within the day, I promise you.'

'Calm down, lad,' Richard said. 'I'll pay for the damages this time, but it has to stop. You keep your hunting to our own land from now on.'

With an inarticulate exclamation, Oliver pushed his chair back, threw his napkin down on the table and left the room. Hunting! What his brother and friends were doing wasn't hunting, it was wilful destruction.

Most of the village turned out for Sarah's funeral two days later, filing into the church, scrubbed and clad in their Sunday best, even the men who worked on the Dewhurst estate taking time off to attend.

Nathaniel sat beside his son at the front, not really taking in the kind words spoken by the vicar about Sarah Jane King because anger was still simmering inside him. When it was time to carry the coffin out, he left Tom to look after Gregory and took his place as one of the leading pallbearers.

The coffin felt so light he could have wept. She'd faded away before his eyes and yet had been so plump and bonny when they'd wed.

It was only as he reached the end of the aisle that he realised Oliver Dewhurst was there, isolated in a rear pew, with everyone avoiding his eyes.

The young man stood up as they passed. 'I'm sorry for what happened, Mr King. Most truly sorry.'

Nathaniel nodded. He had no quarrel with Oliver, who was as kind as his elder brother was brutal.

But what good did saying you were sorry do? Sarah had died in distress, seeing her precious flowers destroyed, and the fact that he was helpless to punish those who'd done that to her continued to rankle sorely with Nathaniel.

That evening Walter came in to dinner looking angry. 'Do you know what happened today?' he demanded, even before he'd sat down.

'What are you talking about?'

'Our workers took time off to attend that King woman's funeral. I hope you're going to dock their pay for that, Father. And to crown it all, my dear brother attended the funeral as well.' He shook out his napkin with a crack of starched linen and glared across the table.

Richard looked at his younger son. 'Is that true?'

'Yes.'

'Why? The woman meant nothing to you, surely?'

'I felt we owed her some mark of respect to make up for how she died.'

'You need a lesson in loyalty,' Walter sneered. 'Your own family comes first.'

'I feel no loyalty to someone who terrorises those weaker than himself, and I never shall.' Oliver threw an angry glance in his brother's direction.

'I've a right to do what I like on our own property,' Walter threw at him.

'Not when tenants are paying a fair rent for the land. They have a right to its undisturbed use.'

'Oh, be done!' Richard commanded. 'I've told you two before about quarrelling. You give me indigestion.' He raised his spoon and took a mouthful of soup, murmuring in appreciation.

Walter ate perhaps half of his, then pushed his bowl away so carelessly he splashed the immaculate white tablecloth. 'So, are you going to dock their pay, Father?'

'Lexham advises not. There's bad feeling about this. Best let it die a natural death, he says.'

'Lexham's an old woman. I don't know why you continue to employ him as your land agent.'

'Because he knows his job. Rent arrears have fallen since he took over. The tenants respect him.'

'The arrears would fall still further if he wasn't so soft with folk.'

Richard scowled at his son. 'One thing I learned when I was making my fortune was to find someone who knew how to do things better than I could, hire him and leave him to it. You'll be no good as an employer until you learn that. I'll have to find some way of teaching you about running an estate.'

'The land agent does that,' Walter snapped. 'You just said to find someone who can do the job and leave him to it.'

'Nonetheless, I shall look into matters.' Richard looked sideways at his younger son. 'I haven't decided yet what to do about your future, Oliver. You're not as sickly as you were, but you're not strong either. Still, you can't live your life in idleness, so we must find you some way of earning a living. Your godmother's legacy isn't enough to keep you in the manner to which you've become accustomed here.' He cast a proud glance round the huge room, with its wood-panelled walls and ornate plasterwork ceiling.

Oliver didn't reply but ate his meal in silence. He kept remembering the packed church and the tall man with the grief-ravaged face walking in with his hand on his son's shoulder. He'd never seen the villagers so united and was relieved they hadn't taken their anger out on him, though there had been a few dark glances thrown his way.

Only another month to go, he told himself as he pushed his plate away, suddenly sickened by this excess of rich food when many people in Lancashire hadn't enough to eat because of the Cotton Famine. In a month's time he would come into his inheritance and have the power – and the money – to start making changes to his life. He didn't need a luxurious lifestyle or a massive house like Marton Hall, just a modest home and a quiet, peaceful life. He'd said nothing to his father yet about his plans, and wouldn't till he turned twenty-one.

There would be hell to pay when they found out what

he intended to do, but he didn't care. He just wanted to get away from Walter. And if his brother ever came and damaged *his* land, he'd prosecute him, brother or not.

In Blackfold village, too small to have a railway line and too far east of Nathaniel's smallholding for him to visit easily, his niece Ginny Doyle went to church with her family, her mother, stepfather and two half-brothers. She couldn't settle during the service because she was too upset by the way her stepfather had shouted at her mother before they left home. He was a cruel man and she hated him. Even when she sat in church the hatred simmered in her – and the fear. Her gentle mother didn't deserve such treatment. None of them did. She sighed and tried in vain to concentrate, but his presence nearby made it impossible.

After the service she walked out of church behind her mother, eyes demurely downcast, hands clasping her prayer book to her chest, praying he wouldn't see the excitement rising in her. As her parents stopped to talk to some neighbours, she slipped across the church-yard to talk to her best friend Lucy Porter.

'Is it all right if Ginny and I go for a walk along by the canal?' Lucy asked her mother. 'Just for a few minutes.'

Mrs Porter smiled at them. 'Bless you, yes. I'll tell your father, Ginny. You can always walk home on your own if they want to leave before you get back.'

'I don't think Mam likes your father,' Lucy said as they walked away, arm in arm. 'She always pulls a face when he's mentioned.'

'He's not my father, he's my step-father!' Ginny

corrected. She never let people call *him* her father if she could help it, but even Lucy forgot sometimes.

Ginny grabbed the other girl's arm as she saw Nick Halstead waiting for them near the canal. 'He's there.'

'I knew he would be. If he wants to walk with you, I'll fall behind.'

'Not out of sight,' Ginny said quickly. It was one thing to risk her step-father's anger, another to make him explode with fury. She'd seen him so enraged a time or two she'd thought he was going to kill someone and the mere memory of it made her shiver. And the way he treated her mother upset her greatly. Her own father had never hit her mother. Indeed the two of them had laughed and had a lot of fun together. Her mother didn't often smile nowadays. Why had she ever married Howard West?

He'd started threatening Ginny too this past year and had slapped her a few times. Hard. She was afraid of him now and her two half-brothers had always been wary of their father, though he didn't hit Edwin and Andrew nearly as often as he did her.

As they reached the canal bank, Nick stepped forward and raised his hat to them. He nodded first to Lucy then his eyes settled on the girl he'd come to meet.

Ginny smiled at him.

'Are you going for a walk, Miss Doyle?'

'Yes. Yes, we are, Mr Halstead.'

'So am I, as it happens. May I join you?'

'That would be – nice.'

As he fell in beside them, Lucy seized the opportunity to nudge her friend and let them move ahead of her.

Ginny hardly noticed, she was so conscious of Nick. He was much taller than she was – did he mind that she was so short? She loved his blue eyes and his soft brown hair which always flopped over his left eye, giving him a boyish look. And not only was he easy to talk to, but he seemed to enjoy chatting to her as much as she did to him.

Time passed so pleasantly she was surprised when Lucy pulled her to a halt and said apologetically, 'I think we'd better be getting back. You know what your step-father's like.'

With a start, Ginny came back to reality. 'Yes. Yes, I suppose so.'

'I'll walk back with you,' Nick offered.

'No, better not,' Lucy said quickly. 'Someone might see us. Her father's very strict.'

'Perhaps I should call on him and ask his permission to take you out walking, Ginny?'

'No! Don't do that. He'd not appreciate the courtesy.' The mere thought of the confrontation that would ensue made Ginny shiver. The less her step-father knew about this friendship the better. He didn't like any of them having friends or doing things outside the home.

'Well, then, I'll say goodbye. Until next week, perhaps?'

Ginny spent the whole of the ten minutes it took to walk back telling her friend how handsome Nick was and how interesting to talk to.

Lucy hid a smile as she listened. The man was well enough looking, but by no stretch of the imagination could he be called handsome, though her friend was a very pretty girl, a little plump but with lovely curly hair of a light brown that was sun-gilded at this time of year. Ginny was lively and fun to be with – except when her step-father was around and then she grew very quiet. She helped on the family farm, always bustling about doing something, a hard worker everyone agreed.

Lucy sighed at the pity of it all. It was silly to keep meeting Nick, really. Mr West was staunchly Church of England and would never allow Ginny to walk out with a young man whose family were Methodists. Never. Even she knew that. Ginny's father had also been a Methodist and Mr West wouldn't even have his name mentioned – though how you could hate someone who had been dead for twelve years just didn't make sense to her.

What worried her most was that the attraction between her friend and Nick glowed as brightly as any star in the night sky whenever they were together – which made it even more dangerous for them to go on meeting. You couldn't keep things secret for long in a small village like Blackfold.

Hannah looked up to see Louisa tapping on the kitchen window in the old way. Smiling, she wiped her hands on her apron and went to greet her friend at the door.

'I have some news,' Louisa whispered.

'Not here.' Hannah looked up to see Patty standing in the doorway, scowling at them. 'I'm just going for a little chat with my friend.'

'It's not very convenient just now, Mother Firth. I want to feed John and you still haven't finished the baking.'

Louisa gaped at her, then looked at Hannah as if to say she couldn't believe what she was hearing.

'Oh, there's nothing that will spoil.' Hannah pushed her friend into her bedroom, shutting the door with a bang. As Louisa opened her mouth to say something, Hannah whispered, 'Shh. Keep your voice down. I'm sure she eavesdrops when she can.'

'I'd never have believed that if I hadn't seen it with my own eyes. Who does she think she is, ordering you around? Does Lemuel know?'

Hannah nodded.

'Oh, my dear. No wonder you want to leave.' Louisa clasped her hand for a moment, then remembered her news. 'I've heard of a job as a housekeeper. Relatives of the Cowpers. They live in Blackburn. I told the Cowpers about you. Was that all right?'

'Oh, Louisa, thank you so much.'

'They're coming over here to visit at the weekend so you can meet them then.'

Hannah had to take two or three calming breaths before she could speak, and even so she couldn't keep the tears from her eyes. 'I do hope they like me.'

'Of course they will.'

In their excitement both women forgot to keep their voices low and the listener on the other side of the door heard enough to find out what was going on.

When she realised Louisa getting ready to leave, Patty whisked quickly upstairs and began to feed her son. If her mother-in-law thought to leave, she was in for a big surprise. Only how to stop her from getting this job?

It was only as Patty was giving little John the soothing

drops that kept him from troubling her too much that she realised she was holding the solution to her problem in her hand. A smile of satisfaction curved her lips.

Hannah hummed as she got ready, putting on her Sunday best and taking special care with her hair. Even Patty had been in a better mood today, making a pot of tea after their midday meal and pouring a cup for her mother-in-law.

'Are you going out, Mother Firth?'

'Just to see Louisa.'

For a moment Patty's smile slipped, then she retrieved it and shrugged. 'Well, don't be too long. We still have a lot to do.'

Hannah knew what that meant. Patty still had a lot for her to do. She prayed she would be offered this position today and then she'd leave as soon as she could. As she reached the door, she felt a wave of dizziness and stopped for a moment to shake her head in puzzlement. She'd felt perfectly all right this morning. Surely she wasn't coming down with something? Well, if so, it could wait.

But by the time she got to Louisa's she was feeling so dizzy and distant it was an effort to speak to her friend.

'Oh, you do look pale, love. Are you all right?'

'I'm not feeling very well, but this is too important. I'll have to manage.'

But the swimmy-headed feeling got no better and by the time she reached the Cowpers' house, she had to stop and lean against the wall. After a moment or two she took a deep breath. This wouldn't do. Gathering all her determination together, she pushed open the gate and knocked on the front door.

When she was invited in, the dizziness overcame her again and she had to put out one hand to the wall to steady herself.

'Are you all right, Mrs Firth?' her hostess asked.

'Just – a trifle under the weather. A little dizzy.' Once she was sitting down, she'd be better, she was sure.

But it grew worse. Hannah found it hard to concentrate and answer their questions, and though she did her best, she knew she was failing to impress by the way Mr and Mrs Berenwood looked at one another.

When she left they said they would let her know about the position as they had other women to see. She knew then that she'd failed to obtain it. The fresh air made her feel even dizzier and she staggered as she crossed the road and made her way back to Louisa's.

Once inside Hannah burst into tears. 'I've never felt like this before in my whole life,' she sobbed. 'I can't think clearly, can't even stand up without feeling faint.'

In the end, Louisa had to call in her husband to help get Hannah home, and they walked one on either side of her to support her.

Patty must have seen them coming because she had the door open before they got there. 'What's wrong?'

'Hannah's not well.'

'She's not having another of her dizzy turns, is she?'

Hannah tried to contradict her but the words wouldn't form and she could only groan and let Louisa help her into her bedroom.

'Let me take your things off, love. You need to lie quietly for a while.'

When Louisa went back into the kitchen, Patty was waiting. 'She's had a few of these turns lately,' she said in a low voice. 'She denies it when I ask, but I know something's wrong with her.'

Louisa stared at her in surprise. 'Hannah hasn't said anything to me.'

'Well, she wouldn't, would she? She doesn't like to show weakness.'

'I'll come round tomorrow to see if she's all right.'

'She's always been fine the next day. She may not even remember this clearly.'

Louisa walked away, feeling worried. Surely Hannah would have confided in her if something had really been wrong?

As she passed the Cowpers' gate, Mrs Cowper came out. 'How is your friend?'

'Not very well. She must be coming down with the influenza.'

'Has she had these turns before?'

Louisa hesitated.

'She has, hasn't she?'

'Her daughter-in-law says she has, but Hannah hasn't mentioned them to me. I'm sure it's nothing.'

Mrs Cowper's lips pursed. 'Well, I'm afraid my cousins weren't impressed by her. They've decided to look elsewhere for help. Will you tell her, please?'

Louisa's heart sank. If Hannah really was ill, this would be the final straw. She wished she could think of something to do to help her friend, but if Hannah continued to have these attacks, the best place for her was with her family. Lemuel would always look after his mother, she was sure, whatever happened. Growing older could be painful, it could indeed. She hoped she never had to depend on anyone else.

But why had this happened so quickly to Hannah? She was only forty-two, after all, two years younger than Louisa and had been perfectly all right before her husband died.

CHAPTER THREE

October 1863

Ginny's step-father looked at her across the breakfast table. 'There's to be no going off walking today after church.'

She stared at him in dismay. 'Why not?'

'Because I say so.'

'But I always have a walk with Lucy and—'

'Aye, down by the canal where all the riff-raff go. I'm not having *my* family seen down there. If you want to go walking, you'll do it on our own land or not at all. You're at an age where you need to be watched and I take my responsibilities seriously. Mind you obey me!'

With that, Howard pushed his empty plate away and went out to continue work, because animals still had to be fed, Sunday or no Sunday.

Ginny looked at her mother, her lips trembling with the effort not to cry. 'He's so unfair and you never stick up for me! How can he say I need to be watched? What sort of person does he think I am?'

'He's just being careful.'

'No, he's not. He's being nasty, forbidding my pleasures for no good reason. I need to get away from him sometimes or I'll go mad. And why shouldn't I have friends? Everyone else does. I can't wait till I'm married and can leave here.' She saw the sadness deepen in her mother's expression and went to give her a hug. 'I don't want to get away from you, Mam, but he hates me and the older I get the worse he treats me. Why?'

'He's a careful sort of man,' her mother repeated. 'Just make sure you do as he says.'

Ginny stepped backwards. 'I might have known you'd take his side.'

'He's my husband. I owe him obedience and loyalty.'

'Obedience! What are you – a servant? He certainly treats you like one. And you let him hit you, don't fight back or—'

Christine West stared at her aghast. 'How do you know about that?'

'Do you think the rest of us are all deaf? Or blind?' Ginny pointed to a bruise on her mother's arm.

'What happens between a husband and wife is no one else's business.'

'I can't watch you being hurt and not care!'

'Ginny, *please.*' Christine glanced over her shoulder as if afraid of him overhearing. 'Some men are like that. There's nothing I can do about it.'

'If he hit me, I'd fight back.'

'That only makes him worse.'

'How do you know? You don't even try!' The girl flung out of the kitchen, taking refuge briefly in her bedroom, then as she calmed down, going into the dairy to start work separating the new milk.

After church she stood demurely behind her mother and when Lucy came across, whispered the new edict.

'Oh, Ginny! What are you going to do?'

'I don't know. Will you go and tell Nick for me?'

'I suppose so.'

Inspiration suddenly struck. 'Tell him to come and meet me next Sunday after church in the wood at the top of our north pasture.'

'Ginny, it's too dangerous . . .'

'I'm not stopping seeing him.'

Lucy made her way down to the canal on her own, feeling very nervous. Nick Halstead was waiting there, but his face fell when he saw only her.

'Ginny's step-father has forbidden her to walk here any more,' she announced.

'Why? Did someone see us talking? Has he got something against me?'

'No one saw you that I know of. He's just being nasty. Mr West likes to prevent people enjoying themselves.'

'He has a reputation as a mean man to cross.'

'It's well earned. Ginny hates him.'

'How am I to see her, then?'

Lucy took a deep breath and passed on Ginny's instructions.

Nick's face lit up. 'Thank you. You're a good friend to us both.'

Lucy watched him stride away, thinking that if she really cared about her friend she'd not have passed on the message. This could only lead to trouble for Ginny.

The following Sunday after church, Ginny changed out of her best clothes and announced that she was going for a walk.

'You'll stay on our own land,' Howard ordered. As she walked past him without replying he caught hold of her arm and swung her round so hard she bumped her head against the wall. 'You hear me, girl?'

'Yes.' She pulled away from him and set off, heading for their small patch of woodland, a place she'd always loved. It was so pretty, especially in spring. She went to sit on a rough wooden bench outside the ruined cottage there, looking up eagerly as she heard rustling sounds. Someone was walking through the woods. Could it be him? Yes, it was. 'Nick! I'm over here.'

He came to clasp her hands, pulling her gently towards him. 'I can't believe we're truly alone at last.'

Ginny smiled trustingly up at him. 'And can be every time the weather is fine. I'm forbidden to leave our land, but you can easily get to this cottage without anyone seeing you and it's only just over our border so *he'll* never know.' Her smile faded. 'I have to get away from him sometimes. You don't know how hard he is to live with.'

They spent about an hour sitting on the bench, talking of themselves and their hopes, then she looked at the way the sun was slanting through the branches and said reluctantly, 'I'd better be getting back or he'll throw another fit.'

'You'll be here next week?'

'If it's fine.' When he dared to kiss her she gave him her lips willingly and carried the memory of that kiss away with her like a candle glowing inside her heart. He hadn't said so yet but she was sure he loved her. As she loved him.

That evening when all the children were in bed, Howard looked at his wife. 'I think we should marry

Ginny off quite soon. She's far too pretty for her own good and that's bound to lead to trouble.'

'Marry her off! But she isn't walking out with anyone.'

'I know that. I wouldn't have allowed it. No, I mean to marry her to a sensible older man, one who'll know how to manage her. With a father like that, it's no wonder she's turned out flighty.'

'She's not flighty!' And there had been nothing wrong with her first husband either, though Christine had learned never to say that because Howard was insanely jealous of him.

He glared at her. 'Are you contradicting me, woman? I say your daughter's flighty and we need to watch her carefully.' After a pause during which he observed his wife's gaze falter and her whole body droop, he continued, 'Fortunately I have a man in mind, a widower who is looking for a wife to care for him and his two young children.'

'A widower! Who?' Then she suddenly realised. 'Not your friend Peter Gordon?'

He nodded, looking smug. 'Yes. He's well set-up and she'll want for nothing. It'll be a good match for her.'

Even fear of his anger didn't stop Christine from protesting at this. 'He's too old for her, Howard, far too old.' And was like her second husband in nature. She didn't intend Ginny to be as unhappy as she was. That at least she could prevent, whatever it cost her.

'He's a man in his prime, as I am. He's already spoken to me and I shall give him my answer tomorrow.'

'I won't be part of it,' Christine declared.

The answering blow knocked her off her chair and sent her sprawling on the floor.

'You'll do as you're told.'

'Not in this, not even if you beat me till I'm black and blue.' She screamed then as his fist lashed out again.

In the morning Ginny came down cautiously, having heard the sounds of the beating and knowing how her step-father's unpleasant moods could linger for days. He wasn't in yet from the early chores but her mother was there, with a massive bruise on the side of her face and others on her arms.

The girl ran to hug her. 'Why did he hit you this time?'

Christine looked cautiously over her shoulder and said in a low voice, 'Because he wants to marry you to his friend Peter Gordon and I won't support him in this, not if he breaks every bone in my body. Don't say I told you and don't contradict him if he mentions his plans. If necessary I'll find the money to send you to my brother Nathaniel. I won't let Howard do this to you.'

'Oh, Mother!' Ginny touched her bruised cheek lightly. 'It's not fair. You don't deserve a man like him.'

'It's too late for me, but not for you.'

Which made Ginny want to weep for her. Even her two half-brothers were afraid of their father and hardly even opened their mouths when he was around. But at least Edwin and Andrew had each other to play with and talk to. Ginny had no one.

No, that wasn't true. A smile lit up her face. She had Nick now.

★　　★　　★

Hannah felt down-hearted after that terrible day when she'd failed to gain the position she was sure she could have coped with easily. She didn't suffer a recurrence of the dizziness but did notice her daughter-in-law looking at her with barely suppressed triumph from time to time.

Even Louisa kept asking her how she was, and when Hannah tried to discuss the dizzy turn, her friend told her Patty said it'd happened a few times now.

'But that's not true! It only happened once, on that day of all days.'

Louisa frowned. 'She said you wouldn't admit it, but Hannah, surely you know you can trust me?'

'Of course I do. And if I'd had other dizzy turns, I'd tell you, but I haven't, I promise you.'

'Then why did Patty say you had?'

'I don't know. She's up to something and I mean to find out what.'

As the days passed people in the village also started looking at her warily and Hannah guessed that Patty was spreading the tale. Why? She lay in bed worrying about it. All she could think of was that her daughter-in-law didn't want to lose her help in the house. Well, if things went on like this, she'd go into Blackburn and apply for work at a domestic employment bureau, taking anything they offered, however hard. But the trouble was, she didn't have any references and that worry held her back, because if anyone asked about her in the village, the rumours would surface and then she'd lose any chance of finding a decent job.

If she had more money, she'd have left and found

lodgings while she sought work. It didn't seem fair that she received no reward at all for her hard work, not even a share of the egg money, so one evening she went into the workshop before Lemuel shut up for the day and asked him if she could have some each week. 'Just a little pin money so that I can buy things if I need them.'

He looked at her and frowned. 'Why should you need separate money, Mam? If you want anything, you've only to tell Patty and she'll give you what you need.'

'It's humiliating to have to ask her for money, Lemuel. Surely you can be more generous to me than that?'

From the uncomfortable expression on his face she guessed he had already discussed this with Patty, who seemed to hold the purse strings very tightly in her plump white hands.

'I never thought you'd treat me so shabbily.' Hannah couldn't prevent the tears from welling in her eyes for all her efforts to control them.

'But you lack for nothing, Mam . . .'

'Except dignity.' She left the workshop, walked through the kitchen, ignored Patty's demand to know where she'd been just when it was time to serve up the evening meal, and shut herself in her room, sitting weeping on her bed.

A few minutes later the door crashed open and Patty stood there, eyes glittering in triumph. But her voice was gentle enough as she said, 'This won't do, Mother Firth! You need to eat properly if you're to get better.'

'Get better! There's nothing wrong with me except low spirits.'

'Now you know you've had a few dizzy turns lately. I'm sure it's nothing, but we have to keep an eye on you.'

Hannah bounced to her feet, anger drying the tears. 'I've had one spell of dizziness, *one,* and that's all. I don't know why you're telling these lies about me.'

With a sigh, Patty turned away and went to lean against her husband. 'I can't do anything with her when she gets like this. See if you can persuade her to eat her tea, Lemuel.'

Hannah watched him pat his wife on the arm and then come into the room.

'Come on, Mam.' He took her arm and pulled her to the table, using his superior strength, even though she resisted. When he let go of her she stood stiffly by her normal chair for a minute then turned back towards her room, furious at being treated like this.

But he stopped her, this time sitting her forcibly on her chair. 'I'll tie you there if I have to. You need to eat, and Patty has enough on her plate without worrying about you.' His eyes went to his wife's stomach, pride shining in them, and she guessed that they'd started another child.

Speechless, unbearably humiliated, Hannah sat there, but didn't even try to force any food down. It would have choked her, she was sure.

Patty ate a hearty meal and Lemuel cleared his plate with his usual thoroughness.

Afterwards he took his mother's meal and ate that too. 'Hunger will maybe teach you to eat the good food that's set in front of you,' he said as if he were talking to a child.

'Honour thy father and mother,' she threw back at him.

He flushed scarlet.

When they eventually allowed her to go to bed, Hannah lay awake for hours, not hungry but puzzled. Why was her daughter-in-law so determined to treat her as an unpaid servant and keep her obedient? Why was the need so urgent?

That question was answered the following week when a cart drew up outside the house and a woman got down from the back. Hannah recognised Patty's sister and wondered why she had come on a cart.

Patty wiped her hands and went outside, her sharp tones carrying clearly in the damp air. 'You've brought her, then?'

'Yes. I've done my share. It's your turn now.'

'Bring her in and I'll show you where she'll be sleeping.'

Patty's father climbed down from the driving seat and on to the back of the cart while his daughter stood waiting. He lifted up an old woman in nightgear with a blank expression on her face, carrying her in his arms like a child.

This must be Patty's mother, Hannah guessed. Poor thing. She was definitely suffering from softening of the brain. They'd all seen that blank look before and pitied the families of sufferers. But where was Susan going to be staying? In the baby's bedroom, she supposed.

'Lemuel! Come and help us as you promised,' Patty called.

He came out of the workshop, looking embarrassed

as he took Hannah's arm and led her back inside. 'We didn't tell you before because we didn't want to upset you, but the only place we can house Patty's mother is with you.'

Hannah stiffened. 'You can't mean that, son!'

'I'm afraid it's the only place where there's room,' he repeated. 'With the new baby coming, we'll need the other bedroom upstairs.'

That, Hannah realised, was why Patty had been so eager to keep her living with them. She wanted someone to care for her mother.

'If you do that to me, I'll leave,' she said firmly. 'Even if I have to go on the tramp. Do you really expect me to share my bed with a woman who'll be incontinent? I can't believe you'd treat your own mother like that. How will you humiliate me next, Lemuel Firth? Your father must be turning in his grave.'

He ran a hand through his lank hair which was already growing thinner. He'd be as bald as his father by the time he was thirty, Hannah thought, staring at him with the eyes of a stranger and not liking the weakness she saw in him.

'I have other people to think of besides you, Mam. We must all manage the best we can. I'll – um – see if I can find you a straw mattress of your own.'

'That's the best you can offer me?' she asked, aghast. 'A straw mattress on the floor? Can I not even keep my own bed?'

'Well, Mrs Riggs will need to be strapped in, you see. She wanders otherwise. Patty explained it to me. It's a dreadful affliction, but we must just do the best we can for her. We can't send one of our own to the asylum, surely you can see that? I mean, it must be a comfort to you, given the circumstances?'

'What circumstances?'

'Well, your dizzy spells. Whatever it is that's wrong, you know we'll always care for you.'

The way he stared at her made Hannah realise with a sense of shock that he was wondering if she too was succumbing to softening of the brain.

'There's nothing wrong with me apart from one day's dizziness,' she said with her old crispness. 'That and the pain of finding that my son won't carry out his father's last instructions to take good care of me.'

'Mam!'

'Will you at least give me some money, so that I can go and find myself employment? I can't – *I won't!* – stay here under those conditions.'

Patty's voice spoke from behind them. 'No, he'll not. Let alone we've no money to spare, families help one another and we need your help now. It's your bounden duty to stay, Mother Firth. And anyway, you've nowhere else to go.'

Hannah looked beyond her to where they'd already laid the old woman in her bed, tying her arms loosely to the bedhead. She was whimpering, looking terrified.

Patty's sister Ruth came out of the bedroom. 'She needs to be fed soft food or she chokes. And she'll need changing like a baby. I've washed her clouts, all except those she wore on the way here.'

Mr Riggs stood behind her, a stern expression on his face. 'It's your turn now, Patty. If there were anyone else to help us, I'd not impose on you in your condition. But there isn't. And at least you're not on your own here.' His gaze rested briefly on Hannah, then back on his daughter.

Patty didn't protest. Indeed she always became very quiet when her father was around and Hannah guessed that she was afraid of upsetting him, even now.

'I can't afford paid help,' he went on, looking at Hannah. 'This war in America has played havoc with the cotton industry. I'm lucky I've still got a maintenance job in the mill, very lucky, but it only pays half-wages.'

'And I'm lucky that my Harry has got himself a new job in the south,' Ruth said. 'Well, Father, we'd better get off again.'

Patty went to see them out, waving to her father. But her smile faded as she turned back towards the house and hissed at Lemuel, 'I'm relying on you to make her accept this.'

But Hannah wasn't accepting anything. She walked out, ignoring the inclement weather, and went to Louisa's because she had nowhere else to go. Her friend, however, was distracted because one of her daughters was ill, so Hannah didn't get her usual sympathetic hearing.

This was not the time to ask if she could stay for a while.

That evening she found it difficult to eat but forced some food down because she intended to keep her strength up. When the meal was over Patty said in a casual tone, 'You'd better take the slops and feed my mother. Make sure you mash up the food well.'

Hannah cleared the table, mashed up some food and

went to feed Susan. There was a smell of urine to the room already. Grimly she spooned food into the mouth that opened like a child's and then cleaned up the old woman.

When she took the soiled linen out, she said, 'I need my straw mattress tonight, Lemuel. I can't sleep in a wet bed.'

'What straw mattress?' Patty demanded.

'I promised my mother her own mattress. It's a reasonable request, Patty love,' he said soothingly.

'Well, we can't get you one now, can we? You'll have to wait till it's convenient, Mother Firth.'

'Then I'll bring down the spare quilt and sleep on that in front of the kitchen fire.'

Patty opened her mouth to protest, but Lemuel stood up. 'I'll get it for you, Mam.'

When he'd gone upstairs, Patty turned to Hannah and said very quietly, 'Be careful not to anger me, Mother Firth. I *will* be mistress in my own house and you're in a very delicate position here.'

Hannah said nothing, but that threat only increased her determination to leave. She wouldn't tell them, just go. As far as she was concerned, Lemuel wasn't treating her with anything like the respect a son owed to his parent, and Patty was using her to avoid the unpleasant task of looking after her own poor mother.

If only Malachi were still in the country she'd go to him. Or if she had enough money she'd follow him to Australia.

Hannah sighed as she tried to get comfortable on the floor. That it should have come to this! Not even a bed of her own on such a bitterly cold night. She knew John would have been horrified.

Her own son, treating her like this!

She couldn't help weeping.

CHAPTER FOUR

October 1863

Richard Dewhurst read the letter and studied the pages of figures that had come with it carefully, his lips growing tight with anger. 'Is this a true accounting, do you think?' he asked his agent.

'Yes, I believe it is,' Jack Lexham replied.

'Then why were the other damages we've paid so much less?'

'For several reasons. Firstly, King is more intelligent than most and knows how to produce a complete reckoning.' The land agent tapped the top sheet of figures. 'I couldn't have set this out better myself. He must have a gift for figures.'

His employer grunted.

'Secondly, a market garden has all its crops in a small compass, so it's easier to wreak greater damage in a short space of time.'

Silence. Then, 'This fellow could be exaggerating.'

'Well—' Jack hesitated.

'Speak out, man!'

'When I heard what had happened I thought the rumour of such destruction must be exaggerated, so I rode past the place myself to check on your behalf.' He looked his employer directly in the eyes as he added, 'It looked to me as though someone had deliberately caused as much damage as possible. People merely riding through after a fox wouldn't have caused a tenth of the havoc I saw. I have – er – suggested before that you ask your son to take a little more care when he's hunting.' Playing at hunting, he added mentally, just as the young brute plays at being a gentleman, something he'll never be.

'My Walter's a lively young chap, too full of energy for his own good.' After drumming his fingers on the desk, Richard added, 'I'd better find him some occupation. I'd thought to raise him as a gentleman, but he's too much like me to spend his days idly without bursting out from time to time. I'll tell him he's to start working with you from Monday onwards. You can begin teaching him the business of managing an estate.'

Jack Lexham stared, unable to conceal his horror at the mere thought, then shook his head. 'I can't do it, sir.'

'Eh? What do you mean, you can't do it?'

'I have no way of controlling your son. He'd not listen to me, would order me to act differently and thus would undermine my standing with your tenants. I couldn't work like that.'

'Nonsense! I'll give him strict orders and—'

Utterly determined, Jack reiterated quietly, 'I can't and won't work with him. If you want my resignation because of that, then you can have it. I shall have no trouble finding other employment. And when we renew my contract next month, I shall need it to be with you and to end immediately if anything should happen to you.'

'It's just a young fellow's natural liveliness.'

'It's gone beyond that, sir. He and his companions

are feared in the district and if you want the truth I'd already decided to leave my job when Walter inherits.' After another hesitation Lexham added, 'What's more, your elder son has been offensive to my daughter and now Flora's afraid to walk out without her mother in case she meets him. And she's not the first girl he's upset. That's not the behaviour of a gentleman.'

Richard stared at him, lips pursed, brow furrowed in a deep scowl. 'Hmm. I'll reconsider the matter, then. But I'm still determined to find him some occupation.'

'Perhaps in one of your remaining businesses in the town, sir?' Jack suggested.

'Perhaps.'

Richard heaved himself to his feet and walked heavily from the estate office, horrified by the thought of Walter frightening that nice young lass. He went out into the gardens but his eyes were blind to their beauty as he walked to his favourite seat near an ornamental fountain. As he sat there, enjoying the sunshine, the realisation slowly sank in that he himself wouldn't want his son and heir working in one of his other businesses, wouldn't trust Walter to do a decent, sensible job, especially in these hard times when the mills weren't earning their keep for lack of cotton.

He looked round. This estate, which he'd bought with the wealth he'd worked so hard to acquire, was one thing, but his other businesses – for he had interests other than cotton mills – still brought in what he considered the bread-and-butter money. As he sat there he faced the situation squarely, for he had always prided himself on calling a spade a spade.

'Eh, I've made a right old mess of bringing him up,'

he muttered as he stood up to return to the house. 'Well, what do I know about raising a gentleman?'

At dinner that evening he stared at Walter as if he'd never seen him before, then picked at his food, sighing from time to time.

'You're very quiet tonight, Pa,' Walter said. 'Are you feeling all right?'

'Aye. But I still mean to find you employment. Jack Lexham hasn't the time to keep an eye on you – he has too much to do for me – so we'll have to find some other way of harnessing your energy.'

'I don't see why I should have to work, not when we're rich and—'

'I'm the one as is rich, not you, and don't you forget it.'

His father continued to stare at him and Walter felt impelled to fill the silence. 'The chaps and I get a lot of exercise riding and shooting, you know. We've been wondering where that fox got to, whether it came back to King's place and—'

'Aye, so that you can cost me another small fortune! Hunting! What's the worth of that? It don't bring in money and you can't even eat the damned creatures if you catch 'em.'

Oliver sat very still, staring covertly from one to the other. It was unusual for his father to become annoyed with Walter. Very unusual indeed. His brother had been the favoured one for as long as Oliver could remember; the one who was fit and healthy, who laughed readily and made their father laugh too, the one who hadn't looked sickly as a child. Their mother had died when Oliver was ten, but he could still remember her kind nature and the way she had spent time with him when he was ill, reading to him or just sitting with him in the beauty of their well-kept gardens.

He was intrigued by what his father was saying, but knew better than to join in the conversation, so concentrated on his food.

After another silence, Richard demanded harshly, 'Do you know how much that little jaunt of yours on King's property has cost me?'

Walter shrugged.

'Don't you shrug at me!' His father turned a deeper red and spluttered with rage as he named the sum.

Even Walter was surprised, then waved one hand dismissively. 'He's trying to trick you. It couldn't possibly have cost that much.'

'That's what I thought, so I asked Jack and he said he rode past that same day. He thinks King was accurate in his calculations and was surprised by how much damage you did.' He thumped down his fist on the table. 'Dammit all! What were you thinking of? That wasn't a meadow, it was a market garden, chock full of crops at that time of year. You should have kept out of it.'

'And you even trampled down Mrs King's flowers,' Oliver added, unable to keep quiet over this, 'though it must have been obvious that no fox could have been hiding among them. She died unhappy because of that.'

Walter surged to his feet, fists clenched. 'Look, you mealy-mouthed—'

'*Sit down!*' roared Richard.

After a moment's hesitation, Walter subsided, but the look he threw at his brother boded ill for later.

'If you cost me anything like that much money again, I'll sell that bloody horse of yours and put you into a cotton mill to learn the business from the bottom up, as I did, every step of the process.'

'I'd not do it,' Walter threw back at him, 'and you couldn't make me.'

'Then how would you live?' His father leaned back, his colour subsiding a little and a smile twisting the corners of his mouth briefly as he saw doubt and then consternation on his son's face. Ah, he could still handle him, there was nothing like the power of money. 'Just take more care what you do from now on and don't put people's backs up. That's no way to get us in with the county folk in this area.'

With a sullen expression on his face, Walter applied himself to his food.

Oliver took a sip of water, ignoring the half-full glass of wine standing untasted by his plate. He was quite sure nothing would get his family accepted by county folk, especially now that everyone knew what Walter was like, and for himself he didn't care. The Dewhursts weren't gentry, however much Walter played at it, so why pretend they were? Oliver ate as lightly as usual, refusing dessert, then excused himself as soon as he could.

When Walter burst into his brother's bedroom later, he found it empty. He contented himself with sweeping everything off the desk and kicking some of the books across the room. Damned puppy! He'd teach him to cause trouble.

A little later, when he'd heard Walter go out for an evening's drinking with his friends, Oliver left the attic where he regularly took refuge from his brother's anger. He'd become an expert at hiding over the years, or disguising himself occasionally if he wanted to go out, even if that was a cowardly way to behave.

Not long now, he told himself as he began to clear up the mess in his room. Not long at all.

He hated the feeling that he was a coward, but Walter was a very strong man and Oliver knew he'd stand no chance against him if it came to a fight.

Hannah made careful preparations to leave, working out what to take with her and what to leave behind. She would be foolish to try to carry a heavy bundle, she decided.

She needed to retrieve her money from Louisa's but found it impossible to get away from Patty for a day or two. And since she knew Louisa's daughter was still ill, she waited with as much patience as she could muster, aware of how closely her daughter-in-law was watching her but trying not to show it.

One morning Hannah experienced a second attack of dizziness. She was unable to think clearly let alone walk straight. Patty watched her for a minute, making no attempt to help her, then called Lemuel in from the workshop.

He helped his mother to lie down on her mattress. 'You see, you're not well and you need us as much as we need you.'

She didn't try to answer, and when sleep took her drifted away thankfully.

In the evening she awoke feeling exhausted and sluggish, but got up and attended to her needs, then to those of the old woman, whose incontinence was stinking to high heaven and who clearly hadn't been touched all day.

'Ah, you're better, are you?' was all Patty said when Hannah went into the kitchen.

'Yes. Could you not have helped your mother?'

Patty looked at the bundle of dirty linen and wrinkled her nose in disgust. 'That's your job. And such things make me ill in my delicate condition. You'll have to have another washday tomorrow, I suppose. It's very inconvenient having a woman in that condition in the house. I hope you don't get like that when your turn comes.'

Hannah stopped short and spun round. 'Stop saying such things! You know they're untrue.'

'What I know for certain is that you have dizzy turns and afterwards you're vague and distant. And that's how my mother started.' Patty smirked as she said that.

Biting back a sharp retort, Hannah went to put the wet sheets to soak, then carried on with her duties in silence.

Only when she was lying on the prickly straw mattress alone in the blessed privacy of darkness did she try to understand what had happened to her. Why had she suddenly had this attack, so like the first one? And why did Patty keep telling people she'd had more than two attacks? She hadn't, she knew she hadn't. What's more, even if what Patty had told her about how her mother's illness had started was true, it was a cruel thing to say.

But was any of it true?

Something deep inside Hannah refused to accept

that her brain was softening, that old age was setting in. She felt well the rest of the time, well and energetic, and her mind was only too active, chafing at the boredom and drudgery of her daily routine. Her thoughts went round in circles for a long time as she thought about what she had done, what she had eaten and drunk before each attack of dizziness.

It was only as she was drifting off to sleep at last that she remembered Patty making a pot of tea and pouring out a cup for her each time – an unusual occurrence. Hannah stiffened on the prickly, uncomfortable mattress. Had her daughter-in-law put something in her cup of tea? Surely not? Even Patty couldn't be so wicked.

Hannah lay awake a little longer and finally resolved to take great care what she ate and drank from then onwards. She also came to the conclusion that she didn't dare tell anyone about her suspicions. Lemuel simply wouldn't believe her and outsiders would think it another manifestation of her going stupid in old age. Why, even Louisa had doubted her word. Her daughter-in-law had been very cunning.

Hannah knew she herself wasn't cunning, had too open a nature. Well, she'd have to learn to think carefully about what she was doing. Very carefully.

Patty watched her mother-in-law like a hawk from then on and one day sent Hannah to the shop, a job she usually reserved for herself, so that she could check through the older woman's things. She studied the top drawer and realised a few things had been taken out since last time. It didn't take much thought to realise that what had gone was a spare set of clothes and some extra underclothes.

'What is she doing?' she murmured to herself, putting them back carefully. 'She has nowhere to go. Surely she's not going off to tramp the roads?'

As she turned to leave the room, her mother gibbered at her from the bed and Patty glared at the old woman. 'Be quiet, you filthy old hag!' The smell of this room sickened her. She hated old people, hated them.

Why did her mother-in-law not look old as her mother did? That galled her. Hannah was still slim and upright while Patty herself was starting to get fatter. Having babies did that to you. Lemuel said she was as pretty as ever, but she knew she wasn't. Still, he was easy to manage, which was why she'd chosen him, so it didn't really matter what she looked like. Love might fade – and she didn't believe in it, anyway – but the marriage ties still bound you, so you put yourself in charge if you had any sense at all.

She was disappointed that the cooperage business wasn't doing as well as she'd expected, though. Lemuel said things would pick up again, but she'd heard that times were changing and folk were wanting galvanised buckets, which were so much lighter than wooden ones. When she'd suggested selling them as well as the ones he made, he'd nearly bitten her head off. But what would they do if business got worse?

Matters came to a head a few days later. Patty had noticed how tense her mother-in-law seemed that morning and a quick glance at Hannah's things while she was pegging out the washing showed the top drawer empty and a bundle hidden under the pillow. This was the day Patty normally went to market and she had guessed if Hannah were planning to leave, it'd be while she was out of the house.

Furious, Patty went back into the kitchen. Trust Lemuel to be away from home when she needed him. She doubted she could keep her mother-in-law here by force, because Hannah was a strong woman.

It was time to take the next step, one that she'd worked out a while back in case her mother-in-law proved too troublesome. She knew the routines of the poorhouse because she'd made enquiries about getting her own mother into the asylum, and would have done so if Lemuel and her father hadn't protested and absolutely insisted on her looking after the old hag at home.

She wrapped a shawl round herself, snatched little John from his cot and tugged at her hair to make it look as if she were distraught. Then she went running through the back streets to the poorhouse, half of which was used as a lunatic asylum for the whole district. She arrived, panting and flushed, and banged on the door. When the porter unlocked it, she fell through, sobbing loudly and pleading for someone to come and help her.

They took her to the Matron and she stammered out her tale of abuse by her mother-in-law who seemed to be suffering from the early stages of softening of the brain and could fly into rages for nothing. 'My husband is away from home and she's grown suddenly worse. I'm afraid for myself and my son, daren't go back.'

'Are you talking about Hannah Firth?'

Patty nodded and squeezed out a few more tears.

'Yes. We've been trying to hide it, but I can't do that any longer, I just can't. I'm too afraid of her.'

'If you're really frightened for your safety—'

'I am, I am!'

'— then I'll send someone to bring her here, but she can't be admitted properly until the doctor has seen her. Can you go back and keep her quiet for a little while?'

Patty dabbed at her eyes and pretended to give it her consideration. 'I think, if I'm careful, I can prevent her from attacking us again. I can always run out of the house and scream for help if she does, can't I?'

Back at the house Patty got the tea things ready and waited for Hannah to return from the nearby farm with some milk.

'Ah, there you are, Mother Firth. Did you get some cream as well?'

'Yes.'

'I'm just making a pot of tea. You'll be ready for a nice hot drink, won't you?'

Hannah looked at the tea things set out on the end of the table. She went to study the two cups and found that one of them contained a little clear liquid in the bottom. 'Were you going to drug me again?' she asked scornfully, tipping it upside down.

Patty jerked up and put the chair between them. 'I don't know what you mean. I mustn't have wiped that cup properly when I washed the dishes, that's all.'

Hannah was suddenly so sickened by the way Patty could lie and look you straight in the eyes that she couldn't bear to stay in the house a second longer. Without a word she went into her bedroom and picked up the bundle of clothes.

When she came out she found the younger woman waiting for her.

'What are you doing, Mother Firth?'

'Leaving.'

'Oh, no, you're not!'

'How will you stop me? Lemuel isn't here to manhandle me this time and I reckon I'm stronger than you.'

Patty heard footsteps coming down the front path and smiled. 'Haven't you learned by now that I always find a way to get what I want? Be warned. Do as I say from now on or take the consequences.'

Hannah gave her a disgusted look and turned towards the back door.

Quick as lightning, Patty barred her way and began to scream for help.

Hannah was so astonished she could only stand and stare at her. Then she heard someone knocking on the front door, and before she could stop her Patty had tugged at both their clothes and scratched her own face. After that the younger woman began screaming again and sobbing wildly, clutching Hannah all the time to prevent her leaving.

'Let go of me! What are you doing?'

The front door burst open and heavy footsteps pounded towards the kitchen.

Hannah tried to shake Patty off, but her daughter-in-law clung like a leech. When hands pulled them apart, she turned in relief, but the two men holding her didn't let her go and Patty was now weeping and thanking them for coming so quickly.

'What's happening? Why have you come here?'

Hannah asked in bewilderment, struggling to get out of their clutches because they were hurting her.

'Stand still and you'll not be hurt,' one said, giving her a shake. 'You understand me: *stand still.*'

He spoke slowly, as if she'd have trouble understanding, then turned to Patty. 'We'll take her into the asylum for the moment, Mrs Firth, and let you know how she goes. When the doctor sees her, he'll probably give her something to soothe her.'

'Thank you. Oh, thank you,' Patty sobbed. 'I was so afraid for my baby.'

When they began to walk Hannah forcibly towards the door, she resisted. 'I'm not mad, just angry at her. Why are you doing this to me? There's no law against being angry.'

They ignored her, and as she continued to struggle one twisted her arm behind her back. She let out an involuntary cry of pain and he said, 'Be quiet, if you have any sense left in you!'

To her great shame, they marched her down the street, but there was nothing she could do about it because they were both strong men. Anger kept her from weeping, anger kept her defiant, but when the heavy door of the poorhouse banged shut behind her, she couldn't hold back a sob.

'They allus realise it when they come inside, don't they?' one of her captors said to the other.

'Aye, and they soon start doing as they're told after we've had 'em here for a bit.'

As he'd kept her arm twisted behind her, Hannah stood still, but when the Matron came in, a woman whom she knew slightly, she gave a sob of relief. 'Mrs

Gregory! Oh, I'm so glad to see you. There's been a dreadful mistake . . .'

The grasp on her arm didn't slacken.

'We caught her attacking her daughter-in-law,' one man said. 'Poor young woman was distraught and had a dreadful scratch on her cheek.'

'Patty did that to herself!' Hannah protested. 'Mrs Gregory, she's been telling lies about me.'

Jean Gregory avoided her eyes. 'Bring her through.'

They force-marched Hannah into the asylum side of the building. By now her anger was giving way to fear mingled with disbelief. This couldn't be happening to her, it couldn't!

Another woman met them there and Hannah was taken into a small room, then the two men left.

Matron pulled a bundle of clothing from a shelf. Inmate's clothing. 'Will you take your clothes off yourself, Hannah, or do we have to undress you?'

'I don't understand what I'm doing here or why I should take my clothes off. Please tell me what's happening? I'm sure it's all a dreadful mistake.'

'Your daughter-in-law has committed you to our care as being unrestrained and dangerous. You'll be held here until the doctor decides what is best for you.'

The last of the anger vanished, leaving behind it a cold fear. 'Patty's lying.'

The other woman took a step forward. 'Well, she's out there and you're in here, so if you have any sense left, you'll do as you're told. Take off your clothes and put these on.'

But Hannah couldn't do it, she just couldn't, and fought them every inch of the way. In the end they had to call in one of the men to help hold her, and then to her intense embarrassment they stripped her naked and dressed her in the coarse underclothes and grey twill uniform of an inmate of the asylum. The man even made jokes about her having a nice firm body still.

Then they took her along to another small room, this time with an iron bedstead in it.

'Do we need to chain her?' the female attendant asked.

Jean Gregory looked at Hannah thoughtfully. 'I think we'd better. Just till the doctor's seen her tomorrow.'

After they'd gone, Hannah gave in to her tears. There was a chain round her waist fastened to the bedhead and she was sitting on a grey, stained mattress with one coarse blanket on it. Beneath the bed, just within reach, was a chamber pot, but there was nothing else in the room.

She heard moaning nearby and someone began to laugh: high-pitched laughter with no mirth in it that went on and on. Footsteps passed the door from time to time, but no one came in to see her. It was damp and cold in the tiny, cell-like room and the clothing she was wearing wasn't warm enough. In the end she pulled the blanket off the bed and wrapped it round her shoulders.

She had never felt so alone or afraid in her life.

Lemuel arrived home late that same evening. He was unharnessing the horse when Patty rushed out and threw herself into his arms, sobbing wildly. He held her at arm's length, astonished.

'What's wrong, love?'

'Your mother went mad today.'

He stared at her in shock. 'What do you mean?'

She resisted the temptation to shout at him and managed a few more sobs against his chest. 'What I say. I told you she'd started the same way my mother did and today she went wild, attacking me. Look at my cheek! She did that!'

He reached out one fingertip to the scratch. 'My *mother* did?'

'Yes.'

'Let me see to the horse and then I'll come in and you can tell me exactly what happened.' He glanced towards the house. 'Is she all right now?'

'She's in the asylum. I was frightened she'd attack John, didn't know what to do with you away all day, so I called for help.'

He stared at her then the house, as if it'd tell him something. 'Nay, I can't take it in! Mother running mad? I just can't believe it.'

'I was shocked too,' Patty said in a soft, weak voice. 'It's a dreadful thing to happen to someone.'

When he went into the house, she had his meal ready and he sat down, but couldn't face eating yet. 'Tell me exactly what happened.'

He listened in silence to her version of events.

'They're getting the doctor in to see her tomorrow,' Patty finished. 'Maybe he'll give her something to calm her down.'

Lemuel pushed the plate away suddenly. 'I must go and see her.'

For a moment his wife scowled at him, then quickly adjusted her expression. 'You can't. The asylum is shut up for the night.'

He stood up and went to stare into the fire in the central part of the cooking stove, taking comfort from its glowing warmth.

At Patty's urging he tried to eat his food, but couldn't force it down.

When they went to bed he pretended to fall asleep but instead lay awake for a long time. He couldn't bear the thought of his mother being shut away, or of her going mad. Not his mother. A thousand memories flickered before his eyes of her playing with him and Malachi, reading to them, making sure they could read, mending their clothes, caring devotedly for them when they were sick.

Tears squeezed themselves out of his eyes and he let them roll down his cheeks, not wanting to wipe them away and disturb Patty.

He hadn't told his wife but he'd failed to get the order he'd gone about, a big one for barrels, because he couldn't produce them quickly enough, working with just his apprentice. And now this – this thing with his mother on top of everything. It was too much.

CHAPTER FIVE

November 1863

Nathaniel was summoned to the land agent's office and found Jack Lexham sitting behind his desk with his usual welcoming smile.

'It's a bad business, this,' he said. 'Sit down, Mr King.'

'Thank you.'

'Mr Dewhurst has approved payment of the damages you asked for. I confirmed that I thought them accurate.'

'Thank you. But I'd rather have had my crops undamaged.'

Jack pushed a small leather purse across the desk. 'I think you'll find this correct.'

Nathaniel counted out the money then nodded. 'Thank you.'

'What are you going to do now?'

'Start getting things in trim for the next planting and look round for some seeds. I shan't be able to produce my own now.'

'I can ask the gardeners at the big house if they have any seeds or cuttings to spare.'

Nathaniel was surprised. 'You'd do that for me, Mr Lexham?'

Jack smiled. 'Yes. And Mr Dewhurst would let me. He's not like his son.'

'That younger boy of his is different too. He came to Sarah's funeral. I was still angry at the time, but I appreciated it afterwards when I'd had time to think about it. It couldn't have been easy for him to do that.'

'No. Oliver doesn't have an easy life. He's a nice lad.'

'Would you tell him thank you for me?'

'Yes. And I'll let you know about the seeds soon.'

'I'm grateful.'

But as he was walking home, Walter Dewhurst passed him on horseback and when he recognised Nathaniel, laughed and ran the horse at him, so that he had to jump into the ditch to avoid it.

The younger man looked down from his horse, not smiling now. 'When I inherit, King, you'll be the first to be thrown out if you don't behave. I shan't let uncooperative tenants stay on. Remember that.'

Nathaniel said nothing, just waited for the other to ride on then clambered out of the ditch, untying his boots to shake the water out of them, wishing he dared punch that lout in the face, then making his way home. Maybe now was the time to look for another property to rent because his tenancy was up in a few months. Only he didn't want to force such big changes on Gregory until his son had got over his mother's death. The poor lad was still crying for her at night, though he denied it, and he looked so sad it tore Nathaniel's heart in two. Sarah had never been too ill to talk to her son.

The hours passed slowly for Hannah. It grew dark quite soon and she was cold with only one rough grey blanket on her bed, but there was nothing much she could do about that. Her thoughts chased one another round in circles until she thought she really would go mad, then she suddenly pictured Malachi, her younger son, and clung to that image. The memory of him steadied her and gave her courage. Gradually her panic began to settle. He had gone off half-way round the world, knowing no one in Australia, and with only his own wits and a few trading goods to rely on after his arrival.

If Malachi could take such a huge step, face so many risks in a strange land, then she could find a way to deal with her own situation. That thought calmed her as she huddled under the blanket, unable to get comfortable because of the chain round her waist that was fastened to the bed. Any unwary move made it chink or scrape on the metal bed head and then she would jerk awake. Whatever she did, she simply could not get comfortable.

Concentrate, she told herself. *How am I to deal with this?*

The question seemed to hang in the air around her and echo in her brain. A phrase of her father's came back to her: *panic never won a battle.* She had been panicking ever since the men captured her, she saw that now.

It came to her in the hush of early dawn that she must accept this new situation quietly and with dignity, she must *show* them she wasn't mad. Could she rein in the anger that still rose in her every time she thought of Patty's deception? She must.

Soon she heard the first sounds of people stirring and prayed that someone would come and at least give her a drink of water, for she was parched. But footsteps passed her door several times before she heard the sound of a key in the lock.

The Assistant Matron looked in.

Hannah said nothing, just sat quietly under her scrutiny.

When the woman approached the bed, Hannah saw the bruise on her arm and guessed she herself had inflicted it on the woman in her wild struggles. She looked down at it, then up. 'I must apologise for hurting you. I panicked, I'm afraid.'

'Well, you're certainly calmer this morning.'

'Yes. I've had time to think. I'm not mad and this is a mistake, but it isn't your mistake.'

'Hmm.' The woman turned to leave.

'Could I have a drink of water, please? I've had nothing to drink since breakfast yesterday.'

'Did no one bring you a drink even?'

Hannah shook her head.

'Well, I'm sorry about that and I'll have one sent in. If you behave yourself, we may consider letting you join the others later.'

'I'll behave.'

It was nearly half an hour before the door opened again and the Assistant Matron brought in a mug of water herself.

'Thank you.' Hannah sipped it reluctantly, seeing the bits floating in it because the water had not been allowed to settle after being drawn from the well. There were dirty marks on the mug too, as if it hadn't been washed properly, but she was so thirsty she forced some liquid down.

'Breakfast will be late, I'm afraid. The cook hasn't arrived.'

'Could I help? I'm a good cook.'

Again that thoughtful scrutiny followed by a quick shake of the head. 'You can't be assigned duties till the doctor's seen you, and not even then if he considers you dangerous.' She picked up the half-empty mug. 'Not so thirsty after all?'

'The water hasn't had time to settle and the mug is dirty. I'm sorry. I'm not used to that sort of thing.'

'You'll get used to it or starve in here.' It wasn't said in a threatening tone, but wearily. 'We have a hard job keeping up with everything.'

'I'm sure you do. Thank you.'

'They'll bring you some food soon.'

But the food was lumpy porridge in another dirty bowl and she just couldn't force herself to put it into her mouth.

It wasn't till well after noon that the doctor came, pausing in the doorway to stare at Hannah in shock. 'Mrs Firth! I didn't realise it was you.' He approached the bed, studying her. 'How are you feeling today?'

'Bewildered, Dr Kent. I don't understand why they brought me here. I was angry yesterday, certainly, but I'm not insane.'

'Your voice sounds husky.'

'I'm thirsty.' Even as she spoke her stomach growled.

'Have they not fed you?'

She shrugged. 'The food wasn't palatable and the bowl was dirty. They seem run off their feet.'

Dr Kent asked her several questions and watched her carefully as she answered. 'Your daughter-in-law says you've had several dizzy turns and you get disoriented sometimes.'

'I've had two dizzy turns. And each time it was because *she* put something in my tea. I can't prove that, but it's what happened.' As she saw him look at her more warily, Hannah added quickly, 'She gives the same thing to her little son to keep him quiet. It's in a blue bottle and I think she gets it from the apothecary in Upper Hetton.'

He looked at her reprovingly. 'That sort of claim will do you no good.'

'I shan't mention it again then, but it's true nonetheless and should be easy enough for you to prove.'

'I shall have to keep you under observation for a while before I come to a decision about your future. If I let you join the other inmates, you won't do anything stupid, will you, Mrs Firth?'

Hannah shook her head. 'No. I've gained control of my anger. It'll serve no purpose to unleash it on these people.'

'It'll serve no purpose to unleash it on anyone,' the doctor said sternly.

She forced herself to say, 'Yes, you're right. Sorry.'

As he walked away, Maurice Kent frowned. The new Board of Guardians were very zealous and where once he would simply have released Hannah Firth into her family's care, now he had to keep her here until they approved her release. It was such a waste of everyone's time. As if he didn't know better than they did when a person was dangerous or not!

He frowned at that thought. Hannah didn't seem at all senile, which her daughter-in-law claimed she was. In fact, Hannah was very young-looking for her age, and was respected in the village as a vigorous and capable woman. Could she be telling the truth about what her daughter-in-law was doing? There was a mixture sold for pacifying babies that came in a blue bottle. He disapproved of it strongly, but mothers would use it.

Why would Patty Firth behave like that towards her mother-in-law, though? It simply didn't make sense.

When they let Hannah into the common room later on, she took an involuntary step backwards at what she saw and had to hold back a whimper of dismay. Most of the inmates were so old! A toothless woman sat rocking on a stool in a corner, mumbling to herself, another was staring vacantly into space, a younger woman was rubbing the table over and over as if wiping it clean and another woman, extremely thin, was cowering in a corner, flinching away from something invisible.

Dear God, how would she bear it here?

An inmate came in with a bucket of stew and thumped it down on the table. She picked up some dirty dishes and started to ladle it out. Hannah looked at them and her gorge rose. 'Is there nowhere to wash these?'

'Fancy, aren't you? Think I've time to fuss over details?'

'I'd be happy to help you.'

'Not till I'm sure you won't hit me over the head when I turn my back, you won't. I'm a pauper, not an idiot like you.' She gestured to a letter P on her sleeve and Hannah looked down at her own, to see I for idiot printed in red. Humiliation welled in her and she had to blink away tears.

When she received her own stew, Hannah knew she couldn't eat it, however hungry she was, and passed it to the woman next to her who was waiting eagerly for her food. She went to stand by the wall, hugging her arms round herself and watching the others eat, wondering what to do with herself.

'You're not eating?'

She looked up to see Matron standing beside her. 'I couldn't. The dishes haven't been washed for quite some time.'

Jean Gregory went to look for herself, then turned to the woman serving. 'Why haven't you washed these, Mary? I told you this morning about that.'

The woman suddenly put on a whining tone. 'I didn't have time.'

Jean turned to Hannah. 'Take one of the empty dishes and come with me.' She led her into the next room and indicated a bucket. 'You can wash your dish in that and then carry the bucket back to soak the others. You must eat something.'

The water had a bit of scum floating in it but was nearly clean so Hannah controlled her disgust and washed the dish as best she could, wiping it on her petticoat. 'I'll be happy to help with the food preparation or cleaning if you're short-staffed,' she offered again.

'As soon as we're sure you're calm enough.'

Hannah looked the Matron in the eye. 'I'm not mad.'

'We'll see.'

She forced down some of the stew, a tasteless, thin liquid filled mainly with potatoes, and ate a piece of stale bread with it. That filled the aching emptiness of her stomach, at least. When the others had finished eating she collected their dishes and set them to soak in the bucket.

The woman who'd brought the food watched her resentfully.

Hannah avoided her eyes. She didn't want to make enemies here, but it cost little extra effort to keep the dishes clean, even if you didn't sweep the floor.

After that, time dragged because there was nothing to do and no one who could hold a sensible conversation. She spent most of the day staring out of the window and wondering when Lemuel would come to visit her.

But he didn't come at all.

For all her resolve, after they were locked in for the night, this time in a communal dormitory with rows of narrow beds down each side to which some of the inmates were chained, Hannah wept herself to sleep on the lumpy straw mattress.

Lemuel started his day's work as usual but finished early and went to call at the doctor's house. Somehow he couldn't make himself go to the asylum, he just couldn't. He had a horror of that place.

Patty watched him wash and put on his Sunday clothes, a sour expression on her face. 'I suppose you're going about *her*?'

'Of course I am. She's my mother.'

'And I'm your wife. Don't I come first? I've had a terrible day and I need your help now.'

For once he didn't let her shrill voice push him into doing what she wanted. 'I need to find out what's wrong with Mam.'

'She's going mad, that's what's wrong. I've *told* you! It's the same as my mother, only it takes years for it to develop. They'll probably let her out once she's calmed down and then if we're strict with her, she can perfectly well do simple household jobs.'

He didn't answer her but left the house and went to knock on the doctor's side door, waiting patiently on a hard wooden bench while Dr Kent finished his meal.

'I came about my mother.'

Dr Kent frowned at him. 'I'd expected to see you earlier, or to hear that you'd called at the asylum.'

Lemuel stared down at the ground. 'I hate that place.'

'Tell me – how often have you seen your mother have these funny turns? With your own eyes, I mean.'

Lemuel frowned and thought back. 'Twice. But Patty's with her more than I am and she's seen it happen several times.'

'Has anyone else seen it?'

'Well, she had one turn when she was visiting her friend Louisa. They had to carry her back. That's when I first saw her like that.'

'Has anyone else seen her?'

'I don't know. You'll have to ask Patty.'

Dr Kent regarded him thoughtfully. 'Hmm. Well, your mother seems calm enough now and is settling in well as an inmate in the Female Idiots' Ward, which is presumably what you want.' He noted with satisfaction that Lemuel winced at that blunt phrase.

'No, it's not. I can't bear to think of her in there. She's *not* an idiot! What I want is for her to come home.'

'The rules say she can't do that until we're sure she's fit to be released. I hope you'll go and see her soon. Inmates derive a good deal of comfort from visits from their families.'

'I'm pretty busy.'

'Too busy to see your own mother?' Dr Kent didn't attempt to hide the scorn he was feeling. 'If she continues to improve, we can let her out under your supervision in a few days' time.'

'It'd be my wife who'd supervise her. I'm in the work-shop all day.'

'Well, it'll still be you who's responsible because she's *your* mother and it's *your* duty to look after her. Surely you accept that?'

'Yes, I suppose so.' Lemuel resumed his study of his feet.

'Now, if you have no more questions?' When the other man didn't speak, the doctor saw him out and locked the door behind him, standing for a moment in the darkness, frowning. Something was wrong, but what? Was Hannah Firth fooling them all? Lunatics could be very cunning. Or was Patty Firth the one telling lies? He didn't like that young woman, he had to admit, but it was no reason to disbelieve her. And it could be hard to be saddled with two ageing women who needed caring for. Very hard.

He suddenly remembered what Hannah had said. It wouldn't hurt to ask the apothecary in Upper Hetton about the mixture Hannah claimed her daughter-in-law used for the child next time he was over there. That would be a start towards finding out the truth.

*   *   *

Hannah woke in the morning and a sick, heavy feeling settled in her stomach when she realised where she was. She went to relieve herself at the communal bucket and then helped one of the old women to do the same. The bucket needed emptying. When the door opened, she had intended to be sitting on her bed, as neat as she could make herself, but another of the old women had started sobbing and she couldn't help going to see what was wrong.

'She'll have soiled herself,' a voice said behind her.

'Yes, she has. If you have clean clouts, I'll change her.'

The Matron's assistant stared at her. 'How are *you* feeling this morning, Hannah?'

'I'm fine physically, thank you. I never ail. But I'm sad to find myself in this place. And that night soil bucket needs emptying.'

The woman studied her, then shrugged. 'Come with me. And bring the bucket.'

Hannah did as she was told and emptied the bucket, rinsing it out as well as she could under the pump in the courtyard, then rinsing her hands several times. She walked back quietly, obeying every order to stop or stand as doors were unlocked then locked again.

'Well, you seem better today.'

'I was never insane, just very angry indeed,' Hannah said with a wry smile. 'And I'd be grateful if you'd find me some work to do, however menial, because time passes very slowly in here and I prefer to keep busy.'

'I'll ask Matron.'

She was back a few minutes later. 'Matron says you're

a good cook and can help in the kitchen, but you're not to touch a knife.'

'Very well. Perhaps I can scour the dishes and make the porridge?'

She worked hard, always under the eyes of someone or other. They didn't talk to her much, looking at her as if she had two heads, so she kept quiet. But she had the satisfaction of knowing she was making a difference to the cleanliness of the place, at least. And the porridge was edible today.

That afternoon she was called out to see the doctor again.

'How are you, Mrs Firth?'

'As well as can be expected, given the circumstances.' She looked down at her drab grey clothing and bit her lip because the shame of being here still upset her, and the fear that she might not be let out again was creeping in. Could they not see that she wasn't mad?

'Matron tells me you've been making yourself useful, so we've decided to give you a few days' trial helping round the place, then we'll reconsider your case.'

'I'll be allowed home again?'

'Only into your son's care, Mrs Firth.'

'Is he not allowed to visit me? I'd expected to see him.'

'Of course he's allowed to visit you. Perhaps he's been busy. I've no doubt he'll come soon.'

With that she had to be content, but she knew now that Lemuel had deliberately not come to see her and that hurt.

She only wept at night when no one could see her, and not for long because she didn't want them to see her with puffy red eyes. But it seemed if she didn't spill a few tears they gathered in her breast and weighed her down like a stone.

Lemuel sent the apprentice home early and sat down in the corner to think. He didn't want to go into the house because Patty had been very sharp lately. Of course she tired more quickly these days. She didn't carry a child easily. He wished his mother were still there to help her. The house was looking very neglected and the smell from Mrs Rigby's bedroom was terrible. When he had mentioned that, Patty had fired up and told him to change the dirty linen himself if it upset him, because she'd been too busy looking after his son and cooking his meals. She had also demanded a washerwoman to help her, but he couldn't afford one and had to refuse. Business was still very slow and he knew he hadn't his father's ability to sense out new jobs, so was feeling panic-stricken when he contemplated the future.

Worst of all at the moment was the guilt he felt for not visiting his mother. He couldn't explain the terror the poorhouse and asylum had always inspired in him. It didn't make sense because none of his family had ever wound up in there – until now! – and he'd never even been inside the place. But sometimes you could hear the lunatics inside moaning and shrieking, especially when the moon was full, and it always made him shiver and feel quite sick with dread. And to end up there in the paupers' side because you were too old to work, well, it was what everyone dreaded except the rich.

In the middle of the night, lying awake again, he knew he would have to face his fears and visit his mother. He wanted to see her and yet was afraid to. What if she really was going mad? He couldn't imagine it, but they wouldn't have locked her up in that place for no reason, would they?

When he was eating breakfast, he said to Patty, 'I must go and visit my mother today.'

'You shan't do it! She'll cozen you into bringing her home again and I'm not having two mad old women to look after. I can't cope with one!'

She started sobbing, but for once her tears and then her angry shouting made no difference. His mind was made up and he was enough like his father to carry through what he had decided, whatever the cost.

In the afternoon he washed off the dirt of his working day very carefully and made his way along the back lane, ashamed to be seen visiting that place. It occurred to him as he walked how bad his mother must be feeling shut up there.

When he rang the bell and asked to see her, the porter gestured him inside. 'Sit on that bench. I'll see if she can be brought down.'

So Lemuel had to sit there with the occasional shrill call or scream echoing around him, making him shiver.

He heard footsteps and looked up to see the porter beckoning to him. 'Matron says you can see her on your own.'

They led him into a little room with two benches and a table. He couldn't bear to sit down but paced to and fro, three paces one way, two and a half the other. When he heard a sound, he swung round and gasped in shock to see his mother standing there, wearing poorhouse garb. For a moment, he couldn't move, couldn't speak.

Then his eyes settled on her face and he realised she hadn't really changed. She looked sad, though, deeply sad.

Hannah didn't attempt to touch him and he didn't approach her.

'Shall we sit down, Lemuel?' she asked at last. 'I've been on my feet helping in the kitchen since early morning and would be glad of a rest.'

He nodded and sat, trying to think of something to say.

Her voice was gentle. 'Can't you even speak to me, Lemuel?'

'How are you feeling, Mam?'

'The same as ever. As sane as you, but deeply shamed to be shut up in this place. Oh, Lemuel, I didn't deserve that of you!'

'It was Patty who did it.'

'And in the six days that have passed since they brought me here, was it Patty who stopped you coming to see me? It would have been a comfort at least to see one of my own, for there's no comfort to be found inside this place.'

Her voice was bitter but quiet and she showed no sign of madness that he could see.

'What happened?' he asked.

'Patty knew I was going to leave and tried to drug me again to make me have another dizzy turn. I found out and grew angry.' Hannah sighed. 'Too angry. I shall not let myself get so angry again. It does no good.'

'Patty wouldn't drug you, Mam. You must have made a mistake.' He realised then that she *was* suffering from delusions, however normal she seemed.

'She drugs your son, too, to keep him quiet. The mixture is kept in a little blue bottle.'

'Mam, I can't help you if you keep repeating such falsehoods.'

Hannah let out a long sigh that was almost a sob. 'I wanted to tell you the truth once, but if you intend to blind yourself to what's going on, I shan't repeat myself.'

'They say you can come home again once they're sure you're – calm. We'll be responsible for you but you must stay with us and behave yourself if you're not to be brought back here.'

'So I'm to spend the rest of my life drudging for your wife, who doesn't even speak to me civilly, with not even a penny piece to call my own? To have people in the village turn away from me in fear? Shame on you, Lemuel Firth, that you've let Patty bring me to this!' She stood up, graceful and quick as ever, and turned towards the door as if to leave.

'Mam!'

She turned to look at him, but her expression was closed and tight now.

'Mam, the only way you'll ever be let out is if you'll agree to submit to our supervision.' He watched her lean against the wall for a moment, her arm covering her face as if she couldn't stand even to look at him, then she rubbed her sleeve across her eyes to dash away tears. Tears! He'd never seen her crying before: not when his father died, not even when his brother Malachi left home. The sight shook him and he was going to go and comfort her but she recovered, sniffing back the tears and straightening her shoulders.

'Well, then, so be it,' she said quietly. 'It can't be as bad as this place. But you'll know, Lemuel, how unhappy I am and it'll be on your conscience.'

When he opened the door and asked to see the Matron, the porter led his mother back up to the ward and she went quietly, without a backward glance.

But the large red letter I on the back of her coarse grey dress seemed to burn into his eyes for a long time afterwards.

Once she was back in the ward Hannah didn't look for a task but went to stand by the window, staring out, one hand clutching a bar, her head resting against that arm.

Lemuel was a weak reed. She'd always known that, but not how weak until now. Very well, she would find a way to help herself instead. She would live this lie with seeming meekness for a little while, but had no intention of spending the rest of her life under Patty's harsh rule.

As she looked across the rooftops it came to her that she would create a threepenny dream for herself, one so splendid it would lighten even her present life. She had no need to consider the first part of the dream, that was easy: to escape from Hetton-le-Hill and build a new life for herself, away from Patty and Lemuel.

But that wasn't enough. Malachi would have called it a mere penny dream. So she let her fancy wander and dared to think of what she had lost and what she would like most in the whole world to regain – her own home and a man to love, as she had never loved her husband. A man with a quick brain and a pleasant nature, who cared for her and didn't just see her as a convenient housekeeper and producer of children. But if this man had children, so much the better. She loved children and had always been sorry only to have had two, but John had never been very energetic in bed and had eventually given up touching her even, let alone kissing her. And Patty deliberately kept her away from her grandson, something which upset her greatly. She worried about that poor baby, who didn't seem to be thriving as he should and who slept so much. But when she tried to help with him, it only provoked temper tantrums from her daughter-in-law, so she had learned to keep away from little John.

So why not dream of finding love again? She had met it once when young and full of so many desires, even though what she had done was called a sin. And it had been every bit as bright as the story books said, for a short time at least. The memory of that man's love had warmed her for many years. But then duty had prevailed, duty and the fact that she had Lemuel to consider, could not bear to run away with her lover if it meant leaving her small son behind. Malachi was the result of that love, the bright shining gift fate had given her when she'd sent her lover away.

It seemed for a moment as if the sun shone more brightly, as if the whole room was filled with the shimmering light of her beautiful dream, then it slowly faded. She stood there for a few moments longer as the sounds of her prison reasserted themselves, then went off to find some task to keep herself busy.

Malachi was gone, she decided in bed that night – the first time that she hadn't wept once the lights were extinguished – and Lemuel was no help. But she still had her wits and would have to rely on them.

She could only wait now. And dream. And watch for an opportunity to escape.

To cheer herself up, she began to picture the home she wanted – and the man. Tall, with dark hair and kind eyes. Vigorous. She blushed to remember how vigorous her lover had been in bed, and she too, with a proper man's touch on her skin.

She fell asleep in a warm glow of hope.

CHAPTER SIX

November 1863

Dr Kent applied to the parson, who was Chairman of the Board of Guardians, for permission to release Hannah Firth. Mr Barnish hummed and hawed, then agreed to sign the relevant document as if he were doing the doctor a personal favour. Annoyed with these delays and increasingly doubtful as to whether Hannah Firth really was suffering from softening of the brain, Maurice Kent then sent a message to Lemuel that he could come and take his mother home.

'I'll go and do that,' Patty said at once.

'Be kind to her and . . .' But Lemuel was talking to empty air.

His wife returned a short time later, looking furious, and burst into the workshop. Seeing a customer there, she bit back the hot words that had been boiling inside her as she walked home.

The man looked at her uneasily and left without buying the wooden bucket he'd been examining.

'It's better if you don't come in here,' Lemuel said. 'Men like to make their purchases in peace.'

'I didn't say a word. Not a single one.'

'But you glowered at him, especially when he said he'd think about it. Look, Patty love, we're not selling nearly as much as we did when Father was alive. I really miss Malachi who was always better than me at selling stuff. We have to be careful how we treat customers or we'll be running short of money.' He looked beyond her. 'Didn't you bring Mother home?'

'No, I didn't! They wouldn't let me, said it needed the man of the house to sign some bit of paper. I told them they were wasting everyone's time and that I know how to write my name as well as you, but they wouldn't listen. So you'll have to go and get her.'

'I'll do it later.'

'Go and do it now. I need help with all sorts of things in the house. I'm exhausted.'

When he'd left, Patty looked round the kitchen and smiled. She'd soon have her servant back and intended to make her mother-in-law work harder than ever.

This time Mother Firth wouldn't dare protest or disobey.

Hannah was summoned to the Matron's office and found Lemuel waiting for her there.

'Your son has come to take you home, Mrs Firth, but you have to realise that an eye will be kept on you and if you seem to be behaving erratically, or if you offer your daughter-in-law any violence, you'll be brought back here. Try to live quietly and not let things get on top of you.'

Hannah kept her hands folded in front of her and her expression calm as she nodded.

Matron turned to Lemuel. 'I'll take your mother to change into her own clothes. Please wait for her in the hall.'

So he had to kick his heels for another ten minutes,

shuddering at one point as a woman began to scream somewhere close by. When his mother came down the stairs behind Matron, she looked so normal he could have wept with relief, but as they walked home, she said not a word and soon he began to feel uncomfortable again.

'Are you glad to be coming home again, Mam?'

She looked at him, her face so expressionless it didn't look like hers any more. 'If you say so.'

'What sort of answer is that?'

'The only sort I shall dare give from now on.'

'Mam, really. This isn't necessary.'

'Nor was it necessary to put me in that place. I can never hold my head up in this village again. How do you think I'm going to feel on Sunday, with everyone staring at me in church and edging away from me afterwards? Or will you let me stay home from church from now on?'

'Patty likes us to attend,' he said uneasily.

'She'll enjoy it even more from now on, then. She loves to humiliate me.'

'You malign her, Mam.'

'Do I? If you say so.'

'Won't you miss the singing at church? You have such a lovely voice.'

'I seem to have lost any desire to sing lately.'

He opened his mouth, then shut it again.

When they got home they went in via the back garden and he stopped outside the workshop, waving towards the back door. 'You know the way into your own home.'

'Aren't you even coming to see how she greets me?'

'Mam, please!'

But when she'd gone inside, he hesitated before creeping up to the door to listen. To his dismay, Patty was gloating and telling his mother how hard she would have to work from now on if she didn't want to be put back in the asylum. That hurt him, but he didn't dare go inside to intervene because he knew it'd make his wife even worse if he did.

Eh, he'd be glad when this new baby was born, though the birth was several months away yet. Surely afterwards Patty would stop being so irritable and unkind to everyone? She'd always been sharp, he knew that, but never as bad as this. The birth of their first child had affected her badly, but then she'd seemed a lot better. Perhaps he shouldn't have pressed for another baby. But he loved children, wanted several.

Hannah took a deep breath before opening the back door. As she had expected, Patty turned round and looked at her with a gloating expression.

'Have you learned your lesson now?' she asked. 'I told you, I always get my own way.'

'I've learned a lot lately,' Hannah replied, folding her hands and waiting near the door.

'Well, go and get your pinny on, then you can clean up my mother. I haven't had time to go near her today.'

The old lady was in great distress, covered in her own filth, and for all her own troubles, Hannah felt sorry for her. She worked hard and not until she'd finished and turned round did she notice that all her ornaments had gone from the shelf. She pressed her lips together and breathed deeply. No matter what happened, she mustn't get angry again.

Out of curiosity she went to her drawers and found some of her underclothes gone, too, the prettiest ones, though none of them would fit Patty, who was much plumper than she was, even when she wasn't expecting a baby. But it was no use complaining. She had more important things to consider now, the main one being winning her freedom.

She worked hard, doing Patty's bidding and not saying a word unless spoken to. But she didn't initiate any task, always waiting to be told what to do.

'You haven't said a word for the past hour!' Patty complained as they set the table for the midday meal.

Hannah shrugged.

'I prefer you to talk to me!' Patty shouted, just as Lemuel came in for his meal.

'I'm afraid of speaking out of turn.'

Lemuel carried the apprentice's platter out to the workshop, because Patty refused to let the lad eat with them, then came back and sat down. He said grace then began to eat, noticing how his mother picked at her food.

'Your friend Louisa's got a new bonnet,' Patty told Hannah. 'It doesn't suit her though. You'll see it on Sunday.'

Lemuel caught his mother's sad expression and winced. He listened to his wife's spiteful remarks, noticing that his mother replied only when pushed, and mainly with a mere yes or no. He couldn't help remembering family meals before he'd married, with them all laughing over something witty his mother or

Malachi had said. Everything had changed so much since then.

After the meal Hannah cleared up and then waited for her daughter-in-law's instructions.

'You'd better do some washing. There are very few clean clouts left for John or my mother.'

'Very well.'

Patty came to the door of the laundry several times, as if checking on Hannah.

She looked up each time, stared back calmly at her daughter-in-law but didn't speak, then got on with her work when the door had banged shut again.

It took several days to get the house back in proper order and Hannah worked in silence most of that time.

Patty grew very irritable and several times slapped her across the face when she didn't reply.

Lemuel was passing the kitchen window on one of those occasions and saw what happened. He came storming in, furiously angry.

'How dare you hit my mother!'

'She deserved it! I have a right to chastise her if she misbehaves.'

'What did she do?'

'She was rude to me.'

'That's strange. I've hardly heard her say a word since she got back from the asylum.' He thumped his fist down on the table, making the dishes on it jump up and down. 'In any case, if you feel there's any chastise-ment to be done, that's my job, and only mine. If I find you laying one finger on my mother again, I'll do to you whatever you do to her.'

'You wouldn't dare!'

'Oh, I would. I've listened to you being rude to her ever since she got back and, heaven help me, I've said nothing. But I draw the line at your hitting her.' He leaned forward and said with great emphasis, 'You can push someone too far, even a quiet fellow like me.'

Hannah watched all this surreptitiously and with great satisfaction, but continued chopping the vegetables.

On Sunday Patty announced brightly, 'We'll all go to morning service together.'

Lemuel looked at his mother. 'Do you want to go to church, Mam?'

'No, son.'

'Well, I'm not having anyone in my house neglecting their religious duties,' Patty declared at once.

'*My* house,' Lemuel contradicted quietly.

She stared at him in shock, opened her mouth, then let it fall shut again as if she didn't quite know what to say.

He turned to Hannah. 'If you wish to stay home, Mam, then I'll understand.'

'I do,' she said.

'Lemuel, no!' Patty pleaded.

'My mother's had to bear enough humiliation. Be satisfied that you've got yourself a servant who daren't answer you back, and leave it at that. Don't forget that you'll need her help even more after you bear the child.'

As they got ready for church, Patty began to list a series of tasks for Hannah to do while they were away.

Again Lemuel intervened. 'This is the Lord's appointed day of rest and my mother has worked extremely hard all week. Sit and take your ease while we're away, Mam. You've earned it. There's nothing you need to do until we get back.'

Patty's look promised both of them retribution but Hannah thought it'd be worth it just to have an hour or two's peace.

When she judged there was no chance of them coming back suddenly, she went up the stairs and into the bedroom which had once been hers and John's. Her ornaments were there jumbled anyhow on the small mantelpiece. In the second drawer was her best petti-coat, with the pretty lace edging she had sewn on herself. She couldn't resist fingering it, but then closed the drawer and didn't look any further. When she went back down she sat with a sigh in front of the fire, staring into the flames and enjoying the simple treat of silence.

When the others came home, Patty was looking thunderously angry.

'Your friend Louisa has invited you to go and take tea with her this afternoon, Mam,' Lemuel said. 'Would you like to do that?'

'Yes, please.' She ignored Patty's spiteful comments, counting the minutes till she could set off.

Louisa was on her own in the kitchen. 'Come in, love.' She hesitated then hugged Hannah, who hugged her back convulsively and bowed her head for a moment as tears welled in her eyes.

They sat before the fire as they had done many a time, but even with Louisa something had changed. There was a wariness in her that had not been there before, and when one of her daughters came into the kitchen to refill the teapot with boiling water, she stared furtively at Hannah as if she expected her to look different.

Once they were on their own again, Hannah said quietly, 'I need my money back now, Louisa.'

'Oh, Hannah, no! You're surely not planning to run away again?'

'I just want my money. You don't need to know why.'

'I don't think I should give it to you.'

Hannah stared at her in deep dismay. 'Louisa, if you've ever considered yourself my friend, I beg of you now to do as I ask and not tell anyone. I'm no more mad than you are, but Patty is making my life an absolute misery. She's even slapped my face several times this week.'

'She didn't! Eh, to think of that.' Louisa hesitated then admitted, 'She's been boasting in the village of having brought you to heel. It fair made my gorge rise and I wasn't the only one.'

Hannah breathed deeply, but didn't let the anger swell. 'The money?' she prompted. *'Please?'* Her voice broke on the last word.

'Oh, very well.' Louisa whisked upstairs and came down with the shabby little purse. Hannah took it from her and slipped it into her pocket.

When she left, she hugged her friend. 'Thank you.'

'I'll come and see you one afternoon.'

'No. It'll upset her too much. Let her get used to Sundays first. If you want to invite me again, that is?'

'Of course I do.'

But Hannah knew she wouldn't be there next Sunday if she could help it.

*   *   *

Over breakfast Oliver's father said, 'Better come to the library later this morning, lad. We need to discuss what to do with your inheritance.'

'Very well.' His heart began thumping in apprehension. He'd been dreading this encounter, absolutely dreading it, and hoping his father wouldn't say anything about his inheritance until after his actual birthday. He took a deep breath then another one. This was no time to be a coward, but he did so hate shouting and rows.

About eleven o'clock he put on his new lounge jacket to give himself courage and made his way down to the library, his favourite room in this huge, soulless house.

'Ah, there you are, Oliver. Come in and sit down, lad.'

He looked across the room and saw Walter standing in the bay window. 'I'd rather speak to you in private, sir.'

'What?' Richard stared at him in puzzlement, then shrugged and turned to his heir. 'Oh, very well. Leave us, Walter.'

'What's the secret? We all know exactly what piddling amount he was left by his godmother.'

'It's not a piddling amount. It's seven hundred pounds a year and that's plenty for me to live on. I'm only grateful Mother's friend remembered me in her will. Besides, the money has been mounting up in the eight years since she died, so I shall have some capital behind me as well.'

Walter laughed scornfully. 'You don't know what you're talking about. You live with your head in books, not the real world.'

'I shall live my life as I choose and it's *my* business what I do with my money, not yours,' Oliver said quietly, relieved that his voice hadn't wobbled.

With a snort of disgust Walter left the room, leaving the door slightly ajar. Oliver walked across and shut it properly, seeing his brother's shadow on the carpet outside, then rejoined his father by the fire.

'I've been thinking,' Richard began, 'that it'd be best to sell that house of yours, now that you can. It's quite old and will need a lot of repairs. You should invest the money you get in Government Bonds. With so little capital, you can't afford to take any risks by looking for higher interest.'

'I don't want to sell the house.' Oliver took a deep breath and added, 'In fact, I'm going to live there.'

Richard stared at his younger son as if he'd suddenly sprouted horns. 'What do you mean? Your home is here and there's no need to set up house elsewhere until you marry, if you ever do, and probably not even then.'

Oliver hid a shudder at the thought of living with Walter for the rest of his life. 'I've been planning this for a while, Father. I love Spinneys and intend to make it my home. I doubt I'll ever marry, though.'

'Well, I'm not having it! What will folk say if a young fellow like you moves out as soon as he turns twenty-one? And how will you look after yourself? You haven't the first clue about running a house.'

'I can hire servants to do that.'

'You're not taking any of *mine*!'

'Only Nanny Parkin.' His old nurse was well aware of his plans and had made it plain that if he didn't take her with him she'd follow him anyway.

'Isn't she a bit old to be of much use?'

'I don't think so and she's determined to come with me. I'd like to have her if you don't mind.'

'She's not doing much here. We won't miss her. What about your capital?' his father demanded testily. 'What'll you do with that?'

'I'll need some of it to renovate the house, but I'm sure you're right about investing the rest in secure funds. I'll get my lawyer to look into it.'

'*Your* lawyer? We have a family lawyer. What's wrong with Dawson? I chose him carefully to look after things for you once I'm gone. Walter can look after himself, but you need help. And I *trust* Dawson, which I don't most lawyers. You'll tell this fellow you've changed your mind.'

'I'm sorry father. I think it's better that I have someone of my own.'

His father's face turned so deep a red, Oliver held his breath for a moment.

'You cheeky young hound! If you leave here, not a penny will you get from me!' Richard thundered. 'This is the thanks I get for trying to protect you after I'm gone.'

'I don't think I need protecting financially. My needs are very simple and I'm careful with money. I shall have more than enough from my legacy.' But he could tell that, having made one of those impulsive decisions to which he was prone, his father wasn't going to back down.

Face still dark red, voice still loud and angry, Richard gestured to the door. 'Then if you won't take the advice of one who knows better, you'd better get out of here today. And don't ever cross my doorstep again.'

Oliver hadn't expected this, because it was two weeks till he reached his majority, but he wasn't going to plead. 'I'm sad you're taking it that way, Father. You'll always be welcome in my house, though Walter won't.' He could see the stubborn expression on his father's face and bit back a protest. After all, this would get him away from his brother sooner and he'd easily be able to live on his savings, because his father had always made him a very generous allowance and he'd got plenty saved.

'What do you mean, "Walter won't"?'

Oliver had held his tongue for long enough. 'He's made my whole life a misery, bullying me for as long as I can remember. He still thumps me sometimes, even now. If I never see him again, it'll please me greatly. I expect he'll be waiting for me upstairs now and will hit me a few times before I go – where it doesn't show, of course. But it'll be the last time he gets the chance.'

'I don't believe you! And if someone hits you, you can hit them back, can't you?'

'You know I'm much weaker than him. Besides, I've found it only makes him hit me harder if I try to fight back.'

'Get out! Get out at once!'

But after Oliver had left, Richard snorted and muttered to himself then rang the bell. When the butler arrived, he said, 'Find Walter and send him to me at once, Robbs. In fact, go and fetch him yourself. Then get someone to help Oliver pack and tell them to stay with him till he leaves. He's moving out. Put a carriage and a cart at his disposal. He'll want to take his books and his writing desk, his mare too. Oh, and if you find Walter bullying him or hurting him when you go up, I want you to let me know, though you're not to say anything to the other servants.'

'They're already aware of what goes on, I'm afraid, Mr Dewhurst.'

'You mean – he does bully the lad?'

'Often, sir.'

Shocked, Richard gulped, ashamed of being the last to know.

It took longer for Walter to arrive than he'd expected.

Upstairs Oliver found his brother waiting for him inside his bedroom with the contents of the desk scattered all over it and a few papers torn up on the floor nearby. But he had learned many years ago to conceal any items that were important to him. Walter had never found his hiding places because he was too lazy to search, and the servants who could have told him where to look had very kindly kept quiet.

'Well? What was the big secret?' his brother demanded.

'None of your business.'

Walter shot to his feet and grasped Oliver by the front of his jacket. 'Anything that happens here is my business and don't you forget it. One day this house will belong to me, and if you're living in it, you'd better toe the line if you know what's good for you.'

Oliver pulled his jacket out of his brother's hands and gave Walter a push that took him by surprise and sent him staggering backwards.

His face lit up. 'If it's a fight you want . . .'

Oliver moved quickly behind a chair and picked it up

to use as a barrier, though he knew his brother would soon drag it out of his hands. 'You know it's not.'

'Then you shouldn't provoke me, should you?' Feinting to one side, Walter moved quickly to wrench the chair from Oliver with a caw of triumph. He then twisted his brother's arm behind his back and shoved his face against the wall. 'Now, answer – my – question.' To emphasise his point he banged Oliver's head hard on the wall with each word.

There was a knock on the door.

'Go away!' Walter yelled.

'I'm sorry, sir, but your father wishes to see you at once. Very urgent, he says.'

After a moment's hesitation Walter let go and straightened his clothing. 'This is only postponed,' he warned his brother as he left.

As he sauntered down to the library, the butler moved in front of him to announce his arrival.

Richard looked up. 'Where were you?'

'With Oliver, having a brotherly chat.'

'Sit down. I've something to tell you in a minute.' His father moved to the door and followed the butler out. 'Well?' he asked in a low voice. 'What was he doing?'

In an equally low voice, Robbs replied, 'Twisting Mr Oliver's arm behind his back and banging his head against the wall. And some of the things in the room had been thrown about and destroyed. Which has happened many times before, the maids tell me.'

Richard breathed deeply and slowly, keeping the anger at bay and thinking furiously. 'Mmm. Bring us a tea tray.' With a growl of irritation, he went back into the room and sat down by the fire, staring into its dancing flames and wishing yet again that his wife hadn't died so young. He was beginning to worry about his heir. Why had he been so blind before? Too busy earning money, that's why. As he glanced at his elder son, he saw only a good-looking young fellow with the glow of good health and outdoor living on his face. Even now, nothing of Walter's cruel nature showed in his face. Strange, that.

'Oliver's moving out,' he said abruptly.

Walter straightened up suddenly. 'Moving out? Where to?'

'That house he inherited.'

'It's a hovel. Why is he leaving?' He glanced at his father. 'And why are you allowing it?'

'I told him if he leaves, he'll not come back again. I'll disinherit him.'

Walter relaxed and leaned back in the big, velvet-covered armchair. 'You could still have stopped him going if you'd wanted.'

'Oh?'

'Yes, get a doctor to say he needs caring for and keep him here with a nice, strong attendant. It'll look bad, him moving into that place when he could live here with us.'

'If he wants to go, he can. Anyway, I don't see why you're complaining. There'll be more for you now when I turn up my toes.'

A smile settled on Walter's face. 'You really are dis-inheriting him?'

'I told him, if he goes he's no son of mine.'

'Very wise.'

'But once he's gone I'm not having you visiting him, mind. Do that even once and you'll lose half your inheritance to charity. Do it twice and I'll leave you nothing, either.'

Walter gaped at him. 'You can't mean that!'

'Oh, but I do. I've found myself with one disobedient son. I'm not having two.' Richard raised an eyebrow. 'Did you ever know me go back on what I said?'

'No, but surely someone's got to keep an eye on him?'

'Why?'

'Well – to make sure he doesn't disgrace us.'

'If I've disowned him, it won't matter what he does.' Richard scowled at his heir. 'I mean it. Go near him and you'll lose your inheritance.'

Walter stood up.

'And you'll stay here with me now till he's gone. I'm not having any plotting with him behind my back.'

'Really, Father, as if I'd—'

'Do as you're told or take the consequences!'

Walter looked at him uneasily. The old chap was getting stranger by the day. However, if he really had disinherited Oliver, Walter wasn't going to do anything to upset him. He settled back in the chair and stretched out his legs to the fire, wishing, as he had many times before, that they were as long as Oliver's because every time he looked in the mirror he could see that they were too short for his body. He wondered what to talk about and was grateful when his father showed no inclination to chat. Silence fell and both men sat staring blindly into the flames.

*   *   *

Oliver watched his bags being loaded into the carriage and then a groom led his horse round and tied it to the rear.

'Your father's orders, Mr Oliver,' the young fellow said, his eyes bright with curiosity. 'You're to take her with you.'

Oliver went to pat Beauty, the gentle-natured chestnut mare he'd been riding for three years. He was touched by this gesture and felt it held some hope for a future *rapprochement* with his father, as did the fact that he'd been allowed to bring his writing desk and other possessions.

As the front door opened again, he swung round to see Nanny Parkin moving stiffly down the steps. 'You're sure of this?' he asked gently, coming to offer her his arm.

'Of course I am. You'll need someone to look after you and manage your servants. Besides, if I stayed, who'd come and talk to me? I may have a comfortable bedroom and sitting room of my own, but it's lonely up there. That brother of yours has never visited me, not once, though I raised him too, and the maids only come in to clean the room.'

'Well, you can help me hire a servant or two, and I promise faithfully you'll not be lonely at Spinneys. I'd just like to tell you that I'll never let you want for anything, whatever happens to me. I'm going to make a will as soon as I turn twenty-one, leaving you an annuity, just in case . . .'

She reached up to pat his cheek. 'Bless you, I know you'll look after me.' She smiled at him fondly. 'You can't even pass by a dog in distress, let alone desert your own. Only now, if you want a dog, you'll be able to keep one with no Walter to torment it.'

His face lit up. 'I shall, shan't I? But I'll get the house sorted out first.'

The journey to Beckleton took over half an hour and Oliver hoped that the distance alone would be enough to win him some respite from Walter, but just in case his brother came to torment him, he decided to hire a strong manservant for protection.

When they arrived the house looked forlorn, for it had been shut up for a decade, and the gardens were in a sad state too.

'Have you been inside lately?' Nanny asked abruptly, frowning at the building.

'No. I didn't dare show an interest. That groom of Walter's always kept an eye on my comings and goings. But I know Lexham has made sure the house is weatherproof.' He helped her out and they stood staring at Spinneys, her arm tucked comfortably under his again. For all its air of neglect, it was a pretty place, built of old-fashioned red brick with a grey slate roof – a square, uncompromising house of three storeys. It had three windows along the first floor and three dormer windows above them.

'Well, come on. Let's go inside.' Nanny turned to the groom and coachman. 'Can you lads carry things in for us? I don't know how we'll manage else.'

''Course we can, Mrs Parkin,' the groom said. 'Just tell us where you want everything.'

Oliver turned the key in the lock with a sense of eager anticipation and flung open the front door.

Inside everything was dark and, with a tutting sound, Nanny went round pulling back curtains, sneezing as this raised clouds of dust. 'The sooner we can find a couple of maids to go through this place, the better.'

The groom paused as he heard this. 'I've a cousin looking for work, Mrs Parkin. Only young, but she's a right hard worker.'

'Send her to see me as soon as you can, Ned.'

The groom looked at the under-coachman, who shrugged and said, 'We can stop on the way back if you want a quick word with her. Don't tell anyone, though.'

'Thanks.' But as the under-coachman walked outside, Ned hesitated then glanced over his shoulder and said quickly, 'If you're looking for a groom, Mr Oliver, I'd be glad to be considered.'

'I think it'll be a groom and general outside man combined. A bit lowly for someone like you, isn't it?'

'That'd suit me fine, actually. I have family near here and I'd be glad to be closer to home.' And glad too to leave the bullying servants Walter was starting to collect around him as the older ones were pensioned off.

Oliver looked at the sturdy young fellow and smiled. 'Better give in your notice then.'

Ned grinned at him. 'I'll do that. Maybe they'll let me go early, seeing it's for you. I'll ask Coachman to speak to Mr Lexham.'

'An extra guinea a year on your present wages all right?'

'Fine with me.'

When Ned left the house, Oliver turned round. Nanny was no longer beside him and he followed the trail of open doors into the kitchen at the rear.

'Very old-fashioned,' she said scornfully. 'We'll need a new closed stove in here, Oliver love.'

'Even before that, we'll need to buy some food.'

But as he was speaking, Ned came in with a big wicker basket. 'Cook said you'd need this. Oh, and you're to keep the basket and all that's in it.'

'Does my father know?'

Ned shrugged. 'He must do.'

'Don't look a gift horse in the mouth,' Nanny said quietly from the pantry doorway. 'You can't afford to now.'

'I'll just go and stable your horse for you, Mr Oliver.'

'I'll come with you.'

They found the stables, like the rest of the house, bare and dusty but with an old trap standing in the small coachhouse at the rear.

'This should be all right to use, with a bit of work,' Ned said, examining it and climbing up to the driving seat. 'You'll have to get some hay and stuff delivered today though. Mr Gritton at Bent Edge Farm is a good man to deal with.' He gave directions for getting there.

'I'll ride over this afternoon.' Oliver patted Beauty's neck. 'I think you'll be all right till then, old girl, eh? I can at least supply you with water.' He turned to the groom, still worried. 'You're sure you want to come and work for me, Ned? You'll have to be prepared to do anything that's necessary.'

'I don't mind, sir.'

It seemed to Oliver years later that joy was threaded through that whole day like a bright, shining tapestry. It was fun exploring the house, finding out what he owned, trying out the various pieces of dusty, old-fashioned furniture and choosing a bedroom. He and Nanny made a quick picnic lunch from the hamper, and just as they were finishing a knock on the kitchen door revealed a strapping, rosy-faced girl with a mop of curly hair and a beaming smile. 'Cousin Ned said you were looking for help in the house, Mr Dewhurst. I'm Penny.'

Nanny came forward. 'Leave this to me, Mr Oliver.'

'Thank you, Mrs Parkin.'

He could see how much Nanny was enjoying being in charge of domestic matters. Smiling, he went off to the room which he had chosen for his main sitting-room, where the alcoves on either side of the fireplace contained well-stocked bookcases, even if the books were old-fashioned, and there was a bay window into which his writing desk would fit nicely. He had vague memories of his godmother sitting writing letters there, could imagine himself doing the same, or just staring out into the garden knowing he wouldn't be interrupted.

Nanny came in, so full of self-importance he couldn't help smiling. 'Well?'

'I've hired her. She's only fifteen, but seems strong and cheerful. I can't abide a sulker, never could. What's more, as she's Ned's cousin, I'll not have to worry about her background. She needs to bring her things over but says her father will help her do that, and she's going to put word round that I'm looking for a cook and a daily scrubbing woman. So you get off now and see about the hay and whatever else you need for that horse of yours. Oh, and on your way, you can call in at the village and send whoever runs the grocery shop out to see me. They'll be glad of our custom, I make no doubt.'

He rode out to find that the clouds had cleared and a weak winter sun was shining, even more welcome than the summer warmth at this chilly time of year. It seemed another omen and he couldn't prevent tears of joy from welling in his eyes as he rode down a narrow lane.

At last he was free!

CHAPTER SEVEN

December 1863

Ginny continued to go for walks every fine Sunday, in spite of her step-father's grumbling about her wasting her time. She stuck to her excuse of needing fresh air and exercise, but really she went because it was the only chance she had to see Nick, with whom she was deeply in love and who said he loved her.

One Sunday she happened to glance back just after she entered the woods and caught a glimpse of a head bobbing down behind a wall.

Someone was following her!

She could see it was a man, but wasn't very good at making out details from that distance. It could only be her step-father, though, because what other man was around the farm at this time on a Sunday? Anyway, why would the cowman or the labourers want to follow her? Thank goodness she'd noticed him! She'd have to take a lot more care from now on because if he caught her meeting a young man – any young man – he'd beat her senseless, she was sure, and never let her out alone again.

Instead of making for the ruined cottage where Nick would be waiting for her, she walked past the path to it, loitering in the woods, scuffing up the fallen leaves and pretending to be unaware of her pursuer. She went to sit on the wall at the top and stare out across the fields, then set off walking again, growing colder and colder because it was a very chilly day, but determined to stay out of the house as long as she usually did.

She was terrified that Nick would come looking for her, but could do nothing about that except pray for him not to appear.

Eventually she made her way home again, wondering if her step-father was still watching her. The question was soon answered. Once she heard the sound of a stone being kicked behind her, another time a twig snapped beneath a heavy foot.

She hated him! He spoiled everything.

When she went into the kitchen her mother said, 'You're back early.'

'*He* was following me. That took away all the pleasure.' She looked up at the mantelpiece clock. She wasn't all that early coming back, thank goodness.

Her mother shook her head and put one finger on her lips, then changed the subject determinedly. 'Well, I hope you enjoyed your walk.'

'Yes. I always do. I'll go up and change, then come and help you.'

'No need. I've nearly finished here.'

'I might as well. I like to keep busy.'

Her step-father said nothing when he came in, just sat down to read his newspaper, and Ginny avoided speaking to him.

As she was going to bed, he said, 'I don't trust you to go off walking like that. You're to stay home next Sunday.'

'That's not fair!'

'Don't you dare answer me back!' A slap sent her stumbling sideways and she hurried up the stairs, heart racing in case he followed her to emphasise his point. But this time he didn't, thank goodness.

In bed that night she shed a few tears because she knew she wouldn't be able to see Nick again and she couldn't bear it. Other girls were allowed to court young fellows openly, why not her? Her step-father hadn't said anything further about her marrying his friend, though, so maybe her mother was mistaken. She wouldn't do it, whatever he said or did. Peter Gordon was going bald and had a paunch on him. His little daughters always looked cowed, just like her half-brothers, and she guessed he ill-treated them. Well, he wasn't going to get the chance to ill-treat her.

And she was going to meet Nick this Sunday somehow, whatever anyone said, because he was going away for a week or two to visit his grandfather over Bradford way and she had to see him before he left, whatever it cost in beatings and scoldings.

Nathaniel found it heartbreaking to work on his ruined market garden. There were some plants which he could save, but where was the guarantee that Walter bloody Dewhurst wouldn't come and wreak more havoc once he had things set up again? He was so concerned about this that he went to see Mr Lexham about it.

'I can't promise anything, Nathaniel,' Jack admitted. 'Mr Dewhurst has told his son to be more careful in future, but who knows what'll happen in the heat of the moment?'

'Why do I pay good money to lease the land if it's not mine to do with as I wish?'

Jack sighed but didn't dare let himself comment, though he was fully on the tenants' side in this.

Afterwards Nathaniel walked home slowly, lost in thought. His five-year lease would be up in a few months. It was a fine piece of land, but he definitely couldn't stay under these circumstances. At worst, he'd take an annual lease on it. He was sure Mr Lexham would understand why. Eh, decent men and women were starving in the industrial towns of Lancashire because of the Cotton Famine, and that young ruffian was wasting the food produced by men's honest toil in a part of Lancashire where fortunately there was still work. Where was the justice or sense in all that?

He got home to find a letter from his sister awaiting him.

My dear Nathaniel

I'm sorry it's taken me so long to write. I was very sad to hear of Sarah's death and hope you and dear Gregory are bearing up under your loss. The Lord gives and the Lord takes away.

Howard doesn't know I'm writing this extra bit, only that I'm writing to offer you our condolences, so please don't mention it when you write back. Ginny isn't getting on well with him. He can be rather violent at times, I'm afraid, and I fear for her safety. I wanted to know if you would take her to live with you if things get worse? She's a good

*little housewife and maybe you find a lack of a
woman's touch now?*

    *If you're agreeable, underline your name
when you write back.*

      —*Christine*

He felt very sad as he read this. He knew she was
unhappy in her second marriage and it was common
knowledge that Howard beat her. Nathaniel had kept
away from them once he found that out, because he
knew he couldn't have kept his hands to himself if he
saw anyone ill-treating his gentle sister. But who could
intervene between a man and wife when they were as
one before the law?

    Ginny, though – yes, he could help there. And would
be happy to.

    He didn't hesitate but penned a brief response,
underlining his name before writing a postscript,
sending his regards to Howard, scowling as he wrote
that lie.

When planning her escape, Hannah decided it would
be best to act quickly and leave before Christmas. Patty
was already nagging Lemuel to insist his mother go to
church with them once more, playing on the fact of her
unborn child and her worries that it'd be born into a
godless household.

    Hannah had already worked out how she was going
to start her flight, but didn't make the mistake of getting
a bundle of things together in advance this time. The
following Sunday morning she did don two of every
garment she could when she dressed, knowing she was

slender enough to carry that off without anyone guessing. Then she yawned her way through her morning chores and breakfast, saying she had slept badly the previous night.

She sank into a chair even before the others had left and sat there, feigning sleep and waiting until they'd had time to get away. Just as she was about to get up Patty burst into the kitchen and stared at her as if disappointed. 'I forgot my handkerchief. Run up and get me one.'

Hannah pursed her lips and did as she was told, but as she handed it over, she held on to one end and said softly, 'Aren't you ever afraid of pushing a madwoman too far?'

Patty gaped at her open-mouthed, then took a hasty step backwards. 'I'll tell Lemuel what you said.'

'He won't believe you. No one will. I'm so very meek nowadays. Now, what was I doing? Oh, yes, having a nice nap.' She settled down in the chair and waited, her nerves stretched unbearably. But the clock ticked on – much more slowly than usual, surely? – until she knew the service would have started. She was fairly certain Patty wouldn't walk out in the middle of that. Patty set a lot of store on keeping up appearances – her own, anyway – and fussed over the new parson, who for some reason seemed to think her a model parishioner.

Hannah stuffed the things she planned to take with her into a pillowcase, including her best petticoat, retrieved from upstairs. Then she took the purse from its hiding place and made up her mattress to look as though a figure was sleeping on it. That might buy her a few more precious minutes. In the kitchen she took one of the new loaves from the pantry plus a big piece of cheese and wrapped them in a cloth. That would see her on her way and if Patty cried thief after her, well, it was a risk she'd have to take. But she didn't think even her poor weak Lemuel would allow his wife to do that, because it would mean sending his mother to prison.

If he did . . . well, she would have lost two sons and might just as well be in prison.

She went out into an icy wind and a sky black with clouds, hurrying along the back lane and up towards the moors. She had worried that someone would see her go, but she doubted many would be out on a day like this, and most of those would be at church. It was a day for huddling over fires and keeping out the draughts, for mulled ale and preparations for Christmas.

Where would she be this Christmas?

In spite of the weather she felt a sense of freedom as she made her way up to the lower stretches of the moor. The paths were muddy, but her shoes were sturdy and she was nimble enough to avoid the worst bits, leaping from stone to stone like the girl she'd once been and laughing aloud as she did so.

It took her an hour to reach the shepherds' hut, which was deserted, but she hesitated by the door, looking back over her shoulder towards the village. It was too close. They'd soon catch up with her here. Surely there'd be another hut she could shelter in further afield? As she decided to press on she heard footsteps behind her and swung round, her heart skittering in her chest.

The shepherd, Tad Mosely, stood there. 'I saw you coming up the hill. You're running away, aren't you?'

Hannah nodded.

'They say you're losing your wits.'

'My daughter-in-law says that because she wants a free servant, but I'm as sane as ever I was.'

Silence hung in the air between them and just as Hannah thought she could bear it no longer, he said quietly, 'She tried to cheat me once, your Patty did, over a few pennies. I've never forgot that. And there are other folk in the village who say they don't believe you're losing your wits, so you have a few friends still.'

Hannah sagged in relief and a groan escaped her.

'They'll come looking for you, Mrs Firth, and they'll soon find you if you hide here.'

'Then I'd better walk on.'

'It'll be teeming down within the hour – look at them rain clouds coming in from the west – an' it'll be misty too. There's many who've perished trying to cross the tops in such conditions.'

'I can't go back. I'd rather die trying to escape.'

He nodded, his brow wrinkled in thought, and after another pause said, 'I'll show you a safer hiding place, then, one as few know about, an' I'll come and tell you when it's safe for you to set off again. If you can wait a day or two in patience there, I reckon you'll have a better chance of getting away once they've given up hunting for you. The roads are full of folk on the tramp since they stopped bringing in the cotton. You'll not be alone.'

'Thank you. I'm grateful.'

'Come on then, lass. We'll need to hurry up if I'm to get you settled afore it rains.'

Before they left he went inside the shepherds' hut to

take a couple of the old sheepskins kept there, making a mark on the wall.

She watched him anxiously, terrified she'd misjudged him. 'What's the mark for?'

'To let the lads know I've took the sheepskins.' He smiled at her. 'Nay, I wouldn't betray you, lass. We use these for all sorts of things an' count 'em in and out.'

Hannah had no choice but to trust him. She thought she could, she really did.

He took her up on the tops, leaving the track and following a narrow path, then zigzagging across a rocky patch, by which time she was panting with exertion.

'Not far now. Can you keep going?'

She nodded, too out of breath to speak. She could work all day in a house but her legs weren't used to climbing hills.

He led her past a big rocky outcrop and into what looked to be a mere crack, but was actually the entrance to a shallow cave. 'It's sheltered from the worst of the winds here an' I doubt many folk know of it. With them sheepskins you should be warm enough. I've already got a couple of old pelts here, see, just in case I ever get caught out in the snow. I'll bring you some food tomorrow if I can.'

'I have some.' She gestured to her bundle.

'Well, it'll be safer for you if I don't come tomorrow, I must admit. You'll find pools of water in the hollows in the rocks, so you'll not be short of a drink neither. Just bide here till I come for you.' He looked at her with another of his gentle, friendly smiles. 'I'll not let you down, lass, I promise.'

When he'd gone she went to peer through the entrance crack but already Tad had disappeared behind the rocks and there was nothing to see but wind flattening the grass and cloud shadows chasing one another across the tops. The air had a dampness to it that said rain wouldn't be long, so she went back to make a nest of the old sheepskins in the rear of the cave.

Even before she'd finished, rain began hissing down outside and thunder rumbled in the distance. Poor Tad would be soaked to the skin before he got home and she had better get inside the sheepskins before she lost what body warmth she still possessed. It was cold now, but would get even colder when night fell.

She used the bundle of clothes as a pillow then had nothing to do but lie and watch the play of light across the narrow entrance to the cave. When she tired of that, she followed the play of her own thoughts and hopes for the future. The hours seemed to pass very slowly, but eventually she realised it was getting dark. She left the warmth to relieve herself again, made a hasty snack of a piece of bread torn from the loaf and a few bites of cheese. After that she settled down again.

She didn't expect to sleep, but as the storm died down and the world grew quieter around her, she did fall asleep, waking once during the night to jerk upright in the darkness and wonder for one terrified moment where she was. Then it all came back to her and she lay down again, drifting for a moment or two in drowsy relief before falling asleep.

She had escaped! That was all that mattered for the moment.

★　　★　　★

When Lemuel and Patty got home from church, she stared round. 'Where's your mother? I knew it! I knew she'd run away again.'

He opened the door to his mother's bedroom to see Mrs Rigby drowsing on the bed and a shapeless form on his mother's mattress. He knew at once it wasn't her but shut the door and said, 'It's all right. She's asleep in there. Perhaps she's sickening for something. It's not like her to be so drowsy.'

'Let me see!'

But he held Patty away. 'Don't wake her. If she needs some sleep, let her have it.'

Her voice rose. 'And who's going to help me if she lazes around?'

He pushed her back and laid his hand across her mouth. 'Shh!'

'You don't care about me, only about her!'

'You know that's not true.' But he was fed up with reassuring her and deeply ashamed of how he had allowed her to treat his mother.

She shook him off and went to swing the kettle over the heat, grumbling in a monotone as she did so.

He sat down at the table, though he'd usually have gone into the workshop and pottered around because it was more peaceful in there.

'What's the matter with you?' Patty demanded a few minutes later, coming to stand in front of him, arms akimbo. 'You don't usually stay in the house after church.'

'I'm tired today, like my mother, so I'll sit and have a cup of tea with you before I go out to the workshop.'

Her eyes narrowed and she looked at him suspiciously, then across at the door of the bedroom. But she said nothing until she had to go to the pantry to get out some more milk. Making a quick dash for the bedroom door, she flung it open so that it bounced against the wall.

He sighed as he watched her vanish inside, then come rushing out, shrieking, 'She's gone! You must have seen that and yet you said nothing. Are you mad? How else am I to get help in the house if we don't keep her here?'

'You could have had her help willingly if you'd treated her right.'

'Not everyone is as soft as you, Lemuel Firth, and not everyone lets themselves be taken advantage of. I soon saw that your mother didn't intend to pull her weight, so I made sure she had no choice. And when they let us have her back, I'll—'

'What do you mean by that?'

'Why, we'll have to report her to the Guardians and they'll insist on taking her inside for a bit. That'll teach her to behave! You're still responsible to them for her so they'll help us search for her.'

'I'm not doing it.'

'*What?*'

'I'm not setting them after her. If she hates it so much here – and I don't blame her, the way you treat her – then let her go and make a new life somewhere else. I shan't stop her and so I'll tell them.'

'Well, if you won't report her, I will.' She went to the door and snatched her shawl from the wooden peg next to it. 'See! Her shawl is gone. Why didn't I notice that when we came in? We've wasted so much time.'

He went and held the door closed as she tried to get out. 'I forbid you to do it.'

Patty shoved him back so hard he stumbled and fell, and while he was righting himself, she went running to the neighbours, calling for help, her voice shrill enough to be heard above the wind.

Lemuel closed his eyes for a moment, wondering what other men did with nagging wives like Patty, then went to sit in a chair. Let her do it all. He wasn't setting folk to hunt down his mother like a wild animal. He hoped she got away. Hoped it desperately. She wasn't insane, and so he would tell Dr Kent and the people from the poorhouse.

But would that stop them pursuing her?

In spite of the approaching rain, people in the village ran out to find what was wrong with Patty Firth and then gathered in small groups to discuss Hannah running away again.

Patty eagerly told them all she knew, but one man looked at her disapprovingly and said, 'That's all very well, Mrs Firth, but why isn't your man here telling us this?'

'He's too upset.'

'I'll go and see him then.'

'No, don't—'

But he was off before she could stop him.

He found Lemuel sitting in the kitchen with his head in his hands.

'Eh, lad, don't take on. We'll soon find your mother for you.'

Lemuel raised a face ravaged by pain and said, 'I

don't want you to find her, Vincent lad. Let her go free. She had a dreadful time here with Patty.'

'Nay, you can't mean that.'

'I can and I do.'

'Well, I doubt the Poor Law Guardians will agree. Your mother's still bound to them for good behaviour, isn't she?'

At which Lemuel groaned aloud and buried his face in his hands again.

Vincent returned to the group, looked at Patty disapprovingly and said, 'He wants us to let her go.'

At which they all began arguing about the rights and wrongs of doing that while Patty ran home to screech at her husband till he walked out to the workshop and locked himself inside.

Louisa said nothing when her neighbour told her the shocking news, but afterwards she went back inside the house and indulged in a hearty bout of weeping. 'It's not fair,' she sobbed into her husband's chest. 'Some of them are talking about her as if she's a wild animal and dangerous – and she's still Hannah, my dear friend. She isn't mad, she isn't!'

He patted her shoulders awkwardly. 'Not if you say she isn't.'

Someone pounded on the back door and when Ralph shouted to come in, another neighbour peered inside. 'They're getting up a search party to look for Hannah Firth, though Lemuel won't join it. Are you coming?'

Louisa bounced to her feet. 'No, he isn't! Hannah's no more mad than I am. How can you forget what she's like? She's helped many people over the years, been a good neighbour. How can you speak of her like that?'

'They don't shut folk up in that asylum for nothing and I want to sleep sound in my bed of nights, not worry about a madwoman breaking in and murdering us all. If I were that Patty, I'd not have her back this time.'

She could only gape at him in shock then turn to her husband and plead, 'Don't go. Please!'

Ralph set her aside gently. 'I think I'd better if such hotheads are to be in the search party. They'll need someone to make sure she's treated right when they find her.' Just before he left he asked in a lower voice, 'Did she tell you she was going to run away?'

She hesitated, then admitted, 'She asked for her savings.'

'Eh, Louisa, love, you should have stopped her.'

'How could I when she was so unhappy and being ill-treated by that woman?'

He shook his head. 'You were wrong, love. Poor Hannah will be in far worse trouble now.'

But Louisa didn't, couldn't, agree with him, and prayed hard that her friend would escape.

By the time Ralph went outside, the rain had started and the sky was as dark as dusk. Thunder rumbled in the distance and even the hotheads in the group suggested they gather in the church to discuss what best to do, instead of rushing out into a storm and catching their deaths from cold and damp.

The parson was waiting for them and conducted the meeting, hardly allowing anyone else to get a word in. But he did agree that it was no use going out in such a bad storm. He only hoped, with many shakes of his head, that the poor madwoman didn't fall and break a leg, or die of exposure.

While folk were making their way home again, the doctor drove past one group in his gig and reined in. 'Is something wrong?'

'That Hannah Firth's run off again. We're getting up a search party for tomorrow first thing. The parson says we're to find her, even though her son doesn't want her brought back. But Parson's one of the Guardians, so he knows what the law says.'

Maurice Kent suppressed a sigh. The new parson was over-zealous, in his opinion, and Lemuel Firth was in the right. They should let the poor woman go. 'Well, unless you want to get soaked to the skin, I'd suggest you get yourselves home.' He shivered even as he spoke.

There was much muttering and grumbling by those who had regarded this as an adventure and wanted to go out after her right away, storm or no storm, so Ralph took the opportunity to say quietly, 'She'll not get far in such weather.'

When he went home he found Louisa still tearful and upset, and had to agree with her that it was a shame to pursue her poor friend who had now lost everything.

Maurice Kent drove his gig home, wishing he'd got back before the weather broke. The canopy usually saved him from the worst of the weather, but today the wind was driving the rain almost sideways and he was wet through. He frowned in thought as he handed the horse over to the garden lad to stable and legged it to the house. Why had Hannah Firth run away this time?

Then he thought of what her daughter-in-law was like and pulled a wry face. He'd not like to live with that one whose true nature showed in the peevish lines of her face.

He'd spoken to the apothecary from Upper Hetton the day before and found out that Patty Firth did indeed buy the Infants' Soothing Mixture regularly, and that it was sold in blue bottles as he'd thought.

'I told her not to give the baby too much but she wouldn't listen, said she needed her sleep,' the apothecary had confided in him. 'Perhaps you can have a word with her, Dr Kent, and advise her not to use so much? That little lad of hers can't spend much time awake if she's using so much and what'll it be doing to him, eh?'

The memory of this kept Maurice thoughtful for the rest of the day. He'd always liked Hannah and been surprised to see her in the asylum – though it did happen that people could suddenly turn strange. And the two porters had assured him she'd been attacking her daughter-in-law, though after questioning they'd admitted they'd not seen it themselves, only heard the screams and seen the scratches on the poor young woman's face.

But Mrs Firth had definitely struggled like a madwoman when they took her away, they insisted, which just showed she was out of her mind.

Maurice rather thought he'd have struggled too if someone had suddenly accused him of being insane and tried to cart him off to the asylum. Hannah had seemed sane enough to him whenever he examined her, though he'd had to follow the rules about dealing with her once she'd been admitted. And if she'd been drugged . . . if she'd never been insane . . . well, he hated even to think of the injustice of that.

The following morning as he did his rounds in the poorhouse one of the porters told him that a search party had gone out early that morning looking for the madwoman.

'She'll not get away from them, Doctor. They've got dogs and her old skirt to sniff. But her son won't go with them, still says he hopes she gets away.'

Maurice also found himself hoping that the impossible would happen and Hannah would make her escape. He knew he'd have trouble locking her away again.

Lemuel insisted on seeing him later that day and begged him to call off the chase.

'Why do you say that?'

'There's nothing wrong with my mother.'

'It's not as easy as that. There are rules and procedures to be followed, and I answer to the Guardians who're in charge of all inmates of the poorhouse.'

'I should have helped her get away before, but you insisted she stay with me and Patty . . .' Lemuel's voice trailed away.

'You'll have to tell me more if you wish me to understand.'

'Patty's been ill-treating her, making her work like a skivvy. And she – Patty – makes things up, I know she does. I've caught her at it many a time. My mother *isn't* mad and should be left in peace to live her life as she chooses.'

'Unfortunately the law says differently now that she's come under its control.'

Lemuel stared at him from a face so haunted by anguish that Maurice felt sorry for the poor devil.

'When Hannah is brought back you'll have to stand firm, make your wife—'

Lemuel thrust back his chair and stood up. 'How the hell can I? I'm not in the house with them, and anyway, you don't know Patty. She'll get her own way whatever you decide. How I'm to stand living with her for the rest of my life, I don't know.'

And he was gone, leaving what sounded suspiciously like a sob hanging in the air behind him. Life, as Maurice was regularly made aware, did not always treat people kindly.

Hannah woke with the dawn light, though that came late at this time of year, and went to relieve herself, coming back into the cave shivering with cold, which always seemed to bite more deeply in damp weather. She settled down again among the sheepskins with a sigh, glad of her warm cloak for an extra cover.

Time passed so slowly she grew impatient and considered setting off and making the best time she could across the tops. She felt she would in truth go mad if she had to spend several days here with nothing to occupy herself but her own unhappy thoughts. But almost immediately she told herself not to be foolish. Tad had said he'd come when it was safe and set her on her way. She must wait for him.

Her stomach growled with hunger and she pulled out the bread and cheese, studying them and working out how many portions she could eke out. Both had gone a bit hard by now, so first she went outside again and scooped up drinking water from depressions in the rocks. Although she ate the portion she'd torn off very slowly, the food was soon gone and she knew she only dare eat in the morning and evening.

It was hard for a vigorous woman like her to face a day of inaction. After lying still for a while, she stood up and moved around, windmilling her arms and even jumping up and down like a child, trying to touch the fractured rocky ceiling. And it did set her blood flowing more warmly through her, so she decided to do it at regular intervals. She didn't intend to be one of those who perished on the moors.

When she was glowing with warmth from her exertions, she pulled her cloak round her and went to stand by the entrance to the cave, stiffening in apprehension as she saw small figures leaving the village in groups. She narrowed her eyes, trying to make out the details, but it was hard at this distance. Surely those were a couple of dogs frolicking round them? Search parties! She was sure of it. Why else would groups of people be leaving the village on a Monday morning?

What if they found her? Shut her up in that place again? She shivered at the mere thought of it.

She was glad now that she hadn't set off today and left a new trail for the dogs. Her scent from the previous day would surely have been washed away by the rain and unless she was very unlucky the dogs wouldn't find her. It would be hard to stay here while they searched all round her, but it would be her best chance. Tad was right.

Soon she found herself shivering and crawled back into the huddle of sheepskins, sitting up with her back against the wall of the cave. If they found her, she wanted to see them coming, to face them calmly and insist she wasn't mad.

It was the only weapon she had left if they caught her, but she doubted it'd make much difference.

The Sunday after he'd followed his step-daughter, Howard West lingered behind after church to speak to his friend Peter Gordon while Ginny walked home with her mother. The lads scampered along in front of them, happy as always when their father wasn't around.

'I'm going out for a walk,' Ginny said quietly as they reached the farm.

Her mother stared at her in consternation. 'No. Oh, no, you mustn't! He'll be *furious.*'

'He always finds something to be angry at me for. I'm going.'

'You're meeting that Nick Halstead, aren't you?'

Ginny hesitated, then nodded. 'Yes. He's going away for a few weeks, so this is my last chance to see him before he leaves. Tell *him* you didn't notice me go, then maybe he won't be so angry with you.' But she knew he would and felt guilty about bringing more trouble down on her poor mother.

She hurried up to her room, changed quickly and slipped out the back way, running up the hill as fast as she could, then pausing at the top to check that *he* hadn't come home and seen her. But there was no one in sight, just clouds scudding across the sky and an icy wind whistling over the fields, setting the bare branches lashing to and fro.

At the ruined cottage she fell into Nick's arms, forgetting the bruises still showing on her face.

He held her at arm's length and stared in shock. 'What happened, love? Did you fall over?'

'No, *he* hit me.'

He pressed her closer to him. 'The man's a brute. I wish I could take you away from him. I will do one day, I promise.'

It was so wonderful to be in Nick's arms that she instinctively lifted her face to his, and one thing led to another: caresses, wonderfully tender; more kisses. She had ached for this, dreamed of it. When he would have stopped, she begged him not to. 'Love me properly, Nick. Make me your own.'

'Oh, Ginny, we shouldn't.'

'I need to belong to someone. I need to know I'm loved.' She began to sob.

He stopped her tears with kisses then said huskily, 'Well, we're definitely going to get married, so if anything happens . . .'

'One of my friends says you can't fall for a baby the first time,' she whispered.

'Oh, Ginny!' And he was lost.

Afterwards they lay in one another's arms and she felt blissfully happy, loved as never before, her body soft against the lean muscle of his.

'We'll be married one day,' he assured her. 'Soon. I'll find a way.'

It suddenly occurred to her that if she was expecting Nick's baby, they'd have to get married, even her stepfather would say so, and she let out a gurgle of laughter, sharing her thoughts with her beloved.

'That's not the way I want to marry you, my darling, not out of shame, but out of joy.'

'I'll marry you any way I can.'

When she arrived home, *he* was waiting for her. He beat her and assured her he'd not let her out of his sight from then on. She didn't care. She and Nick would find a way to be together permanently. They would! She had to believe that.

Afterwards Ginny saw her mother favouring one arm, so knew he'd taken out his anger on her as well.

But Ginny remained stubborn in the face of the tongue lashings he heaped on her whenever they were together, buoyed up by the thought of Nick's love. She'd be eighteen in a few months. Surely then they'd be able to do something? At eighteen you were definitely a woman.

And Nick was twenty-one already, a man in every way that counted.

CHAPTER EIGHT

December 1863

When Nick arrived home, he found his mother in tears and his father frantically busy.

They both greeted him with, 'Where have you been? We need your help.'

'What's wrong?'

'It's your grandfather.' His mother applied her handkerchief again. 'They sent to tell us that he's not likely to last the week. He wants to see us, all three of us. So your father has called in his cousin to look after the farm and we're leaving by the evening train.'

'Why can't I stay here and look after the farm?'

His father glared at him. 'Weren't you listening to your mother? Because your grandfather wants to see us all.'

'He always promised he'd leave me the farm,' she said, more tears rolling down her face. 'That's why he wanted you to go and visit him. But I'd rather he was still alive. I don't want to profit from his death.'

Nick told himself this trip would be no different from the visit they'd already planned and he'd only be away for a week or two, then he'd come back and ask Mr West openly for Ginny's hand in marriage. He'd decided on the way home that he wasn't going to continue with this dishonest courtship. He was proud of his darling girl, loved her deeply, was going to marry her whatever that step-father of hers said.

As if she'd read his mind, his mother waited till his father was outside and said abruptly, 'I know you've been seeing that girl.'

'I intend to marry *that girl*! Her name's Ginny.'

'I don't care what her name is. She's the daughter of a horrible man and we'll all regret it if you tie us to Howard West.'

'You've said things like that before but you'll never explain yourself.'

'You're too young.'

'I'm twenty-one, Mother, a man by anyone's standards.'

'But too young to marry without help from us.'

'Oh, there's no talking to you! And there are no threats that'll make me give up Ginny.' He flung out of the room.

When the cousin's wife came in, Jane took her upstairs to her bedroom. 'I need to speak to you privately, love. It's very important. And – I want you to keep this to yourself.'

Mary stared at her in surprise. 'Eh, whatever's up?'

'It's our Nick. He's seeing that Ginny Doyle and I'm not having it.'

'She's a nice enough lass.'

'Oh, I've nothing against *her*, but I don't want any connection with her step-father. So if she comes looking for Nick or asking where he is, you're not to tell her or give her our address.'

'Well, you'll only be gone a week or two, won't you?'

Jane shrugged. 'I don't know. When someone's

dying, you can never tell. But just in case, you think on! You're not to let her know where Nick is. And if any letters arrive here for him, put them in another envelope and send them to me.'

Mary looked uncomfortable. 'I don't like to interfere with other folk's letters.'

'You'll do as I ask if you want to benefit from what I think's going to happen with the farm.'

Two hours later, Mary's husband drove the Halsteads to the station and she stayed behind, looking round the kitchen with a proprietorial air. She would do nothing to upset Cousin Jane. Definitely not. This could be a good chance for her family, too.

The following Saturday evening, Howard West looked at his step-daughter across the table and said abruptly, 'You'll soon be eighteen, Ginny. Time you were wed.'

'I've no mind to wed yet,' she said, trying to speak lightly. 'I'm too young.'

'Best time to wed is before you get set in your ways. My friend Peter Gordon has spoken for you and—'

In spite of her mother's advice, Ginny couldn't pretend. 'No.'

'*What did you say?*'

'I said no. I'm not marrying an old man like him.'

'You'll do as you're told.'

She shook her head. 'Not in this. I don't even like the man.' His backhander caught her on the side of the head and knocked her to the floor. She tried to scramble away, but he stood up so quickly his chair went flying and dragged her to her feet by one arm, shaking her hard and raising his hand again.

Her mother stepped between them and Ginny sobbed as he turned his anger on her. She couldn't bear to watch this happening again and snatched up a chair, thrusting it between them.

That startled Howard so much he stood panting for a moment, his expression ugly and menacing. 'This has nothing to do with my mother, so leave her alone. This is *my* life we're talking about and there's no way you – or she – can make me marry anyone I don't like.' Ginny spoke quietly now, her eyes meeting his squarely. 'You can't put the words into my mouth in church, nor can you make me say yes to your friend.'

A nasty grin curved his lips. 'Oh, can't I?' He wrenched the chair out of her hand and twisted her arm behind her back, forcing her upstairs to her bedroom. Throwing her inside, he locked the door on her from outside. 'You'll stay there,' he yelled through it, 'until you change your mind.'

'I'll *not* change it!' she yelled back.

'See what you say when you're thirsty.'

She heard her mother scream after he'd gone down. Two sets of footsteps pattered up the stairs and she knew her half-brothers were hiding in their bedroom.

She stood by the window, letting her tears fall freely now. Howard West proclaimed himself a respectable member of the community, attending church every Sunday, yet he behaved like a savage. She frowned. Was he well-respected, though? He didn't seem to have a lot of friends in Blackfold. In fact, there was only Peter Gordon, who was probably as bad as him once the door of the house was closed – as well as being old and ugly.

She went to lean out of the window, then as rain spattered against her face, rushed to get her washing bowl, holding it out in an attempt to catch something to drink. But her arms soon began to ache and she'd caught so little, a tiny puddle which wouldn't last long. She looked down at the ground instead, wondering if she could climb out during the night and run away. Only, where would she go? Her Uncle Nathaniel lived too far away, over the other side of Preston, and she'd need money to reach him. And she didn't know where Nick was.

When she saw her step-father striding across the farmyard she pulled the bowl inside, afraid he'd come and take it off her, but remained standing by the window. Why had he got so much worse lately? He'd always been strict with his womenfolk and had never shown any open affection, even to her mother. He hardly ever hit his sons, though they too lived in terror of him. Was it – could it be because Ginny was almost a woman now? He made nasty little remarks about her growing up all the time these days, insulting her father's memory and saying she'd better not take after him – though what her father had ever done wrong, she couldn't work out.

Well, she wouldn't do what he wanted this time, no matter how much he hurt her. The mere thought of marrying an old man like Peter Gordon made her feel sick. Besides she was promised to Nick and she had let him make love to her. As far as she was concerned they were man and wife now, in all the ways that truly mattered.

*　　*　　*

The following morning her step-father threw open the door of her bedroom and roared, 'Get ready for church, you!' Then he noticed her bruised face and scowled at her as if it was her fault. 'Look at that face of yours! You'd better tell anyone as asks that you fell down the stairs.'

She said nothing. When she went down he didn't allow her anything to eat or drink and her mouth was uncomfortably dry, which only bolstered her determination to disobey him. Could she, dare she, defy him openly? She had to or things would get worse, she was sure.

When they arrived at church he began smiling and nodding to people, but she felt dreadful with her swollen, painful face. She could see people staring at her. Well, bruises like those couldn't be hidden and she wasn't going to lie about them.

'Eh, Ginny love, whatever did you do to your face?' Mrs Grindle exclaimed as they all paused near the entrance to let another group of people go inside.

'She fell down the stairs,' her step-father said quickly.

'No, I didn't. *He* hit me.'

The old woman gasped in shock and Howard swung round towards his step-daughter again, his fist bunched and his face darkening in rage.

Ginny dodged behind the woman, yelling, 'He did it because I wouldn't agree to marry his friend Peter.' She was aware that everyone round them had stopped talking to listen, some open-mouthed in shock. 'And I won't, whatever he does to me.'

Her mother was by her side. 'Oh, Ginny, hush. You're only making things worse.'

Mrs Grindle looked upset, then stared in shock as Mrs West's sleeve slid back and showed part of a huge, livid bruise.

'See! He hits my mother too!' Ginny yelled.

'Get the boys into church while I deal with her.' Howard pushed his wife forward so hard she stumbled into a little run, but Ginny slipped out of his grasp and made for the water fountain, shouting, 'He hasn't let me have anything to eat or drink since yesterday.' She gulped down as much water as she could before his fingers dug into her shoulder and he began to drag her away.

By now people had stopped going into church, with others joining the circle of onlookers every second and asking what was happening.

Ginny wondered if her step-father would have an apoplexy, he looked so furious. She also wondered if he was going to kill her for this.

The parson's wife appeared beside them and said in a calm voice, 'Your step-daughter is distraught, Mr West, and in no condition to attend the service. Let me take her home with me and try to calm her down.'

Parson Crawford appeared behind them. 'Best thing for the moment, my dear fellow. I'm sure my wife will bring her to a more reasonable frame of mind.' He frowned at Ginny. 'You behaved very badly just now.'

'I told the truth!'

'Some things should be kept within the family.'

Mrs Crawford shot a quick frowning glance at her husband, but said nothing.

For a moment it seemed as if Howard was going to refuse the offer, then he stepped back and said in his usual smooth manner, 'That's very kind of you, Mrs Crawford. I hope you won't be taken in by her lies, though.'

She gave him a very level look. 'I try not to be taken in by anyone's lies.' Then she put an arm round Ginny's shoulders and led the girl away. When she looked back she could see her husband talking soothingly to Mr West. Trust him to take the man's side, whatever the justice of the case. She was tired of appearing to support him, tired of everything lately, it seemed.

When they were sitting in the Parsonage kitchen she said quietly, 'You don't need to tell me anything if you don't want, but sometimes it helps to talk.'

Ginny felt tears trickle down her cheeks. 'This may be my only chance to let people hear my side of the story.'

'Then you talk while I tend to your poor face.' Mrs Crawford got out a bottle. 'Arnica. Good for bruises.'

'It won't help the bruises he'll give me tonight, probably where they don't show this time.'

The older woman bent her head for a moment, an expression of pain on her face, then she looked up and sighed. 'I don't want to come between father and child—'

'He's *not* my father!'

'– but I think people in the village are more aware than you realise that Mr West can be rather,' she hesitated, searching for a word, 'a violent man.'

'They don't try to help us, though.'

'People don't think it right to interfere between husband and wife.'

'Well, they should if they have any pity in their hearts. It's my mother I feel for most. He's been thumping her for years, but he only started hitting me last year. One day I'll get away from him, but she has to spend the rest of her life with him. I wish he would drop dead!'

'You must never wish that, dear.' The parson's wife hesitated then said sadly, 'I pity your mother and wish I could help, but I'm afraid the law is on his side. A husband is allowed to chastise his wife within reason.'

'He goes beyond reason.'

Mrs Crawford shook her head helplessly then went on in a more normal voice, 'There. That's your face attended to. Have you any bruises elsewhere? There's no one in the house, so if you want to remove any garments and let me tend them . . . ?'

Ginny did as she asked, hearing how the other woman sucked in a shocked breath at the sight of her bruised back.

When Mrs Crawford had finished, she made some sandwiches and a pot of tea, urging Ginny to eat as much as she wanted.

Time passed so quickly and pleasantly that she was startled to hear someone knocking on the back door. When Mrs Crawford opened it, she saw her mother standing there with *him* grim-faced behind her. Her heart fell as she realised the service must be over.

'Are you all right now, dear?' Christine asked.

Ginny nodded.

'Then let's go home.'

The parson arrived back just then. 'Could I just have a word with you, please, Mr West?' he asked.

With a suspicious look, Howard followed him through to his study.

Knowing there was nothing more the parson's wife could do to help, Ginny put on her bonnet and cloak again and moved towards the door, where her mother gave her a quick hug.

She turned and tried to smile at Mrs Crawford. 'Thank you for putting arnica on my bruises. And for the food. I was very hungry.'

A few minutes later, her step-father rejoined them, smiling as if he'd had a pleasant chat, and she saw that the parson had a smug expression on his face, too. Howard didn't say a word on the way home, but anger radiated from him. When they went into the house, he glared at Ginny and snapped, 'Get out of my sight!'

She went up to her bedroom, not locked in this time but still a prisoner. She wondered what Mr Crawford had said to him. She didn't really like their new parson, who looked down his nose at ordinary people.

Her biggest consolation as the next few weeks dragged past was that Peter Gordon announced his engagement to marry a widow of his own age, so one threat at least was lifted.

But another was looming, one that was so much worse.

Very early on her third morning in the cave, before it was fully light, Hannah heard boots on the rocky ground outside and scrambled out of the sheepskins to face whoever it was. She stayed inside the cave in case it was just someone walking past, then sagged in relief as she saw Tad approaching. No mistaking his upright figure, even in the half-light.

'Time to go, lass.'

'Give me a moment to get ready.'

'I'll wait up the hill a bit.'

She joined him ten minutes later and he thrust a cloth bundle containing slices of bread and mutton into her hand. 'Here. You must be hungry.'

'Yes. Thank you.' She bit into the piece with relish.

'Folk went out searching for you the day after the storm. Did you see them? Yes, I thought you would. You did the right thing to stay where you were. Your son wouldn't join them, though, and he told the doctor you should be let go.'

Hannah stopped walking to look at him. 'Lemuel did that?' She felt like weeping and laughing at the same time. She hadn't lost her other son, then. She hadn't! And she knew how much it must have cost him to go against Patty in this.

'But Parson Barnish says it's against the law now that you've been in the asylum and you must be brought back to answer to the Board. I think he believes what your daughter-in-law says about you.'

She sighed but said nothing. The news that she was acting against the law upset her. It was all so unfair. Why should they treat her so badly, just on Patty's word?

They walked across the tops for a couple of hours, ignoring the occasional light shower and speaking only when necessary. Hannah found Tad's company very restful, craved peace like some drunken sots craved pots of ale.

When the track began to angle downhill Tad stopped. 'You should be all right on your own from here.'

She hated the thought of losing his protection but forced herself to say, 'Yes. Yes, of course I will. I can't begin to thank you for your help.'

'I never did like to see anyone unfairly treated. Now, at the bottom of the track where it meets the road you can turn left for Blackburn or right for Preston. I should make for Preston, if I were you. They've enough folk seeking work in Blackburn and few jobs going.'

'Are there more jobs going in Preston?' she asked in her usual blunt way.

'No. But they say the Cotton Famine hasn't hit folk as hard in the countryside beyond it and I got to thinking that they may still be taking on maids in the big houses. They're still taking on gardeners, that I do know, because a cousin of mine got set on only last month. Any road, I reckon that'd be your best bet, lass, but it's up to you.'

He stretched out his hand and when she took it, clasped hers in both his big warm hands for a moment. 'You should change your name, too.'

'Yes, I suppose so.'

'Call yourself Mary or Susan, some right common name,' he said with a wry grin. 'It won't suit you because there's summat special about you, Hannah Firth, but what does that matter?' With a final wave, he turned on his heel and strode off up the hill again.

Only then did she become aware of the coin he had pressed into her hand, warm, as if he'd been holding it for a while. She gaped down to see a whole half-sovereign and almost ran after him to give it back, then shook her head and turned resolutely in the opposite direction. One day she'd repay him, that she vowed, but at the moment she had to survive and a sum like this would help a lot.

She was grateful that the weather was fine but it was a very chilly day. As she walked along the road she met others on the tramp. Some of them had the famine look on their faces, with gaunt cheeks and hollow eyes. She felt deeply sorry for them, guessing they were cotton operatives who'd been long without work. Some exchanged the time of day, some avoided her eyes, as if they were ashamed of what they were doing. There were whole families tramping along together, with what she guessed were their remaining possessions in a hand-cart or simply carried in bundles. She felt sorry for the little children, who looked so weary.

Eh, times were hard in Lancashire, they were that!

She spent the first night in the lee of a hedge, shivering and not sleeping well in spite of putting on every piece of clothing she possessed. As it grew light she saw frost riming the edge of the water in a nearby ditch and knew she'd have to find somewhere better to sleep than the open air.

After eating the rest of the bread and mutton she set off with her determination to escape unbroken. She would get as far away from Hetton as her two feet would carry her before looking for work. Her money would last a while if she was very careful, thanks to Tad's gift. But on that thought, she frowned. What if someone attacked her and took it?

That night she found the remains of a haystack

and burrowed into it, glad to be out of the biting wind.

In the morning she removed every wisp of hay she could from her clothing, wanting to appear as respectable as possible, then spread the coins about her person and bundle as best she could, with the half-sovereign inside her chemise. Finally, before she set off again, she found herself a stout stick to use in self-defence if necessary.

She needed it two days later. Hearing a woman's screams for help, she moved cautiously forward to see two louts attacking an older woman who was more prosperously dressed than the usual traveller.

'Hoy!' Hannah yelled at the top of her voice. 'Stop that! Come on, quick!' She turned and gestured behind her as if urging other people to join her and then rushed forward, brandishing the stick.

After a moment's hesitation the two men ran off and Hannah stood in front of their victim, stick raised, until she was sure they weren't coming back. Only then did she try to help the woman to stand up, to find that she had hurt her ankle.

'I don't know what the world is coming to, I really don't,' her companion muttered. 'If a body can't walk into the village without being attacked, it's a poor look-out, it is that.'

'If you lean on my stick and take my arm, do you think you could move? I'd like to get away from here before they come back.'

'I shall have to, shan't I?' Wincing and making little whimpers of pain the woman began to limp along, leaning heavily on Hannah.

'We'll have to rest,' she gasped after a while.

They found a fallen log behind which they were out of sight of the lane and Hannah was glad of that when she heard footsteps from the road. She raised her head cautiously to see one of the men moving along it again. Turning, she put one finger to her lips and the woman nodded, understanding. They lay there on the muddy ground until he'd walked back.

'I think it's safe now,' Hannah said, helping the woman sit on the log. 'Are you all right?'

'Yes. And it's more than time we introduced ourselves. I'm Frances Hill, under-housekeeper at the Hall.'

'Hannah –' she broke off, annoyed with herself for saying her real name, but added, '– Mellor,' quickly, and hoped her companion hadn't noticed the slight hesitation over the surname.

'You're not from round here, are you?'

'I'm from the other side of Blackburn. I'm seeking work.'

'You're a cotton operative?'

'My husband was. He's dead now.'

'No children?'

Hannah shook her head.

'What sort of work are you seeking?'

'As a maid, I thought. I was always considered a good housewife and it surely can't be much different?'

'It is different. Very. The gentry have their own ways of doing things. But there's nothing you can't learn if you set your mind to it.' Frances hesitated then said, 'I'll ask the housekeeper if we can set you on at the Hall, if you like? Young Susan's getting wed after Christmas and we'll need another maid when she's left.'

'I'd be grateful.' This place was closer to Hetton than she'd wanted, but you didn't turn down such a kind offer. And anyway, who in Hetton socialised with the gentry? None of the folk Hannah knew, that was certain.

Heverbrook Hall was an imposing modern house, built on a gentle rise near a narrow river for the present master Mr Champley. Hannah thought she'd never seen such a pretty place. Even in the depths of winter the gardens were still attractive, with paved walkways and stone walls zigzagging down to the river. The land round here was flatter than Hetton, softer somehow, though the moors still sat on the horizon to the north and east. She couldn't remember a time when she hadn't seen them every day, but she supposed if she went further she'd get right away from them.

'Us servants use the back door,' Frances whispered.

Hannah looked at how much further that was but didn't say anything. She could see the pain on her companion's face as she limped along and thought it foolish to stick to a rule in these circumstances.

When they got to the kitchen, there was a chorus of exclamations from Cook and a young kitchen maid at the sight of Frances limping so badly and with her clothing muddied. The girl went running and a lady arrived, looking so grand in her black silk dress that Hannah was surprised to find this was only the housekeeper not the mistress.

Frances explained what had happened and how she owed her safety to the kindness of a stranger and they all turned to stare, making Hannah blush. 'I'd be glad of a cup of tea and no doubt my new friend would, too.'

Frances looked at the housekeeper. 'If you have a moment, Mrs Hallows, I'd appreciate a word with you.'

When the two older women had left, Cook waved Hannah to a seat. 'Sit yourself down, love. It never takes me long to make a pot of tea and I have some scones just out of the oven.'

A few minutes later another young maid came in. 'Mrs Hallows wants to see Mrs Mellor, if you please, Cook.'

It took Hannah a few seconds to remember that was her new name and stand up.

'If you'd follow me, Mrs Mellor?'

The housekeeper had her own sitting-room, so grand it took your breath away. Hannah wasn't asked to sit down but was told to approach the table behind which Mrs Hallows sat, with Frances on a chair to one side, nodding and smiling at her.

'I believe you're a widow, Mrs Mellor?'

'Yes, ma'am. My husband died a few months ago.'

'And you're seeking work, but have no experience in service?'

'Yes, ma'am. Though I was always accounted a good housewife and I'm not afraid of hard work.'

'We don't normally take anyone without references but Mrs Hill has asked me to give you a trial because of the service you rendered her. She's also agreed to provide you with a basic outfit.'

'An outfit?'

'Clothing suitable for your position.'

Hannah felt her face heat with embarrassment. 'Yes, I see. I had to sell everything when my husband died. That's why I only have the few things I could carry.'

'Times are hard, but to risk your life for another is very praiseworthy and has earned you this chance. See that you don't waste it. By the way, how old are you?'

'Thirty-six.' The lies were coming more easily now, though she hated having to be untruthful.

'Then we can also assume you have a little more sense than a younger woman, I hope.' She smiled and made a gesture of dismissal.

As they left her room, Frances leaned heavily on Hannah's arm again and said quietly, for her ears alone, 'There are all sorts of rules in a place like this, Hannah love. If you don't understand something, you come straight to me. If it weren't for you, I might not be here today.'

'I'm sure someone else would have heard your cries.'

'Someone else probably did, because a man passed me not long before it happened. But he made no attempt to come back and help me while you did, at some risk to yourself. I never forget a kindness, my dear.'

And then began a whirlwind day during which Hannah tried to cram so much new information into her brain that she thought her skull would burst.

She'd fallen lucky and she'd make sure she didn't waste this valuable opportunity. If she could just stay here for a while during the worst of the winter, then perhaps she could gather herself together and decide what she wanted to do with the rest of her life.

Though she might not achieve all her dreams – well, fancy thinking of finding another husband at her age – she'd have a good try at making a better life for herself.

CHAPTER NINE

December 1863 – January 1864

When he heard the sound of hoofbeats ringing on the frozen earth and wheels rumbling a dull counterpoint, Oliver stood up to peer out of the window. Spinneys lay at the end of a lane so it could only be someone coming to see him. To his astonishment it was Jack Lexham, driving the neat gig in which he did Oliver's father's estate business.

He went to open the door himself, hoping it wasn't bad news and then daring to hope that his father had forgiven him.

'Good morning, Mr Oliver.'

'Lexham. Do come in, my dear chap.'

As Ned came hurrying round the corner of the house to climb into the driving seat and drive the vehicle round to the stables at the rear, Jack remained outside for a moment or two staring up at the house before following his host inside.

'Not bad news, I hope?'

'No. But there are a few matters which need clearing up in connection with your inheritance.'

Oliver rang for a tea tray and Penny went off with her usual abundant cheerfulness to fetch it. Nanny had decided they could manage with her, a cook and a daily scrubbing woman for the time being, and it suited Oliver to live quietly.

Jack made no bones about his curiosity, going to stand by the window and study the gardens. 'I see you've set yourself up comfortably and are starting to get the place into shape.'

'I love living here and I'm grateful you kept the buildings in such good repair for me.'

'I'd be a poor agent if I hadn't.' Jack hesitated, hating to destroy the hope shining in the young man's face, then said bluntly, 'Although I bear a message from your father, he hasn't changed his mind about severing all relations with you, I'm afraid.'

Oliver moved his fingertips slowly and carefully along the line of brass upholstery tacks on his chair arm, trying not to show how much this news hurt. 'I'm sorry about that.'

'However, as he's still concerned about your welfare, he wishes to continue paying your allowance and—'

That needed no thinking about. 'No. If he won't see me, then I won't be obligated to him.'

Jack looked at him. The young man's tone was firmer somehow and, in fact, Oliver looked more in control of himself and his surroundings than he ever had before. He might not be a gentleman born but he took after his mother and had a gentlemanly heart. Jack knew which of his employer's sons he preferred, by hell he did!

'Your father was afraid you'd say that but still insists on helping so he's deeded you a piece of land near here, one of no importance to the main estate. He purchased it together with a parcel of other small properties.' He held up his hand as Oliver would have voiced another refusal. 'Let me finish, if you please. Walter knows nothing of this and the land has already been transferred into your name. Your father won't take it back and refuses to discuss the matter any further.'

Oliver frowned. 'But if he wishes to treat me,' he hesitated then said the word, 'so kindly, why won't he even see me?'

'Who knows with your father? But he's set on it, so let him do this for you at least, lad.'

Oliver walked to the window, stared out, then shrugged and turned back to the agent. 'Oh, very well. Tell me about this land. What does it consist of?'

Jack explained the details of the thirty or so acres which abutted Spinneys. It had a tumbledown cottage on it, which Oliver had already seen from the garden, and the land consisted mainly of a haphazard collection of fields. These were presently leased out in summer to a couple of nearby farmers who wanted more pasture for their stock and who had tried to buy the fields outright. 'I wouldn't advise you to sell them at present, though. The place could be made quite productive with a little care – if the cottage was made more habitable, for instance, there are a couple of fields round it which would make an excellent smallholding. I'm afraid the roof needs attention, though, if you don't want the place to deteriorate still further. There are quite a few tiles missing and the rain has already damaged the inside.'

'I don't know what to say.' Oliver gave a wry smile and threw up his hands in a helpless gesture. 'My father tends to do this, doesn't he? Makes it impossible for one to do other than what *he* wants. Oh, very well. I'll accept the gift of the land, but if he won't see me, that must be the last thing I take from him.' After a moment or two spent frowning in thought, he said slowly, 'I suppose he feels I need it to give me the requisite status as his son.'

'Or the additional income?'

'My tastes are very simple and I'm living quite comfortably on what I have. I'm not like my brother, you know, constantly wasting money. Has Walter damaged any more good men's livelihoods?'

'No. In fact, he's been rather more circumspect lately. He's taken up shooting at targets, which I suppose is less harmful. They tell me he's set out to make himself into a crack shot.'

Oliver stared into the fire. 'I hope it holds his interest for a while, then. I can certainly do without his attentions. Walter can bear a grudge for a long time, whether it's justified or not. And look, if Nathaniel King ever needs help, could you let me know? Or tell him to come to me. My brother blamed him for my father's anger over the destruction of the market garden and I'm afraid he'll try to get back at him.'

'You'd be better staying out of your brother's affairs altogether.'

'I will generally, believe me. But I can't forget King's face at the funeral – or that of his son – so humour me in this, if you please. Ah, here's the tea tray. Thank you, Penny. Let me pour you a cup, Mr Lexham. I'm becoming quite adept at this, you know.'

Jack decided as he drove away that although Oliver looked better, there was a loneliness about him that tugged at your heart strings. If only *he* had been the elder son instead of Walter! Everyone who lived on the estate would have been grateful for that. As it was, a tenant with a pretty young daughter had just given notice that he wished to quit his lease and had been quite open about the reason why – Walter's unwanted attentions towards the young woman. Nothing Jack had said or done had made the man change his mind, because he had already sent the daughter away and wasn't bringing her back, hoped never to see 'that nasty sod' again after he left. It was always a pity to lose a good tenant.

Well, when Walter inherited, he'd lose a good agent, too. Jack would never work for a man like him.

Christmas passed with little cheer in the West household. Ginny had hoped to hear from Nick, but there was no sign of a letter, and she knew from what Lucy told her that the Halstead family had not returned to the district. Lucy had heard that a relative was dying, but if so, it was taking a long time and surely Nick could have come back to see her?

She decided that as soon as life settled down into its January routine, she'd find some way to get a letter to him. If she addressed it to the farm, surely whoever was looking after things would send it on? Or she could even call there and ask for his new address. She desperately needed to see him.

Nick's grandfather died suddenly on the sixth of January and the family was caught up in preparations for the funeral. Nick was fretting to get back to Ginny but couldn't refuse to play his part in the proceedings.

After the funeral the solicitor came back with them and read the will. Everything had been left to Nick's mother, so they now owned their own farm instead of having to lease one, and a good farm it was too.

When the solicitor had left, his father solemnly poured them all a glass of port and toasted, 'Our new home.'

Nick couldn't bring himself to drink to this.

'What's wrong, lad?' his father asked genially.

'I don't want to live here.'

There was a sudden silence, then his mother set her glass down, wiping her lips with her handkerchief and losing her smile in the process. 'It's that girl, isn't it?'

Nick nodded.

'Ginny West,' his father said in tones of loathing.

'She's Ginny Doyle. West is only her step-father, not a blood relative. And yes, I still love her and want to marry her.' He saw his parents exchange grim glances and his heart sank.

'She's not for you, son,' his father said gently. 'West won't let her marry a Methodist.'

'Then we'll run away.' He looked desperately from one to the other, finding no softening in their grim expressions. 'I shan't change my mind about this.'

'And we shan't change our minds, either,' his mother said. 'Your father won't tell you so I must.'

'Jane, no!'

'He needs to know why, Sam.' She turned back to her son. 'West tried to have his way with me once before I was wed, and if your father hadn't heard me screaming, the man would have raped me.' She shuddered at the memory. 'Till he got all religious he had a bad reputation with women. Our mothers told us to keep away from him, but there was no one to keep him away from us.' She closed her eyes on the memories, then opened them again to say earnestly to her son, 'I've never forgotten what he tried to do and how scared of him I was, and I never shall.'

'So you see why it's impossible for you to marry the daughter,' his father added. 'We won't deal with that man, not in any way, nor with anyone connected to him.'

'But that's not Ginny's fault,' Nick protested.

'She's related to him now. You couldn't force that connection on your mother, not if you care about her at all.'

He jerked to his feet. 'I shall have to – think about it.'

When he was out of sight of the house, he stopped and dashed the tears away from his eyes. This was the last thing he'd expected to hear.

And it did make a difference to his decision. He had loving parents, to whom he'd always been close because he was their only child. He couldn't bear the thought of upsetting his mother so deeply.

But could he bear to give up Ginny? He didn't know.

More tears followed. But none of them helped him make a decision and when he returned to the farm to carry out his normal duties he turned his face away, not speaking to anyone.

What use were words now? His life was ruined.

One weekday in the middle of January Christine waited until she knew for certain her husband was at market and the boys were at school, then went to find her daughter.

'Do you have something to tell me?'

Ginny swung round to face her, her expression apprehensive. 'What do you mean?'

'You didn't have your last monthly and you're nearly due the next one.' Ginny sucked in a breath and looked at her mother, tried and failed to smile, then burst into tears.

Christine cradled her in her arms. 'Is it Nick? You've – lain with him?'

A nod was the only answer and a gulp that changed into a sob. 'He asked me to marry him and I said yes. I know he meant it but he's been away for so long. I've been waiting for him to come back before I said anything.'

'Oh, dear Lord, what are we to do?'

'I was going to run away, go and look for Nick, only I don't know where he is and anyway, I've no money.'

'Running away would only lead you into greater difficulties if he refused to help you.'

'What can be worse than being beaten senseless by *him*?'

'Being on your own at the mercy of anyone stronger.' Christine stroked the hair back from Ginny's forehead, murmuring endearments and trying to think rapidly. 'I'll have to write to my brother.'

'Will Uncle Nathaniel help?'

'Yes. I've already asked him if he'd be willing, because I thought Howard would insist on you marrying his friend. I'll write to him next week when Howard is at market and somehow we must find a way to post the letter.' Lately her husband even resented her going into the village alone, questioning her closely about what she did there and who she talked to.

But he came home early from market the following week, in a rage about an imagined slight, something that happened from time to time. Whether these slights were real or not, Christine could never work out. Her husband was always so ready to take offence. How deceived she had been when he'd come courting her! He'd hidden his true nature then and had seemed a kindly man.

She didn't hear him coming so he found her with the writing things spread out on the kitchen table. Before she could prevent him, he had twitched the piece of paper from beneath the shaking hand with which she'd instinctively tried to cover it.

As he began reading what she'd written, his face turned so deep red with rage, the veins standing out like cords on his forehead, that when Ginny appeared in the doorway, Christine yelled out, 'Run for your life!'

The girl turned and sped off, running to such avail that she was up in the woods at the top of the fields before her step-father was even half-way up the hill. His bellowing and shouting as he chased behind her was to haunt her nightmares for months, as was the sight of the enraged face he had turned towards her, like a maddened bull about to charge its victim.

She knew better than to stop in the woods, for he would quarter them searching for her, she was sure. So she ran on, making for Nick's family's farm, hoping against hope that the Halsteads would have come back so that she could beg them to help her.

But a stranger opened the door and it was a moment or two before Ginny could gather enough breath to inquire about Nick.

'The family's gone for good now. Mrs Halstead's father died and left them a farm. They wanted to get out of here quick, so we're looking after things for them until they can move their stock and furniture.'

Ginny cast a distracted glance over her shoulder. 'I need to contact them – well, contact Nick, actually. It's really urgent. Could you please give me their address?'

'Are you Ginny?'

She nodded, her face lighting up. He'd left a message, then. She should have come here sooner.

'I can't give you their address. Mrs Halstead asked special for me not to tell you, said it was better if you and Nick didn't see one another again.'

The world seemed to spin around Ginny and next thing she knew she was lying on a wooden settle in the kitchen and the woman who'd answered the door was fanning her face.

'In trouble, aren't you?' She looked suggestively at Ginny's stomach.

'How did you . . . ?'

'I've daughters of my own. I know the signs.' She sighed. 'I wish I could help, but I can't. You'd better go back to your family and let them deal with this, my dear.'

'I can't. My step-father hates me and I'm terrified of him. He'll beat me senseless.'

'Ah. I heard about him hitting you before.' Mary bit her lip then took a decision because she felt so sorry for the poor girl. 'Look, this is what I'll do. You write your letter and put a stamp on it then give it me. I'll write the address on it and post it for you. Bring it round here any time.' She stood up, clearly ready to get back to her day's work.

Ginny dragged herself to her feet and hesitated near the door. 'Could I stay in your hay barn until dark? *Please?*'

After a moment's hesitation, the woman shook her head. 'No, better not. They want nothing to do with that man, or any of his family.'

Ginny gaped at her. 'What's my step-father done?'

'I've said more than I should. Please leave. But I *will* post a letter for you.'

So the girl left the farm and trailed down to the river where she hid in an old shed until it grew dark, then made her way up to the ruined cottage in the woods. She was cold and hungry, had no blankets or way of keeping warm and no idea of what she was going to do. When she got to the cottage, she huddled on the bare earth, weeping.

Exhaustion at last allowed her to sink into an uneasy sleep but she kept waking, shivering, chilled to the bone, and there were noises in the darkness, noises that made her jump. She had never been as terrified in her life. Or as cold.

Had Nick known about his family's move? He'd talked about his grandfather's farm once or twice. It sounded a lovely place.

As the dark night dragged on and on, she had to wonder if he'd meant a single word he'd said.

What was she to do if he never came back?

Hannah woke up feeling more cheerful than she had for a long time. She'd been here at Heverbrook Hall for nearly a month now and was used to the ways of the household, strange though some of them seemed to her.

Eh, rich folk were certainly different from the people she'd known. Even the gentry in her small village hadn't lived like this, so wastefully and waited on hand and foot. And as for Christmas, well, the food they'd consumed, the presents the family had given one another would have kept a whole village for a year. It didn't seem right.

The Champleys even gave her a present: a length of material to make a new petticoat. She said thank you and tried to feel grateful, but she was missing Malachi and Lemuel more at Christmas than ever before and a deep sadness filled her. She and Malachi had always sung together, carols and hymns, one after the other. He had a lovely voice. And Lemuel had joined in quietly, knowing his voice wasn't anything special, but still wanting to be part of the celebrations.

This Christmas was lonely even though she was surrounded by crowds of people, and she grew so low in spirits she couldn't even summon up her lovely dream to keep her warm. Well, it was a daft dream, wasn't it? What man would look twice at her? She was too old for such foolishness.

After the festivities were over she pulled herself together. This was to be her life for a while, so she set herself to learn all she could and fit in. Frances said she was a good worker and Mrs Hallows spoke to her in the New Year, saying they'd be happy to keep her on though she'd have to find herself some decent clothes. If she was a good needlewoman, they might find her a few lengths of material to make herself up some more dresses.

Today was Sunday, the third in January. It was

always an easier day than usual, though all the staff had to go to the early morning service before they did anything else, a service attended mainly by servants and villagers. The Champleys were sticklers about that, though they didn't go themselves until Evensong, with the rest of the local gentry. But Hannah didn't mind. The church choir sang beautifully and she really enjoyed listening to them.

She got through her duties quickly then went to make herself tidy, walking to the church beside Frances who was a comfortable companion, not burdening you with too much talk.

During the short sermon Hannah let her thoughts wander where they would, joining in the singing and letting her voice soar. Afterwards she walked sedately home with Frances. A quiet life this, but it suited her for now and why she had let herself get so down-hearted at Christmas she didn't know.

The Vicar's wife came up to Mrs Hallows after the service and asked without preamble, 'Where does that new maid of yours come from, the one who sings so beautifully?'

The housekeeper looked puzzled. 'From the other side of Preston. Why do you ask?'

'And her name?'

'Hannah Mellor.'

'Ah, Hannah.'

Although the two women could not have been classed as friends, they had a great deal of respect for one another so Mrs Hallows repeated her question, 'Why do you ask?'

'Because I have a friend staying with me and she's sure she's seen the woman before. Yes, and heard her sing – that's what drew her attention to her. Only the last time wasn't in the best of circumstances.' She hesitated, looked round and said in a low voice, 'This is not the place to discuss something so serious. Would you come and take tea with us tomorrow afternoon? I really think you should talk to my friend.'

'Hannah's a good worker.'

'Yes, I'm sure she is. But can you *trust* her?'

Which left Mrs Hallows feeling puzzled.

The following morning she called Frances into her room and asked, 'Is Hannah doing all right?'

'Yes, of course she is. A nice, steady worker.'

'You haven't noticed anything – odd about her?'

'Odd? In what way odd?'

'I don't know exactly, but I'm taking tea with the Vicar's wife this afternoon. She says she has some disturbing information about Hannah, so I just wanted to warn you to keep an eye on her for the rest of the day until I find out what this is about. We may not be able to keep her on.'

'Yes, of course I can.'

When the housekeeper had left, Frances went to check the linen, a task she kept for times when she needed to have a think. In the quiet, shadowed room, with its rows of shelves and neatly folded sheets, tablecloths and towels, she found a peace that was sometimes difficult in a house which kept ten indoor servants and fourteen outdoor staff.

Something was wrong. But what? How could Hannah be under suspicion of anything? Her friend was not only a good worker, but had put her life at risk to rescue Frances who owed her a lot. And anyway, she *liked* Hannah.

It came to Frances half an hour later as she was checking on the upstairs rooms that she could do no less for Hannah than put her own comfortable life at risk in return.

She bustled up to the nursery floor and found her friend just finishing cleaning the bedrooms. 'I need to speak to you, love. It's urgent.'

At the sight of her worried face Hannah's heart lurched in her chest and she followed her to the linen store.

'I don't know how to tell you this, love, but the Vicar's wife has a friend staying with her from over Hetton way. This woman thinks she knows you and—' At the sight of Hannah's terror, she knew something was dreadfully wrong and said simply, 'Tell me. Trust me.'

Hannah swallowed hard. 'Perhaps it's best you don't know.'

'Not if you consider me your friend, as I consider you mine.'

So Hannah stumbled into her story, shame colouring her cheeks and words tripping over one another as she relived those dreadful months of living with her daughter-in-law. When she had finished she hardly dared raise her eyes but found Frances looking at her, her own eyes full of tears, and then was swept into a big hug.

'You believe me?' Hannah asked, dazed.

'Yes, of course I do.' Frances frowned. 'We'll have

to get you away from here quickly, though, because you've no way of proving your innocence that I can see. We don't want them taking you back to that place.'

Tears were trickling down Hannah's cheeks. 'Oh, Frances, you don't know what it means to have someone believe in me.'

'It sounds to me as if several people have believed you. That friend of yours, the shepherd and even your son – though he's a weak reed, if ever I heard of one.'

At midday Frances supervised the servants' meal and the housekeeper, butler and the master's valet dined in rather more state in her room. As usual, Frances carried in the dessert.

'You're keeping an eye on her?' Mrs Hallows asked sharply.

'Oh, yes. Definitely.'

'Good. I shall be back about four o'clock. Make sure she doesn't leave the house.' She didn't explain her remarks to the gentlemen, who were used to her sharp commands in connection with the maids.

Frances carried Hannah's bundle of clothes outside for her, pretending it was some unexpected washing, and met her beyond the laundry which had its own separate building behind the house. She had to be dissuaded from accompanying Hannah further and surprised them both by bursting into tears. 'What shall you do? Where shall you go? Oh, I can't bear to think of you on your own!'

'I'll go back towards Preston,' Hannah said. 'I'm hoping it'll be easier to hide in a big town.'

'Will you write to me?'

'Oh, Frances, I daren't.'

'No. No, I suppose not. But if you ever can . . .'

Hannah picked up the bundle and set off towards the Preston road, stopping at the bend to turn and wave to her friend.

What the Vicar's wife had to tell her sent Mrs Hallows back to the Hall feeling very shaken. She called the butler into her room and told him what she had learned about their new maid, then begged him to find two strong men to help her capture the madwoman.

While he was doing this, she rang the bell for Frances. When her assistant arrived, she said only, 'Please wait here with me. I have something to tell you.'

Frances stared at her grim face and guessed that this was something to do with Hannah. She felt shivery in her stomach for she had never disobeyed an order before and was terrified she was going to lose her job.

When two of the young grooms appeared, Mrs Hallows turned to the butler. 'Perhaps you'd like to tell them, Mr Meadows?'

He explained the situation and warned the two young men very strictly to say nothing to anyone afterwards.

Frances burst into tears and in the end Mrs Hallows had to speak sharply to her to get her to stop weeping. 'Be quiet now. Tell us where Hannah is working this afternoon.'

'She should be getting the nursery floor ready for the night.'

Frances lowered her eyes and waited until the men had left, then dared to say, though her speech was punctuated with more sobs. 'I don't believe it. Hannah's *not a* madwoman. You haven't even heard her side of the story.'

'And you have?'

She nodded. 'She told me a while back.'

'You should have passed the information on to me.'

The butler returned just then. 'She's not there.'

They both stared at Frances, who slowly turned red.

'You helped her escape, didn't you?' Mrs Hallows said.

'Yes. She saved my life. I couldn't – I simply couldn't! – allow them to lock her away again. Please let me tell you what really happened.'

Mr Meadows stared down his nose at her. 'What *she* says happened is of no relevance. They don't shut people up in asylums for no reason. Why, this woman could be a danger to herself as well as to others. We're lucky she hasn't run amok while she's been here. Very lucky.'

'If you wish me to leave, I'll understand,' Frances faltered.

'She's been taken in by the woman,' Mrs Hallows told the butler. 'We all have. These people can be very cunning. And she *was* a good worker.' She waited till Frances had calmed down a little and said gently, 'The best way to help her now is to tell us where she's gone, so that she can be recaptured with as little fuss as possible.'

It took the two of them over an hour to convince Frances of that.

'Hannah was making for Preston,' she said at last. 'I saw her set off down the road.'

'Ah.' Mr Meadows stood up. 'I'll go and tell Mr Champley. He'll no doubt send men after her. He's very conscientious when it comes to the safety of his workers and his public duty.'

At which Frances began sobbing all over again and wouldn't be comforted. 'I've betrayed her. Why did you make me betray her? I'll never forgive myself.'

A letter arrived for Lucy Porter, something which had never happened before. Her mother picked it up and stared at it, then went into the kitchen.

'Who is writing to you?'

Lucy gaped at the envelope. 'I don't know.' She stretched out her hand for it, but her mother held it back.

'I think we'll let your father deal with this.'

'But it's addressed to me!'

'We're not having you receiving letters from strangers. We want to know what's in it.'

The letter sat on the mantelpiece all afternoon and when Lucy's father came home for his evening meal, it was produced and handed over to him.

He looked sternly at his daughter. 'You're sure you don't know who this is from?'

'No, Father.'

He took a knife and slit open the envelope, read it, breathed deeply, then read it again.

When he passed it to his wife, she did the same, then both of them looked disapprovingly at Lucy.

'You've been helping Ginny Doyle meet Nick Halstead secretly, haven't you?'

She could only nod.

'He's expecting you to pass this letter to her without her parents' knowledge, but *I'm not having that!*' He thumped his hand down on the table. 'And if you ever do such a thing again, you'll be shut in your room for a week on bread and water.'

She began to sob, worried for her friend more than for herself.

'I'll send it back to his mother.'

Lucy stared at them in dismay. 'But if it's for Ginny—'

'Did you hear what I said? I'm having no underhand behaviour in my house.' He folded the letter and put it into his pocket. 'Go to your room and don't leave it until morning.'

She lay on the bed sobbing, feeling she had let Ginny down.

In the morning she sobbed even more loudly as they forbade her to associate with Ginny again, or even speak to her.

When the letter was returned to its sender, Jane Halstead stared at it, tore it open and gasped as she read what her son had written. He'd already asked *that girl* to marry him.

She didn't show him the letter, but she did have a long and serious talk with her husband, a talk that ended up with her in tears and him angry – and the letter burnt in the stove.

CHAPTER TEN

January 1864

Ginny was so desperately cold and hungry that the following morning she went to the Parsonage for help, remembering how kind Mrs Crawford had been to her before. She waited outside until she could catch that lady on her own. Feeling nauseous, as she did every morning now, she hid at the end of their back garden and watched the house. When she saw Mrs Crawford come out, she watched anxiously, but to her shuddering relief the other woman made her way through the graveyard and vanished into the rear of the church, her arms full of greenery.

Ginny followed, casting hasty glances over her shoulder in case anyone else approached. But it was another chill, damp morning and there was no one around so she gained the rear of the church safely. Pushing open the door she crept inside, but it slipped out of her numbed fingers and its weight swung it shut with a bang that echoed through the building.

'Who's there?'

'Me.' Taking a deep breath, Ginny moved forward, ready to make a dash for it if anyone tried to detain her.

Julia Crawford stared at her, saw the poor girl was ready to flee and said in her abrupt way, 'Better come into the flower room. No one will see you there.'

As tears welled in Ginny's eyes and she swayed dizzily, Julia dropped her secateurs and rushed forward to catch the girl in her arms. 'Dear heaven, how cold you are!'

'You won't – send me back to him?'

'Has he been hitting you again?'

'No. But he'll kill me if he catches me and . . .' sobs threatened to stop her speaking and she had to make a huge effort to gain some control of her voice '. . . anyway, you may not want to help me now.'

Julia tugged her forward. 'Nonsense. If Our Lord could help sinners, I can do no less. And anyway, what have you done that's so bad?' She opened the door of the flower room and led Ginny inside, wishing she dare take her somewhere warmer because the child was white with cold, racked by shivers. All she could think of was to find a length of old green baize which they sometimes used to cover stands upon which they were massing flowers, and cast it around her companion's shoulders.

After Ginny had explained the situation she sat with head drooping, fingers clutching the improvised blanket. Suddenly she was so tired she couldn't have run away even if *he* had come into the room. She could only wait for judgement.

'I need to speak to your mother,' Julia said slowly. 'If this uncle will take you in, and if that's what *she* wants, then I'm sure it'll be the best solution.'

'My step-father's always nearby. You'll not catch her on her own.'

'Then we must find some way to distract him. In the meantime, I'll go and bring you some food then we'll find you a better hiding place than this. Will you trust me, dear? Will you wait for me here and not run away again?'

Ginny was too spent to do anything but nod. When Mrs Crawford had gone she leaned her head back and knew nothing more until someone shook her arm gently.

'Sorry to wake you, dear, but you need to eat something, and look, I've brought you a cup of tea. I sometimes bring tea across to my husband and—'

'What are you plotting now, Julia?' that same husband said, following her into the room with a stern expression on his face.

Ginny could take no more. With a gasp she slid to the floor in a faint.

Julia turned to her husband and explained rapidly what the problem was.

'We can't keep her here,' he said instantly. 'Her parents are the ones in charge of her and she must be returned to them.'

'Well, I'm going to contact her mother. I said so.'

'The man is the head of the household and must make decisions about matters like this.'

'How can you be so cruel? You know what Mr West is like. He'll beat her for this.'

Her husband drew himself up. 'I'd beat her, too, if she were my daughter and had got herself in trouble.' He turned and locked the door by which he had entered, then pushed his wife through the other one and locked that, too, leaving Ginny lying on the floor.

'You might at least have let me give that child something to eat and drink.'

'She doesn't deserve that sort of cosseting.'

Julia stalked ahead of him to the house, furious. They had disagreed over so many things lately, but most of all about a man's right to chastise his wife and make all the family decisions.

When she heard him telling the maid to get ready to take a note to Mr West, Julia couldn't hold back an angry sob. She went storming up to their bedroom, preferring not to show the servants how at odds they were, how angry she felt.

Later, Godfrey came looking for her. 'I've sent for Mr West.'

She stood up and faced him with her arms folded across her body. 'I meant what I said. I'll never forgive you for this.'

'My dear wife, the law is quite explicit about a woman's place in this world.'

'And would you beat *me* if you felt I was not behaving as I should?'

He smiled and made a condescending little sound. 'The question doesn't arise. You were raised by careful parents and will always do your duty.'

'No,' she said quietly. 'Not if I disagree with what you're doing. And what's more, I refuse to continue as we are.'

He frowned at her. 'What do you mean?'

'I've made up a bed for myself in the back bedroom. What you've done today was so cruel the mere sight of you sickens me. In bed you think only of yourself and don't care whether you please me, so the only way you'll get me to do my wifely duty from now on will be by force. And,' anger made her voice shake, 'I hereby withdraw from all my parish duties as well. I shall not help in Sunday School, nor shall I do the flowers, nor shall I convene the Ladies' Auxiliary. You'll get nothing more from me until you change the way you behave towards me.'

A pulse began to beat in his throat and dusky colour rose in his cheeks. 'You're not thinking clearly.'

'Oh, but I am. I'm thinking very clearly indeed. I've made the best of our marriage so far because I could see nothing else to do once I'd made my vows, but you've treated me as if I were a slave with no brain ever since the day we were wed. You were only pretending to be kind when you were courting me. You don't love me any more than you love your fellow man, and I certainly don't love you.'

He took a step forward, fists clenched by his sides. 'Be silent! How dare you speak to me like this?'

'I've been silent too long. I've watched you supporting men who ill-treat their wives like Howard West. I've done my best to help women in distress. But it's never been enough, because *you* weren't supporting my efforts and the people in this parish knew that. I despise you, Godfrey Crawford. If I had anywhere to go, I'd leave you tomorrow.'

She stormed out of the room and he took a hasty step after her, then stopped. 'Their female brains are easily overset,' he muttered. 'I must give her time to come to her senses.'

Half an hour later there was a pounding on the front door and the maid let in Mr West, showing him into the parson's study.

'Do you have her safely held?' Howard asked, not bothering with preliminary courtesies.

'Yes. I'll take you to her in a minute. But first I must warn you that she should not be hurt. A woman with child is too delicate and whatever the mother's sins one must think of the baby.'

Howard muttered something and after a minute the parson took it for agreement and escorted his visitor across to the church. When he opened the door to the flower room, Howard said, 'Ah!' in a tone of immense satisfaction and Ginny screamed.

She screamed again as he slapped her across the face, then curled up, trying to avoid the blows she knew would follow.

But Godfrey Crawford stepped between them. 'Sir, I have warned you.'

'Sir,' mocked Howard, 'this is *my* step-daughter and I shall treat her as I see fit.' He took Ginny by the arm and force-marched her to the church door, tossing over his shoulder, 'Thank you for restoring her to my care. We shall now deal with our shame ourselves – in any way I see fit.'

Godfrey watched him go, open-mouthed, then decided not to describe this encounter to his wife. It would only make matters worse. Julia would come to her senses soon and no doubt regret her little rebellion.

When Nathaniel heard nothing more from his sister, he began to worry. Christine had sounded so desperately anxious about Ginny that he couldn't help but fear for them both. He had begged his sister not to marry Howard West because something about the man didn't ring true and he had a mean mouth. But Christine had hated being a widow, and indeed hadn't managed very well. He wondered if Howard had scented his disapproval because invitations to visit them were few at first and then stopped altogether.

It was sad to be estranged from your only sister so Nathaniel had continued to write the occasional letter – but had received few answers and those only scrawled notes which, it often seemed to him, must have been written secretly.

'What's the matter, Dad?'

He looked up to see Gregory standing there, as solemn-eyed as ever, and suddenly decided to tell his son the truth. 'I'm worried about your Aunt Christine.'

Gregory pursed his lips, then began to draw with his toe in the soft earth, avoiding his father's eyes. 'She doesn't feel like an aunt. I don't even remember what she looks like.'

Nathaniel stared at him in shock. 'But surely – is it so long since you've seen her?'

Gregory nodded. 'Not since I was little.'

'She wrote to me recently, said she was sorry about your mother and then – well, she said she was worried about your cousin's safety.' He was talking as much to himself as to the boy. 'Ginny was such a bonny little lass, always smiling, just like her father. How can that second husband of Christine's not get on with her?' He put one arm round his son's narrow shoulders and gave him an absent-minded hug. 'Eh, I wish I knew what was going on.'

'Couldn't we go over and visit them? Other people go to visit their families.'

Nathaniel stared into space. 'Trouble is, that might make things worse. Fellows like him can take huffs over nothing. And Blackfold isn't an easy place to get to because it's not on a railway line.'

'Why did my aunt move so far away?'

'To live with her first husband.'

'She should have come back here afterwards.'

'Aye, she should that!'

And he should have asked her to come back. Only Sarah had just started being ill and Nathaniel had had as much on his plate as he could cope with. Christine had turned instead to this West fellow and lived to regret it.

'What shall we do, Dad?'

'Wait a day or two longer. If we don't hear, I might go over to Blackfold and call on my sister.' He'd visit the local parson first, ask if he knew anything.

'Can I come with you?'

'I'd thought to leave you here with Tom.'

'Please let me come, Dad. I've never been anywhere. And besides – I don't feel safe if you're not with me.'

Which made Nathaniel hug him again and wish he could wring Walter Dewhurst's neck, because this clinging dependency of Gregory's had started after *that incident*. The lad went out of his way to avoid the landowner's son now, hiding if he saw him coming.

Eh, life didn't get any easier, it definitely didn't. If one problem was solved, another two rose to take its place.

Oliver strolled down into the village, turning aside to visit Beckleton's small church which he had not yet attended. It was a pretty stone building, only about twenty years old, he'd judge, but without the rawness of some of the newer churches hereabouts which were being built in red brick.

He supposed he should start going to church and getting acquainted with his neighbours, but it had been so blissful to live quietly and, as he called it 'unto himself', that he'd not made the effort yet.

Pushing open the small door cut into one of the huge double doors which were only opened on Sundays, he went inside, to stop entranced and stare at the row of stained glass windows down one side. Not grand windows these, because it was a small church, but particularly pretty with delicate colours that the eye was drawn to. A shepherd with his sheep. A woman with a plump baby – presumably Mary with the infant Jesus. And then a window looking like a garden full of summer flowers with an angel hovering over it, dedicated to the memory of one Lady Ann Turner. Turner? Weren't the local landowners called that? They lived in London mainly now, but he'd heard that one of the family was in residence.

Near the door were more flowers, real ones this time, with evergreens setting off their delicate colours in the vase. How did anyone get spring flowers so early? These seemed so gracefully displayed, not standing stiffly to attention, that he moved towards them, entranced. When he saw a young woman near the altar at work on a second flower arrangement he stopped. She could not have heard him come in because she was humming to herself as she worked.

He didn't speak for a moment or two, but stood and

watched her as she selected one bloom after the other and threaded them into another beautiful arrangement. She was small and dumpy, with a plain face and reddish hair, but there was something altogether wholesome-looking about her. The Vicar's daughter, perhaps?

Deciding that she might be startled if she turned and saw him staring at her, he waited for a break in her humming and loudly cleared his throat.

She swung round at once. 'Oh! I didn't hear anyone come in.'

'I know. I didn't want to startle you. I was admiring your flower arrangements. They're so beautiful. I hate to see flowers standing stiffly to attention.'

'So do I.'

'Yours are a joy to behold.' Oliver pointed to the stained glass window. 'They remind me of that.'

She beamed at him. 'I'm so glad. Lady Ann was my grandmother and she designed the window herself. She's the one who taught me how to arrange flowers, too.' She wiped her hands on her coarse sacking apron and came towards him, hand outstretched, as un-selfconscious as a child. 'I'm another Ann Turner. Are you our mysterious new neighbour?'

Oliver took the hand, bemused. 'Mysterious?'

She chuckled, a rich sound, and her smile lit up her face so that it no longer seemed plain.

'Well, I'm Oliver Dewhurst and there's no mystery about me.' He saw a shadow pass across her face and she recoiled ever so slightly. 'I take it you know of my family?' He was unable to keep bitterness from his voice.

'I met your brother once, briefly.'

'Then you'll not want to further your acquaintance with me.' He bowed slightly and turned to leave.

'Wait!' She moved to his side. 'It's wrong of me to judge you by – by others.'

For some reason it was important to tell her, 'I'm not like him, not at all. In fact, I've left home to avoid him.'

Her eyes searched his face. 'That's very sad. I don't know what I'd do without my brothers.' Especially with a father as strict as hers, one who had believed children should be seen and not heard but had rarely even seen them during their childhood. And her mother was terrified of him so had followed his example, handing her babies over to nursemaids and governesses when ordered to continue attending dutifully to her husband's needs. Ann shook off the unhappy memories and saw the stranger give a wry smile.

'It may sound sad, but I'm far more comfortable not living with Walter. He's a bully and I'm not very strong so have never been able to fight back physically.' He looked down at his own spindly body and wished it were not so frail.

'And what are you going to do with yourself in Beckleton?' she asked.

'I don't know yet. Enjoy the peace, mostly.'

'Do you ride?'

'A little.'

'Hunt?'

'No. I couldn't bear to, nor could I shoot helpless animals.' He spread his arms in a self-deprecating gesture. 'Not a very manly person, I'm afraid.'

'I like you the better for it. I don't hunt either, and

that makes my father furious.' She looked back at the vase. 'I'm like my grandmother. It's flowers and gardens that I love.'

'I do too. I have a whole garden to rescue, and I want to grow lots of flowers in it.'

'If you should need any advice . . . ?'

'I'd welcome any help you could offer me. I know nothing about horticulture, though I mean to learn.'

Her face lit up with mischief. 'My old governess and I sometimes go for walks. If we're passing, perhaps we could call in and see your garden?' They'd have to be careful, though. The servants had been instructed to keep an eye on her because sending her here to a remote and deprived little estate in Lancashire was supposed to be a punishment for not obeying her father and marrying the man he'd chosen. She loved being here, but knew it couldn't last. One day her father would come after her with more demands and she must either obey him or flee.

Oliver watched her lose herself in her thoughts and it seemed to him they weren't pleasant ones. Well, he could understand that. Her father the Marquess was notorious and ran his estate harshly, with no thought for his tenants' welfare. Lady Ann seemed as unlike her father as he was to Walter. Only when she came out of her abstraction and gave him a quick smile did he speak again. 'You'd be more than welcome to come and see my garden. Not that there's anything to see yet, except the shape of it.'

He dreamed of her that night, a plain young woman but with a smile that made her whole face glow with life. And although others might not like red hair, he loved the way the sun had turned hers into a bright, happy colour.

In the morning he mocked himself for daring even to think about her. A woman like Lady Ann Turner was not for him. His young maid had been happy to talk about the great family of the neighbourhood when he'd asked her this morning and now he knew that Lady Ann was two-and-twenty and still unmarried, sent to the Priory in disgrace by her father the Marquess of Iffingham though no one in the village knew exactly why.

It was hard to leave a friend when you had only one in the world, Hannah thought as she waved one last time to Frances. Harder still to deceive her. She waited until Frances had walked back into the grounds of the Hall then turned in the opposite direction to Preston, cutting through one of the fields and keeping in the lea of the hedge, praying harder than she had ever prayed before that no one would see her go this way.

She had no idea where she was heading, but this time intended to make sure she didn't stop until she was far enough away for no one to recognise her. She'd go to Australia if she had the money, but there was no guarantee she'd find her son Malachi if she did, because there hadn't been a letter from him before he left and now she wouldn't know even if one did arrive. Where was he? Was he all right?

She walked until nightfall then found a sheltered spot behind a hedge and made herself as comfortable as she could, given the bitter cold. Winter was definitely not the time to be tramping the roads. In the morning, she'd smooth the ground before she set off. No need to leave any sign of where she had been.

Running away was all she could think of doing. She hated it, had always preferred to face up to trouble but what choice did she have now? They believed Patty, not her.

The next day Hannah found a quiet little road which seemed to lead roughly in the direction she wanted, away from Preston. Later that morning she found herself talking to a family who were travelling the same way. They seemed more friendly than most tramping folk and let her put her bundle on top of theirs on the rickety handcart for a while.

Suddenly a man came riding up behind them and shouted, 'Hey there! Have you seen a woman on her own, tall and with a wild expression?'

They looked at one another in astonishment and he added impatiently, as if they should have known it already, 'There's a madwoman on the loose. They're looking for her. You'd better make sure you stick together.'

'We've seen no madwoman,' the father of the family replied, not even glancing in Hannah's direction.

'What's she done?' the mother asked.

'Escaped from the asylum, they tell me.'

'Has she hurt anyone?'

'Not that I know.'

'Then why are you hunting her like this?'

'Her daughter-in-law has set up a hue and cry for her.'

'Well, we'll keep our eyes open.'

He nodded and was off again, hallooing as if enjoying himself.

'Don't say anything,' the mother warned Hannah, her eyes going to the two children. 'You can stay with us till nightfall then you should make your own way.'

'Thank you.' Hannah's voice was shaking with reaction.

'A daughter-in-law should be looking after you, not setting folk to hound you,' the man said disapprovingly. 'I can't abide families that don't look out for one another.'

'I don't need looking after. I'm *not* mad.'

'You don't seem it to me either,' the woman said. 'But you can only stay with us till nightfall. We don't want to get into trouble. We've enough problems already.'

'You're very kind and I'm grateful.' Hannah tramped along beside them in silence, moving unobtrusively to the other side of the group as the horseman rode back, and already dreading the approaching darkness.

They'd catch her in the end, unless she was very lucky. If they had a hue and cry out after her, with men riding out along the roads, what chance did she have of evading them? Dear Lord, what had she ever done to deserve this?

That night she could summon up no dreams to warm her darkness. Nor could she do more than sleep fitfully. It was bitterly cold and although it wasn't raining, the air was damp and it would rain soon. She'd been lucky so far with the weather. She'd have to find better shelter the next night or she'd catch her death of cold. If she hadn't done so already.

But as colour returned to the world, her spirits rose again. They hadn't caught her yet, had they? And she'd do her best to make sure they didn't today. One day at a time, that was how to take this.

CHAPTER ELEVEN

January 1864

Nathaniel set out to see his sister two days later, taking enough money to see him through and also, he hoped, pay Ginny's fare back. That wouldn't leave him with a lot left for emergencies, but family came first.

He and Gregory travelled by train as far as they could, but Blackfold was a small village and quite far from the nearest branch line so they had to finish the journey by carrier's cart. Finding transport delayed them so they didn't arrive until dusk and Nathaniel decided it was best not to do anything further at this hour. He guided his son towards the village inn, saying cheerfully, 'We'd better get something to eat first and see if there's a bed to be had.'

Just before they got there, he stopped and stared round. 'Eh, I've got a bad feeling about this and I wish now that I'd not brought you with me, son.'

'I'll be all right with you to look after me, Dad.'

Nathaniel knelt so that he was at eye level with his son. 'I shan't always be able to protect you, Gregory, so if we're ever in a fight where the odds are against me, you're to run away and hide – or fetch help. I'll do better if I'm not worrying about protecting you. And, who knows? You may be able to help me afterwards.'

Gregory scowled at him. 'I don't want to be the sort of person who runs away.'

'He that fights and runs away may live to fight another day,' Nathaniel quoted.

The boy avoided his eyes. 'Is that why you didn't try to stop Walter Dewhurst?'

'Yes. He's got money and power on his side, not to mention his father owning our bit of land. If I ever see a way, though, one day I'll make him sorry he hurt us, I promise you. But even then I shan't do anything that'll land me in prison. That'd help no one. A man should abide by the law of the land, else there'd be nothing but chaos.'

The boy nodded solemnly and they continued walking.

At the village inn Nathaniel persuaded the landlady to sell them some bread and cold mutton, even though it was late, and to let them have a room for the night. When she inquired what they were doing here in Blackfold, he said frankly he'd come to visit his sister, Christine West.

'Christine's brother, eh? I'm Nancy Feathers.'

He nodded, waiting, hoping she'd say something more.

She hesitated, opened her mouth as if to speak, then shut it again and walked to the door of their tiny bedroom. 'Well, I'll let you get some sleep.' Another hesitation and she added, 'I daresay your sister will be glad to see you. She's been looking a bit peaky lately.'

In the morning, he decided to stick to his original plan and see the parson first. Maybe he could win the man's support. Knowing the gentry didn't rise early, he fretted around till ten o'clock before going to the Parsonage, which he remembered from his previous visits. He knocked on the back door, one arm round his son's shoulders.

The maid who opened the door looked at them in an unfriendly manner.

'I'd like to speak to the parson, please,' Nathaniel said politely. 'It's Mr Beavis, isn't it?'

'No. He died. It's Mr Crawford now and he doesn't usually see people like you till the afternoon.'

'It's important.'

'Come back later, then.'

When she tried to close the door he put his foot in the way. 'Go and ask him to see me now. This is too urgent to wait.'

With a squeak of dismay she backed away. He didn't attempt to follow her inside, but pulled Gregory to stand in front of him so that the warmth from the house would touch the lad first and his back be protected from the biting wind by his father's body.

Heavy footsteps came towards the door and Nathaniel braced himself.

'Well, what's so urgent, my good man?'

This new parson seemed a starched up sort of fellow and Nathaniel's hopes plummeted even before he made his plea.

'I'm sorry to disturb you, sir, but I need your help and advice.'

'I don't give money to tramping folk.'

'I'm not short of money and I'm not on the tramp. I only came here for your advice. I'm Christine West's brother and, well, I'm a bit worried about my niece.

Since I don't get on with my sister's husband, I'd thought to inquire how things are at the farm before I go there. I don't want to cause any trouble, but I am worried.'

'Ah.'

A woman came up behind the parson. 'Let the poor man inside, Richard. It's a bitterly cold day.'

'Who knows if he's even telling the truth? Besides, as I told you earlier, this is not our business. West is perfectly within his rights to chastise his step-daughter, especially in the circumstances.' He began to close the door. 'I'm afraid you've wasted your journey. You'd be best advised to mind your own business and leave your sister to mind hers. That's the only advice I intend to offer you.'

Nathaniel stuck his foot out again. 'Beg your pardon, sir, but what circumstances are you talking about?'

Godfrey Crawford breathed deeply then gestured to him to enter a cheerless room near the back door, furnished only with a table and one wooden chair. When his wife would have followed them inside, the parson snapped, 'Leave me to deal with this, Julia, if you please!' and closed the door in her face. Sitting down, he gestured to his visitor to approach the table. 'The crux of the matter is that your niece is with child.'

'*Ginny?*'

'Did I not say so? Have the courtesy not to interrupt me again, because I don't intend to repeat myself. She is with child and her step-father, quite rightly, does not take the matter lightly.'

'He's beaten her, you mean?' Nathaniel said flatly.

'Of course. As I would myself.'

'I'm here to ask them if she can come and live with me. My wife's recently dead and I need help in the house. Maybe that'll solve all our problems.'

'I doubt Mr West will allow her to take such an easy way out. In fact, he has spoken to me about putting her in the House of Correction until the child is born, to teach her a much-needed lesson.'

Nathaniel was horrified at this information, delivered in such an off-hand way too. 'There's no need for that. I can look after her.'

'Did you not hear me? There is every need to teach her not to behave in such a wanton manner in the future. I fully agree with West about that.'

'Then you'll not support me if I offer to take her back with me?'

'Certainly not.'

'In that case, I'll bid you good day.' Nathaniel walked out without looking at the parson again, sickened that a man of God could approve of treating a young lass so harshly.

As he walked along the rear of the house on his way back to the street, a window opened and someone hissed at him. He looked round to see the parson's wife putting one finger to her lips. 'Speak quietly, Mr King. I don't happen to agree with my husband about this and I too am worried about your niece. Mr West is known as a brutal man, violent with his womenfolk. If you take my advice, you'll go out to the farm straight away and force that man to let Ginny go. I really do fear for her safety.'

A door behind her opened and her husband erupted

into the room, slamming the window shut and drawing the curtains.

Nathaniel hesitated for a minute, then walked on.

Inside the house, Godfrey roared, 'Never disobey me again, madam!'

As he raised his hand to hit her, Julia jumped backwards, seized a chair and used it to keep him at bay. 'I'm not a weak woman like Christine West,' she shouted. 'If you raise your hand to me again, be sure I'll fight back every time. I won't tolerate such ungentlemanly treatment.'

'I have every right to chastise you. I've been too lax with you and things are going to change from now on. You're not even fulfilling your wifely duties.'

She glared at him. 'I don't consider it my wifely duty to let you hit me. And, heaven help me, I'm not sure I can even continue as your wife if you won't change your attitude.'

'How dare you speak to me like that?'

'I dare do a lot more.' She didn't set the chair down but watched him warily.

'I'm warning you: I shall not tolerate any more of this disobedience.' He left the room and Julia listened to him stamping along to his study then set the chair down very precisely so that it was at right angles to the table. She sat upon it, hands folded tidily in her lap, trying not to give in to her despair. She took a few deep breaths in a vain attempt to control her emotions but couldn't help weeping, letting the tears trickle down her face as she sat upright on the chair.

After a while she raised one hand to brush the tears

away. Unlike poor Mrs West, she wasn't quite without resources, but it would take time to gather them together and make her plans.

When she went upstairs to wash her face, she removed the key from the lock of her bedchamber and took the spare one from the key cupboard to be sure *he* couldn't enter the room when she was asleep. She was glad Godfrey hadn't got her with child by now and intended to make sure he never did. She hadn't really wanted to marry him, but her parents had insisted it was a good match and her mother had been ill, desperate to see her safely settled, so in the end she'd given in to their persuasions. Now they were both dead, for her father hadn't long survived his beloved wife.

After their marriage Godfrey turned almost instantly into an arrogant tyrant. When she'd protested at the way he was behaving, he had informed her that the law was totally on his side and he had a right to treat her as he pleased since she was now in every sense his possession, with no legal rights of her own. Even the clothes on her back belonged to him.

From then on things had slowly grown worse because she was not and never could be the meek, obedient woman he clearly expected. But he'd never raised his hand to her until recently.

How dare he do that? He'd find out she had teeth and knew how to bite if he tried it again.

Well, she didn't need the money and comfortable way of life he could bring her, had only ever wanted affection and companionship. Since he wasn't capable of giving them to her, she would seek them elsewhere.

Three days later she left Blackfold, choosing her time

carefully when her husband was at a diocesan meeting. As the cab drew up, she was watching for it and ready.

'This is for me,' she told the maid.

The cab driver looked at the pile of luggage and pulled a face.

'There'll be a good tip if we can do this quickly. I'm in a hurry. A relative is dying.'

His face cleared. 'Ah.'

Not until she was sitting in the train and it was pulling out of the station did Julia's heart stop pounding. What she was doing was against the law. She'd had no right to take her jewellery and had besides broken into her husband's cash box, removing every penny it contained.

By the time he came after her she'd be on her way to America or Australia. He'd never think of her going there. She hadn't yet decided which country she preferred but perhaps Australia, because it was the furthest away from him.

She intended to become a spinster again and make a new life for herself. Selling the jewels would give her a decent nest egg.

She only wished she could be back at the Parsonage standing invisible in a corner when he found out what she'd done. A smile curved her lips. He'd just about explode with fury! And serve him right. Then she thought of poor Christine West and sighed. Other women were not as lucky as she was, had no money to escape with and children to tie them to brutish husbands.

Nick's father stopped him one day as they were walking the boundaries checking the dry-stone walls. 'You've been very quiet lately, son. I hope you're not still thinking about that girl?'

'Yes, I am. I've written to her and am waiting for a reply.'

His father's face darkened with anger. 'Didn't I tell you to have nothing more to do with her?'

'Yes. But this is my life, not yours, and I'm old enough now to make my own decisions.'

Anger rumbled in his father's throat, but the days were past when he could thump his son. Nick was now as tall as he was and did a man's work on the farm.

Later, as they were approaching the house, Sam Halstead stopped again. 'You'll say nothing about this to your mother!'

'I'm waiting for Ginny's reply before I decide anything.'

When Nick had gone out to the local pub with a young fellow he'd grown friendly with, Jane Halstead looked at her husband. 'What's wrong?'

'Nothing.'

'There is. You can't fool me. I know you too well.'

Sam breathed in deeply. 'He's written directly to *her* this time.'

Jane swallowed hard and put one hand to her throat. 'Oh, Sam, no!'

'Well, we'll know what to do if a reply comes. Burn it like we did the other.'

She bent her head for a moment, then raised it and said, 'I still feel guilty for doing that. It was his letter not ours.'

'Well, keep on doing it and feeling guilty, if you don't want that man's daughter marrying our Nick.'

*   *   *

The farm itself was quiet, with men working in the far field. A dog came out to investigate the intruder, growling in its throat, and Nathaniel spent a little time gentling it for he had always had a way with dogs. In the end it followed him along, tail wagging.

He walked round the house to the kitchen and all his intentions of being conciliatory vanished when his sister answered the door and he saw her bruised face.

Christine dissolved into tears and he took her into his arms.

'Get away from her, you!' a harsh voice said, and Christine staggered backwards as her husband yanked her away.

'Can a man not give his sister a hug?'

'You're not welcome here, as I told you last time.'

'This is just a short visit and I'll not be staying, but surely you can offer me and my lad a sup of tea and a bite of food? Or do you not offer hospitality to relatives now?'

Howard hesitated.

Christine watched him but didn't move until he nodded, his lips a tight, sour line and the frown lines very marked on his forehead. When he jerked his head at her, she hurried to get out some tea cups and a cake, setting the table rapidly then making a big pot of tea.

'What are you doing in this district?' Howard asked as he helped himself to a slice without offering the plate to his guest.

Nathaniel passed it to his son. 'I've come to ask you a favour.'

'I've no money to spare.'

'I don't need any. Now that my wife's dead, what I need is help in the house and I wondered if Ginny could come and live with me for a while. She should be old enough to run a house now.'

'No, she can't.'

'Oh? Is she needed here?'

Howard breathed deeply then said in a harsh voice, 'You'd better know how she's let us all down. She's with child and the only place for a whore like her is the House of Correction, so that's where I'm putting her.'

Christine sobbed aloud and dropped her cup so that tea splashed across the tablecloth.

Nathaniel grasped the edge of the table tightly to prevent himself from punching the man opposite, who was looking triumphant. 'Better to let her come to me, surely? Keep things quiet and in the family.'

'No I said and no I meant. She'll be punished as she deserves and the child taken from her after it's born. We're having no bastards in this family.'

'Howard, please!' Christine begged. 'Don't do this! Let Nathaniel take her, for pity's sake.'

He swung round to her, fist raised, and Nathaniel said quietly, 'Go and wait for me outside the gate, lad.'

Gregory looked from one to the other, fear in his face, then fled from the kitchen.

Nathaniel stood up, and only then did it become plain how very much bigger he was than Howard. 'Fetch your daughter to me, Christine, while I make sure this one doesn't try to stop you.'

She looked from one to the other, then hurried up the stairs.

'Come back this minute!' roared Howard.

She glanced back once, looking terrified, but continued up the stairs.

As Nathaniel moved round to bar the way to the back door, Howard said, 'The law is on my side in this.'

'Then we'll have to break it, won't we?'

'They'll come after you and lock you up in prison. In fact, I'll make sure they do.'

Nathaniel smiled grimly, a smile as terrifying as another man's scowl. 'If you try that, I'll make sure *you* have two broken legs before they put me away. I've always been a good fighter and I'll settle your hash for you, that I swear.'

Howard went white and took a step backwards.

'Two broken legs,' Nathaniel repeated, though he knew he'd do no such thing. But he could see this bully believed him. Such men always did believe others were as bad as themselves.

Christine came in with Ginny behind her, a bundle in her hands.

It sickened Nathaniel to see how afraid of Howard they both were. He took the bundle from his niece and said quietly, 'Stand up to him, Christine. If you don't, you'll never have a minute's peace again.'

'He's stronger than I am.'

'But he can't watch his back every minute of the day. If he's hitting you anyway, make sure you hurt him in return when he's not expecting it.' He looked beyond her to Ginny. 'Will you come and live with me, lass?'

She nodded.

'Wait for me outside the gate. Your Cousin Gregory's there.'

He moved across the room and then the sight of his

sister's bruised face shattered his self-control and he couldn't resist one swift punch to his brother-in-law's jaw that sent him sprawling on the floor. 'I meant what I said about your legs.' Howard made no attempt to get up or fight back. Typical of such a bully, Nathaniel thought. Hurts those weaker than himself, but doesn't try to stand up to anyone stronger.

He looked one last time at his poor sister. 'Remember what I said.' Then he left, feeling bitter that the law was on that bully's side when it came to ill-treating a wife. Not that decent men needed that sort of law. Nathaniel had never raised his hand to a woman in his life; nor, he'd guess, had most of the men he knew.

At the gate, he found Gregory trying to comfort Ginny who was sitting weeping on the milestone. 'Come on, lass. Dry your eyes and put your best foot forward. We've a fair way to go and we can't wait for the carrier today.' He doubted his brother-in-law would carry out his threat to bring down the law on them because that sort hated scandal, but he wasn't going to stay in the village and risk it, not with that snotty parson clearly on Howard's side.

He regretted hitting his brother-in-law now. It had been a stupid thing to do and would only make Howard angrier, which wouldn't help Christine at all. But, by hell, it'd been satisfying!

They walked through the village then on towards the next town. Nathaniel doubted they'd get there before nightfall, but he'd slept rough before and was sure his niece wouldn't complain. Already she was looking more cheerful, chatting quietly to Gregory and giving her uncle an occasional shy smile.

When they sat down for a rest, she said, 'I'm worried about Mum.'

'Aye, me too. But he's her husband and there's nowt much we can do about that. Now, let's see if we can find a farm that'll sell us summat to eat. And before long we'll have to find somewhere to spend the night.' He could have gone on walking, but Ginny was looking exhausted now, though she was trying to hide it. He wasn't doing anything to put her baby at risk.

As soon as his brother-in-law had left, Howard pulled himself to his feet and left the kitchen, not saying a word to his wife who had been waiting in terror for another beating.

He came back a few minutes later looking triumphant but still said nothing, only asked for some food, ate it and went outside again.

She fed the boys and got them to bed, worrying as it grew dark, wondering what Howard was up to. He'd not tell her, but when he got that look on his face, someone usually suffered.

But surely Nathaniel and the children would be out of Howard's reach by now?

The three men walked briskly along the road, Howard in the lead. When they found no sign of their quarry, he turned to the one behind him and snarled, 'You said you could find them for me.'

'And so I can. Where dost think they can go at this hour? There's no village for another three mile an' he's not had time to get there. Ah!' He pointed to some flattened grass. 'They stopped for a rest there, see.'

Howard nodded. 'You take the lead, then.'

The other man walked along quietly behind them, wishing he hadn't let himself in for this because Ginny was a nice lass. But it didn't do to refuse an employer like this one.

'Ah!' The first man stopped again. 'See! They turned off towards that farm. They'd be looking for summat to eat, I dare say.'

'Did they come out again?'

'Not that I can see.'

'We'll wait for them a bit further along the road then, catch them by surprise.'

Nathaniel led the way back down the farm lane, feeling better for having a full stomach. He'd had to coax Ginny into eating, but had made sure she got some good food into her. He never had to coax Gregory, who was growing rapidly and seemed always ready to eat these days.

As they walked along he wished he'd asked to sleep in the hayloft at the farm, but Ginny had looked a bit brighter and he was eager to get home. If they could make their way to the next station before dawn, they could catch the early milk train.

As they turned a bend, three men suddenly stepped out from the hedge, one of them his brother-in-law. Nathaniel barely had time to yell, 'Remember what I told you, Gregory!' before he was defending himself from a vicious attack where boots were flying as well as fists. And Howard, damn his hide, stood and grinned, only taking the opportunity for an occasional kick or thump when he wasn't risking himself.

Gregory pulled Ginny's hand and whispered, 'Quick! I know what to do.'

'But my uncle—'

'Come on!'

Even as they moved away, Howard came and grabbed her arm. 'You're going nowhere, young lady, except to the House of Correction.'

She whimpered and flinched away from him so Gregory darted out of his reach and looked round for a weapon. He found a stone near the hedge and hesitated, knowing he shouldn't attack an adult. But then Mr West clouted Ginny round the ears and made her cry out in pain, so the lad forgot his scruples and threw it at the man's head from behind.

'Ow!' Howard let go of Ginny's arm, to clutch his head and curse in pain.

'Run!' Gregory yelled, then lowered his voice to add quickly, 'You go into the woods and I'll go for help.'

And this time she heeded him, pounding off into the gathering darkness beneath the trees.

Howard hesitated, then turned back to share in the pleasure of beating his damned brother-in-law senseless. He'd find the girl later. She couldn't go far in her condition. Neither would King, if they took his wallet.

CHAPTER TWELVE

January 1864

Another two days passed and Hannah travelled cautiously, trying to stay invisible rather than make good speed. One rainy day she had the luck to find a kindly woman who let her sleep in an outhouse and gave her a hunk of bread and dripping. It seemed like an omen that her luck had turned.

But the next day her spirits sank again as it rained continuously, a miserable soaking rain that seemed to hang heavily on every fold of her clothing. Her cloak, skirt and petticoat hems were soon thickly splashed by mud, even though she'd kilted them up as much as was decent. In the afternoon she stopped trying to travel on and sought shelter at the nearest farm. A hard-faced woman told her to be off, but when Hannah offered her threepence for a night's shelter in the hay loft, she changed her mind, and grew almost affable when Hannah offered a further threepence for some food.

She changed into her spare skirt, which was damp but not dripping wet like the one she'd been wearing, and hung her wet clothes on the nearest beams to dry. The woman brought her out some fried ham clapped between slices of bread and a big tin mug of tea. The ham was juicy and Hannah licked every bit of grease off her fingers, sighing with pleasure. Never had food tasted so good.

In the morning it was fine again and she set off feeling refreshed, having brushed as much mud as she could off the hem of her travelling skirt and put it on again damp. As if to mock her for daring to feel more hopeful, she came upon a small, crudely printed poster nailed to a tree and offering a reward for information leading to the capture of 'one Hannah Firth, escaped mad-woman'. It said people should apply to Lemuel Firth of Hetton-le-Hill, 'son of the poor deluded woman', with information. Had he given in to Patty's nagging again? Or had she done this without reference to him?

Hannah would have to be even more cautious from now on, though it wasn't a good likeness.

The following evening was cold but didn't feel like rain so she decided to sleep in the woods to save money, choosing a copse a little distance away from the road for safety and stopping before it grew fully dark. She gathered up small branches and twigs brought down by the winter's storms to lie on because she'd learned that such things made a warmer bed beneath her cloak than the damp earth, however lumpy they felt.

She found it hard to settle and after a while sat up again with her arms clasped round her knees, watching the darkness gather. She heard someone passing by in the lane and thought it was late for anyone to be out. Afterwards she heard a small animal creeping along nearby, making rustling noises among the remains of the dead leaves. In the distance an owl hooted twice, an eerie sound when you were all alone in the darkness of the countryside.

Then suddenly the near silence was broken by hoarse shouts and cries, a woman's scream and a man's yell of pain. Hannah jerked to her feet, not certain whether to flee or go and see what was happening. It sounded like another robbery. *Stay out of it!* she told herself. She'd been lucky to escape injury when she saved Frances, but she doubted she'd be that lucky again. You had to be sensible, after all, and look after yourself first. She simply couldn't afford to get involved in any sort of trouble that would bring her to the attention of the authorities.

Only she found it impossible to sit there and listen to more cries and shouts so in the end she crept towards the lane she had left earlier, telling herself it could do no harm to see what the trouble was. The yelling was punctuated by what sounded like fists thumping into bodies and grunts of pain.

Suddenly a figure came running through the trees towards her, running so fast she didn't even see Hannah and bumped right into her, bowling her over. As they both scrambled quickly to their feet, the moonlight showed Hannah that this wasn't a robber trying to attack her but a young lass fleeing from something.

The girl hesitated, looking back over her shoulder as if she didn't know what to do next.

'Sorry,' she gasped.

'What's happening?' Hannah asked in a low voice.

'Three men are attacking my uncle. My cousin's gone for help and I'm supposed to hide. Oh, please, can't you help him? It's my step-father who's doing this. He'll kill Uncle Nathaniel if we don't stop him.'

'Three men attacking one, you said?'

'Yes.'

'Then we can't do much on our own. Why is your step-father doing this?'

'Because my uncle came and rescued me from him.'

As she raised her tear-stained face, Hannah saw how puffy and bruised it was and sucked in her breath in dismay. 'Who did that to you?'

'My step-father.'

'Why?'

'Because he likes hitting people and – and because I'm carrying Nick's child. But Nick loves me, I know he does, and if I can only let him know about the baby, he'll come back and marry me. He promised he would.'

Hannah didn't try to contradict her. This lass wouldn't be the first to be taken in by loving words and promises and she wouldn't be the last either. 'I'll go and see what's happening.'

'I daren't come with you. If *he* catches me, he'll put me in the House of Correction. He said he would.'

'He sounds a brute. You wait here and look after my bundle.' Hannah slipped away, telling herself she was a fool to get involved, but when had she ever been able to stand aside and let injustice happen?

As she stopped near the road, she saw a man lying there curled up, another kicking him while two others stood to one side, edging uneasily from one foot to the other.

'Are you murderers as well as thieves?' The scornful words rang out before she could stop them.

The men all swung round in her direction and at least the cowardly one stopped kicking his victim.

'It's only a woman,' the leader said scornfully. He

moved towards Hannah, fist raised. 'Get away while you can and mind your own business!'

'I might say the same to you. Help's on its way. We don't take kindly to robbers in this part of Lancashire.'

One of the two silent men shifted uneasily and cleared his throat.

The leader laughed. 'We're not robbers and we were finished anyway.' He moved forward and grasped Hannah's arm suddenly. 'Did you see a girl back there?'

When she didn't answer, he shook her hard so she slapped his face and kicked his shin for good measure, jerking away from him quickly before he could grab her again and stooping to pick up a small rock from the side of the road to protect herself.

While he was hesitating, voices and footsteps could be heard in the distance and he swung round to the others. 'We'd better go.' He turned to Hannah. 'Tell him there's more where that came from if he doesn't send the girl back where she belongs. I know where he lives and I'm going to set the authorities on him.'

One of his companions sighed audibly with relief as they walked off down the lane.

Hannah moved across to kneel by the still figure. He was still alive, but dear Lord, they'd hurt him. Even if blood looked black in the moonlight, she could see that he'd shed plenty of it.

When two men arrived, puffing and panting, she stood up. 'Three men have beaten this one senseless. Can you help us, please?'

'Eh, what's the world coming to if the roads aren't safe?' the older man exclaimed. 'We'd better carry him back to the farm and let my missus tend him. She's good with sick folk.' He looked round. 'The lad said there was a girl, too? Don't tell me they've taken her away with them?'

'No, she's hiding in the woods. I'll go and fetch her.'

She found the girl on her way to join them, lugging Hannah's bundle, and stopped her to ask urgently, 'Can you pretend I'm with you?'

Ginny stopped to stare at her. 'Are you in trouble?'

'Yes. But like you, I don't deserve it.'

'All right.'

They reached the road to see that the boy had arrived and was crouching by his father.

'I think we'd better fetch the cart,' the farmer said. 'He's a well-built chap. Will you be all right with him, missus? I don't think they'll come back again.'

When they'd gone, the girl turned to the lad. 'This woman helped Uncle Nathaniel and now she needs our help. Can we pretend she's Uncle Nathaniel's wife?'

He stared at her then looked down at his feet, avoiding her eyes. 'My mother's dead and I don't want anyone pretending to be her.'

'But this one *helped* us, Gregory. I'm sure your father would agree to it.'

'It's only pretend,' Hannah urged.

After another silence and much screwing up of his face, he shrugged and said, 'All right. But you're *not* my mother.'

'I could pretend to be your step-mother, your father's second wife. Would that be better?'

His face cleared a little and he nodded.

He must have loved his mother very dearly, Hannah thought, and that made her wonder if Lemuel cared half as much for her. She knew Malachi did, but was never as sure of her elder son's feelings. 'You'd better tell me your names, then.' This time she didn't make the mistake of calling herself Hannah but used a pet name her lover had once had for her – Nancy. She didn't even try to invent a surname, since she would be calling herself King from now on. The youngsters didn't seem to notice the lack.

When they took Nathaniel back, the farmer and his son carried him into the stables, directing Hannah to spread some clean hay in an empty stall and cover it with a horse blanket.

'We haven't a spare bed in the house,' the farmer said cheerfully, 'what with our son's wife near her time and all the grandchildren.'

The farmer's wife came out to join them, tutting and shaking her head. But in spite of her unceasing comments, she proved very capable and with Hannah's help soon got the unconscious man's clothes off and began to bathe his battered body.

He groaned, though he didn't open his eyes. 'There, there. Soon be over,' she told him, and smiled at Hannah. 'I like to think they can hear you even when they're unconscious. I don't believe anything is broken, dear, though they may have cracked his ribs. Eh, but he'll be sore all over tomorrow.' She got to her feet and stepped back to stare down at him. 'I think that's all we can do for now.' Then she looked at Hannah with a frown. 'You weren't with them earlier.'

'No. I was to meet them but I got lost. He's my husband.'

'Oh?' The woman still sounded suspicious.

Ginny came to the opening of the stall. 'How is he, Aunt Nancy?'

'Badly hurt, but nothing seems to be broken, thank goodness.'

Gregory joined them, his face twisted with anxiety.

'He'll be all right, love,' Hannah said automatically. 'He's a strong man.'

He looked at her, his gaze unblinking, as if uncertain whether to believe her.

'Your mother knows what she's talking about,' the farmer's wife said, picking up the bowl of reddened water.

'She's not my mother,' Gregory said without thinking, then saw her dart a suspicious glance at him and added hastily, 'She's my step-mother. *My* mother died.'

'Ah, I see. That explains why you don't look like her at all. You're going to be a sturdy fellow like your father and she's the thin, wiry sort. I always envy them.' The farmer's wife chuckled and looked down at her own plump body then walked out, calling as she opened the barn door, 'Don't forget to put out the lamp before you go to sleep. I've hung it on a nail, but you can't be too careful with hay. It catches light so easily.'

'We'll be very careful indeed, I promise you,' Hannah called back. 'We're grateful for your help.'

Only when the door of the barn had clacked shut behind their hostess and rattled into stillness did Hannah let out her breath in a long sigh of relief.

Howard arrived home in the early hours of the morning, roaring for his wife to come and get him some food. 'Beating up brothers-in-law is hungry work.'

She came down and stopped at the foot of the stairs. 'What did you say?'

He grinned at her. 'I said: beating up brothers-in-law is hungry work.'

Her voice was flat. 'So you've hurt Nathaniel as well now.'

'I have, and I'll do the same to anyone who crosses me. I didn't get that impudent daughter of yours back, but I'll do that, too, believe me. Now, brew me a pot of tea and find something to eat. I'm ravenous.'

She got the fire burning more brightly but they had to wait for the kettle to boil and Howard enlivened the time by describing exactly how he'd trapped Nathaniel and taken his money, leaving him unconscious in a country lane. Christine didn't say anything but got on with her work, anger seething behind her expressionless face.

When she passed him on the way to get something out of the pantry, he kicked her in the backside, laughing as she stumbled and fell. Even he had never done such a thing before, but tonight he seemed drunk on violence. As she crouched there on hands and knees, anger and humiliation overflowed and when she got to her feet again, she picked up the kettle and slung it at him, showering him with boiling water.

As he screamed in pain, Christine picked up the poker and held it out in front of her, screaming right back at him, *'That's it*! I've reached my limit! You may beat me and hurt me, but I'll always find a way to hurt you back from now on. This was only the beginning. You'll never feel safe with me again, the same way I don't feel safe with you.'

He got to his feet and she waited for him to come and thump her but instead he staggered into the scullery and began to pump cold water into the slopstone, splashing it over his face again and again, groaning and cursing.

For a moment she felt guilty, knowing how badly he must be hurting, and nearly went to help him then shook her head. No, he deserved it, deserved far worse. And she'd meant exactly what she said.

When he came to the door of the scullery a few minutes later, an ugly look on his face, she was sitting by the table sipping a cup of tea. She gave him a long, level look and to her surprise he lowered the fist he'd been holding up.

'You've run mad.'

'If I have, you've driven me to it.' She found herself smiling. 'But it feels good.'

He looked at her, fists bunching up again, then shook his head. 'I'm going to bed. Don't come near me till you've regained your senses.'

As if she would go near him and let him hurt her! As if going to bed with him had ever been a pleasure! She waited for half an hour, wondering how he'd get back at her but determined not to give in to him meekly again. Nathaniel was right. She shouldn't just accept the beatings. She should fight back, then every time he hurt her she could remember hurting him, too, and plan for the next time.

She wasn't sure how she would manage to keep that up, because he was a man who paid back a grudge if he had to wait years, but at least she could try.

Going into Ginny's bedroom, she locked the door and lay down on the bed with a sigh. She wished she knew where her daughter was, wished she could find out if her brother was all right.

She was so tired she slept soundly and for the first time in years didn't have Howard's breakfast waiting for him, didn't even stir till he worked out where she was and came to hammer on her door and roar at her to bloody well get up and set about her duties.

Even then she took her time and when she went down to the kitchen he slapped the side of her head as she passed him. Without even hesitating she threw the contents of the milk jug into his red, scalded face and grabbed the poker again to defend herself. She might have to buy another poker to keep in her new bedroom, she decided. A poker was a very handy weapon for a woman.

'You *have* run mad,' he muttered, and used one of her kitchen cloths to wipe the milk off his face, keeping a wary eye on her as he did so. While she stood waiting, he snatched up a piece of bread, slathered it with butter and jam then stormed out, slamming the door behind him with a bang that echoed round the kitchen.

Only when it had grown quiet again did Edwin and Andrew come down and she held out her arms to them, gathering them to her and taking comfort from their warm little bodies. They were timid lads, and no wonder. What sort of family life did they lead? She'd let them down, hadn't managed to protect them or give them courage. If she needed a reason to continue fighting her husband, now that Ginny had escaped, it was her sons. He hadn't started beating them yet, but then he hadn't done more than slap Ginny when she was small, either.

*   *   *

Nathaniel groaned as pain shot through him. He tried to open his eyes and sit up but his body wouldn't obey him, so he waited a minute then managed to open his eyes.

'Don't try to move,' a woman said from close to his head.

He rolled his head sideways and saw the owner of the voice sitting beside him, leaning against the wall by the flickering light of a single candle-lamp. He didn't recognise her and as he stared round, didn't recognise where he was, either. It felt as if he needed about a year's sleep, but he was also desperately thirsty. 'Is there anything to drink?'

'Yes. Wait a minute.'

He heard the blessed sound of trickling water and then she was back, lifting his head and supporting him while she let him sip, refusing to allow him to gulp the water down. When she took the tin mug away, saying too much might make him sick, he lay back and stared at her. 'Who are you? What happened?'

She hesitated then said, 'I helped rescue you when you were attacked.'

'Ah!' He looked down at himself, raising one hand to study the puffy knuckles and grazes. It was coming back to him now. West and some friends had jumped out at him. 'Is my son all right?'

'Yes, and your niece. They had enough sense to run away and fetch help.'

'West?'

'Went away with his two friends once he heard help coming.'

He sighed and closed his eyes again, hating the humiliation of having been beaten up like that. 'Nothing I could do with three to one. Once they got me down, I was lost.' Then he blinked and turned his head to stare at her again. 'That still doesn't explain why you're looking after me – or where we are.'

She chuckled. 'For a man who's only just regained consciousness, you ask a lot of questions.'

He tried to smile, but his lips were swollen and felt as if they'd crack. 'Do you know any of the answers?'

'Yes. I'm looking after you because I've had some experience with injuries. Ginny and Gregory were so tired they almost fell asleep standing up.'

'As long as they're all right.'

'They're in the next stall – we're in the stables at the farm you visited earlier, by the way. Gregory fetched the farmer and his son to help you and they carried you in here.'

He nodded and it was a while before he spoke again. 'I'm grateful for your help.'

'I thought you'd fallen asleep.'

'Nearly.'

She hesitated then said, 'There's something else you ought to know. We're pretending I'm your wife. I'm having my own troubles, none of them my fault and I've done nothing wrong, I promise you. It'll help me not to travel on my own.'

The desire to sleep left him suddenly. 'You're acting as my *wife*!'

'Yes. Do you want to know all the details now or can they wait until morning? You really should—'

'Now, if you please.'

She explained her situation in a low voice, then waited. After a silence which went on so long she was beginning to worry, he said, 'Hmm,' and studied her face openly.

A few moments later, he tried to smile but failed so just muttered, 'Your daughter-in-law sounds as bad as my brother-in-law. All right. We'll pretend you're my wife. It'll hurt no one. I'm tired now and you should be getting some sleep. Blow out that candle and let's make the most of this nice soft hay.'

Even before she had stood up to reach the candle lamp he was breathing deeply, but he'd talked sense, which showed he was starting to recover, and she thought things would be all right in the morning. She'd have been in trouble if he'd rejected her.

When the doorbell rang, Oliver went to peep out of the window. People so rarely came here, he couldn't help being curious. What he saw made him rush across to the mirror to check that he didn't have any ink on his face and smooth down his hair.

Nanny came bustling in, full of self-importance. 'It's that Lady Ann you told me about, but she won't come in, says it'll look better if she meets you in the garden. She's got a woman with her, dry old stick of a thing.' She tugged his arm impatiently. 'Come on! You can't keep a ladyship waiting!'

He followed her out and saw his visitors standing on the gravel, studying what ought to have been a fountain but was a mess of weeds and mud instead. 'How nice to see you again!' He held out his hand and Lady Ann took it, giving him one of her lovely smiles before turning to introduce her companion. He wished he could have held her hand for longer.

'Miss Lewison, my former governess and now, for her sins, my companion.'

He shook the governess's hand and was at once aware of being scrutinised by a pair of very sharp grey eyes. 'Pleased to meet you.'

'We were passing by and thought we'd take up your invitation to look at your garden,' Lady Ann went on.

'I'd be delighted to show you round and listen to your advice. I've been meaning to hire a gardener, but it's no use doing that until I know what I want doing, is it?'

They paced out the garden, all of it in a state of extreme neglect, then Lady Ann retraced her steps, frowning as if in thought. Oliver didn't interrupt, leaving her to think and pacing slowly behind her in case she had any questions.

When she stopped walking and turned round, she smiled. 'Very rude of me to ignore my host like that.'

'Could I offer you a cup of tea now?' he asked.

'No. Better if we don't come inside. I'm not supposed to visit any neighbours.' She looked round and then back at him. 'Do you really mean you'll let me design your garden for you?'

'Yes. I haven't the faintest idea how to start.'

She gave a blissful sigh. 'I can't think of anything I'd enjoy more. The gardens at the Hall are all well established and the Head Gardener is very jealous of his territory. I've never had the chance to create something from scratch before.' She cast a proprietorial glance around. 'The first thing to do is come back with sketching materials and make a plan of the garden.'

'I could do that for you. In fact, I've got it half done already. It seemed a sensible way to start.'

'Oh, good. When you've finished, please make me a copy. In black ink, if you please, then I can work on it with a pencil.' Another look round, then, 'In the meantime, you could perhaps hire a couple of men to dig over the ground. The village labourers are always short of work in the winter and will be glad of some extra money.'

'I'll do that, then.'

'See Farmer Price at Copton Farm. His wife has been giving me some cuttings and she says he always worries about his casual labourers in winter. I should think he'll know who is available. Oh, and they're not to remove the bushes or trees, just dig over the soil. And if they find any bulbs, they're to brush the dirt off and put them in the shed.'

He walked them to the end of the lane, sorry to see them go, sorrier still that they felt propriety prevented them from entering his house.

She was a lady, fancy title and all, while he was a mere nobody, someone who didn't even have much money. And yet he really did like her, especially her breathy little gurgle of a laugh. How had such a delightful young woman escaped being married? She might not be pretty in a conventional sense, but he found her very attractive. And why was she living alone at the Priory? Usually the nobility kept their daughters with them until they were married off. Even he knew that.

CHAPTER THIRTEEN

January 1864

In the morning Hannah woke first. It was quite early but the farmer was already at work just outside. He gave her a cheerful greeting and added, 'I'll tell my wife you'll be needing breakfast soon.'

'We can't impose on you—' she began, but stopped when he laughed.

'There's so many of us here we'll not notice another four. And if you can't help someone in trouble, you're a poor sort of creature. There's no one ever been turned hungry from our door, nor ever shall be while I can break a crust in half.'

When she got back to the stable she found the youngsters awake but Nathaniel still sleeping. She didn't dare think of him as Mr King, in case she forgot she was supposed to be his wife and called him that openly, and besides, she liked the name Nathaniel. It had such a solid, reliable sound to it.

'Go and knock on the kitchen door,' she told Gregory and Ginny, keeping her voice low. 'The farmer said they'd give us some food.'

When they'd gone she turned round to find Nathaniel awake and studying her, his dark eyes shrewd in his battered face. He might be a good-looking man normally, but he looked dreadful now. Well, no use offering him pity or drawing attention to the state of his face. 'How are you feeling this morning?'

He moved incautiously and winced. 'In pain. But I want to see how well I can walk.'

'Should you?'

'Aye. We need to leave today. I've work waiting for me at home and I don't want West catching up with us.'

With her help he stood up, sucking in his breath sharply once or twice. When he was holding the side of the stall, he asked, 'Have you seen my jacket?'

'I hung it on a beam to dry. I'll fetch it.'

She did so and he felt in the pockets one after the other, his frown deepening into a black scowl.

'Is something wrong?' Though she'd guessed already.

'They've taken my money. I've nowt left for our fares.'

'Do you have far to go?'

'Far enough that we needed to travel by train.' He growled something under his breath and leaned his head against his arm for a moment, eyes closed.

She didn't say anything, waiting for him to come to terms with his situation.

When he opened his eyes again, he said abruptly, 'We shall just have to walk home then. It'll take two or three days, perhaps four if Ginny can't keep up, but that'll not kill us.' He looked her up and down, as if assessing her strength too. 'What about you? Where are you going?'

'Anywhere I can find work that's as far away as possible from Hetton.'

'You can travel with us if you like. You seem a strong

woman and it'll be good for Ginny to have your help if she needs it.'

'You too might need some help at first.'

He pressed his lips together in a tight line and gave her an annoyed look. 'I can manage. I'm bruised but there's nowt broken.'

'Well, I'll be glad of the company, I must admit. They're looking for a woman on her own, not a married woman with a family. You – don't mind us continuing to pretend to be wed, do you?'

He gave her a smile which lit up even a face so battered. 'Nay, of course I don't. You helped us all last night. If we can help you in return, I shall be glad to do it.'

'Thank you.' She spoke softly, her face flushing a little – she didn't understand why – and for a moment they stared at one another, each conscious of a feeling of warmth flowing between them as if they were old friends.

Then the farmer came in to tend to his horses and the spell was broken. If it *was* some sort of spell. If she wasn't just imagining things.

After that there was no further opportunity to talk privately, which Hannah admitted to herself she was sorry for. She wanted to get to know Nathaniel King better, not just as a father and uncle but as a man.

Which thought sent more blood rushing to her face as she remembered her threepenny dream in the asylum. She was being very foolish today, she decided with a shake of her head, and at her age she ought to know better.

An hour later they left, set on their way by the

farmer's son in his cart, for when the family had discovered they'd been robbed of their fares, they insisted on helping, putting together a bundle of food as well as giving them a start along the road. Hannah found room for the food in her half-empty pillowcase. She noticed Nathaniel eyeing it but he didn't offer to carry it for her. She'd guess he'd find it hard enough to carry himself today, while his son was holding their bundle and Ginny carrying her own.

When they got to the far side of the next village, the farmer's son reined in his horse and shook Nathaniel's hand. 'I wish you luck, Mr King. You and your family.'

Hannah saw how it hurt Nathaniel to get down from the cart, but he didn't moan or make any sound of distress.

'Best foot forward, eh?' he said after they'd waved goodbye.

'Best foot forward,' the two youngsters echoed cheerfully.

They didn't make good time, though, and no one offered them a lift, though several empty carts passed them.

'I think my face is putting them off,' Nathaniel joked, then winced as he stumbled, putting one arm round his ribs as if they hurt.

'Let's rest for a minute or two,' Hannah said. 'It never hurts to spell yourself when you have a long way to go.'

She noticed how hard he found it to get up again, but said nothing. What was there to say? He was doing what he had to, they all were.

She thought nothing of it when a horseman trotted

past them and then reined in. He turned and stared at them, shouting, 'That's her! It's the escaped madwoman!'

Hannah was dismayed to recognise one of the grooms from Heverbrook Hall staring at her with a gloating expression, no doubt with the reward in mind.

When he dismounted and came running towards them, arms outstretched as if to catch hold of her, Nathaniel moved between them and put his arm round her, tucking her protectively against his body.

'Let go of her, fellow!' the groom called, tugging at his arm. 'She's a madwoman and there's a reward for capturing her.'

'Nay, you're far and out there, lad. This is my wife Nancy and we've been wed several years now. A madwoman, indeed!'

Ginny stepped forward. 'Think I don't recognise my own auntie?'

The groom laughed. 'I don't know how she's persuaded you to say that, but if you won't give her up, I'm going to fetch the nearest magistrate.'

'You do that,' Nathaniel said easily. 'He won't take your word against three of us.' He gave Hannah a quick kiss on the cheek. 'Come on, love. Pay no attention to this fool. We've a long way to go yet.' Then he set off walking, his arm still round her shoulders, completely ignoring the man who stood by his horse watching them with a scowl on his face.

'Do you think he'll go for the magistrate?' Hannah asked when they were out of his hearing. She was unable to stop her voice quavering at the mere thought of being shut up in the asylum again.

'I don't know.' Nathaniel's expression softened. 'It must have been bad in that place.'

She nodded, unable to put her dread into words.

'We won't let them take you back, I promise.'

She looked at him and again something blossomed between them. Oh, she was being stupid. Dreaming again. But what a wonderful dream!

The groom watched them till they were out of sight, a frown on his face. He could have sworn she was Hannah Firth. No, he *knew* she was. Two women couldn't look that much alike. It had to be her. Only where had the others come from and why were they telling lies about who she was?

He stopped off at the next alehouse to fortify himself for the ordeal, then asked to be directed to the nearest magistrate.

They kept him waiting for over an hour, then showed him in to an old gentleman who was sitting behind a desk in a comfortable room with a roaring fire in the grate.

'Well, fellow? What's so urgent?'

The groom pulled out the poster. 'It's this. I've seen her.'

The magistrate glanced at it and gave a sniff of annoyance. 'You're the third this morning. The other two were following poor women on the tramp. You could see at a glance they weren't anything like this. I'm damned if I'm going out on another wild goose chase.'

The groom gathered his courage together. 'But, sir, she used to work at the Hall so I *know* her personally. It's my master there who's sent me out looking for her.'

The magistrate heaved a sigh. 'Well, tell me your tale.'

When it was finished, he pursed his lips and said peevishly, 'I suppose we'd better go and search for them, then, though it's a damned cold day. But if you've been lying to me, I shall be most displeased and be sure your master will hear about it. And why didn't you come to see me more quickly? Think I can't smell the ale on your breath? They'll have had enough time to hide by now.'

The groom breathed deeply, thinking of the hour he'd sat kicking his heels, waiting to see this man, but didn't dare contradict him.

At the next crossroads Nathaniel stopped and frowned up at the signpost. 'If I had any money, I'd hire us a ride in a carrier's cart and put as many miles between us and that fellow as I could before nightfall.'

'I have a little money,' Hannah volunteered. 'How much would we need?'

'Let's find out.' He limped on into the next village and asked if there was a carrier who might set them a few miles along their way. Within minutes a man with a cart had been found who offered to take them as long as they paid him in advance, but said he needed to be home before nightfall.

Nathaniel entered into a bargaining session which gave them a ride of about ten miles. After he'd finished he looked questioningly at Hannah and she nodded. She had that much money.

She went behind a hedge to retrieve some of her coins, hidden about her body, paid the owner of the cart and with sighs of relief they all climbed on board. The youngsters took places near the front while she and Nathaniel sat together at the rear.

'I'm sorry to take your money, lass,' he whispered. 'But this'll give us a good start if anyone comes after us and I'll pay you back when we get home.'

'It's worth it. What use is money if I don't have my freedom?'

They rumbled along for nearly three hours, then the man told his horse to stop and turned to look at them. 'This is as far as I can take you.'

Nathaniel got down, unable to suppress a groan, and turned automatically to help Hannah off, but she had already managed and was lifting down her bundle.

When the cart had driven away, Gregory said tentatively, 'I'm hungry, Dad.'

'We'd better wait to eat until we stop for the night, son. We have to make the food last.'

'Oh.'

'You'll not die of going hungry for a day or two,' Nathaniel said with a grin at Hannah.

She smiled back, remembering times when her boys had eaten every meal as if no one had fed them for a week.

The magistrate jogged along on an elderly horse that was nearly as fat as he was, followed by his court officer and the groom.

When they got to where the groom had last seen Hannah, the magistrate looked round as if he expected to see her standing waiting for them.

He might be gentry, the groom thought, but he wasn't very clever.

'If we ask in the next village, sir,' the officer ventured, 'we may find someone who's seen her.'

'Yes. Yes, ride on, then.'

In the village their arrival caused angry looks and people found reasons to slip inside houses or nip round corners.

'Hey, you!' the magistrate yelled.

A man turned reluctantly and stood still.

'Well, come here, fellow. Now, have you seen a madwoman wandering about?'

The man goggled. 'No, sir.'

'This is her,' the groom volunteered, passing him the crumpled poster.

He studied it. 'Haven't caught sight of any madwoman.'

'She was with a family: a man, a young woman and a lad. Maybe you saw them?'

Another man who'd been hovering came over to join them. 'We haven't seen anyone like that, have we, Bill?'

'No. No families like that.'

'But you must have!' the groom insisted. 'There was no other way they could have gone but through this village.'

'Think us have nothing better to do than stand around watching folk pass through?' the second man asked scornfully.

'No,' the magistrate snapped. 'I think you're the fellows I sent down for poaching last year.'

'Well, we've learned our lesson, sir,' the man said at once. But then the two of them clamped their mouths shut and answered only in monosyllables, still insisting they'd not seen anyone.

When the group had ridden off, one winked at the other. 'Wouldn't hand my worst enemy over to that sod. He's too fond of sentencing poor folk to prison.'

'I hate all rich folk. And that woman didn't look mad to me, though someone had given the fellow a right old pasting.'

They walked away, discussing where they'd set their traps that night.

When they got back to his residence, the magistrate glared at the groom. 'It's clear you were mistaken. Get back to your master and don't waste my time again.'

'Yes, sir.' The groom knew when he was beaten. But he also knew he'd seen Hannah Firth and so he'd tell his master, who was a stubborn fellow and didn't like to be bested on anything.

As the early winter dusk fell, the travellers found a ruined barn on the edge of a field and inside it signs that they weren't the first people to shelter there. There was even a stream nearby which looked clean enough to drink from.

Hannah sent the youngsters to have a drink first and while they were gone took out some of the food, keeping enough back for the following morning. 'Eat it slowly,' she warned Gregory, who came back suspiciously quickly. 'It'll seem more filling then.'

Nathaniel sat silently, exhaustion in every line of his body, but the food seemed to revive him a little. Hannah watched him bend to cup his hands and drink from the stream afterwards, her heart aching to see how the movement hurt him.

Ginny fell asleep as soon as she had eaten, looking so

white and drained that Hannah was worried. Gregory protested that he wasn't at all tired, but it wasn't long before he too fell asleep, pressed against his cousin for warmth.

Which left Hannah and Nathaniel sitting in the darkness next to one another, their backs against the wall. She shivered involuntarily.

'We'll keep warmer if we sit close,' he said.

'I'd – rather not.'

'Nay, I'm not going to attack you, lass. I'm in no fit state for that sort of thing anyway.' He winced as he moved too suddenly.

So she gave in to temptation and moved to lean against his warm body.

He sighed. 'It's strange how life treats you, isn't it?'

'Yes.'

'Did I tell you how my wife died?'

'No.'

So he told her the tale of Walter Dewhurst's spree, deliberately distracting her from her own worries.

She found herself relaxing against him and before she knew it she was sliding towards sleep.

He eased his arm from round her shoulders once he was sure she was sleeping and let her head fall against his chest as he tried to get more comfortable. But he hurt in so many places, it was impossible, so he lay pondering their situation. Who'd ever have expected a simple journey to visit his sister to turn out like this? He looked down at Hannah's soft dark hair straggling across his chest and smiled. He'd bet when she wasn't travelling rough she was a fine figure of a woman. He liked her courage and her direct gaze.

His ribs were hurting again so he moved into another position and she murmured a sleepy protest. Against all his expectations he fell asleep a short time later, waking only as some drops of rain blew in through one of the gaps in the roof.

Hannah moved to sit up, yawning and easing her shoulders. 'I thought the weather was going to turn. This'll make travelling even more difficult.'

'We must just press on as best we can. I promise I'll pay you back the money you spent on the ride once we get home.'

'No need. We only had to spend that because of me.'

He chuckled. 'Are we going to argue about it? If so, you won't win. I'm a terrible stubborn fellow.'

She couldn't help smiling at him, though it was probably too dark for him to see that. 'I won't argue now, at any rate, Nathaniel. Shall we wake them and set off? It's nearly morning.'

'No, let them sleep as long as they can. We'll not make good time today.' He liked the way she said his name. Indeed, he liked everything about her. Eh, what had got into him? This was no time to go fancying a woman!

They made only five or six miles that day, by Nathaniel's reckoning, trudging along the muddy lanes with an icy wind cutting through their clothing. The detours added to their journey, but it seemed sensible to avoid the main roads.

Ginny went more and more slowly and in the afternoon stumbled several times, once measuring her length in the slippery mud. As Gregory helped her up she burst into tears. 'I can't walk any further. I'm sorry, Uncle Nathaniel, but I just can't!'

The way she was looking at him said she was half-expecting him to thump her, which upset him. He went and put his arm round her instead, giving her a hug. 'It's hard going for all of us. We'll have a bit of a rest, eh?'

Hannah looked at the girl's white, exhausted face. 'I think it's time we were looking for somewhere to sleep. I've a few pence left to pay a farmer to let us use one of his barns.' She saw Nathaniel's frown. 'We'll *all* freeze to death if we stay outside in the wet on a night like this.'

At the first farm a sour-faced woman took one look at Nathaniel's battered face and told them to be off or she'd set the dogs on them.

At the second farm they were luckier. A cheerful young woman said she'd ask her mam, and came back a short time later to say they were welcome to use the hay barn and no need for payment, but if they wanted some food, they'd have to pay threepence each for it, but it'd be good hearty fare.

After she'd showed them where they were to sleep she said she'd bring out their food later.

'I'm getting quite used to hay barns now,' Hannah said once they were on their own. 'I miss real beds and clean linen, though.' And she hated not being able to wash her own body properly, though it'd be asking for trouble to try to wash in an icy stream at this time of year.

It wasn't only Ginny who was exhausted. Nathaniel eased himself down into a sitting position, his back against a wooden partition, trying not to show how much he was hurting. Hannah busied herself making things as comfortable as possible, getting Gregory to help her since the other two were slumped in utter exhaustion. He was a nice lad, she thought, bearing all these discomforts without complaint but watching everything with those big, solemn eyes of his.

'Dad looks so tired,' he whispered. 'Is he all right?'

'Yes. It'll take him a few days to recover but it's only bruising.'

He thought about this and nodded.

She'd have liked to give him a hug, but didn't dare. He was at that difficult age, between childhood and manhood, and wouldn't accept hugs from strangers, she was sure.

When the daughter of the house brought them a big pot of hearty soup and hunks of crusty bread and even some pieces of cheese, the smell preceded her and they all sat up straighter in anticipation.

Hannah stood up to help. 'That looks wonderful! I'll bring the empty dishes back to the house once we've finished.'

'Come to the back door.' She looked across at Ginny and lowered her voice. 'Eh, your daughter looks proper done in.' She lowered her voice. 'She's carrying, isn't she?'

Hannah didn't bother to contradict her about relationships. 'Yes.'

'Poor thing. She needs a proper home at a time like that.'

'We do have one to go to, but the thieves who attacked my husband stole our money so we're having to walk back instead of taking the train.'

'Eh, the wickedness of some people. They should be whipped for it, that they should.'

When she'd gone, Hannah ladled out the soup into the bowls and there was silence as they all ate. The warmth of the food was as wonderful as its taste and they would have eaten up every crumb if Hannah hadn't set some bread and half the cheese to one side.

'We need to save something for morning, remember. I can't afford to buy us breakfast as well, I'm afraid.'

Gregory sighed.

Nathaniel scowled. 'I'm ashamed that I'm not looking after you all better.'

Hannah began to pile up the dishes, speaking matter-of-factly. 'You've done your best. No one can fight off three men. Anyway, we're managing, aren't we?'

Ginny lay back, letting Gregory take her bowl and not even offering to help Hannah. 'I feel a bit better now. The soup was lovely. But I'm so sleepy. It's all I want to do lately, lie down and sleep.'

'I was just like that with my first.' Hannah picked up the tray and went towards the door.

As she looked back, she could see all three of them leaning back with their eyes closed, and she smiled.

But Nathaniel didn't let himself fall asleep yet. Once again, he watched the two youngsters settle into a sound sleep then, when Hannah returned, gestured to the hay beside him. 'Come and share body warmth, Hannah lass.'

'You'd better call me Nancy, just in case someone overhears.' She moved across, feeling suddenly shy.

'You don't seem like a Nancy. Hannah suits you. It's a name I've always liked, an honest sort of name.'

She smiled and lay down beside him, feeling a little nervous and trying to cover that by talking. 'Tell me about your home. What shall you do when you get back? Do you think there'd be any work for me in your village, or should I travel on?'

He wrinkled his brow in thought then looked sideways at Ginny and said slowly, 'Perhaps you should stay with us for a while? You fit in well and that poor lass could do with a woman's help.'

'I don't want to get you into trouble.'

'I don't like to think of you out there tramping the roads on your own – especially after we've used up your money. At least stay with us for a few days.'

'I have a little money left still.'

'Not much, I'll wager.' When she didn't contradict him he asked, 'Well, will you stay with us?'

'How can I? I'm not a relative. It'd look strange for you to take me into your home – and people would be bound to think the worst. It's one thing to tell everyone I'm your wife as we travel, because they'll never see us again, but it's another thing altogether for us to live together in a place where you're known and respected.'

'Hmm.'

She lay back and closed her eyes for a moment or two, feeling their shared warmth begin to counteract the dampness of her clothing and the piled hay keep her warm on the other side. When she turned her head she found him watching her, his face very close to hers. She could feel her cheeks getting warm.

'It's a funny way to meet, isn't it?' he said quietly.

'Yes.'

'You must have been lonely travelling on your own.'

'Yes. And a woman on her own stands out because women usually travel with their families. Well, those who're suffering because of the Cotton Famine do.'

'I'm always glad I didn't have to work in one of those mills. Dirty, noisy places, and the work itself comes and goes so they're often on short time from what I hear. I saw a mill once and it looked like hell come to earth. Big square place with a tall chimney pouring out black smoke next to it.'

'I'm glad I've never had to work in one, either. I don't like being shut up indoors.'

'It must have been bad in the asylum.'

She nodded, her throat suddenly thickening with tears. 'I just – couldn't understand what was happening at first and when I did, I got angry. But that did me no good at all. It wasn't till I calmed down that they let me out, only they sent me back to my daughter-in-law and that wasn't good either.'

His hand was warm on her shoulder and then he trailed his fingers down her cheek, catching the tears she couldn't hold back.

'I'm sorry. I've not had anyone to talk to about it.' More tears came, faster and faster, and when he pulled her into a close embrace she gave in and wept against his chest, trying to muffle the sound, not wanting the youngsters to see her weeping.

She didn't allow herself to cry for too long, but when she tried to draw away he wouldn't let her.

'I reckon you needed a good cry. My wife always said it did her good when things went wrong to cry out her sorrows. I used to envy her. Us fellows aren't supposed to do that sort of thing.'

'I did need it. Thank you for –' oh, dear she was blushing again '– comforting me.'

'Eh, I think a lot of you, Hannah Firth. And I'm not taking no for an answer. You'll come and stay with us and hang what other folk think.'

She didn't say anything but lay awake for a while, wondering what exactly he meant by 'think a lot of you'. He couldn't . . . surely he couldn't mean . . . She didn't dare allow herself that hope. But she did admit to herself that she liked him, too. Very much indeed.

Howard West was working in the field nearest the road when the postman came walking along the lane, whistling.

'Got a letter for your Ginny, Mr West,' he called. 'Is she back yet?'

'Not yet. I'll take it for her.' He stared at the envelope, wondering who it could be from. Not until the postman was out of sight did he tear it open, his fingers leaving smears of dirt all over the single sheet of paper it contained.

As he read it, his temper rose. That young sod was daring to write to her now. Well, she'd never see this letter, never see her lover again either, if he could help it. And this bloody Nick of hers could wonder how she was all he liked. No one was going to write back and tell him.

He stormed back to the house and waved the muddy piece of paper in his wife's face. 'Your daughter's lover is writing to her, *missing her*, but his family lives somewhere else now.' He let out a short bark of mirthless laughter. 'Well, she's never going to find out where he is because I'll make sure all his letters go where they belong'. He tossed this one into the glowing embers of the stove, watching with satisfaction as the paper curled and blackened and the loving words were consumed one by one.

When he'd gone, Christine sighed. Poor Ginny! But there was nothing she could do and at least her daughter was safe. All her efforts from now on would go into looking after her boys. And trying to find the courage to stand up to Howard.

CHAPTER FOURTEEN

January 1864

Lemuel first saw the Wanted poster for his mother when he heard something crackling at the back of the kitchen drawer. He pulled it out to see what was stuck, and smoothed out the piece of paper to find a crude likeness of his mother and the offer of a reward for her capture that shocked him to the core, especially as it was made in his name.

Hearing a sound, he turned and saw Patty looking angry. She rushed across the room and tried to snatch the paper out of his hand, but he held it out of her reach and used his other hand to force her to sit down on one of the hard wooden chairs.

'*What's this?*'

She gave up struggling to get away and folded her arms, giving him a scornful look as she said sharply, 'You can see perfectly well what it is.'

'How did you find the money to do this?'

She shrugged and when he continued to look at her expectantly, muttered, 'Parson Barnish paid for it because he's angry she escaped and he's quite determined to get her back into the care of the Guardians.'

'But it's in my name! Why didn't you tell him I don't want her brought back?'

'Because there's too much work here for me and *I* need her help, even if you don't.'

'But they'll take her into the asylum, not send her to us.'

'Only till she's calmed down and this time she'll learn her lesson properly so she'll do as I want from then on. And I won't let *you* undermine me as you did last time, Lemuel Firth.'

'It's you who's been undermining me,' he said grimly. 'But no longer.' He went to stand just inside the room which had once been his mother's, wrinkling his nose against the sour smell as he stared at its filthy condition. 'For a start, we're going to put *your* mother into the asylum. She needs better help than you give her, and without her to care for even you should be able to manage the housework. Other women do.'

'What do you mean "even me"?'

'We both know you're not a good housewife.' He looked pityingly at the old woman lying in the bed with her usual vacant expression and added quietly, 'She's beyond noticing who looks after her but she still notices if she's dirty.'

Patty came across to join him in the doorway, grabbing his arm and giving it a shake. 'Do you think I don't want to put her in the asylum? Only I can't. My father will be furious and he'll—'

'Then he can take her off our hands instead. You're my wife, owing your first loyalty to me and your first care to our son.'

She let go of him and folded her arms across her breast. 'You know my father has no one else to look after her.'

'Well, *you* aren't looking after her properly, so he can either make other arrangements or put up with it.' Suddenly he was sickened by his wife and her cheating ways, and went to don his hat and overcoat. What upset him most was that he'd let her hurt his own mother because of his cowardice. Well, no more. 'I'm going to sort this mess out once and for all,' he said loudly.

As he started to open the back door, Patty barred the way, arms spread out. 'Where do you think you're going?'

'Out.'

'*Where?*'

'Where I choose.'

She burst into tears, but he knew how she used that as a weapon and didn't let it stop him either, and as he closed the door she abandoned tears to shriek threats that she'd make him sorry. Only he was already sorry, very sorry indeed, for what he'd done – or rather, not done to help his mother.

He walked briskly through the village and was relieved to find Dr Kent at home. When they were seated in the doctor's cosy consulting room, Lemuel found it difficult to start and sat turning his hat around in his hands.

'Something's obviously bothering you, Mr Firth. Tell me what it is.'

It was hard, Lemuel thought, to lay bare your wife's failings, even to a doctor. He faltered through his tale and then looked earnestly at the other man. 'So – I don't think there was ever anything wrong with my mother. Patty has a little blue bottle and she uses the mixture from it on our son, to keep him quiet. Is that all right?'

'No, it's not. A child shouldn't be drugged like that.'

'I thought not. I'll tip the stuff away when I get back. But I don't know how to stop people from hounding my mother. Can you help me?'

'There's not much either of us can do until we can prove her sane. To do that, she'll have to be brought back, I'm afraid. The new parson is a stickler for abiding by the rules.'

'Then I hope they never find her. She doesn't deserve such treatment.'

'No, I agree. But as long as I'm here, I promise you that if she is brought back, I'll try to see justice done.'

'*Try?*'

Maurice sighed. 'You can never promise anything for sure with so many other people involved.'

Lemuel took a deep breath then said the other thing he'd come for. 'There's also the question of Mrs Riggs. My wife isn't looking after her properly and the poor soul can't even talk properly now. I think she'd be better off in the poorhouse. Is that possible?'

'I'm not sure she will be better off there. They do their best, but—'

'Patty hates even going near her, leaves her lying in her own filth all day and doesn't feed her properly.'

Maurice stared at him in shock. 'Are things that bad?'

'Yes, I'm ashamed to say they are. Patty's not a good housewife – well, she's downright lazy – but she's worse when she's expecting. She was bad last time, but worse with this one.'

'You'll have to make an application to the Board of Guardians for admission.' The doctor hesitated then said, 'If I come back home with you now, what shall I find?'

'A stinking mess that shames me.'

'If I do, I shall be able to bear witness to the need for taking Mrs Riggs into parish care.'

'Then come.' Lemuel stifled his embarrassment because he had set himself to do something about the intolerable conditions at home and would carry this through even if it tore him apart. As they walked along the village high street together, he had another thought. 'We can find that damned blue bottle and destroy it while you're there, and you can look at my son and tell me if she's harmed him.' He held back any further words because his bitterness might overflow and then he didn't know what he'd say or do.

When they walked in through the back door, Patty didn't look up at first, just snapped, 'If you want anything to eat tonight, you'll tell me where you've been, Lemuel Firth.'

'To fetch the doctor.'

She spun round, shock making her mouth drop open.

'This way, Dr Kent,' Lemuel said grimly, determined to get it all over and done with.

When she saw him opening the door to her mother's room, she screamed, 'No! Lemuel, don't do this!'

But he ignored her.

Maurice stared into the room and felt sickened by what he saw. He looked at his companion and said in a low voice, 'You were right to come to me.'

Patty was still standing by the stove when they went back into the kitchen, her hands clasped at her breast.

She looked from one man to the other, but didn't seem to know what to say or do.

Lemuel went to search the drawer of the dresser. 'Where's the bottle of stuff you've been giving our John?'

'I don't know what you mean.'

The doctor looked at her sternly. 'I've spoken to the apothecary in Upper Hetton and he tells me you've been buying the mixture regularly, more than other women usually purchase or need.'

'I've only had a bottle or two, just to help me get some sleep when John was sickly.'

The doctor's voice was implacable. 'Show me.'

Still she hesitated, darting an angry glance at her husband, but Lemuel's face wore an expression she'd never seen on it before, an expression that frightened her and stopped the angry words in her throat.

He came across and took her arm, shaking it. 'Do – as the doctor – asks.'

She pushed his hand off and went to the pantry, bringing out a blue bottle.

Maurice examined it. 'There's hardly any left here. Do you have any more?'

'No, I told you. I only use it now and then.'

'That's not what the apothecary told me. He said you bought three bottles last time.'

'I didn't! That's all I have.'

'You stay here with her, doctor.' Lemuel went up the stairs two at a time, going first into his own bedroom and finding nothing, then into his son's. He upended each drawer on the floor and found two more of the blue bottles hidden among John's clothes and the things waiting for the new baby. Both were full. He stood still for a minute, hand pressed against his eyes, then went to the cradle and picked up his son, holding the baby awkwardly against his chest. John seemed sleepy and hardly stirred.

When he went down, Patty came across automatically to take the child, but Lemuel fended her off. 'Will you look at him, Doctor? He's always so quiet. Now that I know why, I'm feared for him.'

Maurice nodded and took the infant, going to sit near the window and study the child's face which was paler than he liked, with dull eyes. John wasn't well cared for either, his skin looking dirty with a red rash round his nether parts. 'He's been given too much of the mixture. It'll take some time to get him well again,' the doctor admitted, hating to see the look of suffering on the other man's face.

'What must I do?'

'Give him to me!' Patty shouted suddenly. 'He's my son and I'll look after him how I choose.'

'Behave yourself.' Lemuel didn't even look at her but turned back to the doctor and repeated urgently, 'What must I do to help him?'

'I'd like to see him looked after by someone experienced with sick babies for a few weeks. He'll miss the mixture, you see, and will cry and fret because he's not getting it. It'll take careful nursing to bring him back to normal after so many months using this stuff.' He glared at the blue bottle. 'If I had my way, they wouldn't sell it at all.'

Patty started weeping as noisily as a child and shouting, 'Give me my son!'

Both men continued to ignore her.

'Is there someone who'll take him?' Lemuel asked. 'I'll pay whatever's necessary.'

'Yes. There's a woman over Hetton way who's a born nurse. I've sent her other ailing children and she's helped some I'd given up hope of saving.' He looked across at Patty, not hiding his disgust with her, then down at the child, his eyes softening. 'Can you pack his clothes and clouts, Mr Firth? I'll take him now. The woman I'm thinking of won't refuse to take a sick child.'

Again Lemuel went upstairs, his steps slow and heavy. Patty made no attempt to help him, just collapsed on to a chair next to the table, put her head on her arms and continued to bawl loudly.

'You'll do yourself and the new baby harm if you go on like this,' Maurice told her gently. 'Try to calm down.'

She looked up briefly, anger twisting her face so that she looked like a gargoyle. 'What do *you* care about me?'

'I care about anyone who isn't well, and I think you need my help, Mrs Firth. I want to come and see you in a day or two, to check that the new baby's growing as it should.'

'You'll not touch me!' she shrieked, hurling the nearest item at him, a teacup half-full of cold tea.

Lemuel stood in the doorway, shocked rigid. '*Patty!*'

The doctor stood up. 'I think your wife isn't well. I'd like to come and see her in a day or two, but let's deal with your son first. If you'll carry those things round to my house, I'll drive the child over to the nurse. Oh, and don't forget the bottles of soothing mixture. We don't want your wife using them again.'

Lemuel went into the scullery, pulled the cork stopper from each one and emptied the contents down the drain.

Patty sat there once they'd left, still weeping, though more quietly now. Her mother began to make noises that said she needed help but Patty paid no attention, lost in her own woes.

When Lemuel returned, his wife became hysterical and all he could do with her was carry her up to their bedroom and lay her on the bed. Then he went down and did his best to help his poor mother-in-law. It might not be man's work to clean an old woman's body, but he hated to see anyone suffer.

Only – what was he going to do with Patty?

If only his mother were still here. He had never needed her help so much in all his life.

They arrived at Nathaniel's market garden two days later just as dusk was falling, all of them exhausted and bedraggled. Ginny was so white her uncle had walked the last mile with his arm round her waist for support and encouragement, murmuring to her from time to time.

'We're here, lass,' he said gently because when he stopped she didn't look up, just sagged against him. 'Open the door, Gregory lad.'

But it was locked.

'It's never locked,' the boy exclaimed, looking back at his father.

'Here, let me take her.' Hannah shifted her bag to the other shoulder and waited while Nathaniel felt above the lintel.

He found a rusty key and opened the door to the kitchen but stopped dead in the doorway, exclaiming in shock. 'What the hell's happened here?'

As he moved forward the others followed him inside. They didn't need a lamp to see that the place was in a mess, furniture tossed around, shards of broken crockery underfoot, flour scattered like dirty snow across the floor and sugar crunching underfoot.

Hannah thought she heard someone approaching so went to tug on Nathaniel's sleeve and gesture behind her. He nodded, put one finger to his lips and crept back ready to pounce on the man who was creeping towards them through the lengthening shadows.

'Is that you, Nathaniel?' an old voice quavered.

'Tom!'

Hannah remembered that this was the name of the old man who helped out in the market garden.

'They come here three nights ago, Nathaniel lad, and if I hadn't been down at the privy, they'd have beat me up. I crep' down the garden behind the muck heap and heard 'em looking for me.'

'Who came?' Nathaniel asked, easing the old man gently down on a chair because Tom was shivering like a leaf in a high wind.

'That groom of Walter Dewhurst's, Colin he's called, and two other fellows. I never seen 'em afore and I hope I never see 'em again. They didn't know I was listening so they was laughin' as they broke your things, saying that'd teach you to do as the young master ordered in future. They broke some of your tools, too.' He began to sob, dry thin sounds as if he didn't even have enough breath to weep properly.

'There was nothing you could have done to stop them, Tom. I'm relieved they didn't hurt you,' Nathaniel said gently, bending to give the old fellow a hug. Tom clung to him, still shaking with emotion.

'I let you down. I didn't look after things,' he sobbed. 'They pissed all over the ham so I threw it away. Such a nice flitch, it was, too.'

Nathaniel patted him on the shoulder. 'What could you have done against three men? A ham means nothing compared to your safety.' He pointed to his own face. 'I was beaten up by three men, Tom, and you can see what they did to me. You were better off hiding.'

The old man raised one shaking hand to touch the younger man's face, a curiously tender gesture. 'Why did they hurt you, lad?'

'It was my brother-in-law who did it because I was taking my niece away, bringing her here to look after her.' After a moment or two he straightened up and his voice grew more brisk. 'Right then. The first thing we need is a light. If they've left any lamps intact.' He searched the cottage, his expression growing grimmer all the time as he discovered more destruction, eventually finding two old lamps on a high shelf. He lit them and set one on the table, holding the other up and turning in a circle to inspect more closely the damage that had been done.

Hannah felt sorry for him and would have gone to stand beside him, but just then Ginny swayed. Quickly she picked up a chair that was more or less whole and guided the girl to sit down on it. 'There you are, love. You sit quietly while I help your uncle to straighten up a bit.' She went across to Nathaniel and, without realising what she was doing, linked her arm in his for a moment, giving him support in the only way she knew how.

He looked sideways at her, bewilderment in his face. 'Why would a rich man do such a thing? It's Walter Dewhurst who ordered it, can't be anyone else. All because I refused to open my gate and help him destroy my livelihood.'

'He sounds downright wicked to me. But what we need now is a fire in that stove and some warm food in our bellies – if they've left anything undamaged. You see to the fire and I'll inspect your pantry.'

She found oats and a crock of dried currants in one corner. 'Look, I can make some porridge. Pity we don't have any milk. It's heartier with milk.'

Nathaniel looked up. 'Gregory lad, see if you can find a bucket and nip down to the farm for some milk.'

Hannah wouldn't let Gregory leave until she'd scoured the bucket out with fine sand that she found in a box in the scullery.

'Take care how you go,' Nathaniel called to his son. 'If you see anyone coming down the lane, hide till they're past.' He stood back from the stove and watched as flames rose in its belly, nodding in satisfaction. 'It always was a good burner.'

They both turned as Ginny laid her head down on her arms and sighed, but the girl was simply exhausted, as was the old man.

'What about the rest of the house?' Hannah asked Nathaniel. 'We need to make up some beds.'

'I'd as soon sleep in here with you tonight, if you don't mind, lad,' Tom said. 'I've been afeared they'd come back, hardly slept a wink. We can bring my bedding up from the hut, can't we?'

'Of course you can sleep here,' Nathaniel said heartily, then drew a deep breath. 'Right then, I'll go and see what the rest is like.'

'I'll come with you,' Hannah said at once. If he had to face further destruction of his possessions, she wanted to be with him.

Upstairs he held up the lamp as they went from one room to the other. The intruders had broken the bed frames and left dirty footprints on the bedding but had left the family's clothing more or less intact, though it was tossed around.

He led the way back into his own bedroom, set down the lamp on the mantelpiece and picked up the largest piece of a broken vase, staring at Hannah in dumb bewilderment. 'I bought Sarah this on our first wedding anniversary. She was expecting Gregory then and it was before she fell ill. She loved it and always had it where she could see it, right to the end.' His voice broke as he added, 'Why do folk do things like this? *Why?* What good does it do anyone to smash my little treasures?'

'Some folk seem to have evil born in them,' she said in a low voice, going once again to thread her arm in his.

He clasped her hand and looked down at it, putting his other hand over the top. 'I'm glad you're here. Don't leave us, Hannah.'

'People will talk.'

'Not if we get wed.'

She looked at him in shock, unable to believe she'd heard rightly.

He gave a near-noiseless laugh. 'Eh, listen to me. What a way to ask you! I meant to do it properly, in a day or two.'

'You really mean it, then?'

'Of course I do.'

'But – we hardly know one another. And you've only recently lost your wife.'

'I'm not pretending it's a love match, though I do like and respect you. But we both need help. You need a home and I need a wife to work alongside me. So why not help one another?'

She liked him too, but suddenly remembered her dream of finding a man who would love her as she'd once been loved. Bending her head, she looked at their hands, still joined, and said slowly, 'I'll have to think about it, Nathaniel. You've – rather taken me by surprise.'

'I surprised myself if truth be told.' He let go of her hand and went to pick up the lamp. 'But I suddenly saw how well it'd work for us both and the question popped out before I could stop it.' He managed a wry smile from his bruised face. 'You take as long as you like, lass. But I hope you'll say yes.' When he got to the door he turned again and this time gave her a smile full of genuine amusement. 'Eh, you've never even seen what I really look like.' He gestured to his face. 'It's a wonder this hasn't frightened you away.'

She smiled back. 'That's only the outside. It's what people are like inside that counts with me and I know you're a good man.'

'And you're a good woman.' Again that feeling flared between them then he changed the subject by gesturing to the room. 'You and Ginny can sleep in here. I'll go in with Gregory and we'll leave Tom down in the kitchen. He'd have trouble with the stairs anyway. He's not very spry at the best of times, though I've never seen him so feeble-looking. He taught me most of what I know about growing fruit and vegetables, and I owe him a lot.'

She could sense that he employed Tom Ringley out of compassion for she had seen in her own village how old folk would do anything rather than be taken into the workhouse – and she didn't blame them. It was a dreadful place and the memory of it still made her shiver.

Downstairs they found the fire burning brightly and Ginny sound asleep.

'Should I carry her up to bed or shall we wake her and make sure she eats?' Nathaniel asked.

'I think she should eat then she can sleep as long as she likes tomorrow. Besides, I haven't sorted out the beds yet.'

Gregory came back a short time later with a bucket full of milk and a clean cloth tied across the top. He was followed by Farmer Sawyer, shocked to hear that the cottage had been broken into.

'Nay, I'd never have believed it if I hadn't seen it with my own eyes!' he exclaimed in shock. 'And Gregory says it was Walter Dewhurst's man who did it.'

'Best not spread that around,' Nathaniel said. 'We've no proof and we don't want *him* causing more trouble.'

'I saw 'em do it,' Tom said. 'Aren't I proof?'

'Nay, old friend, we'll not have them coming after you. Least said, soonest mended about this, I reckon.'

Farmer Sawyer nodded. 'You're right. I hate to see them get away with it, but who can go against the Dewhursts?' He looked at Hannah and then back at Nathaniel questioningly.

'This is our good friend Hannah. She's been helping me with my niece. Ginny's not been well and she's coming to stay with me for a while.'

The farmer nodded at the newcomer. 'Poor sort of welcome you've had, missus.' He held out a parcel wrapped in another cloth. 'The wife sent a loaf and a pat of our own butter.'

Hannah took them automatically. 'Tell her thank you.'

'I will. I'll tell her what's happened too, but we shan't say a word about who did it to anyone else.'

Nathaniel escorted him out then came back, looking irritated. 'I hate taking charity even from neighbours!'

'So do I, but we do need help just now.' Hannah set a large pan of milk on top of the stove, measuring out some oats into it, then putting the lid on. She'd add the currants later. 'Do you have a broom, Nathaniel?' She gestured to the floor. 'I'll give it a good scrub tomorrow, but if we don't clear this lot up we'll be treading flour and sugar all over the house.'

'I used to have one.' He came back from the scullery holding a broom that had had the long handle snapped in two. His lips were set in another of those tight lines.

'Well, the brush part is all right and bending down never hurt anyone,' Hannah said cheerfully, taking it from him.

'I'll do the sweeping. You make the food. It's a good bargain because I'm not the best of cooks.'

So she stirred the porridge, put on a kettle of water to heat and cleared up the broken pieces of crockery from the dresser shelves. There were enough plates and dishes left intact or only chipped for them to eat from, so she washed them and set them out ready.

'I knew you'd be a good housewife,' Nathaniel said quietly as he passed her to take out the first lot of sweepings.

She looked at him in surprise. 'How can you tell from this?'

'Just the way you set about things.'

It was nice to receive a compliment. She knew she could easily accept Nathaniel's offer of marriage because she did like him.

But would it be the right thing to do? Would it be fair to him, given her circumstances?

And could she bear to give up her dream of finding love once again?

CHAPTER FIFTEEN

February 1864

Walter leaned back in his seat in the alehouse, laughing with his groom at what King would have found when he returned home. 'He'll know who arranged for that,' he gloated, 'but he won't be able to do a thing about it.' When he had finished his pot of ale he stood up, though the other man was still drinking. 'Right, let's go for a ride.'

With a sigh Colin drained his pot and followed him, wondering why his master was so edgy lately. 'You're not going over to Beckleton, are you?'

'I may come back that way.'

'Your father warned you to stay away from your brother. Mr Oliver has lost his inheritance so why bother about him?' Colin, who had been Walter's groom for several years, was the only man who dared talk to him like that.

'Mind your own business. I'm not going near Oliver, am I? Just riding through the village. It'll be enough if he hears I was there. He'll be trembling in his bed for days if I know him. We may stop for a sup of ale there, too, to find out what he's doing. You're good at getting folk to talk to you.'

Colin sighed. He had gone and messed up King's cottage on his master's orders, though had not done it as thoroughly as ordered. Nor had he beaten up Tom, though he'd seen the old fellow hiding behind the muck heap. Well, what good did that sort of thing do anyone? The best course was to make money out of other folk's stupidities and Colin was much more interested in that. He had a decent amount saved now and it wouldn't be long before he left this job and probably left Lancashire too.

As they rode into Beckleton later that day, a lady came out of the church and Walter automatically raised his hat to her then recognised her and stopped, sitting on his horse to watch her walk down the street. He'd met her once, when she was talking to the parson here, and had remembered her several times since. Oh, yes, he'd remembered her and vowed to have her one day.

'What's wrong?' Colin asked.

'Nothing's wrong. I'm just enjoying the sight of the daughter of the Marquess of Iffingham taking the air.' Walter classed most females as whores or drudges, but every now and then you met one like this, a *lady* in every way, different from the others. For some reason he found this one particularly attractive. Her very neatness made him want to pull her clothing off piece by piece and take away all that prim propriety. Though you could only do that to noble ladies if you married them because their families were very powerful and always kept them closely guarded.

But when he inherited his father's money, things might change. He'd be very rich indeed then.

He watched her till she'd disappeared from sight, then went into the inn with his groom. It was a comfortable place and as usual Colin got the landlord talking about the local inhabitants, including the new tenant of Spinneys, which was the purpose of this visit. Walter might be forbidden to go near his brother, but he was going to keep an eye on him all the same.

Afterwards Walter turned the conversation to Lady Ann and the landlord was happy to chat about her.

'They say she's helping Mr Dewhurst with the garden at Spinneys. She has green fingers that one, lady or not, just like her grandma. Does the flowers in the church beautiful. Never seen anything as pretty. Gives you something to look at while the parson's droning on.' He chuckled.

'Does her father ever come here?'

'Not if he can help it. The Marquess of Iffingham lives on one of his other estates in the south. He thinks this place very small and shabby and makes no secret of his feelings. It used to be his grandmother's.' He leaned closer to add in a lowered voice, 'They say Lady Ann's in disgrace with her father for not marrying the man he chose, and that's why she's been sent here. All I know is she's as civil to a cat as to a king and a nicer lady you couldn't hope to meet.'

After the landlord had gone to attend to another customer, Walter sat staring into his ale, lost in thought. Suddenly he knew she was *meant* for him. Marrying her would help him gain his rightful place in county society. Besides, he wanted her.

As they were riding back, he said abruptly to Colin, 'Find out more about Lady Ann. See if you can get to know one of their grooms. I want to meet her again, as if by accident.'

'Nay, Mr Walter, she's not for you. They guard their daughters well, the nobility.'

His master didn't even seem to hear this, but rode home lost in thought, a smile on his face – a surprisingly gentle smile for him. But that worried Colin all the more.

Oliver was walking into the village when he saw his brother in the distance, riding that showy black stallion which Oliver never quite trusted, any more than he trusted Walter. He moved behind a clump of trees and kept watch, wondering if they were coming to Spinneys, though Lexham said his father had forbidden it. But Walter and his groom sat slumped on their horses watching something in the village, oblivious to what the rest of the world thought of them.

Oliver slipped quickly across the road and, keeping to every piece of cover he could find, moved forward until he could see what they were watching. Lady Ann! Surely Walter wasn't interested in her? The daughter of a Marquess was well above the touch of a Dewhurst socially.

Once she was out of sight, the two men dismounted and the groom took their horses round the back while Walter went into the inn.

Oliver turned round and walked home again, lost in thought. It might be cowardly, but he wasn't going into the village if Walter was there.

Was this just a chance visit on the way to somewhere else, or was his brother about to start tormenting him again?

*   *   *

Nick turned up in Blackfold on the first Sunday in February, a crisp frosty day with the sun shining but giving no warmth. He went to church, feeling uncomfortable with the rituals of the Established Church after his own Methodist chapel, but determined to find a way to see Ginny. There was no sign of her, however, only her step-father, mother and the two little boys.

After the service Nick lingered outside, talking to a fellow he knew slightly, waiting for Lucy to emerge so that he could ask her about Ginny.

But after one startled glance in his direction she walked straight past him, keeping her eyes lowered and staying close to her mother.

Nick's companion grinned at him. 'Why didn't you ask me to act as go-between?'

'What do you mean?'

'I've seen you and Lucy walking down by the canal. Doesn't want to know you now, though, does she? Perhaps she's found herself another lad.'

'It's Ginny Doyle I was walking with, her I've come to see.'

His companion let out a long, low whistle. 'Rather you than me, with a step-father like that! Any road, you won't be able to see her.'

'What do you mean?'

'She's left Blackfold, lad. No one's seen her for weeks. Just up and vanished.'

'People don't vanish into thin air.'

'*She* did. I heard my mum talking to the neighbour about it. No one saw her leave, but no one's seen her for a while now. You can't ask Mr West and you never see Mrs West on her own in the village, so folk gossip about them but no one really knows.' He grew thoughtful. 'It was about the time that Mr West got scalded that she vanished. You can't see how bad his face is with that hat on, but it's all red in patches. No one knows how that happened, either.'

Nick closed his eyes and groaned, not the least interested in Ginny's step-father or the local gossips' opinions. 'I have to catch the six o'clock train back. What am I going to do?'

'You could ask at the inn. I did hear Mrs West's brother was staying there about the time Ginny disappeared, just for the one night, though no one spoke to him either. Maybe Mrs Feathers knows something.'

Nick went straight to the back door of the inn, begging for information. The landlady took pity on him and told him all she knew. Which was a little more than his friend, at least.

'Did the uncle mention where he lived, Mrs Feathers?'

'Nay, he didn't. Somewhere t'other side of Preston, I think, but he never spoke the name of it, or if he did, I don't remember.'

'If you do remember anything, could you *please* let me know?' He pulled an envelope out of his pocket, on which he'd already written his address. 'I've put a stamp on so you'd only have to write his address and slip this into the post.'

Her expression softened. 'Eh, you must be fond of her.'

'I am.'

When Nick got home, he had to face his family. He admitted he'd been trying to see Ginny. 'Only I haven't found her. She seems to have vanished off the face of the earth.'

'Well, that's that, then,' his father said briskly. 'You'll just have to find another young woman to court.'

But Nick's mother didn't like the sound of what her son had said. The usual reason young women vanished and their families refused to talk about it was that they were expecting and there was no father around, so they'd been sent away to preserve their good name. Was that possible with Ginny Doyle? Jane didn't like to ask her son whether it was, but the idea worried her. Oh, please, she prayed, please let him forget the girl!

Only – if there was a baby, it'd be Nick's child too, and her first grandchild. She did so long for grandchildren.

She couldn't banish that sense of guilt about keeping him and Ginny Doyle apart, she just couldn't.

Nathaniel got up as soon as there was any hint of dawn brightening the sky, leaving his son still fast asleep. Downstairs he walked quietly round Tom, who was curled up on his old mattress near the stove, snoring gently. After opening the damper to get the fire burning up, Nathaniel went outside and leaned against the wall, oblivious to the chill air because he loved being home, even under these circumstances. As soon as there was enough light he'd go round and check for damage outside, though Tom said the intruders had concentrated mainly on the cottage.

Rotten sods!

When he heard the door opening and a sound behind

him, he didn't need to ask who it was. Who else walked as quietly as Hannah?

'Did you sleep well, lass?'

'Yes. It was wonderful to lie in a proper bed again.' She leaned against the wall beside him, her eyes on the sky. 'I love to watch the dawn.'

They didn't say anything, just enjoyed the play of light from grey to blush pink. Even before it paled to the clear frosty light of a fine winter's morning, he pushed himself away from the wall. 'I need to check that my money is safe.'

'I'll go inside and leave you in peace.'

'Nay, I've no secrets from you, lass. If they found my savings, we shall be in trouble, though.'

But she went inside the cottage nonetheless.

They hadn't found his small hoard of coins, buried in a corner of the garden, and he breathed a loud sigh of relief as he dug up the little tin box, removed some money and buried it carefully again, stamping down the earth until only he would know where to look. He went into the kitchen with something in his pocket, at least, a man able to provide food for those who depended on him.

Tom was sitting at the table and Hannah was already getting breakfast ready. He nodded to show her things were all right and she smiled back. There was only bread and butter to eat, but it was welcome nonetheless.

'I've a few cabbages, carrots and potatoes still in clamps, and some onions hanging in the shed,' he said, 'but we'll need to buy meat in the village. Someone will have slaughtered a beast, because it's market day. You and I could go there together, Hannah lass. You'll know better than I do what's needed here.'

She considered this, head on one side. 'I think it'll look better if Ginny comes too.' Even so people would gossip about what she was doing at Nathaniel King's house – well, they would if they were anything like the people of Hetton-le-Hill.

It was a small market and Nathaniel was clearly well known to all the stallholders. He was greeted and offered commiserations on what had happened to his cottage, and took the opportunity to introduce both his niece and her friend to everyone they met.

Hannah watched his face as he struggled to keep his expression calm when people went on and on about the intruders. She could see that folk thought well of him; indeed, one man took him aside to ask his advice about some problem. Someone respected in his own small world, she guessed, and it would upset him to leave here, as he might have to. Eh, he was such a lovely fellow and didn't deserve the troubles he'd had – but then, when was life ever fair? She didn't think she'd deserved her troubles, either.

Stallholders were generous in weighing their goods and she didn't say anything about that, hoping Nathaniel hadn't noticed. Soon they had a half-flitch of bacon and a sack of flour in the handcart, as well as some pieces of pork that would make a fine raised pie, eggs nestling in straw in the bowl she'd brought for that purpose, since Nathaniel hadn't kept his own chickens since his wife's illness.

As they moved round she added flour, sugar and honey, a nice piece of cheese, and some dried peas and rice, going to the village shop as well as the market. Nathaniel clearly wasn't used to skimping on food and didn't complain about how much she was spending. She added oatcakes to the basket, liking the look of those offered on one stall: the same flat oat pieces that had been used in her grandmother's time instead of wheaten bread because oats could be grown so much more easily than wheat in the cooler climate of the north, and which some now thought old-fashioned. She'd always enjoyed them, though, especially with honey, and they were a good stand-by with a hungry lad for whom meals were too far apart.

In the end she said, 'That should do for the moment, don't you think?'

Nathaniel nodded and paid the last stallkeeper.

But when they got home, they found more largesse on their kitchen table and Tom beaming at them across a cake, another loaf, a bag of apples and a big meat and potato pie.

'Neighbours brought 'em,' he told Nathaniel.

'You should have told them I can manage.'

'Nay, why should you, lad? It's a poor world if we can't help one another.' The old man grinned. 'But you allus were stiff-necked and independent, so I were glad they come while you were out.'

Hannah smiled as she listened to the conversation, then set to and scrubbed down the pantry shelves before putting the provisions away. She found Ginny a willing helper in the task of cleaning up the cottage once the girl had got over her morning sickness.

In the afternoon there was the sound of a horse riding

up and she went to the window, wondering who was visiting. 'Who's that?' she asked Gregory.

'Mr Lexham, the landowner's agent.'

A short time later Nathaniel brought the visitor in, his tight expression back in place. 'We've been cleaning up so there's not much to show you now, Mr Lexham.'

'But you know who did it?'

'No.' Nathaniel sent a warning look at Tom, who was hovering near the door. 'I was away, fetching my niece and her friend to live with me.' He introduced Hannah and Ginny.

'I think you do know,' Jack Lexham said quietly as they walked back to his horse.

'And *I* think no good will come of trying to prove it.'

'Tell me anyway, if you please.'

Nathaniel sighed. 'Walter Dewhurst's groom and two strangers. Tom saw them.'

As if Jack hadn't guessed! He hated to hear it confirmed, though. ' If Mr Dewhurst dies, I'm giving up this job and leaving the district. I'd advise you to get out too – sooner, if you can. I'll not work for Walter Dewhurst and I'm sure you'll find him a bad landlord. Indeed, I've heard him say he'll have you out the minute he's in charge. He's really taken against you.'

'I need to find another piece of land first. I've been looking already, but it isn't easy.'

'I'll keep my ears open.'

'Thank you, Mr Lexham.'

Richard Dewhurst gazed at his agent in dismay. 'Why should Walter do that to King?'

'I'm afraid your son holds grudges, sir. I've seen it happen before. He gets others to do his dirty work for him and you can never prove anything. Indeed, it'd be risky for the people concerned even to try, so I hope you won't tax him with this or the old man who saw them will certainly suffer.' He sat quietly, waiting for an answer.

Richard sighed and stared into the fire, saying at last, 'I've bred a bad 'un there, haven't I?'

'It's not for me to say, sir.'

The old man raised haunted eyes. 'Nay, you're the only one as will speak to me frankly about what Walter's doing, and I'm grateful for that, very grateful. Only what's to be done?'

'Get King out of the district, for a start. Which means finding him another smallholding and cottage. I'll ask around, but it'll take time. Changes of lease don't happen overnight.'

'Can we make it up to King? Give him some money?'

'He'd not take it. He's a proud man and it galls him to accept help.'

Another silence, then, 'Send a message to my lawyer. Ask him to call on me tomorrow.'

'Very well, sir.'

Walter was riding through Marton the following week just as the market was in full swing. He saw King there and scowled to see the fellow looking so hale and hearty. Even the bruises that had been the talk of the village had almost cleared up now and King was smiling at a tall woman beside him, dark-haired and capable-looking. What, had the fellow got himself a lady friend now? Was there no stopping him?

Reining in, Walter gestured to Colin and the two of them watched the small group make its way round the stalls. King's lad was with them and another stranger, a plump young woman who'd probably make a comfortable bed companion. 'Find out who the young one is,' he murmured. 'It's been a while since there's been any new delicacies in the village.'

Colin nodded and dismounted, helping himself to a crisp apple as he passed one stall and laughing as the stallkeeper bit back an exclamation of annoyance. He enjoyed being able to do things like this. It made up for the number of times he'd been beaten as a lad by fat stallkeepers for taking an apple or some other trifle because he was near starving to death. He was getting a bit concerned about the wild threats his master was making about getting his own back on those he bore grudges against, though. In Colin's opinion, Walter had already got his own back and should set his mind to enjoying life, not harping on the past.

He went to talk to a crony and soon found out what he needed to know, strolling back to his master and taking another apple as he did so, this time not even pretending to eat it but shying it at a mongrel which was sniffing round the rubbish at the back of the stalls. He hit the mangy creature in the ribs and sent it off yelping, while a hovering urchin snatched up the battered apple and bit into it with relish.

When he'd remounted, he moved his horse closer to his master's and explained in a low voice that the young woman was King's niece and the older woman had been introduced as a friend of hers – only everyone reckoned she was really King's fancy piece.

'She must be short of bed play if she can stomach *his* attentions,' Walter said. 'But she's too old for me. Perhaps *you* should have a try for her?'

'I prefer them willing, sir.'

'You don't know what you're missing.'

Neither do you, thought Colin.

As they rode back, Walter said thoughtfully, 'I'll go after the younger one, I think.'

'Isn't this a bit too close to home, sir?'

'Adds to the sport. Anyway, my father's getting too old to notice what's going on. He surely can't last much longer.'

When she and Ginny got back from market the following week, Hannah put the food away, then went outside to find Nathaniel, who was working in his potting shed making up trays of seeds which he'd bring into the house to persuade them to start sprouting a bit early.

He was whistling as he worked and didn't hear her coming. She stood watching him for a moment or two from the doorway, feeling unaccountably nervous about what she'd come to tell him. In the end, she took a deep breath and walked into the shed. As he caught sight of movement he spun round quickly, all trace of relaxation leaving his body. But his tension vanished as soon as he saw it was her.

'Hello, lass. I was just thinking about you.'

'Yes. I owe you my answer, don't I? We said a week, didn't we?'

'If you're ready. If you need more time to think about it and get to know me better, you have only to say.'

'No, I don't need more time. I – I should be honoured to become your wife, Nathaniel. I'm sure you're right and it'll be a good bargain for both of us.'

His face lit up and he looked down at his earth-stained hands with a rueful smile. 'I'd like to take you in my arms and kiss you to celebrate that, but as you can see, I'm in no fit state to be touching anyone.'

'That's all right.' The thought of him kissing her in broad daylight made her feel unsettled.

'How soon can we be wed?'

'As soon as you like.'

'Then we'll go and see the parson this very afternoon and arrange to have him call the banns, if that's all right with you?'

'Yes, Nathaniel. That's fine.'

'Hannah?'

'Yes?'

'You've no need to be nervous, lass. I shan't force my attentions on you till you're ready.' The memory of her nervousness had made him decide to hold back on the bed play at first, because he didn't want to push things along too fast. He wanted everything to be right between them, at first and in future years.

As she walked back to the house, Hannah wondered why he had said that. Did he only want her as a house-keeper, not as a woman? She hoped not. She sighed, still not certain she was doing the right thing. Marrying him made sense, but she'd dreamed of more. Nathaniel didn't love her and she was unsure of her own feelings about him. They worked well together and were never short of something to talk about, but she'd had the bliss of true love once and, oh, she wanted it again!

Fool! she told herself. You've got more than you could ever have hoped for when you were shut up in that place. Just be grateful for the respect of a good man.

A good man who'd never even kissed her, beyond a chaste peck on the cheek. Perhaps he wasn't a very passionate man. John hadn't been.

But she was a passionate woman, given the chance. Feelings long suppressed seethed inside her, but she forced them back. It *was* the right thing to do, the best thing for them both. She must take her satisfaction from that and not go chasing after rainbows.

CHAPTER SIXTEEN

February – March 1864

Ginny looked up from pegging out the washing to see a gentleman on horseback staring at her over the fence. She looked away and continued her work but he stayed where he was, staring. He had a heavy, brutal face and the way he was looking at her made her feel so uncomfortable that in the end she went inside, leaving half a basket of washing sitting beside the line.

'There's a man staring at me,' she gasped to Hannah. 'I don't like him.'

Hannah went to peer round the side of the cottage and the stranger immediately tipped his hat to her. She didn't respond. Why would a gentleman be hanging about here? She wished Nathaniel were at home, but he'd heard of a piece of land for lease, borrowed the farmer's gig and gone to look at it.

'I'll finish hanging out the washing,' she told Ginny. 'You stay indoors.'

Hannah doggedly ignored the stranger and when she had finished, set the clothes prop in place so that the washing began swinging in the breeze. It was wonderful to have a fine day.

As she turned the man called, 'You have a pretty daughter, ma'am. Does she ever go walking?'

She knew then that he was up to no good so still didn't answer, apart from a brusque, 'No!'

In the kitchen she found Tom peering out of the window, looking scared.

'That's Walter Dewhurst out there,' he said, 'the landowner's heir.'

'Ah! So now I know the face of our enemy.' She refused to give in to the feeling of apprehension that shivered through her and said as cheerfully as she could manage, 'We'll work indoors until we're sure he's gone.'

'Yes, but what's he after now?' Tom wondered. 'Why is he hanging around?'

From what the man had said, Hannah guessed with a sick feeling that Dewhurst's fancy had settled on Ginny. The baby wasn't really showing yet so they hadn't told anyone about it, but the girl had that attractive bloom to her face that some women got when they were carrying.

When Nathaniel came back he was radiating disappointment and Hannah knew before he spoke that he hadn't found them another place to live.

'It was spoken for just two days ago.' he sighed, 'It'd have been perfect for us.'

It wasn't until they were sitting at their evening meal that Hannah told him about Walter Dewhurst sitting on his horse and staring at Ginny, then making that suggestive remark.

Nathaniel looked so angry she was frightened for him. She waited until the youngsters were in bed and Tom had gone outside to smoke his final pipe of the day, since she refused to have the nasty smelly thing in her clean kitchen. 'You won't – try to do anything about Walter Dewhurst, will you?'

'Not if he leaves Ginny alone. Trouble is he's known for pestering young women – seems to prefer them reluctant. Even *he* doesn't have the right to ravish them, though, and I won't stand by and let him hurt Ginny. One farmer has left the district already because Walter was after his daughter. He didn't say it was that, but everyone knew the real reason. Trouble is, you see, old Mr Dewhurst is the magistrate hereabouts so how can you complain? He seems all right, the old man, and treats you fairly if you do as you should. He isn't severe in his punishments as a magistrate, either, but if it came to his own son, well, he'd not put *him* in jail, would he? I've spoken to some of the fellows in the village and we're agreed that we'll bite our tongues about the other things Walter Dewhurst does, but not about our womenfolk.'

Which didn't reassure Hannah.

The following day was Sunday so they dressed up in their best and went to church, walking into the village together, meeting other families on the way, glad of another fine, crisp day.

Hannah followed the service half-heartedly, feeling nervous about what was to come. And sure enough, when the parson called the banns for her and Nathaniel, heads turned and there was a buzz of conversation.

They waited for the gentry to leave first, old Mr Dewhurst hobbling along with the aid of a silver-topped walking stick. He paused at the end of their pew to say, 'Congratulations, King. I hope you and your good lady will be happy.'

'Thank you, sir.' But Nathaniel was more conscious of the younger man standing behind him, leering at Ginny.

When everyone had filed out, he forgot Walter Dewhurst as he was approached by one neighbour after the other, offering their good wishes to him and his betrothed. It seemed to go on for a long time and he'd really rather have gone straight home, but he was proud of the quietly dignified way Hannah accepted their good wishes, proud of how bonny she looked, too.

The following day at noon, Colin slouched into the village inn and demanded a glass of ale. The landlord served him and would have left him alone, but he showed signs of wanting to chat.

'Funny turn-up, isn't it?' Colin said.

'Eh? What is?'

'That King fellow getting married again. He's only just got shut of one wife. You'd think he'd want to enjoy a taste of freedom before putting his head back into parson's noose. After all, they're living together already.'

'She seems a nice enough woman.'

'Where does she come from, though? She's not local.' Mr Walter thought there was something fishy about the way no one had been told about her family background except that she was a widow, hence Colin's present visit to the inn.

'How should I know where she's from? I mind my own business and leave others to do the same.'

But just as Colin was lifting his pot to drain the last inch of beer, a man came into the inn, a stranger, so he set the glass down after a mere sip and waited to see if there was anything of interest to be gleaned.

'A glass of your best beer, landlord,' the man said. 'And my master would be grateful if you'd put this Wanted poster somewhere people will see it.'

The landlord drew the glass of beer, took the man's money, then picked up the piece of paper, glancing at it incuriously and setting it aside almost immediately.

Colin drained the beer, got up and carried his empty pot to the counter, a courtesy he didn't usually bother with. 'Mind if I have a look?'

'The more folk as see this, the better. He's in a right fussation, my master is, and there'll be no living with him till the madwoman's caught. I've been everywhere you can think of leaving these pieces of paper. Waste of time, I reckon. If the woman's got away, it's less expense on the Poor Rates, in my opinion.'

Colin read the poster quickly, sucking in his breath sharply. 'If you've got another of these, I think my master would be interested as well.'

When he had left, the landlord read the poster properly and exclaimed in dismay. After the stranger had gone, he didn't nail the poster up as he usually would have, but took it through to his wife and showed it to her.

'Nay, who'd have thought it!' she exclaimed. 'She seems so nice.'

'I'd better go and show this to Nathaniel,' Chas said heavily. 'Can't let it come as a nasty surprise, can I?'

The landlord was relieved to find Nathaniel working in the garden, turning over the soil. He called a greeting and went through the gate to join him.

'What brings you out here, Chas?' Nathaniel asked, thrusting his spade into the soil and stepping back to wipe his brow on his sleeve.

'Bad news, I'm afraid.' He hesitated, then said, 'There's no easy way to tell you this, so you'd better read it for yourself.'

Nathaniel took the poster, read it in growing anger, then screwed it up and ground it under his foot. 'I knew about that already, and it's all lies. And to think of her own son being involved in hounding her . . . well, I call that downright disloyal. I don't want you to mention the poster to her.'

'No, of course not.' Chas closed his eyes for a moment in sheer relief. 'You knew, then?'

'Yes, of course I did. Hannah wouldn't lie to me. She was falsely accused by her daughter-in-law and had to run away.'

'Then why are they pursuing her? I never heard of folk sending out posters this far for a madwoman.'

'Sheer spite, I suppose. How should I know?' He looked at Chas. 'You haven't told anyone else about this?'

'No. Nor I shan't put the poster up on the wall.' He hesitated before adding, 'If you're *sure* she's not, well, fooling you.'

'I'm very sure. My Hannah's a fine, decent woman.'

'Well, I'll say nothing more of it, then.'

Only on the way home did the landlord remember that Colin had taken away the second poster, but by that time his feet were aching and he wanted nothing so much as a glass of his own good beer. He'd tell Nathaniel about Colin on Sunday after church.

＊　　　＊　　　＊

Walter laughed aloud when he read the poster. 'We've got him!'

'What do you mean?'

'I mean, I'll write to this Barnish fellow and tell him where to find his madwoman.'

'Is it worth the bother?'

'Oh, yes. It's always worth the bother to make sure a man learns to obey his master.'

But he didn't mention it again, so Colin decided he must have thought again about doing anything.

In church the following Sunday the parson called the banns for a second time. Even as he spoke, a man in clerical garb came striding from the back of the church and shouted, 'I protest! The woman is in no fit state to marry. She's a lunatic, wanted by the Poor Law Guardians of Hetton for escaping their legal custody. We're here to take her back.'

A burly man came to stand at the end of Hannah's pew and Dr Kent moved forward to join Parson Barnish at the front of the church, looking at her sympathetically as he passed.

She clutched Nathaniel's hand, so terrified she couldn't speak for a moment or two.

He put one arm round her. 'I'll not let them take you.'

'How can you stop them?' she asked in a voice that shook. 'There are three of them and one's a parson, another a doctor. They can say and do anything they want and the law will be on their side, not mine. You surely don't think anyone will take my word against theirs?'

He felt sick at the mere thought of them taking her away from him, hurting her again. The son must be a nasty sort to do this to his mother.

The church was abuzz, with everyone exclaiming and asking one another, what next?

In the front pew Walter leaned back, one ankle crossed over the other, and smiled, a smile of pure malice.

Richard Dewhurst frowned at the cleric speaking earnestly to their own parson, then looked sideways, surprising a triumphant expression on his son's face. Was this more of Walter's nasty meddling? He heaved himself to his feet on a sudden impulse and left the pew to join the two clergymen.

'I'm the local magistrate, with jurisdiction over this parish, so I think you'd better explain this to me before you do anything in Marton.'

'There's no need for you to trouble yourself, sir,' Parson Barnish said in a condescending voice. 'We only need to take the madwoman back with us.'

Richard stiffened. Here was another supercilious bugger looking down his nose at him, as so many had since he moved to the country. He slammed his cane down on the floor. 'Oh, but I insist. I take my duties as magistrate very seriously indeed.'

He turned to find Walter at his elbow.

'There's really no need for you to get involved, Father. It's a minor matter. Leave them to deal with it.'

Then he was utterly certain his son was to blame and his heart lurched in pain to think what he had spawned. 'Get out of my sight!' he snapped. 'I'll deal with you later.' He raised his voice to call, 'Lexham! Come and join me. I may need your help.'

Walter gaped at him and flushed in embarrassment for his father's voice had rung out clearly and caused another buzz of comment. He moved backwards, anger seething through him. When his father got that look on his face it was best to humour him because the old fool still controlled the purse strings. But this was yet another reason to get rid of King as soon as he could. His father was taking the fellow's side against him. Senile, that's what his father was! Easily duped.

Jack Lexham moved to join his employer, feeling sorry for him, for he too had seen the gloating expression on Walter's face and guessed he was somehow involved.

Richard turned to their own parson. 'If you'll tell folk to leave the church, we'll deal with this here and now.'

'Yes. Um – certainly.' With a big donation needed for the repair of the steeple, the parson had no intention of offending the richest man in the district. He made the requisite announcement and people filed reluctantly out, craning their heads to stare at Hannah and lingering outside in the churchyard to discuss this scandal with relish.

'You can leave, too!' Richard told his son. 'In fact, go home and then send the carriage back for me.'

Walter spun on his heel and left, getting into the carriage and ordering the coachman to drive him home, but leaving Colin behind with instructions to keep an eye on what was going on and not to come back till he found out.

Nathaniel turned to Ginny and Gregory. 'Go and wait for us outside, but don't go far.'

Ginny nodded, then turned to Hannah and gave her

a hug, whispering, 'I don't believe what they say about you.'

Hannah gave her a tremulous smile. She had lost her usual confidence at the mere thought of being shut up in *that place* again.

'Come to the front, Mr King, and bring your good lady with you,' Richard called.

She had to force herself to move forward, wanting only to sink back in the hard pew and curl up as small as she could. If she hadn't had Nathaniel's arm to cling to, she didn't know how she'd have walked at all.

'Now,' Richard said, 'tell me clearly what this is all about.'

Parson Barnish went through it all again, impatiently, still speaking in a patronising tone to this fellow who might be the magistrate but had clearly not been born a gentleman.

Richard stared at him, disliking the fellow intensely, and then turned to the man who had accompanied him. 'So you're the doctor, eh? What do you have to say about Mrs Firth?'

Maurice wondered if there was any chance of help from this quarter. He had come along determined to tell the truth and not necessarily to do what Barnish wanted. 'I saw Mrs Firth the day after she'd been admitted to the asylum and could find nothing whatsoever wrong with her. She was intemperate in neither language nor behaviour. I kept her in for observation for a few days, during which time she continued to behave perfectly normally, then released her into her son's care.'

Angry at this, Parson Barnish put in, 'These lunatics

can be very cunning, you know. Even a doctor can be fooled.'

'I wasn't fooled.' Maurice glared at him. 'And since that time further information has come into my hands so that I'm now convinced there never was a reason to admit Mrs Firth to the asylum, as I have repeatedly told you, sir.'

His companion scowled at him. 'Keep to the point.'

'This *is* the point!'

'The daughter-in-law tells a very different tale from yours and *she* lived with the woman for months so should know more about her than anyone. Besides, our rules say that an inmate may not be discharged without careful examination and observation, and then only given into the hands of her nearest relative.'

'Which will be me once I've wed her!' Nathaniel put in, seeing a ray of hope suddenly.

Barnish's sneer was pronounced. 'Silence, fellow! Have you not been listening to what I've been saying? Firstly, you are not yet married to her. Secondly, this creature has fooled you as she's fooled everyone else. I saw the poor young woman she attacked, the scratches on her face – does a rational person do that? – and am quite convinced that Firth is not to be trusted in any way.'

'What further information did you obtain, Doctor?' Richard asked.

'I said there was no need—' Parson Bamish began.

Maurice nodded to Richard. 'Thank you, sir. I feel my new evidence *is* important. Mrs Firth's son came to see me because his wife had been behaving strangely. He was sure she had been giving his mother a certain mixture used to calm infants, which makes those who take it in large quantities very disoriented. The wife had also been using it on their infant son, who was so low physically we had to take him away from her and put him into the care of a trusted nurse I employ from time to time. Since when the child is starting to thrive again.'

'Get to the point,' Barnish snapped. 'This information about the child is not relevant.'

'I venture to disagree with you, sir. In the house we found further bottles of the mixture in question. This lady,' he nodded to Hannah, 'told me when I first interviewed her in the asylum that she suspected her daughter-in-law had given her a potion of some sort on two occasions to induce the disorientation, but it took me some time to prove that the young woman in question had indeed been buying this pacifying mixture – and in much larger than usual quantities.'

'So you're convinced that this woman isn't mad?' Richard asked, enjoying the fury on Barnish's face.

'She's definitely not mad. I would stake my reputation as a doctor on it.'

Hannah sagged against Nathaniel in relief. Surely they would stop pursuing her now that the doctor had spoken up for her like this?

'Well, I am not convinced, and I am the one in charge of the Board of Guardians of the asylum, not you!' Barnish snapped. 'It still doesn't mean she can flout the rules – or you, either, Dr Kent! There are proper ways to do things and I insist they be adhered to.'

'Why are you pursuing Mrs Firth like this?' Maurice asked angrily. 'You've wasted the money of the Board on posters and have brought us across country at some expense. It's ridiculous.'

'Because it is my bounden duty to see that the rules are obeyed and because I am not convinced by your specious reasoning. The people of Lancashire have for too long flouted the nation's Poor Laws – for decades, in fact! – and the union of Hetton and its six parishes has been among the worst offenders, as bad as Todmorden and Rochdale. It is part of my remit as Chairman of the Board of Guardians for our combined parishes to ensure that the rules are obeyed to the letter and I shall do my duty whatever the cost.'

Richard frowned. It sounded as though this silly fool had the law on his side, but he felt sorry for the woman, who was looking white and shaken. Eh, to be shut up in an asylum when there was nothing wrong with you. It didn't bear thinking of! From what Lexham had told him, she was a hard-working woman and King certainly seemed taken by her. Well, he had suffered enough. Why should he lose the woman he was to marry as well? And anyway, Richard believed the doctor, not that prating fool of a parson. Pity the couple hadn't got wed already, then the woman would indeed be her husband's responsibility, not her son's.

A grin slid over his face as he suddenly realised how he could help her. He looked across at King. 'Are you still prepared to marry this woman?'

'I can think of nothing I'd like better, Mr Dewhurst.'

Richard looked at his own parson. 'I believe it's in your power to provide a licence and marry them on the spot, since they're both of legal age?' He cocked an eyebrow and leaned his chin on his walking cane, enjoying the expression of outrage on Barnish's face.

'Well – er – I suppose I could do that, Mr Dewhurst.'

'Right, then. Go and get the licence and we'll perform the marriage here and now.'

The parson looked at the landowner's expression, thought of his steeple, and hurried out.

'Sir, I protest!' Parson Barnish said, his face turning deep puce and his whole body radiating anger.

'I think it's an excellent idea,' Maurice said mildly, 'and I shall be glad to stand as witness to the marriage, if you need one, Mr King. Afterwards I shall supply a statement to you and your wife stating that, as a doctor, I believe her to have been maligned and never to have been out of her senses.' He looked at Richard Dewhurst. 'I hope you, as magistrate, will witness my statement, sir?'

'Delighted.'

'I shall ensure you no longer act as doctor to the workhouse, Kent,' Barnish said furiously.

Maurice smiled. 'Where shall you find another who lives close enough? Though I should be happy to relinquish that task, I will admit. Under your direction, sir, conditions there have become unfair and inhumane, and the food supplied less than is necessary for humans to maintain their health.'

'The conditions are exactly as the Act specifies, less attractive than the worst conditions outside the poorhouse.'

'Then the Act also is inhumane and I thank God for the people of Lancashire who had the courage to resist it for so long.'

As he listened to the low-voiced but nonetheless

vehement quarrel, Nathaniel decided he liked this doctor fellow. He patted Hannah's hand as it lay on his arm and she gave him a grateful but still wavering smile.

As the two gentlemen fell silent just then, he looked across at Mr Dewhurst. 'I can't tell you how grateful I am to you for helping us, sir.'

'It makes up a bit for some other troubles you've had, which you didn't deserve, eh?' Richard said, but his smile was sad.

So money didn't necessarily bring you happiness, Nathaniel thought as he realised what the landowner meant. He knew what Walter was like, did he? Poor man. No wonder Richard Dewhurst was looking older and frailer. It'd fret any decent man to have produced a son like his.

As the parson returned just then, Nathaniel said, 'I'll go and fetch my son and niece inside. I'd like them to be with us on this *joyful* occasion.' He turned to kiss Hannah's cheek and walked briskly down the aisle.

It was at that moment, as she watched him stride away, that she knew she loved him. He was a quiet man, but strong and reliable. And although he might not love her, might only be marrying her for convenience, she could hope that he would come to love her a little. Another dream, and a bright one, too. Was she foolish beyond reason to build up her hopes in this way? She let out a long, shuddering sigh. She needed to marry him if she was to stay free, whether he loved her or not. But she also wanted very much to marry him.

Maurice moved across to her. 'You're looking well, Mrs Firth. I'm sure your son would wish me to tell you that he had no part in sending out the posters. For all his name is on them, he knew nothing about them until he found one hidden in a drawer.'

Hannah looked at him, feeling her eyes brimming with tears of relief. 'Thank you for telling me that, Dr Kent. It upset me greatly that Lemuel would hound me so.'

'He'd never do that. He loves you dearly. It's his wife. She's not only been drugging your grandson but is in a most unreasonable frame of mind altogether. We've had to take John away from her and put him out with a nurse.'

'I'm so glad! I've worried about that poor little lad! And you say Patty is behaving strangely?'

'Yes. This happens sometimes when women are expecting or have given birth, we don't know why. We've also moved old Mrs Riggs into the workhouse, poor soul, because her daughter wasn't caring for her properly.'

Barnish came up to them and glared at Hannah. 'You haven't fooled me, woman. You have flouted the law and I shall write to my superiors about it. If there is any justice, you will still be brought back to answer to us.'

'You leave her alone, you miserable old crow!' Richard called from the front pew. 'She'll be under her husband's jurisdiction from now on. And mine. I can't abide men who waste other folk's money to further their own spite.'

Barnish stared at him pop-eyed with shock at this attack, then walked away to the back of the church to sit in the rear pew, with his arms folded and a dark scowl on his face. The man from the asylum, whom he had brought along to help apprehend Hannah, stood uneasily behind him, shuffling his feet.

Richard winked at Hannah, who felt relieved. If this was her husband's landlord, then he was on their side and that could make a big difference to your life.

The door at the rear of the church opened and Nathaniel came in, one hand on his son's shoulder, the other on Ginny's. They both moved to the front to stand beside Hannah.

'I'm so glad you're marrying Uncle Nathaniel,' Ginny said with a smile.

Hannah turned to Gregory. 'How do you feel?'

He hesitated, then muttered, 'I'm glad, too. I didn't know you before, but now I do – well, I don't mind at all.'

Richard cleared his throat. 'Right then, get on with it, man!'

The parson jerked round and said hastily, 'If the bride and groom will come and stand in front of me, we can begin.'

Nathaniel took Hannah's arm and moved forward, gesturing to the youngsters to stand on either side of them.

'We are gathered here today . . .'

The brief ceremony came to a halt when the parson asked for the ring. Nathaniel flushed and looked at Hannah apologetically, so she pulled off her wedding ring and handed it to him.

'I'll buy you your own when I can,' he whispered, looking embarrassed.

'It's not important.'

'It is to me.'

'I now pronounce you man and wife.' The parson looked at them expectantly and then, when they didn't move, said quietly, 'You may now kiss your bride, Mr King.'

Nathaniel and Hannah stared at one another in silence. He kissed her lightly on the cheek, then on the lips.

Richard Dewhurst's voice interrupted them. 'Well, then, do the rest of us not get our chance to kiss the bride?' He stood up and limped forward, leaning heavily on his cane, to place a hearty kiss on Hannah's cheek. Maurice Kent followed suit then Ginny gave them both a hug and Gregory offered another of his shy smiles.

Hannah wished briefly that Malachi and Lemuel were here, but that was foolish.

'We'll just go and fill in the parish register,' the parson said, 'then everything is complete.'

'I'll come too and sign it in my capacity as magistrate and perhaps you'd do the same in your capacity as doctor?' Richard boomed to Maurice Kent. 'We don't want anyone saying afterwards there's anything wrong with the marriage, do we?' He turned to grin at Parson Barnish, whose narrow face was pinched and disapproving.

When the signing was completed Hannah prepared for the next ordeal, that of facing Nathaniel's friends and neighbours, who knew only that she'd been accused of being a madwoman. And indeed, when they went outside, many of the villagers were still waiting, gaping at her as if she had two heads.

Behind her, Richard Dewhurst growled in annoyance and pushed his way past them to call out, 'Pay attention, please, everyone. It was all a stupid mistake. Hannah is no more mad than I am, and so the good doctor has testified. But while we were all gathered here, we decided to marry them off. So let's hear three cheers for Mr and Mrs King!'

After a moment of shocked silence a ragged cheer arose, growing in volume and enthusiasm, then people crowded round Hannah and Nathaniel to shake their hands and wish them well.

Colin watched all this with his usual detached interest. His master would be in a right old taking when he heard what had happened, though he wouldn't dare to vent his spite on his father. It was a turn-up for the books, the old man publicly showing King support like that. Who'd ever have thought it?

He was quite sure his master wouldn't let the matter drop, though, even if he had to wait years to get his revenge. A waste of effort, but that was his way.

And since there was often extra money to be made out of Walter Dewhurst's little schemes, Colin would wait a little longer to leave.

At dinner that evening Richard Dewhurst raised a glass. 'To the happy couple! Eh, I was glad to best that mealy-mouthed hypocrite who came hounding them.'

Walter, who'd been drinking more than usual and who still felt furious about what had happened, said what he thought for once. 'Well, I wish you hadn't.'

'Oh, you do, eh?'

'I'm the one who sent Barnish news that the woman was living in our village. Bad enough to have a disrespectful devil like King – and why you keep him on as a tenant, I don't know – but to see a madwoman join our community, well, it's just plain stupid to allow that.'

'She's not mad. That doctor said so.'

'Ha! The man didn't want to offend a rich landowner like you. He'd have said anything you wanted. I bet Barnish didn't agree.'

Richard glared at him. 'Well, I'm not stupid enough to be taken in and I reckon Mrs King is a good, hard-working woman. That doctor was a decent chap, too. He'd no need to suck up to me because he isn't living on our land. And I'll thank you for not meddling in my tenants' affairs in future. Keep your spite to yourself if you know what's good for you. You're not in charge here yet, and don't you forget it. I'm not nearly ready to cock up my toes.'

Walter thought it prudent to say, 'Indeed, I hope you're not, Father.' But when he went up to his bedroom, he took the brandy decanter with him and sat in front of the fire there, thinking about his future. It was intolerable living here while his father held the reins so firmly in his hands. And lately the old man hadn't been nearly as manageable as he used to be. He'd vetoed several of Walter's suggestions for getting more revenue out of their tenants and had also made it very clear that his son wasn't to damage tenants' crops when he was out shooting. 'Keep to our own land in future,' he'd ordered.

What fun was that? Half the pleasure was seeing the shock on their faces when he and his friends trampled down their stupid crops.

So now Walter's friends were finding their amusement elsewhere while he was more firmly tied to his father's apron strings than ever before.

Would the old bugger never die?

After a while Walter's thoughts turned to Lady Ann Turner. He knew her family wouldn't even consider him as a suitor, but that didn't mean there wasn't a way to marry her. He smiled and raised his glass in a toast to her. If he had to kidnap her to get her, he'd do it. Once she was spoiled goods, her family would soon permit the marriage. Oh, yes.

After all, Walter would be rich one day, very rich indeed. Money always talked in the end.

He went to bed in a more optimistic frame of mine. He could wait to deal with King. But he *would* deal with him one day.

CHAPTER SEVENTEEN

March 1864

As they walked home after church, Hannah turned to Nathaniel. 'It felt strange, people calling me Mrs King.'

'My mother was Mrs King, too.' Gregory stared at her as if surprised by that and not pleased that she had taken his mother's name.

'She was your father's first wife,' Hannah said gently. 'No one can take that away from her. I'm your father's second wife.'

He nodded, kicking at a stone so that she said automatically, 'Don't do that in your Sunday shoes. It'll scratch them.'

'My mother used to say that.'

'She was right.'

He shrugged but didn't kick any more stones.

'We'll all need time to get used to Hannah being my wife.' Nathaniel ruffled his son's hair then unlocked the back door. 'But it's a good thing for us all, son. A man needs a wife and you need a step-mother to look after you.'

'I'd better move my things out of your bedroom now, Hannah,' Ginny said once they were inside. 'Thank goodness there are two beds in Gregory's room! I'd not like to share a bed with *him*.'

The boy stared at her in horror. 'I'm not sharing my bedroom with a *girl*!'

Hannah looked from one to the other. Ginny was near to tears at this blunt rejection. The poor girl cried so easily these days. 'If you don't object, Nathaniel, maybe we could bring one of the beds down and let Ginny use the parlour? After all, we never sit there.'

'Good idea. Come on, Gregory. You can help me move things.'

The boy's frown vanished again. Hannah smiled as she watched him go upstairs. She'd forgotten how touchy lads were at that age.

Ginny looked at Hannah. 'Thank you. You've been so kind to me.'

'What woman wouldn't be kind to another when she's expecting a child? We'll have to start making some clothes for the baby soon, won't we?'

Ginny's face brightened a little. 'Oh, I'd like that. Only you'll have to help me. I'm a good needlewoman, but I shan't know what to make. My mother and I didn't get a chance to talk about – anything.' She hesitated, then added, 'I'm really glad Uncle Nathaniel's married you.'

Hannah hoped *he* would not live to regret it. She had been in so much trouble lately and he had enough problems of his own.

Going to bed that night seemed a huge obstacle. She sat on in the kitchen beyond her usual time, not daring to be the first to suggest it. Gregory went up early, saying he was tired. Ginny soon followed his example, going into the parlour which she had spent hours rearranging.

'Why don't you go up first, lass?' Nathaniel suggested once the two of them were alone.

Hannah nodded, but could feel her cheeks heating up. Her first wedding night had been a disaster. John had taken little account of her needs and it had been a painful experience. Indeed, it wasn't until she took a lover later that she had discovered how wonderful things could be between a man and woman. She wondered now what Nathaniel would be like in bed. She couldn't imagine him being rough with her, but he had never really kissed her, not with passion, so she was more than a little worried about how they would go on together.

When Nathaniel went up to join his new wife, she was lying in bed looking very nervous. His heart went out to her as he blew out the candle and took off his clothes in the darkness, putting on his nightshirt and shivering in the cool air. Before he even got into bed, he said the words he'd been practising downstairs, not the words he'd have liked to say but the words he thought fairer to her. 'I still think we should wait until we know one another better before we make love, Hannah lass. We're almost strangers and you've had a lot to bear lately. Let's not rush things.'

'I'm happy to be your wife, Nathaniel,' she said, but her voice wobbled and she realised she wasn't ready for him to touch her tonight.

'And I'm happy to be your husband, but I want things to be right between us. So we'll wait a little, eh?'

She lay beside him, conscious of his every movement, expecting to find it difficult to sleep, but so weary she could barely move a limb. Before she knew it the warmth of his body had relaxed her and she was sliding towards sleep, welcoming it.

He lay awake a little longer, listening to her soft, even breaths in the darkness. He wanted her, though he knew it wouldn't have been right for her tonight after so many shocks and what amounted to a forced marriage. But he couldn't persuade his body not to want hers.

He gave a wry smile in the darkness. What a way to get married! But thank goodness for Mr Dewhurst's kindness. As long as the old man was alive, he didn't think he need fear any more troubles at his market garden, which gave him a bit of time to look around carefully for another piece of land.

After Dr Kent told him what had happened in Marton, Lemuel thought long and hard, then decided on the unprecedented step of taking a Monday off and leaving the apprentice in charge of the workshop. He checked railway timetables and made an arrangement with the milk cart which collected churns from the surrounding farms to give him a ride to the nearest station, which was in the next village.

Last of all, he told Patty what he intended. He'd been dreading doing this, expecting her to fly into a rage, but this time she didn't shriek at him, turning cold and vicious instead.

'You'll be sorry for that, Lemuel Firth! I always make folk who upset me sorry.'

'It's only natural I'd want to see my mother and meet her new husband, Patty.'

'Only natural!' she mocked. 'She's a madwoman and I'll prove it one day, see if I don't.'

'Why are you still saying that? You know it was you giving her those drops that made her dizzy. She isn't mad, not in any way.'

Patty looked at him so wildly that for the first time he accepted the fact that it was his wife who was becoming distinctly unbalanced. He wasn't even sure whether it was the result of childbirth, as Dr Kent had suggested, or whether Patty had always had this unreasoning streak. She'd been plump and pretty when he met her, and had seemed so loving, making him feel strong and protective. But she'd started changing the minute they got married and now she was a shrew. She'd lost all attraction for him and took little care of her appearance nowadays. The bulge of her belly stretched her skirt tightly, a skirt that had stains on it and splashes of fat from cooking.

He shuddered as a nasty little smile curved her lips. Her fingers curved too, twitching as if she wanted to scratch someone's eyes out, but her voice was still cold and steady.

'I don't know anything of the sort, Lemuel. Your mother *was* mad and I only gave her the drops to calm her down. Parson Barnish believes me, even if you don't. What's more, I don't want to see that Dr Kent again. He took my son away from me and I'll make *him* sorry for that one day, you see if I don't. John was such a quiet little boy, so lovely when he was sleeping. I miss him.' Her voice took on a crooning tone and she rocked her arms to and fro as if she held a baby in them.

He realised with a shock that after this visit to his mother he wouldn't dare leave his wife alone. And when he got back, he'd have to do something about the business, too. Custom was still dropping and folk he'd relied on were turning to the modern tin buckets, bowls and bathtubs that were lighter and so much easier to use, though luckily for him owners of inns still needed barrels for brewing their beer. He was making these for inns in this and the neighbouring villages, but they didn't need enough barrels to bring him in a proper income, and anyway, more and more of the inns were buying their beer from big companies now and using their barrels.

Eh, he'd been so proud to become a cooper like his father, but what use were his skills now?

The next day he set off before it was light. Patty pretended to be asleep, but he knew she was awake. He was relieved when she didn't follow him downstairs. He took a piece of bread and butter and a quick drink of water, then went out to meet the milk cart in the chill light of a winter dawn.

The horses' breath sent clouds of vapour wreathing upwards and his own left a ghostly trail behind him as he climbed on board. The driver had always been a taciturn fellow and Lemuel was glad of that. He wasn't in the mood to gossip with anyone and was still worrying about whether he should be leaving Patty alone.

He hardly noticed the scenery during the train journey, so lost was he in his thoughts, but when the train arrived at Upper Marton station, he breathed a sigh of relief and got out. After asking directions he decided to walk to Nathaniel King's market garden, which lay between the two villages, striding out in the grey light of a cloudy day, very eager to see his mother now.

When he got to the gate with its neat little sign saying *FRESH FRUIT AND VEGETABLES, N. King Proprietor*, he hesitated, hand on the metal loop that latched the gate to the post. Perhaps he should have written to ask if it was all right to come and see her? No, she might have refused, because his name had been on the posters, though Dr Kent had assured her he hadn't known about that. Or her new husband might not want to see him.

He realised suddenly that someone was speaking to him and turned blindly towards the sound.

'Can I help you?'

'Oh. Yes. I'm looking for Mrs – um – King.'

'My wife? Can I ask your business with her?'

'I'm her son, Lemuel Firth.' For a moment he studied the man, who was tall and well-built with a steady look to him, then rushed into speech. 'I have to see her . . . ask her to forgive me . . . make sure she's all right.'

'I'm Nathaniel King.' The man reached out to unfasten the gate and gestured Lemuel inside before holding out his hand in greeting. 'She'll be delighted to see you.' He was surprised at how careworn Hannah's son looked, his hair thin and lank, his eyes ringed by dark circles and his whole bearing dispirited.

Lemuel closed his eyes, relief shivering through him, then hurried to catch up with Nathaniel. Inside the cottage all was cosy. It reminded him suddenly of how his mother had always had this gift for making places feel warm and welcoming. He stood in the doorway, watching her knead the dough as he had watched so many times before. She raised her head slowly to smile at her husband, then stared beyond him at her son.

'Lemuel?' Her voice was a mere whisper. Then she was running round the table, hugging him, laughing and crying at the same time.

And he was crying too, sobbing so hard that Nathaniel gestured to Ginny to come outside and leave them some privacy.

'He's not at all like her, is he?' she said in wonderment.

'No. He's come to make his peace and I know that'll mean a lot to her. You can help me in the potting shed until they've had time to talk.'

'All right.' She linked her arm in his and he smiled down at her as they walked slowly along the dirt path.

In the kitchen Hannah was the first to pull herself together and stop weeping. 'Oh, look what I've done to you! You're all covered in flour.'

'It doesn't matter, Mam.' He gulped back another sob.

She smoothed back the hair from his forehead. 'Of course it does, love. Let me get a damp cloth and sponge you down, then I'll make us a pot of tea. And I'm sure you must be hungry. You must have set off really early to get here by this time.'

It felt wonderful to have her fussing over him again. 'You do believe me, Mam, don't you? I didn't send out those posters, didn't even know about them. And I told folk not to go after you when you ran away. I wanted you to be free, only that parson wouldn't listen to me.'

'Of course I believe you. And because of all the fuss I met Nathaniel, so it's all worked out for the best.'

'You're happy with him?'

'I'm very happy to have married him. We get on well together.'

'That's good.' A moment later he said fretfully, 'I should have stopped Patty ill-treating you, though! I've been weak, not strong like you and Malachi.' He looked at her, his gentle eyes still pleading for forgiveness, as if he hadn't yet taken it in that her love for him hadn't changed.

'Shh, son. Shh.' She took him in her arms and rocked him a little, as if he were still a little lad, not a man taller than herself. 'Least said soonest mended, eh? I'm so glad you came to see me. I can't tell you how glad. I wouldn't dare go back to Hetton, not with that Barnish there. He's a dreadful man.'

She washed her hands, dampened a cloth and wiped down his overcoat carefully to get the rest of the flour off it, then hung it up behind the back door. She couldn't help noticing that his shirt, although it was his Sunday best, hadn't been ironed, or even washed properly. She made him sit at the table, chatting gently while she brewed some tea. 'I'll call Nathaniel and Ginny in now – she's his niece and the poor girl's expecting, but the lad who's the father has moved away so he doesn't even know and Ginny can't find him. Gregory, my stepson, is at school today, so you won't meet him. You must come again one weekend, when we can all be together.'

He stared down at his hands which had suddenly clenched into fists on the table. 'I shan't be able to come again, Mum, not till Patty's had the baby. She's grown even more – difficult than before, not always rational.

Dr Kent says women get like that sometimes after they've had a baby. It may grow worse so I came now, while I still dared. I needed to see for myself that you were all right.'

She gestured round, reassuring him yet again because he needed it repeating until it sank in. 'As you can see, I'm fine. I have my own home again and you'll like my Nathaniel.'

She went to the door to call her husband in and they all sat talking for a while. Then Nathaniel once again left his wife to chat to her son as she prepared their dinner.

'I'll have to leave soon,' Lemuel said, when they'd shared an excellent midday meal. 'I can't stay away too long.'

'I'll walk with you a bit along the lane,' Hannah said.

But it was raining hard and he wouldn't let her get wet. So she stood in the doorway watching him, remaining there long after he'd gone from sight, with trickles of rainwater dropping in front of her from the little porch that sheltered the door. Then she went inside and wept again, for Lemuel and for poor little John who'd been so badly treated by his mother.

She wept sometimes for Malachi, too, wondering where he was and how he was coping in Australia. Eh, she was turning into a right old watering pot and must stop this. She had a lot to be thankful for and look forward to.

When Lemuel got home, Patty was sitting in front of the stove in his mother's rocking chair, with a roaring fire blazing away in it. The flames were so fierce that sparks were flying out and landing on the rag rug his mother had once made. He moved across quickly to turn the damper down.

'Why have you got the fire blazing so high? You could have set the rug alight.'

'To make sure everything burnt up properly.' She didn't look at him but at the fire, continuing to rock.

'To make sure what burnt?' he asked patiently, used to her making a mystery of things.

'The letter from your brother in Australia arrived today.'

'A letter from our Malachi! Where is it?'

She pointed to the flames, smiling even more broadly.

What she had said sank in suddenly. 'You didn't burn it?'

'Of course I did. I said I'd make you sorry, didn't I?' She waved a torn scrap of paper at him. 'I kept a bit, though, just to show you I'm not making it up. I didn't want you to have any doubt that there really was a letter.'

He snatched the bit of torn paper from her and saw Malachi's scrawling handwriting.

'I'm afraid the address you were to write to got burnt up with the rest. Lovely warm flames, it made.' She smiled at him as sunnily as if she'd just told him some good news.

He drew back from her. 'Heaven forgive you for that, Patty, for I never shall. You know how worried my mother and I have been about him going so far away.'

'Yes, I do. I don't blame him for getting away from her, though. But at least you know he's alive now. Wouldn't you like to know what he wrote?'

He looked at her pleadingly.

'He said – ' she paused and laid her hand across her forehead ' – oh, dear, I've forgotten what he said. Silly me!'

She continued to taunt him for days about the letter. He learned not to react. He spoke to the postman and asked for any letters to be left at the inn from then on and not given to his wife under any circumstances. But nothing would bring Malachi's letter back.

When he could speak about the incident without wanting to strangle her, Lemuel went to see Dr Kent, who said it was a bad sign and she needed careful watching.

But how could he watch her and do his daily work?

The wonderful day with his mother glowed in Lemuel's memory still, but he'd paid a heavy price for his outing. It was a while before he could face writing to let her know what had happened, but he made himself do it because at least it proved that Malachi had reached Australia safely. He knew she too would be devastated by what Patty had done.

Nick went back to Blackfold again two weeks later, attending the church service and this time waiting on the way home for Ginny's family, who always walked to and fro on fine days, he knew.

When the Wests turned the corner, he stepped forward into their path. 'Excuse me, could I please have a word with you, sir?'

'What do you want?' Howard asked.

'I want to know how Ginny is.'

Howard's face grew red with anger. 'So you're the

young devil she was seeing. Get out of our way! We want nowt to do with fornicators like you.' When Nick didn't move, he added with great relish, 'She's where you can't reach her – or the bastard you planted in her belly.'

Nick's face turned white and he stared at them in shock. '*She's carrying our child?*'

Christine turned to her husband. 'Please, Howard.'

'Not a word, or you and the boys will be in trouble,' he snarled. He shoved Nick out of their way, then pushed his wife along so hard she stumbled and almost fell. Grabbing her arm, he began dragging her away as fast as he could while the two little boys trailed behind, looking anxious.

Nick ran after them. 'Why didn't you tell me about the baby? I'd be happy to marry her. There's nothing I'd rather do.'

Howard didn't even look at him. 'Because I'm not having her marry such as you.'

'What's wrong with me? I'm heir to a decent farm now – we own it since my grandfather died – and I'm a hard worker. I can easily support a wife. Why shouldn't I marry Ginny, especially if it's my baby? In fact, it's my duty.'

Howard stopped walking to smile at him, a wolfish grin. 'Because I say so. She's sinned and must wear the badge of her shame. If I had my way she'd be in the House of Correction for what she's done, but certain persons thought differently.'

His wife was sobbing now.

'Mrs West, *please*!' Nick called. 'If you have any pity, tell me—'

'She'll say nothing or she knows what she'll get,' Howard shouted, then set off at top speed, again dragging his wife along, her sobs seeming to hang in the air behind them.

Nick went back to the village and out of desperation knocked on the back door of the inn again. The landlady looked at him and sighed to see how unhappy he looked. 'I've not remembered anything.'

He lowered his voice. 'Mr West just told me Ginny's carrying my child. I want to marry her, but he won't tell me where she is. If you hear anything, anything at all . . .'

'Well, if that don't beat all! He allus was a nasty devil, but he's got worse as he's got older.'

'I think Mrs West wants to tell me where she is, but how do I get near her?'

Mrs Feathers frowned. 'He keeps her close. Never seen anything like it. He's turned into a right jealous sort. Still, if I get the chance I will ask her for you and send off that envelope. I still have it safe behind the clock on my mantelpiece.'

When he got home, Nick's mother could tell something was very wrong. She waited until she was on her own with him, then asked him what it was.

He looked at her. 'What do you care? You don't want me to marry Ginny.'

She sighed. 'I don't want you to be unhappy, either, and I can tell something's gone really wrong. Have you – heard some bad news about her?'

So it all came tumbling out.

When he had finished his tale, he didn't wait for her

to say anything, but went up to his bedroom and slammed the door.

Jane sat very still. They had done wrong, burning that letter. She had worried at the time, now she was certain. If another came, she'd not hold it back from him, whatever it cost her to see him mixed up with *that man*'s daughter.

Hannah wept when she received Lemuel's letter, showing it to Ginny, who gave her a long hug, then telling Nathaniel when he came in for his midday meal. He was by her side immediately, his arm round her shoulders.

'Eh, lass, what a dreadful thing to do. That young woman is the one who's run mad. I pity your poor son, I do that.'

'So do I.' She let out a soft breath of air. 'Well, at least I know Malachi got to Australia safely. But oh, Nathaniel, I can't contact him and – and he'll think I haven't bothered to reply.' She broke down and sobbed against her husband's shoulder.

He cuddled her against him, making soothing sounds in his throat, then as she went on weeping, said, 'I'm sure Malachi knows you better than that, love. He'll think the letter went astray and write again.'

That thought gave her hope, but when her husband had gone to work outside again, she admitted to herself that another thing was worrying her greatly. Nathaniel had still not tried to make love to her. In bed he chatted to her or lay quietly beside her; he often fell asleep after she did, she knew. When they were downstairs, he put his arm round her and gave her quick hugs. But never once had he attempted to make love to her, never once had he even kissed her properly on the lips, as a man kisses a woman he desires.

Why not? Did he think she was too old and ugly? Or perhaps he'd only married her out of pity? She hated the thought of that, absolutely hated it.

Oliver was pleased with the progress of his garden. He'd hired labourers who'd dug the ground over thoroughly, then he'd had them re-lay the stone-paved paths and dig out new ones where Lady Ann told him. She'd visited him several times now while out walking with her companion, always refusing to come inside and keeping up the fiction that it was sheer chance that had brought her that way. She usually walked to and from the Priory across the fields, unless it was very wet and muddy. She'd given him a beautifully drawn plan for the garden and checked their progress with it carefully on each visit. He was sure she was enjoying this work hugely.

When he heard the sound of footsteps hurrying down the lane one day, he was puzzled. It sounded as if someone was running and people never even walked this way usually, let alone ran. He hurried across to the wall and saw Lady Ann stumbling along, looking over her shoulder as if being pursued. For the first time she was without her companion.

'Is something wrong?' he called as he ran across to open the gate for her.

She let out a huge sigh of relief. 'He seems to have stopped following me now, but – it sounds foolish – he made me feel quite nervous and suddenly I panicked.'

'Who was following you?'

She flushed. 'Your brother, I'm afraid. He's turned up in Beckleton once or twice now, just sitting on his horse and – and staring at me. I know it sounds odd, but I don't like the way he stares. He never comes near me or tries to speak to me, and usually I have Miss Lewison with me so it doesn't matter. Only she's turned her ankle and couldn't accompany me today and I had the flowers cut, didn't want to disappoint people. So I drove to the village in the carriage and my footman carried the flowers into the church and then left me. He was coming back for me in an hour.'

She paused to draw in a deep breath that was almost a sob. 'Your brother came into the church and I didn't see him at first or hear him. He must have shut the door very quietly. But you can sense it when someone stares at you and I began to feel uneasy, so I turned round and there he was.' She shook her head as if upset still. 'He smiled at me and came closer. I felt uneasy and I asked him to leave, making the excuse that I couldn't work with people staring at me. Then he said. . . ' she gasped for breath at the mere memory ' . . . he said he intended to spend the rest of his life staring at me and I'd better get used to it.'

Oliver stared at her in shock. 'What can he mean?'

'I took it that he wishes to marry me. As if I'd ever dream of accepting someone like him! There's something about him that makes me shudder.' She looked at Oliver apologetically. 'I'm sorry to say this about your brother but once or twice I've overheard the servants talking about how he pursues young women and does other bad things to get his own back on people who've offended him. He – doesn't have a good reputation.'

'I know exactly what he's like and I hope you don't think I'm in any way like him. He made my whole life a misery with his bullying when I was younger, and even when I grew as tall as him, I was never strong enough to fight back. If I tried it only made him worse. I even disguised myself sometimes to get out of the house without him seeing me. Silly, isn't it? You must think me such a coward.'

'I don't. I really don't.'

For a moment her hand rested lightly on his arm and Oliver wished she would never take it away. It was then he realised he'd fallen in love with her. But he must not show his feelings because someone like her was not for him. 'Just before I turned twenty-one I left home. I think that was the happiest birthday of my whole life, even though there was only Nanny to celebrate it with me, because it meant I was free and in charge of my own life.' He gestured around him. 'I'd inherited this house from my godmother, and although my father has disowned me, I have more than enough money to live on. My tastes are simple and – well, I've never been so happy.'

She looked up at him, seeming a little calmer now. 'I *know* you're not at all like him, Mr Dewhurst. You don't look as if you're even related.'

'No, I favour my mother's side of the family.'

She gestured to the house and garden, a wistful smile on her face. 'I envy you your simple life. My father lives in great state in London, though he can't really afford it. He's sent me here for punishment because I wouldn't marry the man he chose, a man who would have paid dearly for the privilege of marrying a Turner of

Iffingham. I took care to say no in such a way that he won't want to ask me again. Father was furious. He hates it here and thinks living in exile in the north will bring me to my senses. Instead, I'm enjoying my respite from him.' And was wondering what to do when her father summoned her back. Did she dare disobey him? He frightened her sometimes, he was so determined always to get his own way, by fair means or foul.

After a pause Oliver said slowly, 'I think I should warn you – when Walter wants something, he'll stop at nothing to get it. You should be very careful about going out on your own from now on if he's pursuing you. Keep the carriage waiting outside the church and the footman in attendance inside if Miss Lewison isn't able to come with you, and perhaps take a maid, too.'

She sighed. 'It was so peaceful here.'

'I'll take you back to the Priory in my trap now, if you wish?'

'We'd have to pass your brother if you did that. He stopped at the end of your lane and called out that he'd wait for me there. I was surprised when he didn't follow me down it. He may still be there, waiting.' She shuddered again.

Oliver was surprised too. Although he knew his father had forbidden Walter to visit him, when had that sort of edict ever stopped his brother? 'I'll send Ned to check whether he's still there, shall I? Ned's working just round the side and it won't take me a minute to ask him. You'll be quite safe here.' He was back almost immediately, worried by how pale and agitated she still looked. 'I think this is one time you should come inside the house. And perhaps you'd like a cup of tea? It's very comforting, a warm drink.'

'Yes, thank you. I would like one.'

He offered his arm and escorted her into the house. Nanny appeared as soon as they crossed the threshold and Oliver introduced them, saying, 'I think we should take Nanny Parkin into our confidence, Lady Ann. She knows what Walter's like.'

His guest nodded and he explained quickly.

Nanny, who already had her suspicions about how Mr Oliver felt about Lady Ann, saw them confirmed by the way he was looking at her. But to her surprise there was a certain warmth in the lady's eyes as they rested on him, and it was clear he wasn't the only one to be attracted. What a pity nothing could come of it, given the differences in their stations. She dismissed the threat from Walter with a wave of her hand. 'If he comes inside this house, there are enough of us here to throw him out again and I can still scream loudly enough to fetch Ned running.'

Which made Lady Ann give a sudden gurgle of laughter. 'I suppose I could scream, too, though I never have.'

'Why don't you go and sit in the front parlour with Mr Oliver, your ladyship?' Nanny suggested. 'I'll bring you some tea and you can calm down again. We can send Penny across the fields to the Priory with a message for them to send the carriage here, if you like? Ned can stay nearby, just in case.'

'I'd love some tea, but if Mr Dewhurst will escort me, I can perfectly well walk across the fields myself.' Ann didn't want anyone sending messages to her father that she'd been taking tea with someone as totally ineligible as the younger Dewhurst brother. She looked round, loving the casual air of this place, its cosiness after the vast echoing – and often cold! – rooms of her own home. 'You'll stay with us while we take tea, won't you – er, Nanny?'

'Mrs Parkin,' Oliver put in. 'And she's my house-keeper, though she used to be my nanny, and a better nurse a boy never had.'

'Get away with you, Master Oliver,' Nanny said, a little flustered by his compliment and the august company she was keeping. 'I'll be back in two shakes, Lady Ann.'

She returned almost immediately to say, 'Ned's in the kitchen, Mr Oliver, and would like a quick word, if you don't mind.'

Oliver excused himself and went to see his groom and general factotum.

'Well?'

'Mr Walter's still there at the end of the lane, walking his horse up and down. He doesn't look best pleased. He didn't see me.'

'Right. Thank you.' Oliver was even more puzzled by this information. Why his brother hadn't simply pursued Lady Ann up the lane to Spinneys, he couldn't imagine. When had Oliver's presence ever been enough to stop Walter doing anything? 'Look, Ned, after Lady Ann has taken tea with Nanny and myself, I'm going to walk back across the fields with her to the Priory. I'd appreciate it if you'd follow us, just in case I need help.' He pulled a wry face. 'I'm no match for my brother, as you well realise, but the two of us together might stand a chance of keeping him at bay.'

'I'll be there, Mr Dewhurst. I can give a good account of myself in a fight, I promise you.'

Oliver returned to the library and spent a blissful half-hour talking to the woman he was growing too fond of, the woman who was so far above him he didn't dare even dream of marrying her.

But it was a privilege to protect her today and that at least he could do. An opportunity to treasure for a man like him, who had always been the one to need protecting before.

Lady Ann left Oliver at the edge of the formal gardens before her father's house, ashamed that she dared not invite him in but knowing he would understand. He seemed to understand so many things without needing to be told. Such a gentle, considerate companion! She had never felt so comfortable in a gentleman's company before. 'I can't thank you enough for your help today, Mr Dewhurst.'

'It was my pleasure and privilege, Lady Ann.'

The formal words were innocuous, but the look in his eyes made her blush – and wonder – and she kept remembering it at the strangest moments. If the suitors her father favoured had been kinder, more like Oliver Dewhurst, she might not have been so set against them.

When she went inside she was informed that her youngest brother had arrived. Gerald was two years older than herself and had no doubt been sent by their father to keep an eye on her. Her idyll must be coming to an end. Sighing, she rushed up to change her clothes, knowing how her family fussed when she dressed simply to please herself.

She sighed again as she looked at herself in the mirror when she was ready. Rich, fussy clothes didn't suit her, never had, with her plain face and freckled complexion. She had felt ridiculous during her London season and had always been quite sure that the two men who'd offered for her were seeking an alliance with her family rather than wanting *her* for a wife, for they'd never looked at her admiringly even though they'd paid her compliments.

Downstairs, she found Gerald lounging in the drawing room.

'Ah, there you are! Where on earth have you been?' he said crossly.

'I decided to walk back from doing the flowers in church. Our gardens here are so beautiful.'

He gave a scornful sniff. 'Give me London any day.'

She didn't even try to explain what had happened to her. 'What brings you here, then?'

He gave an aggrieved sigh. 'Same as you. Punishment from Father.'

'What for?'

'I got into debt. Well, everyone gambles, don't they? Only it seems the family's running rather short of money. Rural rents aren't what they were and some of our investments haven't done well lately. So Father was furious when he had to pay my debts – only a few thousand! – and now he's looking out for an heiress for me.' Gerald grimaced. 'She's bound to be ugly, they always are. But I'm not to go back to London until he gives express permission and he won't pay any more of my gambling debts.' His gloom deepened visibly. 'This isn't even good hunting country. What are the neighbours like?'

'I don't know. I've been living very quietly. Father said I was not to go out in the evenings or visit neighbours.'

Gerald rolled his eyes. 'Well, you were probably right to stay in, then. To tell you the truth, he frightens me when he gets *that look* on his face. I wouldn't care to cross him then.'

'Even Mother treads carefully with him,' Ann agreed.

When she went up to change her clothes yet again for dinner, she worried over what her brother had been telling her. If her father was short of money and looking for an heiress for Gerald, she was sure he was also considering how he could use his only unmarried daughter as an asset. No wonder he'd been so furious when she'd turned down two eligible suitors.

She was twenty-two, of legal age and in possession of a modest income of her own – well, modest by her father's standards, she realised suddenly. But perhaps it was a generous income by other standards? She didn't even know, had never had to deal with money. She supposed she could refuse to do his bidding, but knew she would hesitate to cut herself off from her brothers and sisters – and would be afraid of making her father angry. They all were.

Her peace had been ruined in more ways than one today and she felt as if something ominous was hovering, even here in the peaceful Lancashire countryside. She smiled at herself for being foolish, then remembered again the way Oliver Dewhurst had looked at her and blushed so furiously she had to turn away from the mirror.

What on earth had got into her? He wasn't and never would be an eligible suitor in her father's eyes.

CHAPTER EIGHTEEN

March – April 1864

By sheer chance the landlady of the inn in Blackfold saw Christine West at a market stall and remembered the unhappy young man who was trying to do the right thing by Ginny Doyle. Mrs Feathers waited until Mr West was a few paces away then edged closer to his wife. 'I have Nick Halstead's address and if you'll tell me where your Ginny is, I can let him know,' she murmured.

Christine was so startled she couldn't speak for a moment and by the time she did her husband had returned and was looking suspiciously at the landlady.

'Is that woman annoying you?' he asked, not troubling to lower his voice.

Christine pulled herself together. 'Good heavens, no! She was merely passing the time of day.'

'*My* wife does not associate with a publican's wife!' He turned his back on Mrs Feathers. 'Have you much more to buy?' he asked Christine brusquely.

'I'm nearly finished now.' She made a couple more purchases and allowed him to hurry her along. Although he hadn't tried to thump her again since she had fought back, he was still inordinately suspicious of everything she did and she was beginning to grow weary of his insistence that she not leave the house except in his company. But she didn't have the energy to fight this edict. She seemed tired all the time lately. It was all she could do to manage her daily tasks.

For the next two weeks on market days Christine tried to find an opportunity to speak to Mrs Feathers, but though she believed she had succeeded in making the other woman realise she wanted to say something, Howard's watchfulness prevented her from actually doing anything about it.

She began to despair of ever achieving her goal. She knew she could do little for her poor daughter now except for this. Howard wouldn't even allow her to write to Ginny and had returned unopened a letter that came from Marton.

Christine felt very unhappy about the prospect of spending the rest of her life living like this. Only what choice did she have? She was not only dependent on Howard herself but had her sons to raise and protect from him as much as possible. She couldn't run away and leave them. But, oh, she felt so helpless and unhappy, weeping often when she was alone in her kitchen.

And when he saw her reddened eyes, he would smile as if pleased by her wretchedness.

Walter rode over to Beckleton, standing outside the church while Colin walked his horse up and down the street. Why hadn't Lady Ann come to arrange the flowers at her usual time? Had he been too abrupt, frightened her off? He'd better tread more carefully for now, but he'd do more than frighten her with words once he had her in his power.

He turned round impatiently and bumped into a tall gentleman, somewhat younger than himself, with a discontented expression on his face. 'Sorry, sir. I wasn't looking where I was going.'

The other man shrugged. 'No harm done.' He stared up and down the street. 'What the hell do people do to pass the time in this benighted place? There are no shops, no polite society, nothing.'

Walter studied him more closely. 'You're from elsewhere, I take it?'

His companion nodded. 'Staying at the family home, the Priory, don't you know. M'father decided I needed to live quietly for a time.' It was his turn to study his companion, who was dressed like a gentleman but looked more like a prize-fighter with that build and those heavy features. Gerald returned to his scrutiny of the street. 'Damn it all, I'll go mad here!'

Walter smiled. 'I sympathise with you, sir. My own father also keeps me tied to the family estate, which is nearby.'

'There isn't any decent hunting in this part of Lancashire, so I hear.' He stuck out his hand. 'Sorry. Didn't introduce myself. I'm Gerald Turner.'

Walter felt a sense of triumph run through him. Fate had been kind to him at last. He shook the proffered hand. 'I'm Walter Dewhurst.' He tried to speak casually. 'Care for a glass of beer? The landlord of the Golden Ball is noted for the excellence of his brew, but the wines he sells are very ordinary.'

'Can't say I know much about beer, but happy to try a glass of the local stuff with you.'

Walter led the way across the street and into the inn

where he spent an hour chatting to Ann's brother and arranging to meet Lord Gerald the following day to shoot pigeons in a wood on the Dewhurst estate.

When Gerald got back to the Priory he went looking for his sister, finding her in the garden kneeling in the dirt and wearing clothes that looked like dish rags. She was humming to herself and didn't notice him at first.

'Aren't there gardeners to do that?' he grumbled, by way of a greeting.

'There are plenty of gardeners, but this was our grandmother's own garden and I like to look after it myself.'

'Father would be furious to see you grubbing in the dirt like a peasant.'

'There's nothing I enjoy more.'

'Come and play billiards instead,' he coaxed.

'No, thank you. I want to finish weeding this flower bed.'

He scowled at her and began to walk up and down a nearby path, hitting out at any tall flower that came within his reach.

'Don't do that!' she shouted, furious to see beautiful blooms wantonly destroyed.

He grinned and hit out at another clump.

She picked up a handful of earth and threw it at him, hitting him smack in the face and wiping the smile off it.

He looked down at himself and tried to brush off the stains. 'What the hell did you do that for? I'll have to change into a clean shirt.'

'I'll do the same thing any time you come here destroying my flowers.'

The anger faded from his face and he smiled reluctantly. 'Regular little firebrand, aren't you?'

'No. But I don't like to see my flowers spoiled.'

'Didn't think anyone would care about a few measly flowers.'

'I love them. I'm like our grandmother in that respect.'

'Sorry. Won't do it again. I was just bored.'

She smiled her forgiveness. Gerald was her favourite brother, though he was as selfish as the others. But he was incapable of entertaining himself and would be pestering her to join him at every opportunity from now on, she knew.

'Well, love them tomorrow. I'm bored and you're not too bad at billiards,' he wheedled.

With a sigh, Ann allowed him to pull her to her feet and went back to the house, casting one longing glance over her shoulder as he held open the small wrought-iron gate that marked the entrance to her grandmother's exquisite garden.

When she came downstairs from changing she found Gerald in the billiards room and took up a cue. She let him break then applied herself. If she had to have him here, she'd prefer him to be in as good a mood as possible.

As they were finishing their first game, he looked at her. 'This chappie I met . . . I wouldn't mind inviting him over here. We could play a few games of billiards – he's bound to be better than you, you obviously haven't been practising – and we could get out the targets and have a shooting practice. He sounds as if he knows how to handle a gun.'

'Oh? Who is he?'

'He's called Walter Dewhurst.'

'*What*?'

'Do you know him?'

'Not as such but he has a terrible reputation. Fathers round here have to protect their daughters from him, and he and his friends trample over crops and destroy people's livelihoods when they're out shooting ground game.'

'He seems all right to me. You don't want to believe everything you hear.'

'I don't. I was introduced to him once, but a few days ago he came into the church and informed me, if you please, that he intended to marry me.' Ann shuddered, as she did every time she remembered that incident.

Gerald roared with laughter. 'There's nothing like being blunt!'

'It's not funny! If you bring him here, I'll write to Father and complain. Walter Dewhurst is *not* the sort of person you should introduce to your sister, believe me.'

He sighed. 'All right. I'll go over and visit him instead.'

'You're not going to make friends with him?'

'Why shouldn't I? I'll go mad here if I have nothing to do. I've not sunk so low as to take up gardening!'

'But surely there are more suitable people than *him*?'

'Not of my own age. And anyway, if you're not allowed out in the evenings – and Father particularly emphasised that – it's a bit hard to socialise with the neighbours, isn't it?'

He changed the subject and with that she had to be

satisfied. Only she wasn't. It made her uneasy to think of Gerald getting on friendly terms with *that man*, whether he brought him to the Priory or not.

Richard Dewhurst stared at the accounts from his cotton mills, which his man of business had just brought, and shook his head regretfully. A good thing he had diversified his holdings or he'd really have been feeling the pinch financially. A good thing, too, he used the Bank of Liverpool, which was also riding this difficult period for the cotton industry quite well. 'We're going to have to close the mills down again. Cotton still isn't coming through regularly enough to keep the operatives on full time.' He saw the other man open his mouth then shut it again. 'Well, what is it? You were about to say something.'

'I was just hoping you could find other tasks to occupy the operatives, sir. There's no other work and they're half-starved as it is. Some owners are taking the opportunity to clean the mills from top to bottom, using their own labour. It's better to find them work than offer them charity, as I'm sure you'll agree. That way we'll keep our skilled workers, ready for when they can start work properly again. People say the war in America can't last much longer.'

Richard chewed the inside of one cheek. Ten years ago he'd have scoffed at the mere idea of paying out good money in charity, but now, well, he had more than enough for his own needs so why not help others, particularly his own workers? Walter would only waste his inheritance when he got his hands on it. 'All right. Tell the managers of the various enterprises to work out how best to do it.' He reached for his pen and dipped it in his inkwell. 'I'll write you a draft on my bank and you can pay out the money as the managers need it.'

He mentioned this plan to Walter over dinner and wasn't surprised when his son was vehemently opposed to it.

'What do they think we are? A bloody charity?'

'It's a drop in the ocean to us,' Richard said mildly. 'I think you should reconsider, Father.'

'Are you telling me how to manage my money?'

Walter breathed deeply and managed to say, 'No. Just offering an opinion.'

'Well, you've offered it now. And you know nowt about running cotton mills, so your opinions aren't worth much. Talk about summat else.'

Walter hated it when his father slipped into the coarse speech of his boyhood. How was the family ever to be taken seriously by those who mattered with a man like that at its head?

He said as much to Colin the next day, but his groom shrugged unsympathetically. 'Those who hold the purse strings hold the reins. And your father's well thought of, for all his lowly background, or they'd not have made him a magistrate.'

Walter met Lord Gerald again to shoot pigeons, after which they repaired to the nearest inn. Over a glass of beer, he discovered how much his companion loved to gamble.

'We could play a few hands of card at my place, if you like.'

Gerald shrugged and spread his arms wide. 'I've nothing to bet with.'

'I'll give you a hundred pounds credit.'

'And if I lost, how would I pay you back? I don't play if I can't pay.'

'Taking tea with your sister would be worth a hundred pounds to me.'

Gerald frowned at him and shook his head, but later boredom got the better of him and he took up his new friend's offer.

Ginny was looking a lot better and taking a more active part in the housework and chores, which allowed Hannah to get outside from time to time and work with her husband in the garden, something she loved. With spring on them there was suddenly a lot of work to do and even Gregory joined in when he came home from school.

'What shall you do if you find another piece of land to lease?' Hannah asked Nathaniel as they pricked out seedlings together.

'Salvage what I can and get out of here quickly.'

She looked at him. 'You're worried?'

He nodded. 'I've seen Walter Dewhurst hanging round nearby again. And that groom of his. I can't help wondering what they're doing. If that man thinks to make use of Ginny, there'll be trouble.'

'Don't get into a fight with him, Nathaniel. The rich have all the power.'

'You'd let him pester Ginny?'

She shook her head. 'No. But maybe we should just keep her closer to home.'

'I thought she was.'

'Well, she nips along to the farm sometimes for milk when Gregory's at school.'

'Where is she now?'

'Getting the milk.'

He stood up, stretching his back and rocking it to and fro. 'I need a break from bending. I'll walk along to meet her. You and Tom carry on here. In future she's not to fetch the milk alone.'

Hannah couldn't hold back the words. 'Be careful, Nathaniel.'

'Don't worry about me, lass. I can hold my own as long as I'm not facing three opponents at once. And round here I have a lot of friends who'd stand by me.'

She worked on, but felt uneasy.

Nathaniel strode along the lane to the farm. As he got near their gates, he heard his niece's voice. She was pleading with someone to let her pass. He speeded up into a run and just round the corner came across Dewhurst's groom barring Ginny's way.

Hearing his footsteps, the man spun round to face Nathaniel, but not in time to duck a cracking blow to the jaw that sent him stumbling backwards to the ground.

'You all right, lass? He didn't touch you?'

'No.' Ginny moved towards her uncle, looking shaken.

'Better stay behind me in case he wants to make a fight of it.'

Colin got to his feet, one hand holding his jaw. 'There was no need for that, King. I was only talking to her.'

'Then why was she asking you to let her pass? And there's no reason for you to talk to her anyway.'

Colin grinned. 'My master doesn't think so. And surely you don't want to offend him again? After all,' his glance flicked to Ginny's belly in a way that was insulting, 'she's not exactly a virgin. He'd pay well for her favours.'

Ginny burst into tears.

Nathaniel glared at the groom. 'This baby was got out of love. She has a family to look after her so you can tell your master to find his pleasures elsewhere, though there's no one in this district would let *him* near their lasses.' He put one arm round his niece's shaking shoulders and walked off down the lane, listening carefully in case the man tried to follow and attack him.

But Colin didn't move. When Nathaniel looked round on reaching the gate, the groom gave a mocking salute and blew a kiss to Ginny.

That night, Nathaniel sat lost in thought. When the youngsters had gone to bed, he looked at Hannah. 'I'm wondering if we should just up and leave.'

'Because of what happened today?'

'Aye.'

'But you'll lose everything and then how will you set yourself up again?'

'That's what's holding me back. Oh, hell, why can I not find another piece of land?'

Two days later Gerald went to find Ann as she was working in the garden. He took care not to tread on any of her precious plants as he wondered how to begin, then decided to come straight out with it. 'I need a favour.'

'Oh?'

'I want you to invite Walter Dewhurst to tea here.'

'I've told you what he's like. How can you even ask it of me?'

'Because if you don't do it, then Father's going to be furious and he'll likely come up here and chew my ear in person.'

'Why?'

'I promised him I wouldn't gamble.' He watched her reactions carefully. 'Only it ain't so easy to give it up. It's, you know, exciting. Anyway, I lost a hundred pounds to Dewhurst and *he* says it'd be worth a hundred pounds to him to have tea with you.'

'I'll give you a hundred pounds myself, but I'm *not* having that man here.'

'I'd not take it. A gentleman don't sponge off his sister, dammit.'

'But he can ask her to associate with unsavoury types like Walter Dewhurst to pay off his debts? No, thank you very much.'

He glared at her. 'Well, he's coming to tea today and I insist on your joining us.'

'Didn't you hear what I said? I won't associate with him.'

'If you don't, I'll tell Father about your visits to Oliver Dewhurst.' Gerald smiled as he watched the expression of consternation on her face. 'If *he* is good enough for you to visit, then his brother is good enough to come to tea.'

'I'm only helping him landscape his garden. I don't go inside the house.'

'That's not what I heard.'

She bent over a patch of flowers, caressing them with her fingertips, feeling trapped. 'Very well. I'll join you for tea – but this one time only,' she said icily.

CHAPTER NINETEEN

April 1864

The tea party was a stiff affair, with Gerald trying to fill the silences with jovial remarks, Ann making no attempt to maintain a conversation and Walter spending most of his time staring either at his hostess or the faded elegance of the room. The Marquess of Iffingham definitely needed money, he thought scornfully, and even if Lady Ann did treat him like dirt now, she'd soon come round when she found out how much he was worth. And if she didn't become more amenable, well, he'd force things along.

He stayed until Gerald tipped him the wink to leave, as they'd arranged, then said farewell to his hostess, raising her hand to his lips and keeping them pressed against her soft skin until she dragged it away. He watched her wipe it surreptitiously on her skirt and his anger grew. By hell, he'd make her pay for that insult one day! he decided as he waited for his carriage to be brought round. He'd have her crawling to him soon enough.

When he got home, he was told his father wanted to see him so went to the library with a sigh of resignation.

'I hear you're sniffing around Lady Ann Turner at the Priory,' the old man said, coming straight to the point as usual.

'Yes. I intend to marry her.'

'They'll never allow it.'

'Maybe I'll make sure they have to.'

His father looked at him narrowly, not troubling to hide his disgust. 'What sort of a marriage would that be?'

'The sort that suits me. It's *her* I want and no other.'

'Yet I hear you're sniffing round King's niece as well?'

'Not with marriage in mind! Why shouldn't I have her? She's carrying someone's child so she's spoiled goods already. But she's not so far along she couldn't give a man a bit of fun in bed.'

'You'll stay away from her.'

'It's none of your business.'

'It is while her uncle's a tenant of mine. In fact, stay away from the daughters of all my tenants.'

'They'll be *my* tenants one day.'

'Only if I choose to leave everything to you.'

Walter stared at him in shock. 'Who else is there to leave it to now?'

'No one. But if you push me far enough, I'll leave my fortune to charity. I'm still in charge here and don't you forget it! Every penny you spend, every mouthful you eat, comes from *my* hard work. What have *you* ever done with your life but destroy things and—' Richard broke off to press one hand against his chest, his face turning dark red and sweat pearling his brow.

Walter waited, hoping the old sod would have a seizure, but gradually his father's high colour subsided and he let his hand fall.

'Help me up to my room,' he commanded abruptly.

When his father had some difficulty standing, Walter moved forward to help him up, then offered him an arm as they walked slowly up the stairs.

Almost at the top, the old man paused again. 'Pain,' he muttered. 'Hurts.' He let go of his son's arm and teetered for a moment.

Walter saw his chance and moved ahead, deliberately pushing him aside. The incredulous expression on his father's face as he shoved the old bugger hard delighted him. He watched with pleasure as the old man bounced down the stairs, cracking his head against the wall and tumbling from side to side like a rag doll until he lay sprawled on the black and white tiles at the bottom.

Running lightly down the stairs after him, Walter felt for a pulse, praying that the fall had done the trick. A slow smile spread across his face as he found no sign of a heartbeat, though he checked again to be quite certain his father was beyond saving before calling for help.

When their guest had gone, Ann scowled at her brother. 'Under no circumstances will I entertain that man again.'

'You will, you know. Or you'll not be seeing your lover again.'

'I have no lover so you can run to our father with whatever tales you like, it makes no difference to me. Walter Dewhurst is –' she shivered, searching for a word and finding only ' – evil. I hate even to be in the same room as him.'

'Don't be stupid! You're letting your imagination

run wild. Dewhurst is going to be a very rich man one day, far richer than your other suitors were.'

'Money wouldn't change my feelings. I'd not marry him if he were the richest man in England. I shall give orders that he is not to be admitted into this house again.'

'I shall countermand them.'

'Then I shall stay in my room while he's here.'

She went upstairs to change out of the clothes she was wearing because she felt soiled by her encounter with such a man.

The minute he heard that his employer was dead, Jack Lexham told his wife to begin packing and went into Preston to find them a house to lease. He wasn't short of money and he wasn't staying in the Dewhurst employ for a minute longer than he needed to. Under no circumstances would he work for Walter.

After some thought he sent a message to Nathaniel King asking him to call the following day. When Nathaniel turned up, Jack didn't mince his words. 'If you'll take my advice, you'll get out of Marton quickly.'

'I've nowhere to go, no way of earning my bread if I leave.'

'And if you stay, what then? Can you face Walter Dewhurst kidnapping your niece and having his way with her?'

Nathaniel had never felt so helpless. 'Surely it won't come to that? This is eighteen sixty-four, not the Dark Ages.'

'Even today rich men can get away with many things that would send poorer men to prison – trampling your crops, for example.' He thought for a moment, then said, 'Oliver Dewhurst once told me to let him know if you were in trouble. He thinks well of you. Perhaps he can help.'

'What can he do?' Nathaniel asked. 'He's not a rich man and I reckon he's had his own troubles with his brother.' He sighed. 'I thank you for your concern, Mr Lexham, but I've no choice except to give it a little while longer. Maybe Mr Walter will be too busy enjoying his inheritance to bother about small fry like me.'

'I doubt it. He harbours a grudge against you, whether justified or not.'

'Well, I'll at least wait till after the funeral and see how things go. I can always up stumps then if I need to.'

Jack watched him go, shaking his head, feeling really worried about the Kings. He scrawled a note to Oliver, who would be coming across for the funeral, explaining that he was concerned about them and asking if he could have a word after the ceremony was over.

A hand-written letter arrived at the Priory addressed to Lord Gerald Turner. He frowned at it, not recognising the handwriting. When he opened it, he found it was an invitation to himself and his sister to attend Richard Dewhurst's funeral. He went to find his sister, whistling cheerfully.

'Look what just arrived.' He handed her the piece of paper.

Ann read it, lip curling in disgust when she realised who must have sent it. 'I shall certainly *not* attend. I didn't know Mr Dewhurst and I don't wish my name to be associated with his son's.'

'Don't be stupid. This is your chance to do well for yourself, if you would only think about it.'

Her brows rose. 'Do well for myself? With *that man*?'

She looked so like their grandmother he blinked in shock then grabbed hold of her arm as she turned away. 'You know what I mean. Walter is now one of the richest men in Lancashire.'

'I loathe him.'

'You haven't given him a chance. And anyway, what does that matter? He's besotted with you. Come on, Ann, you know people of our class don't marry for love but for money and position. At least Walter's a young man, unlike the last one Father found for you.'

'I wouldn't marry men of far better character in London, and no amount of money would ever force me to ally myself with *him*.'

'Father won't see it that way once Walter approaches him. He'll make sure you do the right thing.'

'The right thing by whom?'

'The family, of course.'

She realised yet again how very little her nearest relatives cared for her happiness. The brother who had once seemed closer to her than any of the others was prepared to bargain away her time to win himself gaming money. The father who should be looking after her had sent her away for punishment and made no effort to get in touch with her since – and wouldn't until he needed something from her. Her mother did as her father told her and had rarely spent even half an hour voluntarily with any of her children.

The only person who had ever loved Ann had been her grandmother, who had invited her to visit the Priory several times a year and shown her how to care for flowers and make gardens. They were the golden times of her childhood.

She went to stand by the window. She could sense a crisis approaching. Could she simply abandon her family and set herself up in a home of her own? She was of age, had her own money, but – there was her father. She wouldn't put it past him to take her back to London by force and then find some way to coerce her into doing as he wished. He hadn't tried that when she'd turned down her last suitor because she'd offended the man. Afterwards, however, he'd warned her that it was the last time she would be allowed to oppose his will.

So she had to make it impossible for him to force her into an unwelcome marriage. And quickly. But how?

Oliver didn't receive an invitation but nonetheless returned to his old home for the funeral. He felt desperately sad that he'd not been able to make things up with his father, had never even seen the old man alive again after he'd left.

In Marton Hall he was shown into the library where Walter was sitting in state. His brother stared at him coldly. 'I suppose it'd cause talk if you didn't attend, but you're to leave immediately afterwards.'

'Very well.'

'Sit down. It's not time to go yet.' He began to pace up and down the room and at one stage paused to ask, 'Like living in poverty, do you?'

'My tastes are simple. I have more than enough for my needs.'

'Well, just as long as you don't expect anything from the will – or from me.'

'I don't.'

There was a knock on the library door. 'The carriage is here, Mr Dewhurst.'

Walter scowled at his brother. 'You'd better ride with me, I suppose.'

At the funeral he looked round, smiling when he saw Lord Gerald then frowning when he realised Lady Ann wasn't with her brother. Stupid bitch! She was playing hard to get, but it would do her no good. He had all the power of a vast fortune behind him now and would spend whatever was necessary to get her.

Oliver watched his brother feign a sad expression whenever he remembered that he was supposed to be in mourning; mostly Walter looked smug and self-satisfied. He'd put on some more weight in the past few months and it didn't suit him. His heavy features looked coarse and red against the black clothes, and his hands were as ill cared for as always.

After the funeral and interment he turned abruptly to Oliver. 'You've no need to come back to the house.'

'As you wish.' He had sent the hired carriage to wait in the village and would enjoy the brisk walk to get to it.

'Ahem.'

They turned to see Bentley, the family lawyer, standing next to them.

'I'm sorry to trouble you, Mr Dewhurst, but I couldn't help overhearing what you were saying. The thing is, your father specifically asked that your brother be present for the reading of the will.'

Walter's expression froze. 'Why?'

'I'm not at liberty to say until the reading, sir.'

He turned angrily to his brother. 'Have you been sucking up to Father?'

'No. I've not spoken to him since I left home.'

Walter frowned, pursed his lips, then muttered, 'I believe you. You always were too stupid to look after your own interests.' But his father's wish worried him. He could absolve Oliver from any suspicion of trying to influence the old man, but Bentley had visited the house a few times in the past month or two and Walter just hoped his father hadn't gone soft in his dotage and left any money to his younger son. Because if he had . . . Walter smiled. If he had, then something would have to be done about it.

After all, he'd got rid of his father, hadn't he?

Lady Ann slipped out of the house by a side door and hurried through the gardens. She waited in the grove until she was sure she wasn't being followed, then hurried across the fields to Spinneys. There, she asked to see Mrs Parkin.

Nanny received her in the front parlour, looking as if she'd just woken from a nap.

'I'm sorry to disturb you, but I wonder if you'd give this letter to Oliver the minute he gets back from his father's funeral? It's very urgent indeed.'

'Of course, dear. Of course. I'll put it on his desk.' Nanny was intrigued that the visitor had called him 'Oliver' not Mr Dewhurst. How close were the two of them?

'I'd rather you gave it directly into his hands.'

'Very well. May I offer you a cup of tea, my lady?'

'No, thank you. I have to get back.'

When she'd gone, Nanny picked up the letter, studied it carefully but gained no insight from the simple inscription 'Mr O. Dewhurst' on the envelope, and in the end was forced to contain her impatience.

Ann hurried back the way she had come and spent a little time in the rose garden, making sure her skirt was crumpled and dirty to show she'd been kneeling down.

'We didn't know where you'd gone,' Miss Lewison said in a fluttering, anxious voice when she finally went back inside.

'I was out in the gardens, where else?'

'But I looked and you weren't there. Not in your grandmother's garden, anyway.'

'No. I felt like a stroll first, then got tempted into some weeding.' Ann looked down at her skirt. 'Oh, dear, I'd better go and change.'

The lawyer looked at the two brothers. 'I shall not read the entire will unless you specifically wish it. It's quite complex, but its contents can be summed up easily enough. The majority of Mr Dewhurst's fortune and holdings have been left to you, sir.' He bowed to Walter, then turned to Oliver. 'However, he had a change of heart about disinheriting you and has left you twenty-thousand pounds.'

Walter glanced quickly at his brother's face and saw only surprise. He couldn't blame this on Oliver, annoyed as he was about losing anything. 'Lucky you,' he said sourly, wondering what to do about it. He turned back to the lawyer. 'How much?'

'Pardon?'

'How much am *I* worth, give or take a thousand or two?'

'About a million pounds, if we count the mills and the estate and your father's other investments.'

Walter threw back his head and laughed before turning to his brother. 'Then your measly portion doesn't matter. You can leave now, and don't come here again.'

Oliver stood up, making no attempt even to nod farewell. He was surprised and pleased about the legacy, but could have managed perfectly well without it. For the first time, however, he wondered if it wouldn't be wisest to sell Spinneys and move elsewhere, as far away from his brother as possible.

But that would take him away from Lady Ann, too. And although he had no hope of marrying a woman of her status, he could at least remain her friend, surely?

Outside he remembered Jack Lexham's note so he made his way into the village on foot, calling in at the estate office there.

Jack saw him coming from the window and opened the door to him. 'I'm glad you came. I wanted to say goodbye and to ask your help with King who is, unless I'm much mistaken, about to be thrown off his small-holding.'

'Can my brother do that without notice?'

'Oh, he'll get the lawyer to trump up some charges of mismanagement. It's easily done if you're unscrupulous.'

'I see.'

'Can you help him, Oliver lad?'

'I'll find a way.'

'You'll go and see him before you leave?'

Oliver looked at him in surprise. 'Do you think it's that urgent?'

'Yes, I do. You know how your brother holds grudges and who's to restrain him now?' Jack hesitated then added, 'And I'd be careful on your own account, if I were you. Your father kept your brother away from you by threatening to cut off his inheritance if he went near you, pretending it was because he was angry with you but really to protect you. He asked me to tell you that once he was dead.'

'Ah. That explains it.' It wouldn't keep Walter away from now on, but the nagging unhappiness inside Oliver eased a little. His father *had* cared for him. Even today's legacy had been carefully estimated – not enough to upset Walter, but enough to make a difference to Oliver.

He went to see Nathaniel, who was grateful for his offer of help and admitted freely that he reckoned his new landlord would throw him out as soon as his lease was up.

There was a lot to think about as Oliver was driven home. But the thing that worried him most was: what would his brother do now that there was no one to restrain him? He dreaded to think.

When he got back to Spinneys, Nanny gave him a letter and he stared at it in surprise, seeing Lady Ann's handwriting which he recognised from her garden plans.

'Well, aren't you going to open it?'

'In a moment.' He told Nanny about his windfall from his father and she beamed at him. 'The best thing is, it shows my father had forgiven me. That means a lot to me.'

Afterwards, he went into the front parlour and opened the letter, reading it once, then re-reading it more slowly because he couldn't believe its contents.

Dear Oliver,

I'm writing to ask your help, because I'm in desperate circumstances – or I shall be shortly.

My father is short of money and is pressing those of us who are unmarried to make good matches that will bring money into the family. In other words, he is selling us to the highest bidders. My brother doesn't seem to mind but I find I do, especially as the highest bidder for me appears to be your brother whom I loathe.

I hope you won't think me too forward but I need to get away from my family in such a way that they cannot drag me back and force me to marry – believe me, my father would have no scruples about how he did that. The only way I can be certain of escaping is by marrying someone else.

I have enjoyed your company greatly and I suspect you have enjoyed mine and would, were there not such a difference in our stations, pursue the matter further. That difference means nothing to me and never has. I am therefore asking you to marry me. Will you? If you agreed, I'd prefer to do it by special licence as soon as possible.

I have some money of my own, not a fortune but a reasonable competence, so would not come to you empty-handed, but like you I don't have extrava-

gant tastes and am sure we'd have more than enough to manage on. I shall be quite happy to live at Spinneys.

I shall walk into the village tomorrow with Miss Lewison about ten o'clock in the morning and, if possible, we shall call in to inspect progress on your garden. I shall find some excuse to speak to you alone and receive your answer then.

Yours in hope,
Ann Turner

Oliver pressed his lips to the letter, joy overflowing. He would have walked through fire for her.

He re-read the letter, then ran upstairs and changed out of his funereal black before going out into the garden to contemplate the future, which had never looked so rosy.

He hadn't even hesitated in making his decision. Of course he'd marry her. Life couldn't offer him anything he desired more.

CHAPTER TWENTY

April 1864

The day after old Mr Dewhurst's funeral, Walter received a note from Jack Lexham saying that he would be leaving the district the following day, as per arrangements made with his late employer. Astounded and angry, Walter went to see his land agent to find the whole household in the midst of packing up.

He jumped off his horse, leaving Colin to look after the animal, and stormed towards the estate office which was situated at one end of the Lexhams' house. 'What the hell do you mean by sending me that note?' he demanded.

Jack looked up from his desk. 'It seemed fairly clear to me. I'm leaving.'

'But you have a contract with us, and it's usual for land agents to give at least six months' notice.'

'I think you'll find that my contract was with your father and ended upon his death. I have, of course, left everything in order here and have made some notes to help my successor.'

Walter stepped forward, fists bunched. 'Have you no sense of responsibility?'

'Yes. But not to you. In fact, I won't work for you in any capacity.'

'I'll make sure you don't work for anyone, then.'

Jack smiled. 'I don't need to. I have enough money to live on. But if I do look for a job, I think my reputation will win over yours.'

Walter's words came out in a bull roar. 'How dare you speak to me like that?'

Jack shrugged. 'I'd rather not speak to you at all. Nothing you say will change my mind.'

Walter stormed out again, knowing that if he stayed he'd thump the other man – which might lead to trouble. Jack Lexham was indeed well thought of in the county and Walter didn't dare do anything to get his own back on such a man.

'Something wrong?' Colin asked as he held the horse for his master to mount.

'Aye. Lexham's definitely leaving. We need to find ourselves a new land agent, and quickly.' He settled himself more comfortably in the saddle. 'I'll get my lawyer to put an advert in the newspaper. In the meantime, I'll have to handle a few things myself, instead of leaving them to him. First of all, we're going to see Nathaniel King.'

Colin followed him along the lane. So it had started, had it?

Nathaniel saw Walter Dewhurst riding along the lane, followed by that shifty groom of his, and guessed at once this meant trouble. He stuck his spade in the soil and walked towards the gate. As he passed, Ginny peered out of the shed and he gestured to her with one hand to get back inside. Tom moved from behind her and came out to stand watchfully by, as if he too had sensed that something was wrong.

When Nathaniel got to the gate he stood there, hands resting easily on the top bar, and waited.

Walter reined in and smiled down at him from horseback. 'I'm giving you twenty-four hours to get off this land, King.' He pulled out a large gold pocket watch which had belonged to his father and flicked its lid open. 'It's a quarter to eleven. Let's be generous and say you're to be out by eleven o'clock precisely tomorrow.'

Nathaniel was so shocked he couldn't speak, then his immediate thought was that it was no use pleading with this man – and anyway, even if it was likely to help, he just couldn't bring himself to do it.

'When you've gone,' Walter added conversationally, 'I'm going to take great pleasure in trampling down all those plants of yours. I don't want any sign of you left, you see.' He swung the horse round, turning his head to toss over his shoulder, 'And don't try going to stay with any of my tenants, because if you do, they'll be thrown out too.'

Nathaniel stared at him, hoping he wasn't showing how upset he felt.

With another of his mirthless laughs Walter urged his horse into motion and trotted off down the lane.

Only when he and his groom were out of sight did Nathaniel lay his head down on his hands while he allowed himself a moment's weakness. He heard footsteps behind him, but it took a huge effort for him to turn and face his family. Hannah, Ginny and Tom all knew something was wrong, he could see it in their faces.

He tried to speak, but all that came out was a croak,

so he tried again, forcing the words out. 'Let's go inside and I'll tell you.'

He put one arm round Hannah's shoulders, the other around Ginny's, and started walking.

'Is there any hot water, lass?' he asked. 'We'll all need a cup of strong tea, I reckon.'

'Yes, of course.' She moved to the stove and Ginny got the teacups down from the dresser.

'It's bad news,' Nathaniel said as the two women worked, 'and doesn't take much telling. Dewhurst has given us twenty-four hours to get out.'

They didn't make a sound, staring at him like three frozen creatures, as shocked as he had been.

'Can he do that?' Hannah asked at last. 'Don't you have a lease?'

'Aye, and it doesn't end until October. But I've not got the money to fight him in court, and I'd probably lose if I tried because he can afford a lawyer and I can't.'

'What are we going to do, then?' Ginny asked, her voice barely more than a whisper.

'I don't rightly know,' he admitted. 'I haven't really taken it in yet.'

Hannah poured water into the big teapot and carried it carefully across to the table. She sat down and rested her chin on her hands, thinking hard. She could see that Nathaniel was shattered by the news and her heart ached for his pain.

When he didn't speak, just kept sipping the tea and sighing, she took the initiative. 'We'll have to make plans, then.' She looked from one to the other and saw only despair. 'It isn't the end of the world,' she added quietly.

'It feels like it,' Nathaniel said. 'I never thought even *he* would treat me like this. Refuse to renew the lease and get rid of me in October, yes, but not throw me into the street for no reason and at a minute's notice.'

'Nathaniel, look at me.' They all turned towards her. 'I was locked in an asylum, treated like a lunatic, and yet I won through. We're alive, able-bodied and have one another. That's what really matters. We can find work and make a new life, I know we can.'

Tom stared down miserably at his scrawny old body. 'I'm not able-bodied. Not now. If you hadn't found me work, lad, I'd be in the poorhouse.'

'You're part of the family,' she said firmly when Nathaniel didn't speak, 'and we'll still look after you, Tom.'

'I'm not going to be much help, either,' Ginny said. 'I'm starting to show now and people won't want to give me a job.'

'Nonetheless, we'll manage.' Hannah picked up the teapot and began pouring second cups. 'We'll sit quietly and drink our tea, take time to pull our thoughts together, then you can go and fetch Gregory from school, Nathaniel. We'll need his help in packing.'

He looked at her in wonderment, then he got up and pulled her to her feet, hugging her close. 'Hannah, you're a treasure,' he said huskily. 'The best wife a man could ever have.'

From the circle of his arms she stared up at him, then smiled and took the initiative, kissing him soundly, regardless of the onlookers.

When they drew apart, he raised his hand to run his

fingertip down her cheek. 'Thanks, lass. It fair threw me, but I shall be all right now.'

'Good. The first thing to work out is how we are to get our things away. I don't want to leave them behind for that man to destroy.'

Nathaniel opened his mouth then shut it again, a big grin creasing his face. 'We won't. Not a single thing – inside the house or out.' He pushed his chair back, his whole body radiating energy where it had been listless and defeated before. 'I've friends in the village, Hannah, good friends that I grew up with. I'm going to do something I've never done before and ask for their help. They'll lend me enough carts to take our stuff away, including the shrubs and bushes. Better they die than that *he* gets a chance to stamp on them.'

And he was gone, striding out of the house, head thrown back.

'Eh, that were well done, Hannah,' Tom said. 'He'll be all right now. He's a grand chap, your Nathaniel.'

She smiled at him. 'I know. Now, could you go and start clearing the smaller tools and equipment out of the shed? You're not to tire yourself out, mind, because I don't want to have to nurse you, so be sensible and take regular rests. Can you make a start there for us?'

He brightened and eased his stiff limbs up from the chair. 'I reckon I can do that all reet.'

'There are boxes in the big shed, aren't there? For sending stuff to market?'

He nodded.

'Then you can put things in those. Leave the big stuff for Nathaniel to move, though.'

By the time her husband and a shocked Gregory got

back, Hannah and Ginny had the upstairs bedrooms cleared, except for the bedding. Their clothes were wrapped in spare sheets and blankets, waiting at the foot of each bed to be carried out.

The first helper to arrive was Farmer Sawyer, driving his big cart and bringing his two labourers with him. 'I reckon we can load most of your furniture on this, lad. We'll have to get back home for milking, but until then we're here to help. And we'll come back later, won't we, lads?'

Both men nodded.

'I've sent the wife to tell everyone.'

Nathaniel had to nod his thanks because his throat was thick with emotion at this wholehearted support.

Word spread rapidly and as the day wore on other carts turned up, and men on foot who considered themselves friends of Nathaniel. Some didn't arrive until after dark, afraid of Dewhurst taking out his spite on them, but they brought lanterns, vowing they could work almost as well by their light.

Women came too, bringing loaves and cakes to help out. They worked inside the house, as well as outside, helping Hannah pack the crockery in straw, or making pot after pot of strong tea and platefuls of sandwiches for the men.

All through the night they continued digging up those plants which had some chance of being transplanted. Those which wouldn't survive long, Nathaniel gave to his helpers or used to cover up the salvaged plants and shrubs which were now filling the carts, neatly wrapped in damp sacking or sitting in tubs and boxes of all shapes and sizes.

It brought tears to Hannah's eyes to see them working so silently and wholeheartedly, occasionally stopping to stretch or clap Nathaniel on the shoulder. He would nod when they did that, then go back to work.

No one left to go home and sleep. She had never seen a group of people so united. It was strange to look out of the window and see lanterns bobbing about, dark silhouettes carrying loads to the carts. It spoke volumes for how highly they regarded Nathaniel.

As the false dawn began to lighten the sky she went outside for a breath of fresh air. It nearly broke her heart to see the scene of desolation where yesterday there had been flourishing rows of small plants, shrubs in early leaf or flower, all the flourishing growth of a thriving market garden. She couldn't see Nathaniel and went to ask one of the men where he was.

'Down the bottom of the garden. Said he had summat to dig up ovver theer.'

She picked her way through the mounds of earth and wilting foliage, finding her husband standing by the rear fence staring into space. She slipped her arm in his and looked up to see tears tracking down his cheeks.

'It suddenly got to me,' he said, his voice breaking, his shoulders shaking. 'Eh, I'm being weak again.'

'Of course it got to you. You'd not be normal if it didn't upset you. But you've some wonderful friends and I reckon we'll not only be out on time, but we'll leave that evil man with nothing to destroy.'

'You put new heart into me, Hannah love. Without you, I might just have walked away, I was that upset.'

'Not you.'

He lifted her chin and kissed her, another proper kiss,

and she felt tears of joy welling in her eyes as the kiss deepened and he pulled her into a close embrace.

'I reckon we're ready to be man and wife now,' he said huskily.

'I wasn't sure you wanted to.'

'Nay, whatever gave you that idea?'

'You didn't even try to touch me.'

'I didn't dare or I'd not have stopped.' He gave her a lop-sided smile. 'As soon as we find somewhere private to put our bed, I'll prove how much I want you.' Then his smile faded. 'I'm ashamed that we have to go on the tramp again first.'

'We've lived on the road before and can do so again. Have you any money at all?'

'A bit.'

'I have a bit, too. We'll count it when we have time to catch our breath. The only thing I don't understand is,' she hesitated, 'well, where are we going? You haven't said.'

'We're going to see Oliver Dewhurst first. Remember how he came to see me after the funeral and said if I ever had any trouble with his brother and needed help of any sort, I was to see him? I reckon he meant it. If he can only give us somewhere to store our things till we find work and can set up a new home, it'll be something.'

'He must be very different from his brother,' she said wonderingly, for she had only seen him in the distance, a tall, thin young gentleman standing beside his carriage for a few minutes in earnest conversation with her husband.

'Aye, he is. Chalk and cheese. A nice lad but too

gentle for his own good. He left home as soon as he turned twenty-one and he's living a few miles away at Beckleton now. That's where we're going first.'

By six o'clock in the morning, the house was clear and the last of the plants had been pulled up.

'Better leave now,' Farmer Sawyer said, pulling out his big turnip watch. 'We want to get the carts out of the village before *he* sends someone sniffing around to check on us.'

Nathaniel looked round, easing his aching back a little. He was bone weary but refused to give in to it. 'Well, we dug up all the stuff we may be able to save. I hope folk don't get into trouble because of this, though.'

'I doubt he'll even know who helped. If it isn't too far we're going, we can be back at work by the time he's out of bed.'

'A couple of hours away in the carts.'

'Then I'll leave my Sam to drive you and bring the cart back, and wish you well. It's better if I'm seen around. I'm still a tenant of his.'

The two men shook hands, keeping their hands clasped for longer than usual, then Nathaniel turned to get into his cart. As he gave one last glance back at his former home, he suddenly had an idea. With a smile, he asked the others to wait while he did one final job.

Then the procession of carts set off, making slow but steady progress. The heavily laden vehicles couldn't travel at much more than walking pace, so it was past eight o'clock before they reached Beckleton.

People came out of their houses to stand and stare at them.

'What's up? Are you off to the fair?' one wag called.

No one answered. They were exhausted now after a night without sleep. Those who worked on the estate had gone off to work as normal but those not dependent on the Dewhursts were still helping their friend, driving the carts and ready to offer more help unloading them at their destination.

Nathaniel asked the way to the house called Spinneys and the carts got under way again, turning down the narrow lane and pulling up in front of the house itself.

He helped Hannah down. 'Come with me, lass.'

So she stood beside him as he knocked on the front door and asked the fresh-faced young lass who answered if they could see Mr Oliver Dewhurst.

Penny goggled at the carts lined up down the drive, the drivers slumped in their seats, then rushed to fetch her master.

Her inability to help her daughter was preying on Christine's mind. She knew she had to do something about it or she would never forgive herself. She found an opportunity to scribble the address of her brother and put it in an envelope which she intended to take with her to market, though how she was to pass it on to the landlady of the inn, she didn't know. She had seen her there but had not been able to speak to her because Howard was as watchful as ever.

In the end she decided to address the envelope to Mrs Feathers and drop it, hoping someone would pass it to the landlady. But to have any chance of succeeding she needed to wait until she saw the other woman.

When she spotted Mrs Feathers in the market place, Christine's heart began to thump in her chest as she fingered the letter in her pocket. As soon as Howard's attention was on something else, she pulled it out and dropped it under the edge of a stall after making her purchases.

Terrified he would see it, she turned to walk away and after a few paces was beginning to feel that perhaps she had got away with it.

Then a voice called out, 'Mrs West, you've dropped something!' and she felt a sickening lurch in her stomach.

'Oh, no!' the stallkeeper called out cheerfully. 'This isn't yours. It's for you, Mrs Feathers.'

Howard was across to the stall in a minute, snatching the envelope out of the stallkeeper's hand and scanning it carefully. He cast one ominous glance at Christine, then forced a smile to his face and said, 'Actually, it isn't meant to go to Mrs Feathers yet. My wife wrote it and wishes to deliver it herself later. It must have fallen out of her pocket.'

Mrs Feathers, who had come hurrying up, looked from his face with its thunderous expression to his wife's. If ever she'd seen terror, she was seeing it now. Poor Mrs West was so white she looked as if she was going to keel over at any minute.

Christine knew Howard wouldn't give her an opportunity to communicate with Mrs Feathers again. *Ginny!* she thought. *Oh, Ginny, I've failed you!* That stiffened her spine and she somehow found the courage to call out, 'Tell him to go to Marton, the other side of Preston. That's where Ginny is now.'

Enraged by this, Howard slapped her so hard he sent her flying backwards, not caring for once whether the whole village saw him do it. She landed on the cobble-stones with a thud and he followed her, arm upraised to strike her again.

The people nearby began to murmur and call out, 'Shame on you!' or 'Bully!' and he realised where he was, letting his hand drop.

When Christine didn't get up, he bent to drag her to her feet, still seething with rage. But something about the staring eyes told him what had happened even before he saw the unnatural angle of her neck.

'She's dead,' a voice said into the hush. 'He's gone and killed her.'

'Don't let him get away!' Mrs Feathers cried. 'Call the police, quick.' She watched in immense satisfaction as some of the male stallholders moved forward to stand guard on Howard.

He didn't even try to get away. He wasn't aware of what was happening around him, could only stare down in horror at his wife's face, which still had terror etched on it. It was not until someone took hold of his arm and began to pull him away that he realised what was happening. The man holding his arm was the village policeman wearing the new uniform that made him so distinctive among the crowd. Howard faltered, 'I didn't mean to – it was an *accident*.'

'It wasn't an accident that he hit her,' a woman's voice called. 'He's been beating the poor creature black and blue for years.'

'He should be charged with murder,' another woman yelled from the back of the crowd. 'They should hang him for this.'

When the policeman again tugged at Howard's arm,

he began to struggle wildly and three men who had disliked him cordially for a long time stepped forward and enthusiastically helped subdue him.

Mrs Feathers seized the opportunity to pick up the envelope addressed to her, which Howard had dropped. It was muddy now but she slipped it into her pocket, determined to let that poor young fellow know where his young lady was, for the sake of the woman who'd just died.

She went home and ripped the envelope open, finding inside the full address of Christine's brother. She wrote it down again, just to be sure. Then, with tears in her eyes, she took Nick's envelope and inserted the actual scrap of paper Christine West had written on, which seemed only right. But she couldn't let him meet the girl without telling him what had happened so took out another piece of paper, shook up her bottle of ink and unscrewed the cap, then laboriously penned a few lines before sealing the envelope.

She hesitated, wondering whether she ought to write to Christine's brother as well. No, the police would contact him. They were used to such tasks.

But she could do her bit by giving them his address.

Then it occurred to her that someone had to look after those poor little boys of Christine's. She liked children and could offer to do that. Wiping more tears from her eyes, for she couldn't forget how abruptly that poor woman had died, she went outside again to slip Nick's letter into the postbox. Then she went on to the police station, which consisted of one room in the constable's house.

Drawing a deep breath, she marched inside. 'You'll

need this.' She waved the piece of paper at the constable. 'It's Mrs West's brother's address. Her husband hit her because she was telling me where to find her daughter so that I could let Ginny's young man know where she is.'

He took the paper and scrutinised it. 'Thank you. Very helpful.'

'I thought of something else: there are two little lads to be looked after now. If you want, I can have them till we see who's to care for them? That brother of Mrs West seemed a nice fellow, so maybe he'll take them. Ginny is too young to be responsible for them.'

He blinked and made her explain everything in detail. 'But hasn't West got any relatives who can take the boys?'

'No. He always said he had none left and was glad of it.'

'Well, then, I'd better go and collect the boys from school and bring them round to you. What are their names?'

'Edwin and Andrew.' She looked round. 'Where have you put *him*?'

'In the cell. They'll bring him up before the magistrate, but he'll have to be referred to the Assizes, there being a death involved.'

'Well, just make sure the door's locked good and tight. We don't want that madman getting out and attacking someone else.'

'Or someone attacking him. There's a lot of bad feeling in the village about what happened. One more thing – can I count on you to act as witness to what happened?'

'Oh, yes, definitely.'

'You'll need to give me a statement and be ready to come to court.'

'Happy to.'

After she'd done that, she walked slowly home to get her spare bedroom ready for the boys. She wondered how they were feeling. They always looked so subdued and she'd never seen them playing with other lads. Had that bully beaten them as well?

Just before eleven in the morning Walter rode along the lane towards the smallholding, followed by Colin. He looked down at the ground which was scored by tracks and footprints. 'Looks like they've been busy.'

Colin nodded, giving his master the grin he expected, though he'd felt sorry for the poor buggers, to tell the truth.

As they came to the hedge that marked the beginning of the smallholding, Walter reined in his horse with an oath. 'What the hell!'

Colin edged forward and stared at the bare, trampled earth. Not a plant remained, though there were plenty of torn leaves and shoots scattered around. He hid a grin as his master continued to curse. King had done this, he was sure. How Colin didn't know, except that the fellow couldn't have managed it on his own. But he'd cleared the earth of plants and no doubt the cottage would be equally bare, so there was nothing left to destroy.

Walter urged his horse forward again and muttered in annoyance as he found the gate shut. When he tried in vain to lift the metal loop from the gatepost to open it, he bent to examine it. 'Look at that!' he shouted. 'They've nailed it shut! How dare they tamper with my property? Can you do anything about it?'

'Sorry, sir. Not with my bare hands. We'll have to get someone to come and pull the nails out. Looks like they've made a thorough job of it.'

Walter wheeled his horse round and set off for home at a fast trot. When he got there, he said curtly, 'See that the gate is opened by tomorrow. And check whether any of our men are missing from work today.'

But no men were missing from the estate's farms, gardens or stables. And when Colin slouched into the village inn to ask if anyone had noticed activity from the direction of the smallholding during the night, all he got was blank stares.

On the way back to Marton Hall, he threw his head back and laughed long and loud. Serve the arrogant bastard right!

CHAPTER TWENTY-ONE

April 1864

Oliver hurried to the front door, shocked to see how weary Nathaniel and Hannah looked. King had had so much to bear recently, most of it because of Oliver's damned brother. What had happened now? He glanced at the carts and saw that the other men sitting slumped on them looked equally weary, then turned to find Nanny beside him, also staring. He decided to deal with the simple practicalities first. 'Those men look tired and hungry to me, Nanny. Would you send them round to the kitchen and see they get fed while I talk to Nathaniel?'

She nodded, her eyes brightening in anticipation. She loved looking after people.

Oliver gestured Nathaniel inside, looking questioningly at the woman beside him, assuming it was his new wife. She had steady eyes and a very upright, dignified bearing in spite of her mud-stained clothing, but lines of weariness were etched on her face, too.

'This is my wife, Hannah, Mr Oliver. Can we speak to you?'

'Of course. I'm pleased to meet you, Mrs King.'

The woman came inside but Nathaniel hesitated on the threshold, looking at the polished wooden floor of the hall, then down at his feet. He'd wiped his shoes with a scrap of sacking, but they were still a mess. 'I'm sorry we're so mucky. We've been working through the night, you see.'

'That doesn't matter, truly it doesn't.'

Oliver led them through to the smaller parlour at the rear of the house. Mrs King took the comfortable chair he offered, leaning her head back with a sigh, but Nathaniel insisted on bringing forward an upright wooden chair because of the state of his clothes. He sat staring down at his hands.

'Tell me what's wrong,' Oliver urged.

'Your brother came to see me yesterday. He gave me twenty-four hours to get out of my house and off the estate.'

Oliver gaped at him. 'Why?'

'He didn't bother to give me a reason, just told me to get out.'

'But you'd a lease—'

Nathaniel looked at him grimly. 'You think I can afford to fight a rich man about that sort of thing? Whether it's legal or not.'

'No. No, of course not. I'm sorry. Walter can be very unreasonable and everyone knew he bore you a grudge. That's why I told you to come to me if you were ever in need of help.'

Hannah could see how stiff with humiliation Nathaniel was, so intervened to give him a moment to pull himself together. 'Mr Dewhurst told my husband he'd come to the smallholding after we'd left and trample all the plants down, so we dug them up and brought them with us. That's what's on the carts. We didn't want to give him the satisfaction of destroying them.'

'How on earth did you manage that?'

'I have some good friends – how good I didn't realise till now,' Nathaniel put in. 'We worked through the night. We brought some of the plants with us, gave others to people in the village.' He couldn't hold back a yawn. 'Sorry. Oh, and did you know Mr Lexham's leaving today as well? He won't work for your brother.'

'I already knew he would be leaving and I don't blame him.'

Nathaniel took a deep breath, shame burning in his cheeks as he made his plea. 'I don't have anywhere to go, Mr Oliver, or even to leave my things. I was hoping you'd be able to help – one way or the other.'

'You were right to come here. I'd be delighted to help you and I'm sure my father would have approved.' Someone knocked on the door then and when he called for them to come in, Penny brought in a tray with tea and scones and pieces of fruit cake on it. 'Thank you. Are the others being served? Good. We can manage here now.' He looked at Hannah questioningly. 'Shall I pour or would you like to do that?'

'I'll do it.' She went to the tray, using the skills she'd acquired when working in Heverstock Hall. 'How do you like it, sir?' Deftly she poured him a cup and offered him a plate. He took a piece of cake in order to set them at their ease. She poured cups for herself and her husband and looked sideways at Nathaniel. 'Something to eat, love? Give you heart.'

'I'm not hungry. The tea's good, though.'

She took a scone and buttered it, but Oliver noticed she only crumbled it, eating very little.

'I have a cottage for you,' he said, wanting to put

them out of their misery, 'but I'm afraid it's in need of repair. There's enough land round it for a smallholding, but it's been used as meadows so it'll need ploughing over before you can plant anything.'

Then he snapped his fingers as a solution came to him. 'But I have a kitchen garden here which is still lacking plants and there's no reason why you can't put in your bushes and anything else that will transplant, just for this growing season until we sort things out permanently. Indeed, we'll be delighted to buy produce from you. That'll help us both. The gardens here were a mess when I moved in and we're still working on them. We'll have to find you somewhere to stay, though, until I can have the cottage repaired.'

Hannah was relieved to see Nathaniel straighten a little during this speech and look less defeated.

'Could we see the cottage, sir?' he asked. 'Perhaps part of it is usable.'

'Yes, of course.' Oliver glanced at the clock and ran one hand through his hair, feeling a bit harassed. 'I'll have to show you quickly because I'm getting married this afternoon.' He could feel himself flushing at the announcement.

Again the woman filled the silence. 'Congratulations, sir. I hope you'll be very happy.'

'I'd rather you didn't tell anyone yet. It's a secret. Her family don't approve, you see.'

'We'll not say a word.' Nathaniel set the cup down and stood up. 'Right, then, our friends have to unload the carts and get back to Marton, so if you'll show us the cottage, we'll see if we can use any of it. One room with a roof would be enough.'

'I doubt it's possible to stay there, as the roof's damaged, but if you'll follow me I'll show it to you, then I really must leave you. I'm sure we can find you accommodation here in the house for a few nights, though, just till the roof is repaired.'

He led them outside and walked briskly down to the end of the garden, opening a small wrought-iron gate and leading them across a meadow towards a clump of trees.

Two or three times Nathaniel stopped to pick up a handful of earth, sometimes digging in his heel to loosen the grass. 'Not bad soil. Not bad at all. Needs some muck spreading, of course. And it'll be a while before we get rid of all the grass.'

The cottage was in a bad enough state to make them fall silent. Even the garden gate had fallen off its hinges and lay rotting among the weeds that were thriving everywhere in the walled garden that separated it from the field at the far side from Spinneys. It was larger than most cottages, of one storey only, but half in ruins. The slate roof showed many gaps, the once whitewashed walls were grey and stained, with some of the plaster on them missing, and several of the windows were broken.

'I *will* have it repaired for you,' Oliver promised. 'And as quickly as possible.'

'Can we go inside?' Nathaniel asked.

'Yes, of course.' He gestured to them to go first.

They entered warily, moving slowly and letting their eyes take everything in before they passed from one room to the next.

'It could be very pretty,' Hannah said as they finished their tour.

Nathaniel went back to study the largest bedroom, then made his way outside and stood staring up. 'The roof here is mostly intact, which is why this end of the house is not as bad as the other. I could get up there and move a few tiles. If we could make this bit waterproof, we'd manage.'

Oliver looked at them in astonishment. 'You're surely not thinking of living here?'

The Kings looked at one another, clasped hands and exchanged half-smiles, before nodding to him.

'We're like those plants of mine,' Nathaniel said. 'We need to put down roots again, and the sooner the better. No doubt I've lost most of them, but it was worth giving them a chance. They didn't deserve trampling on.'

Oliver pulled out his pocket watch. 'Damn! I beg your pardon for my language, Mrs King, but I really do have to get ready.'

'You leave us to it,' she said. 'We'll have another quick look round then we'll unload our mattresses and set to work on that roof.'

'There's a shed at the foot of my garden where you can store the rest of your things. It's dusty but quite big and rainproof. It'll be full of spiders, though, because it's not been used for a while. Oh, and the arts can get to this cottage by going back down the lane, heading towards the village and taking the next turning.'

He was already hurrying away, so they let him go.

'Will it do?' Nathaniel asked, gathering her to him.

Hannah didn't let him see her doubts, but buried her face in his chest with a tired sigh. 'We'll make it do.'

'I don't want to live in someone else's house.'

'Neither do I.'

'It's how we're going to make a living that worries me,' he muttered. 'I'll have to seek work or we'll have no money to buy food.'

That worried her too, but she kept her thoughts to herself.

Oliver hurried into the kitchen of his house. 'I have to get ready,' he called to Nanny. 'Mr and Mrs King think they can make part of the cottage habitable,' he looked at Penny as well as he spoke, 'so if you can help them in any way, don't hesitate. And Cook, will you make them all a hearty meal later?'

He turned to the men who'd driven the carts. They'd risen at his entrance and were standing waiting in a group now, cap in hand. 'The next turning after our lane leads to the cottage. And if there are any plants that need to be put in the ground, Nanny will show you where our kitchen garden is. It's not being used this year.'

They nodded and murmured thanks for the refreshments.

He ran up the stairs, hearing murmurs from the kitchen, then footsteps going outside. No time for a leisurely bath now, so he stripped off his clothes and washed rapidly. As he dressed, he wondered if Ann would change her mind, and wondered too how he was going to protect her after they were married. Because he was quite certain that Walter would try to do them harm and her own family would cause trouble. But he'd have risked entering a cage full of lions to win her.

There was a tap on the bedroom door. 'Come in!'

Nanny entered. 'You're going to be late if you don't hurry.'

'You're going to be late too. Remember, you're to be my witness.'

She smiled at him sadly. 'I'd like fine to see you wed, Oliver, but you need me here now to help those poor people. Cook and Penny are good workers but they need someone to tell them what to do. Ned can stand as your witness and look after you, too, if there's any trouble.' She reached up to kiss his cheek. 'I wish you happy, lad. I like your Ann, lady or not.'

So Oliver was driven down the lane in the gig and had to explain to his groom what was happening.

Ned whistled in surprise, having quickly lost any awe of his gentle new master now that he knew him better. 'Eh, Mr Walter's going to be that angry! Everyone in the village here knows he wants her for himself. They've seen him watching her many a time.'

'Well, he's not getting her. Only – well, her family wouldn't approve of me either, so we have to get wed first and tell them later.'

They drew up outside the church and Ned tied up the horse before following his master inside.

Lady Ann was waiting for Oliver in one of the rear pews, her companion by her side. She was wearing a straw hat with a neat little brim and a feather along one side which trailed down the back. Her dress was a soft blue-green colour and it suited her more than anything he had ever seen her wearing before.

As he moved forward, the church seemed to be filled with sunlight shining through the stained glass windows and it blinded him for a moment. 'Is everything all right?' he asked as he stepped out of the dazzling glare, for she was looking worried.

'It's all right now you're here. I saw the parson when I arrived and told him I'd like to speak to him presently. I think he's waiting for me in the vestry. Oh, and Miss Levison and I managed to bring these bags of clothing. I'll get the rest of my things sent to Spinneys later.'

He turned to Ned. 'Can you put them in the gig? We're going straight to the station afterwards.' Then he offered her his arm. 'Let's go and tell the parson what we're here for.'

'He'll be shocked.'

Mr Theophilus Dunhope was more than shocked by their request for him to marry them: he was so horrified he was rendered speechless for a moment, standing with his mouth open and his rather bulbous eyes gaping. 'But Lady Ann, you cannot be thinking clearly—'

She interrupted. 'I'm thinking very clearly, Mr Dunhope. I have my reasons for marrying like this, which are no concern of yours, and my fiancé has the necessary special licence.' She turned to Oliver, who proffered the piece of paper he had obtained the day before.

'Yes, but—'

'You know we're both of an age to marry without anyone's consent. What other difficulty is there?'

'It's – well, does your father approve of this marriage?'

'It's not necessary for him to approve or disapprove.'

'But he's my *patron*! I cannot go against his wishes.'

He sometimes wished he could, but his living depended on the Marquess.

She gave him a glacial stare. 'Do I understand that you're refusing to marry us?'

He swallowed hard and looked from her to Oliver. 'Please, Lady Ann, I beg you to reconsider . . . to discuss this rash move with your family. People of your status don't marry like this.'

'If you refuse to do your duty and marry us,' she said, 'then I shall only go to another church, but afterwards I'll complain about you to my godfather the Bishop, who will no doubt be very angry indeed. I can assure you that if I had had time to ask for his help, he would approve of what I'm doing.' She was quite sure her godfather would only need to meet Walter Dewhurst to understand, and he already knew what her father was like. The two men did not get on.

Mr Dunhope stared at Oliver as if he had two heads. 'Oh, dear. What shall I do?'

Oliver leaned forward, and said earnestly, 'I think you have no choice, sir, but to marry us.'

There was a long silence, then the parson sighed. 'Very well, but I am only doing this under protest.' He paused and snapped his fingers, looking hopeful. 'Witnesses! We cannot marry you without witnesses.'

'We've brought them,' Oliver assured him, watching his face fall. He'd found Dunhope pleasant enough, but the man was clearly terrified of offending Ann's father.

'My companion and Oliver's groom,' Ann added, hiding a smile at the expression on Mr Dunhope's face at the idea of a groom witnessing her marriage.

'Very well. If you'll come to the front of the church,

I'll join you in a moment. I – um – need to get some things and put on my surplice.'

They went to stand at the front of the church with their witnesses to either side. It seemed to take Mr Dunhope a long time to join them.

'You're sure?' Oliver asked softly, taking Ann's hand and clasping it in both his.

'Very.' She smiled at him before turning to face the parson. 'You may begin, Mr Dunhope.'

He began intoning a prayer.

Oliver requested him to proceed straight to the marriage ceremony.

He spoke slowly with many pauses, but the bride and groom spoke their responses clearly and the ceremony was soon over. When he pronounced them man and wife, Lady Ann sighed in relief, and Oliver smiled down at her as he clasped her hands. Whatever the troubles to come, she was his now and he would cherish her to the fullest extent of his capabilities.

They signed the church register and Oliver paid the parson, who said, 'I hope you'll be happy,' but sounded as if he didn't believe this possible.

As they left the church Oliver felt as if the whole world should look different, but it didn't. The village street was nearly empty, the sun was still shining and a solitary dog was scratching itself enthusiastically near the duck pond.

But before they could get into the gig, there was a shout from the far end of the village street and Lord Gerald came galloping down it towards them, looking furious.

'Mr Dunhope must have sent him a message!' Ann

exclaimed. 'Oh, dear, Gerald will try to drag me back, I know he will, and until we've consummated the marriage, they can have it annulled.'

Her brother flung himself off the horse and strode towards them. 'Dunhope said you were getting married. Surely this isn't true?'

'What I do is no concern of yours,' Ann said stiffly.

'No concern? Of course it's my concern! Father asked me to keep an eye on you and he'll have a fit if he hears I've let you get married. I'm sure this can be smoothed over. After all, you haven't consummated the marriage yet. Wait there for me while I speak to the parson. No, I'd better take you inside with me.'

When he reached for her arm, as if to pull her along forcibly, both Oliver and Ned stepped between them.

'We'll wait for you here,' Ann said, as quietly as ever, though Oliver could see a pulse beating frantically in her temple.

The minute her brother was inside the church, she said, 'Quick! Let's get to the station and take the first train to anywhere.'

They scrambled into the gig, finding just enough room for the two of them, so Oliver told Ned to follow them and pick up the vehicle from the station then urged the horse into a fast trot.

As they vanished down the street, Ned saw that the horse Lord Gerald had ridden was standing where he'd dismounted, not hitched to anything. He winked at Miss Levison, went up to it and slapped its rump. It jerked away from him, then when he slapped it again and waved his hands, it whinnied and trotted off down the street.

He turned to the elderly lady. 'Perhaps we too should hurry away, Miss? I know a path that leads along the back of the houses. We can be out of sight in a minute. I'll take you to the entrance to the Priory grounds, then go and fetch the gig from the station.'

'Oh, yes, let's go quickly.'

They had just rounded the corner when the church door banged open and Lord Gerald came out, followed by Mr Dunhope.

They stopped dead when they saw no one waiting for them there. Lord Gerald turned to the parson to ask in bewilderment, 'Where can they have gone?'

Mr Dunhope did not want to become involved any further. He had done his duty in sending a message to the Priory and only hoped the Marquess would bear that in mind. And anyway, he couldn't help feeling sorry for Lady Ann. 'I'm sure I don't know, sir. But if you left them here, they can't have gone far.'

'No, by George! I'll soon find them.' Gerald turned towards his horse, which wasn't his usual mount but one he had found ready saddled in the Priory stables, and again gaped round. 'My horse is gone too.'

'Oh, dear! Oh, dear!' Mr Dunhope retreated to the church porch and watched as Lord Gerald ran first one way then the other, finding no sign of either horse or sister.

People peered out of windows. Lord Gerald's noisy arrival had been enough to gain him a hidden audience. Many were chuckling at his discomfiture because his young lordship's arrogance had not gone down well in Beckleton after his sister's pleasant ways. Prudently, they stayed inside their houses until he'd gone stamping off towards the Priory, then emerged to discuss the situation and wonder what was going on and why Ned had chased the horse away.

When Lord Gerald had found himself another horse and two sturdy grooms to help him get his sister back by force if necessary, he rode at top speed to Spinneys. He didn't bother to knock but tried to walk straight inside. However, the front door was locked. He hammered on it with one clenched fist and waited.

No one answered. 'We'll have to go round the back,' he decided.

When they got there they found the side and kitchen doors also locked. Yelling at the top of his voice, he began banging on the latter. 'Open the door this minute! I know you're in there, Ann.'

Nathaniel, who was directing his friends where in the kitchen garden to put the plants they hoped to save, stopped to frown in the direction of the house when he heard the shouting. 'I'll just see what's happening.'

He strode out of the walled garden towards the kitchen door, stopping at the sight of a very angry young gentleman thumping on it. His friends followed him, welcoming a break in their labours.

'I don't know who that fellow is but he'll have a seizure if he gets any angrier,' one of them said with a chuckle.

Nanny finally opened the kitchen window and shouted, 'Go away, your lordship. Your sister isn't here.'

'I don't believe you. Open that door or I'll break it down!'

Nathaniel stepped forward. While Oliver Dewhurst was away he wasn't having anyone damaging his benefactor's house. 'Oy!' he yelled, standing with hands on hips, glaring at the young gentleman. 'What's going on?'

Lord Gerald turned round. 'Are you addressing me, fellow?'

'Aye, I am that.'

'Then don't be so dashed impertinent. Be off and mind your own business.'

'Not till you've stopped threatening to damage Mr Oliver's house. Who do you think you are?'

Lord Gerald nearly choked at this disrespectful mode of address, and the two grooms who'd accompanied him found it necessary to stare at their feet and swallow very hard to hide their amusement.

'I'm the Marquess of Iffingham's son and I've come here to fetch my sister.'

Nathaniel was beginning to enjoy himself. He was sick of rich sods talking to him as if he were dirt, and damned if he was going to turn away meekly with his tail between his legs. 'Your sister's gone off on her honeymoon.'

'I told you she wasn't here,' Nanny shouted from the window.

'Well, I don't believe you and I insist on coming in to check for myself.'

'You can come in, but you're not bringing those two with you because I won't be threatened in Mr Oliver's home. Mr King, will your friends keep those two out of the house, and will you come in with Lord Gerald to protect me? I'm all of a tremble with him shouting at me like that.'

Nathaniel hid a grin. From the little he'd seen of her, he couldn't imagine Mrs Parkin being afraid of a young man like this – or of anyone, come to that.

Lord Gerald took exception to these conditions, but in the end had to agree to her terms because something about the impertinent fellow standing next to him told him there'd be trouble if he tried to break the door down.

Nanny opened the door with the terse command, 'Wipe your feet properly before you come inside! We've mopped these floors today.'

Lord Gerald made a quick tour of the house, banging doors open and even invading the servants' rooms in the attics.

'The cheek of it!' Nanny said loudly. 'Looking into my bedroom like that. I shan't get a wink of sleep tonight now for fear he'll come back.'

Nathaniel went everywhere with them, standing by with arms folded as the young idiot searched and Nanny made sharp comments, treating him like a naughty schoolboy.

When they got back down to the kitchen, Lord Gerald folded his arms and demanded, 'Where have they gone? I'm not leaving till you tell me.'

Nanny gave him a look which had him feeling as if he was suddenly eight years old again. 'On their honeymoon, and how should I know where?'

Behind her, Cook and Penny stayed very still, not wanting to attract his lordship's attention.

He stared at her and muttered something under his breath, then left, going back to the village to find out if anyone had seen his sister pass through in her new husband's gig. But the mere sight of him galloping back down the main street sent people hurrying inside the nearest house and, although he banged on a few doors to ask, he could find no one who admitted to having seen his sister.

So he went to the station and found out that she and Oliver had got on a train for Preston. He debated briefly going after them, then abandoned the idea. Preston was a large town and it'd be like looking for a needle in a haystack. There was no way he was going to be able to stop the newly-weds consummating their marriage now.

In the end he could think of nothing to do but return to the Priory and write a letter to his father explaining what had happened.

He was sure the Marquess would be extremely angry. Well, *he* was angry too. Fancy Ann lowering herself to marry a fellow who lived in a small house like that. How would it reflect on the family? Had his sister run mad?

For a moment Gerald wondered if she was in love with this Oliver Dewhurst and something almost like envy speared through him. Imagine being able to follow one's fancy in choosing a marriage partner . . .

He didn't send a message to Walter Dewhurst, not yet, hoping somehow they could still keep this in the family and set it to rest quietly.

Oliver and Ann just caught the train to Preston, but only by running in a most undignified way across the platform while the one and only porter panted along behind them with their luggage. They collapsed into a compartment, laughing and breathless.

'Are you all right?' Oliver asked, putting their bags up on the rack.

'Never better,' Ann replied, straightening her hat. 'Where were you intending to go?'

'Preston, actually. I thought we'd find a quiet inn as far away from the station as possible and book a room for the night.' He smiled wryly. 'I'd expected to catch the later train, though, and leave in less of a rush.'

'Preston will be far enough. And tonight we'll consummate our marriage,' she said firmly, having already discovered that he was a little diffident when dealing with her, in fact downright shy at times, which she found very endearing. 'If we don't, they can easily have it annulled and then they'll try to force me to marry your brother.'

'If you're sure? I don't want to – you know, rush you.'

She smiled. 'Oliver, how many times do I have to tell you that I think we'll deal well together and I'm happy to be married to you? I don't like loud people and I don't enjoy London society. My parents despair of me.'

'You can't tell me too many times,' he admitted. 'I'd never dared hope to win you.'

She smiled at him, then leaned sideways to kiss him on the cheek, not raising the slightest objection as he turned and took her in his arms to kiss her properly. She found the experience more pleasant than she had expected and joined in enthusiastically. When he let her go, she tucked her arm in his, holding his hand and resting her head on his shoulder. 'There. I knew we'd deal well together.'

He hoped they would. He'd never made love before, though he'd read about it in books. He was a bit nervous about it all, but even to touch her made him feel a warmth in his loins and her response to his kiss suggested she wasn't unmoved by him, either.

In Preston, a friendly cab driver took them to an inn he knew a little way out of the town centre and promised to come and pick them up the following morning in good time to catch the ten o'clock train to Beckleton.

The landlord was pleased to offer Mr and Mrs Dewhurst his best room and brought his wife to show them up to it.

When they were alone, Ann went to her husband and put her arms round his neck. 'Kiss me again, Oliver.'

Still feeling as if this was the most wonderful of dreams, he did as she asked.

His touch was so gentle, his expression so adoring, that she felt herself melting into him. The bed was soft, the door had a bolt on the inside and they were not seen again until evening, when Mr Dewhurst went down to ask that a meal be sent up to their room.

'I told you they'd just got married,' the landlady said in satisfaction. 'I can always tell. I like to see a young couple who are fond of one another, I do that.'

CHAPTER TWENTY-TWO

April – May 1864

By the time his friends left Beckleton, they had helped Nathaniel move tiles from the rest of the roof into the gaps over the big bedroom and kitchen, making the rooms more or less watertight. They had also planted out – roughly, it was true – the more fragile of the plants he'd brought with him. Eh, was ever a man blessed with such good friends? he thought as he watched them drive away. Or with such a staunch help-meet of a wife?

The anger that had fuelled him to work for two long, hard days without sleep had faded now and he felt as if his boots were lined with lead. He waved a final farewell, knowing he'd miss all his friends, then went into the house through the front door, smiling up at the late sunlight that was coming in through the holes in the roof above the hallway and throwing slanting shafts of yellow light across his path. Make the most of it while you can! he told the setting sun. You'll not be poking your nose in here for much longer.

In the kitchen Hannah was sitting beside their table, on which were several dishes and plates. Her face was drawn and her whole body slumped in exhaustion, but she still managed to summon a faint smile for him.

'They sent some food across for us,' she said in a

mere thread of a voice. 'The others have eaten and the young ones have gone to bed. Poor Ginny was exhausted, and although your lad tried to stay awake he fell asleep with his head on the table, so I got him to bed.'

'Our lad now,' he corrected softly.

A warmth curled through her at this. 'Yes, and a fine lad he is, too. A real hard worker, our Gregory.'

'He's stopped being so quiet, which is partly due to you, I think. A lad needs a mother.'

'He's easy to love.'

'Where's Tom?'

'Outside smoking that horrible smelly pipe of his. He's going to sleep in the kitchen because there really isn't room for another mattress in the bedroom.' She grimaced. 'And although I'm fond of him, I wish he'd wash more often and I'm glad not to share sleeping quarters with him.'

Nathaniel squeezed her shoulder as he passed and sank down into a chair next to her. 'He never did reckon much to soap and water. Says it takes the good oils out of a man's skin.'

'Hmm. Well, if he's to live with us, he'll have to change a little in that respect.' Hannah's tone became more gentle. 'Are you hungry?'

'Aye, lass, but I'm so tired I'll have a hard time lifting the spoon to my mouth.'

'Me, too.'

'Haven't you eaten anything?'

'No, I waited for you. I wanted us to have our first meal in our new home together.'

'That's a lovely thought, but it's not much of a home

to provide for my family, is it?' Nathaniel looked round with shame in his heart: bare boards on the floor, some of them warped, weather-marked walls with brown stains where the rain had trickled in, and holes in the plaster ceiling.

'There's a roof, food and beds – better than we had on the road,' she said firmly. 'We'll be all right, Nathaniel love. It's a credit to you how your friends rallied round and how quickly you found us somewhere to live.' She had seen him in a new light during the past two days, as a natural leader who had directed the other men with quiet suggestions that quickly created order out of chaos. He seemed to have an instinctive understanding of who was suited to what task that got more work done than she would have believed possible.

'I wish . . .' He broke off.

She waited and when he didn't finish his remark, prompted, 'What do you wish?'

There was just the faintest hint of mischief behind the exhaustion as he said, 'That we had our own bedroom and could spend the night together properly. It's more than time.'

That set a glow inside her. 'I wish it, too. But it'll come, Nathaniel. And when Mr Dewhurst sets this place to rights, we'll have plenty of rooms. I've never lived anywhere as big.' She served them some food and, as soon as they'd eaten, called Tom in and helped him lay out his mattress in one corner. Nathaniel damped down the fire and she piled the plates at one end of the table, too tired even to think of washing them.

Lighting a candle, she went into the bedroom, threading her way carefully past the youngsters' mattresses as she held the flickering light high. Neither of the sleepers stirred.

She lay down without undressing, falling asleep so quickly she even forgot to blow out the candle.

Nathaniel wanted to hold her, but his arms felt too heavy so he made a huge effort and reached across her to pinch out the candle flame, then let the velvety darkness wrap him in oblivion.

When the letter arrived for Nick, his mother guessed it must be about the girl. For a moment she was tempted to burn it, even going so far as to hold the envelope out towards the flames. Then she pulled it back. She mustn't think only of herself. Before she could be tempted again, she took the letter out to where her son was working in the far field, holding it out to him. 'This is what you've been waiting for.'

He rubbed his hand down the side of his trousers and took it from her, his fingers trembling a little as he studied the envelope, seeing his own handwriting and knowing instantly that it was from Mrs Feathers.

'Well, go on. Open it.'

He looked at his mother. 'If it tells me where Ginny is, I'm going to her.'

'I know, son. We were wrong to try to keep you from her. A man should take care of the children he's fathered, and of their mother too.'

He read the landlady's brief note and dashed the back of his hand across his eyes. 'She's living with her uncle in a village called Marton on the other side of Preston. I'll be able to—' Then he read the PS and the smile vanished from his face.

'What is it?'

He looked blindly across the field. 'It seems her step-father has killed her mother, hit her across the face in front of half the village. Mrs West fell backwards and broke her neck. I have to go to Ginny at once. She'll be that upset!' He was striding across the field before he had finished speaking.

His mother hurried after him and got him some warm water to wash in before he changed his clothes. She packed him a few spare things, because likely he'd have to stay overnight, and then put together some sandwiches. 'You'll have to find out about trains when you get to the station.'

He paused in the doorway. 'Can I bring her back here?'

It cost her another huge effort but she nodded. 'Yes. And don't worry, we'll make her welcome. There's that empty cottage.' The brilliant smile he gave her glad-dened her heart, for she couldn't bear to be estranged from her only son.

'I'll thank you properly when I get back, Mam. Just now, I can't seem to take it all in. That poor woman dead! I wonder what they've done with Ginny's little brothers?'

When her husband came in she told him what had happened.

'What have you done, lass? He'll bring her back here now.'

'I've said he could and offered them that empty cottage. And Sam – we'll make her welcome because if we don't, we'll lose both our son and our grandchild. I've lain awake worrying about what we did before. It wasn't right. This is.'

'I was more worried about you, love.'

'What's past is done. I'll not let what that man did to me spoil my son's life.'

Nick didn't arrive in Marton until teatime. When he asked the way out to Nathaniel King's smallholding, he received strange looks and people clammed up, saying they knew nothing.

'What's wrong?' he asked finally in exasperation. 'Why won't you tell me where he is? I'm not leaving until I find him.'

'What exactly is your business with Nathaniel?' one man ventured.

'My business is with his niece. I've been searching for her for weeks. I'm going to marry her.'

More of those assessing looks, then they told him what had happened, which shocked him into silence for a few moments. 'How do I get to this Beckleton, then?'

'You'll have to pay someone to take you over there and no one's going anywhere tonight.'

'I'll pay well.'

The landlord of the inn took him aside and said quietly. 'They've only just come back from helping Nathaniel move his things. They didn't get any sleep at all last night and they're beyond tired. I can let you have my old mare and trap in the morning after she's had a rest, because she's had a hard day, too. The lads told me Nathaniel's worked himself into the ground. If you went now, let alone you'd have trouble finding your way in the dark – or finding anyone to ask directions of once you got there – he'd be in bed by the time you got there and wouldn't thank you for waking him after two days without any sleep.'

And with that Nick had to be content. It made sense, he supposed, but he was aching to find Ginny and set things right between them, so it was hard to wait.

In the morning he was ready as soon as it was light and set off after a very hasty breakfast, driven by the innkeeper's son. He was so lost in thought he didn't notice the scenery. He wasn't sure what he'd say to Ginny when he arrived, wasn't even sure she'd welcome him after all this time. But surely her feelings wouldn't have changed?

Beckleton was a pretty village, but all he wanted was to find Ginny. When he asked a man how to find Nathaniel King, the fellow frowned and said he knew no one of that name.

'He came here yesterday, with several carts.'

'Oh, *that* fellow!'

They arrived at the half-ruined cottage just as Ginny was shaking out the tablecloth after breakfast. She froze at the sight of Nick, clutching the cloth to her breast. He turned to the landlord's son and said, 'You can go back now. I've found her.' He threw his travelling bag off the trap, jumped down and ran to Ginny, gathering her in his arms. 'It's taken me all this time to find you. Don't turn me away.'

She began sobbing and a woman came out of the cottage and rushed across to them. 'Let her go, you!'

Ginny raised a tear-stained face. 'It's Nick, Hannah. He's been looking for me.' Then she began to cry again.

Hannah sent Gregory running to fetch his father, who had gone to examine the plants in Spinneys' kitchen garden and water them, then suggested that Nick come inside.

'I need to talk to Ginny on her own first, if you don't mind, Mrs King?'

She studied his face then looked at the young woman. 'You're sure you want to speak to him, love?'

The girl nodded, her eyes starry with hope, though still brimming with tears.

With his arm round her waist, Nick began to walk away from the house, not caring where they went as long as they could be alone. With a smile Hannah picked up his bag and took it inside.

It was over an hour before the two young folk returned, by which time Nathaniel was getting impatient and the kettle had boiled three times.

Ginny's radiant face told the tale even before Nick said, 'Can I have a word with you, please, sir?'

Nathaniel nodded and stood up.

'Wouldn't you like a cup of tea first?' Hannah offered.

Nick shook his head, wanting to get this interview over. When they went outside, he stood with his hands in his pockets for a moment before saying, 'I've been looking for Ginny for weeks. West wouldn't tell me where she was and no one in the village seemed to know, either. I hope I have your permission to marry her? And it's not just because of the child, it's because I love her.'

'Can you support a wife?'

'Yes. We have a decent farm and my mother told me before I left that she'd welcome my wife into the family. Ginny and I will have a cottage of our own.'

Nathaniel held out his hand. 'That's all right then and I'm happy for you both.'

Nick nodded. 'Thank you.' He hesitated, but there was no avoiding it. 'There's something else I have to tell you, sir. I haven't told Ginny yet. I thought – well, you should know first and help me break the sad news to her.'

'Sad news?'

'Yes, sir. I'm afraid your sister is dead. Mrs Feathers, the landlady at the inn, told me how it happened. At market your sister tried to pass a message to Mrs Feathers, telling me how to find Ginny. West caught her doing it and took the note. When Ginny's mother shouted out where you were, he hit her.' Nick paused to swallow. 'It must have been a very hard blow because she fell backwards on to the cobbles and broke her neck. She died instantly.'

Nathaniel had to turn away for a minute as he tried to take this in. Christine dead! He couldn't believe it. He felt as if he were choking with rage at West. 'Have they locked him up?'

'I gather so.'

'I hope they hang him!' He began to pace to and fro, torn between grief and anger, then stopped as if struck by a sudden thought. 'What about the little lads?'

'Mrs Feathers said she'd look after them till you could go and collect them.'

'Me?' Nathaniel stopped and shook his head, feeling overwhelmed. But it took only a minute's thought for him to realise there was no one else. He looked at the ruined house, wondering how quickly Mr Oliver could get it repaired. Thank heavens there were plenty of rooms. 'We'd better go and tell Ginny and my wife,' he said abruptly.

They went inside to find the two women smiling and chatting.

Seeing his grim expression, Ginny asked at once, 'You're not going to stop us marrying, Uncle?'

'What? Oh, no. Of course not. I wish you both happy.'

'Then what's wrong?'

'Sit down, lass. You too, Hannah.' He explained what had happened, letting Nick hold Ginny against him while she sobbed for her mother. While the young man was soothing her, Nathaniel looked at Hannah. 'There's only me to look after the lads.'

'And me.'

He pulled her towards him and kissed her soundly, heedless of who saw him, then wiped the tears from his own eyes. 'It's one thing after another, isn't it?'

'Yes. But we'll cope.'

Oliver and Ann arrived back in Beckleton the morning after their wedding. The porter scurried to send a message to the inn whose gig was the nearest the village had to a cab.

'I think I'd prefer to walk,' Ann said.

Oliver winked at the porter. 'Can you look after our luggage till I send Ned for it?'

He saw the man staring at them round-eyed so added cheerfully, knowing the news would soon spread, 'My wife and I would prefer to walk home.'

One moment of open-mouthed shock, then, 'Er, yes, and congratulations, my lady.'

'I'd prefer to be known as Mrs Dewhurst now,' Ann told him. 'I no longer wish to use my title.'

'Yes, m'lady. I mean, Mrs Dewhurst.' He looked at Oliver uneasily. 'That'll be why one of the grooms from the Priory has been watching the station. He galloped off when you two got out of the train.'

'Thank you for that information.' As they left the station, Ann suggested, 'Shall we walk home the back way? I don't wish to quarrel with my brother in the middle of the street.'

'Certainly.'

They enjoyed the stroll, taking their time, guessing their peace would soon be at an end.

Shortly after their arrival at Spinneys, Lord Gerald rode up, again accompanied by two grooms. Ned slipped across the field to fetch Nathaniel, finding another young man with him who offered to come as well in case they needed extra help.

'Good lad,' Nathaniel said to Nick with a smile.

When no one answered, Lord Gerald again thumped on the door, yelling that he knew his sister was there and they'd better let him in.

Oliver waited until Ned and Nathaniel were behind him, then went to open the door. This time he had no intention of standing aside and letting others do the fighting, if it came down to that.

Ann waited in the parlour, furious at her brother for spoiling her lovely day as she listened to him shouting at Oliver.

'Where's my damned sister?'

She glared at the doorway. How dared he speak of her like that?

'My wife is inside . . .'

Lord Gerald at once shoved Oliver out of the way and the two grooms surged forward behind him.

Some enthusiastic jostling by Nathaniel and Ned had one of the grooms staggering backwards down the steps and the other followed him soon after, upon which Nick shut the door and locked it.

Oliver turned to his brother-in-law and said icily, 'I don't think my wife will appreciate your forcing an entry to her parlour in that rough manner.'

'She certainly won't,' Ann said from behind him. 'How dare you burst into our house like this, Gerald?'

'I've come to take you home. It's not too late to . . .' His voice trailed away as he saw the smile on her face.

'If you're about to say what I think you are,' she said, going to link her arm in Oliver's, 'then it's far too late.'

'But you could swear he never touched you!' he said desperately. 'Surely you've realised your mistake by now? How can you possibly marry a man with no money, one who has to get others to do his fighting for him?' He cast a scornful glance in Oliver's direction.

'There's no mistake. I'm just sorry he isn't as strong as others – though that in no way affects his ability to act as my husband.' She noted the shock on her brother's face with immense satisfaction. 'And if you can't be civil, I shall ask you to leave this house and not return.'

Gerald began pacing up and down the room. 'I sent a telegram to Father yesterday and he's replied, ordering me to take you home and start annulment proceedings.'

'I shall do no such thing. I'm over twenty-one and

have every right to marry whom I choose, which isn't a man like Walter Dewhurst.'

Oliver stepped forward. 'I think my wife has made her feelings quite clear. I agree with everything she's said, including her views on my brother who is a violent man and would make a dreadful husband.'

Lord Gerald's lip curled. 'Well, you would agree with her, wouldn't you? She'll be bringing you quite a windfall.'

'Call Nathaniel in and ask him to throw my brother out,' Ann said furiously. 'And as for you, Gerald, you may send over my clothes from the Priory, after which I wish never to have anything to do with you again.'

'You'll be sorry. You know Father won't let it go at this.'

'I won't be sorry I married Oliver, only that I have such a discourteous family.'

Oliver opened the hall door and found Nathaniel outside. 'Will you show Lord Gerald out?'

Gerald looked at Nathaniel, who was taller and more heavily muscled and left without another word.

Inside the parlour Ann went to hold her husband's hand. 'I was shaking. Did it show?'

'Not at all. I was proud of you. I just wished I could have protected you better.'

'Oh, Oliver.' She looked up at him, her face soft with affection. 'I love you just as you are. I grew up with a crowd of constantly scrapping brothers and a father who egged them on to fight one another. I hate violence.'

His face was bright with love. 'Then you're not sorry you married me?'

'Of course not.' She chuckled. 'Did I seem sorry last night?'

'No.'

He realised then that Nathaniel had closed the door behind their unwelcome guest and was waiting in the hall for instructions, so went and shook the other man's hand warmly. 'Thank you.'

'I'm glad to have a way to pay you back for the way you're helping us.'

'For giving you a ruin to live in? And that reminds me: Ned, will you ride into Beckleton and call at Mr Coxton's house? Tell him I have some urgent building work for him.'

'It's even more urgent than it was,' Nathaniel said ruefully. 'I had news yesterday that my sister's been killed by her husband and I've to go and bring her two little lads to live with us. Nick will also be staying with us until they can call the banns for him and our Ginny.'

'I'm sorry about your sister, but happy for Ginny.'

'Yes. I am, too.'

Oliver watched him walk away and in spite of the sadness on his face, envied Nathaniel for having so many people to care for. He would be relieved not sorry if anything happened to his own brother. Then he smiled and his breath caught in his throat with the wonder of it. He had Ann now. He wasn't alone in the world.

When Nathaniel arrived in Blackfold the following morning, he went straight to the inn and found the boys sitting very quietly in Mrs Feathers' back room. She seemed highly relieved to see him, glancing down at the little lads who at nine and seven were only too aware of what had happened to their mother.

'There you are! Your Uncle Nathaniel's come to see you just as I said he would.'

They looked at him warily as he came across the room to them and flinched when he tried to hug them, as if expecting a slap. He gave up the attempt and sat down opposite them, making no more sudden movements. 'Are you not at school today?'

'They don't want us there,' Edwin said. 'They say we're the sons of a murderer.'

'Children can be cruel,' Mrs Feathers murmured. 'Eh, I'd give 'em what for if I were their teacher, but this one's nobbut a lass herself. A cup of tea, Mr King?'

He nodded and continued trying to make conversation with the lads, neither of whom responded in more than monosyllables. He could only conclude that they had been beaten into docility and wondered how they would get on with his own Gregory who had turned back into his old lively self, thank goodness, and sometimes talked your ear off.

He drank the tea, noticed that the boys accepted a glass of milk but only sipped half-heartedly, then looked at Mrs Feathers. 'Do I have to see someone about the lads?'

'I think you'd better see the police constable. That parson's trying to stick his nose in, saying he was a friend of their father and should be in charge of them, but I told him straight, that's no recommendation. Let alone it doesn't look well for a parson to be a friend of a murderer, I said, your wife left you not long ago so who's to mother them? I don't blame her a bit, Mr King.

Parson Crawford's just like their father: the sort to thump people who answer him back. Men like that are disgusting.'

Nathaniel was amazed that she was speaking so openly in front of the boys, but as she showed him to the door, she apologised for her frankness.

'I know it sounds bad, but they flinch if you move a finger near them. And when my John came in from the bar, angry about something, they slid under the table. So I thought I'd better start telling them other men aren't like their sod of a father – pardon my language, but he was a sod.'

He was grinning as he walked along the street to the police station. You couldn't help liking Mrs Feathers.

The constable was delighted to see him and get the boys off his hands, wanting only to know his address. That was when Nathaniel realised he didn't know the address of the cottage, so he gave his employer's address instead. 'Can I go out to the farm to get the lads' clothes and things?'

The constable pursed his lips. 'I suppose you'll have to. I think I'd better come with you, though. We're not sure what's going to happen to the place till after the trial.'

'We'll take the lads with us, eh? They'll know better than me where their clothes and toys are. Is there anywhere I can hire a gig?'

'Mrs Feathers has one.'

They found the farmhouse uncomfortably neat, even the boys' room where there were very few toys let alone the sort of models lads were always building, or bits and pieces they'd collected. Edwin and Andrew stayed close together and kept glancing over their shoulder, as if expecting their father to appear suddenly. They looked visibly relieved when they left the house again.

'We'll go back to Beckleton tonight,' Nathaniel decided. 'It'll be late when we get there, but that'll give us a good start tomorrow.'

The boys showed a great deal of interest in their train journey, not having been on one before. Had their father never allowed them to do anything? Nathaniel wondered. He pointed out the engine and said another time he'd take them to see the engine driver but now the train was nearly due to leave.

When they got to Beckleton, he asked the porter if there was someone who'd drive him and the lads home.

The man scratched his head. 'Nay, he'll be in bed by now. Is it far to walk?'

'No. I'm living in the old cottage next to Spinneys. But there's too much luggage for me to carry and the lads are only little.' Much smaller than Gregory had been at their age.

The porter's face cleared. 'I can lend you my old trolley, if you like. You'd get everything on that. You can bring it back tomorrow.'

'Thank you. I'm grateful.'

Nathaniel set off, pushing the trolley, with the lads stumbling along tiredly to one side of him. 'This is your village now. We live on the other side of it.'

They nodded and stole surreptitious glances round, as if they didn't dare stare openly.

What was he going to do with them? he wondered. How was he to turn them into proper little boys again, children who could play roughly, rip their clothes and yell out of sheer exuberance as Gregory did?

And how could he put this burden of rearing them on Hannah? Or would West be acquitted and let loose to hurt them again? He hoped not. By hell, if the fellow ever came near him, Nathaniel would beat him senseless. His own loss hit him again – poor Christine! – but he blinked away the tears. This was not the time to weep for his sister.

The following day, as Nathaniel walked back across the field from discussing repairs with Oliver, a grin crept over his face and he stopped to chuckle.

'Is something amusing you?' Nick, who'd kept him company and was helping with the plants and house in any way he could, looked at him sideways.

'Aye. I had this quiet sort of life with nowt much happening and now there's *too* damned much happening! In fact, my life's turned into a right madhouse.'

'And you find that amusing?'

Nathaniel shrugged. 'I can either find it amusing or sit in a corner and moan about it.'

He got back to find that Hannah had been more successful at putting the boys at ease than he had. They were sitting at the table talking earnestly to her and Ginny, with empty plates in front of them, but fell silent when he and Nick came in, looking warily from one man to the other.

'Well,' said Nathaniel, trying to ignore this, 'I'd better do some work on this house of ours. Mr Oliver's sent for the builder, but I don't know when he'll come so in the meantime I'll do what I can. You two lads will have to sleep in the kitchen until we get another room weatherproof.'

But the builder was so eager to see this young man who had married Lady Ann and upset her family that he came to Spinneys within the hour, walking across the field with Oliver soon after that and inspecting the cottage in great detail.

'Soundly built, but needs a lot of work.'

'When can you start?' Oliver asked.

'Soon as you like, sir.'

'At once, then, if you please.'

Walter heard about his brother marrying Lady Ann the next morning and stood staring in sheer disbelief at Colin, his complexion turning dark red and his hands clenching into fists.

The groom watched him warily, ready to duck out of the way.

'I don't believe you. It's a rumour, that's all.'

'The fellow who told me sounded pretty sure. Apparently it's the talk of Beckleton. Mr Oliver introduced her to the porter at the station as "my wife", and Lord Gerald went round to the house to try to drag her back home, only by then it was too late apparently. They'd – um – already enjoyed their honeymoon.'

'Well, I hope she enjoys being a widow, because that's what she'll soon be.' Walter turned on his heel and went off to find his gun, firing round after round into his targets while he thought up and abandoned half a dozen schemes for paying his brother back, then growing furious with himself for missing the targets, something that only happened when he was angry.

How could she? How the hell could she marry a weakling like Oliver?

Later he went for a ride, but could not stop talking about what had happened and what he intended to do to remedy it. He broke off in mid-sentence. 'What's the matter? Why are you looking at me like that?'

So Colin had to remind him of another unpalatable fact. 'She's your brother's wife, sir. You can never marry her now, even if he dies. It's against the law.'

'And the bitch knew it! *That's* why she did it, not because she cared for him.' Walter urged his horse into a gallop, yelling over his shoulder, 'Well, it won't stop me having her – one way or the other. And she'll be a widow soon, I'll see to that too.'

Colin shook his head as he followed his master. He wasn't getting involved in murder for anyone – or in kidnapping a peer's daughter! Only how to get away? Walter insisted on his being in attendance all the time at the moment.

CHAPTER TWENTY-THREE

May 1864

Lemuel stared at his wife, who was near her time and pacing up and down the kitchen, clutching her belly and looking furious. 'Is something wrong?'

'What do you care?'

'You know I care about you.' He didn't really, not any more, but she was carrying his child so he always tried his hardest to keep her calm. It was growing increasingly difficult, though.

She flung him a glance of loathing. 'You probably had a hand in it.'

'In what?'

'In letting *her* get away with it all.'

His heart sank. This was about his mother, then. Why should Patty suddenly hark back to her old grievances? 'I haven't had a hand in anything.'

'You went to see her. Who knows what you got up to there, what you were both plotting against me?'

'It was only the once, to make sure she was all right. I haven't contacted her since.' Why should Patty think anyone was plotting against her? She was getting stranger by the day and he wasn't the only one to think that.

'It was disloyal of you to go to see her. Parson Barnish said so.' Another swift march across the room before she whirled round to shout, 'And now the Poor Law Commissioner has told him that if your mother is off the hands of our Board of Guardians, they should leave things be. Parson Barnish was my last hope. No one where she's living now will know what she's really like. She'll fool them all, like she fooled people here till *I* came. She'll escape what she deserves!'

She paused to clutch her stomach and groan.

He took a step forward. 'Has the birth started?' It was certainly due – days overdue.

'No! No, it hasn't. I'm not going to have a child! I won't! This is indigestion, that's all.'

But he was worried enough to stay and watch her, saw her clutch her belly twice more, then pretended to be going out to the workshop and ran instead for Dr Kent. The doctor was out and all his housekeeper could do was say she'd send him round when he returned, but it'd likely be a few hours yet.

After a moment's thought Lemuel went for the village midwife, with whom Patty had quarrelled several times because she had refused to let Bet check how things were going with the baby. The nurse returned with him and they found Patty upstairs now, curled up on her bed groaning.

At the sight of them in the doorway she screamed, 'Get away! Leave me alone!'

When the midwife went towards her, Patty picked up the carving knife from the side of the bed and brandished it. 'I'll slice you to pieces if you come near me. I'm *not* having another baby. They'll only take it from me so it's best not to have it at all.'

Shaken, the two of them went back down to the

kitchen and Lemuel was relieved when his wife didn't follow them.

'She's not well,' Bet said. 'How long did they say Dr Kent would be? Hours? Oh, dear. I think she's very close to giving birth and she's going to hurt the baby if she goes on this way. Eh, lad, I don't know how to deal with things like this.'

'Things like what?'

The midwife tapped her forehead.

'The housekeeper didn't know how long Dr Kent would be.' Lemuel bent his head, avoiding Bet's pitying gaze. He'd been trying to tell himself it was just the pregnancy, but no one could deny that Patty's behaviour today was very strange.

'Has your wife – um – been acting strange lately?'

He nodded, finding relief in admitting it aloud at last. 'Very. She's been strange all along with this one, but it's got worse the past week or two. I haven't known what to do. I've just tried not to upset her.'

Bet looked at him with sympathy. 'No one knows what to do with these cases. It's not like breaking a leg.' She hesitated then, as a particularly loud scream rang out from upstairs, added, 'I think you'd better ask for help from the asylum, Lemuel. The porters there are used to dealing with people like your wife.'

He stared at her in horror, unable to form a word, so shocked was he by this suggestion. 'But Patty's only having a baby. There's no need to put her in that place.'

'I think she's in a bad way, Lemuel love. You'll have to get help or she might die – and the baby with her.'

So he stumbled along the back lane to knock on the asylum door and ask for help, while Bet sat in the kitchen listening to Patty rant and rave and scream. Eh, she'd never seen a worse case. Well, you might say it served the woman right for putting Hannah Firth into the asylum, but Bet always felt sorry for people who went mad.

As for Parson Barnish . . . a smile crept slowly across her face, and she went outside to hail the first passer-by and ask him to fetch the parson quick. See what he thought of the woman who had told him all those lies now! Maybe he'd consider more carefully in future before hounding innocent people like Hannah Firth on one person's word alone.

The parson came at once and went up to see Patty, full of confidence that he could soothe her and calm her down. Bet stood at the foot of the stairs with arms folded as she listened to Patty ranting and raving, groaning and occasionally screaming, then yelling at the parson to get out or she'd stab him.

He came down looking white and shaken.

'She told you Hannah Firth was mad, but it was her all along who was mad,' Bet told him with great satisfaction. 'Maybe next time you'll listen to what others have to tell you, not just one person.'

'But Patty seemed so genuine, so in need of help.'

'She was. But not your sort of help. I hope you'll have Hannah's name crossed off the asylum records? She doesn't deserve that stain on her character.'

He nodded and left without a word.

The back door opened then and Lemuel came in, looking haggard and beaten down by life. With him were the two burly porters from the asylum. They listened to the sounds coming from upstairs and looked at one another knowingly.

'Got a walking stick, Mr Firth?' asked one.

'Yes.'

'Can't get too close till we've knocked the knife out of her hand, you see.'

They took the stick, which had belonged to his father, and went towards the stairs.

Lemuel pushed in front of them. 'I have to try one more time to talk sense to her. I don't want her hurt.'

They looked at Bet, rolled their eyes and followed him up just in time to see Patty stab him in the arm. She didn't even notice them as she drew the knife back for another blow.

One knocked it out of her hand with the stick and the other rolled her in the bedding before she had worked out what was going on. Then they carried the screaming, squirming bundle down the stairs, complaining about how heavy she was.

'Better go and help Lemuel, Bet,' said one. 'She's stabbed him in the arm. Bad cut it is, too. I reckon the doctor will have to stitch it together.'

She looked towards the stairs. 'Poor man. You have to feel sorry for him. He's too soft for his own good and folk take advantage.'

Just before dusk two men turned up at the ruined cottage in a large cart and asked where they should unload the new planks and roof slates.

Nathaniel indicated a spot then he and Nick helped them.

'We'll be here as soon as it's light tomorrow,' one told him after they'd finished unloading. 'Mr Dewhurst wants the work done as quick as possible.'

'We'll be ready for you.'

After they'd gone, Nathaniel went to fetch Hannah and walk round the piles of materials with her. 'See. Good fine wood, that. Well seasoned. We'll soon have the whole place waterproof.' He lowered his voice to add, 'And we'll have our own bedroom, too, I hope.'

She walked into his arms and they kissed hungrily. 'I can't wait,' she gasped when he'd stopped kissing her and she could breathe properly again. It was wonderful kissing Nathaniel. Eh, she was lucky to have found him, so very lucky.

They turned to discover Edwin and Andrew staring at them as if mystified by what they'd just seen.

Hannah flushed under the boys' unblinking gaze, but Nathaniel seized the moment to say, 'I'm not like your father, lads. Not many men are. I love my wife and it's more fun to kiss her than hurt her.'

They looked at him, brows wrinkled in thought, but still said nothing.

Gregory came round the corner just then, whistling, and stopped dead, his eyes going from Hannah's blushing face to the way his father's arm was still round her waist. 'You aren't kissing again, are you?' He made a disgusted sound in his throat and turned to his cousins. 'They're allus kissing, them two. I'm never getting married if I have to keep kissing someone all the time. Look. I've brought out my cata-pult an' I'll let you have a go with it, if you want. I can make you both one as well. They're good fun, catapults are.'

They nodded and trotted off after him, but Andrew looked over his shoulder once at Hannah and his expression was still puzzled.

Bedtime was a chaos of mattresses on the floor. Nathaniel had managed to scrounge some hay and Hannah had sewed ticking by hand and stuffed it with the straw to create a makeshift mattress for the two lads, promising them a proper feather mattress later. She'd had to borrow blankets for them from Mrs Parkin, they were so short of bedding. She made up a bed on the kitchen floor and the boys went to lie down on it as soon as they'd eaten, looking exhausted. They fell asleep almost at once, cuddled up against one another like a pair of puppies, seeming undisturbed by the people still sitting talking quietly at the table nearby.

But no one sat there for long because they would have to be up at the crack of dawn to be ready for the builders and after that Hannah wanted to walk into the village because Ned said it was market day. Tom offered to take care of the plants, watering them and pulling out the dead ones, of which there were quite a few.

'That'll be a good help,' Nathaniel told him, but watched Tom walk slowly away with a frown on his face. Was it his imagination or was the old man getting weaker? He was definitely walking more stiffly and his colour wasn't good. Was that just because of the sudden move or was it something else? Eh, he'd miss the old fellow when he died.

∗　　∗　　∗

When Ann heard that her father had arrived in Beckleton she could not help worrying about what he was planning. She slipped into the village to see the verger's wife with whom she was quite friendly since they both loved flowers and had exchanged plant cuttings.

'Lady Ann, do come in. What an honour!'

'I'm using the name Mrs Dewhurst now.' She allowed her friend to settle her in the front parlour, a room stiff with polish and lace covers and clearly little used, then came straight to the point. 'Becky, did you see my father arrive?'

'Well, yes. I just happened to look out of the window, since I was expecting a call from a neighbour at the time.'

This was the usual fiction to explain Becky seeing what went on, so Ann nodded. 'Who did my father bring with him?'

'That lawyer who came to see us when they put up our rents and changed our leases.' Becky sniffed. 'No one likes to see *him*. I hope they're not going to put up the rents again or I don't know how we shall manage.'

'I hope not, too. Was there anyone else with him?'

'Another gentleman. No one knows who *he* is. And two other men – not *gentlemen*, if you know what I mean. In fact, they looked more like prizefighters to me. The sort you see in booths at the fair.'

Ann blinked in shock. Why would her father bring men like that? A leaden feeling settled in her stomach. Only one reason that she could think of: he intended to get her back by force.

'Thank you, Becky. Will you keep your eyes open and let me know if any more strange people arrive? And may I leave by the back door? I don't want anyone from the Priory to see me.'

She hurried home, glancing back over her shoulder at regular intervals, her heart pounding with the fear of being pursued.

When she burst in on Oliver, he came to take her in his arms. 'My dear, what's wrong? You look upset.'

'I am. My father's arrived at the Priory and from what Becky tells me, he's brought his lawyer and another stranger and – oh, he's brought two strong men! Oliver, I'm afraid he means to kidnap me and then who knows what Mr Telling will arrange? Father doesn't scruple to turn the law to his advantage.'

'But what *can* he do?'

'Find a way to annul our marriage.'

'We must get away, then, go and hide somewhere.'

'How? You can be sure they're already watching the station and probably this house.'

He was shocked. 'Surely they wouldn't—'

'My father would do anything for money,' she said bitterly, 'and he never comes here willingly. He hates Lancashire.' She laid her head on his shoulder. 'Oh, Oliver, I should have found another way to avoid marrying your brother. I shouldn't have embroiled you in this, put you in danger. Only,' she looked up at him shyly, 'I like being your wife. We could be so happy together if only people would leave us alone.'

But they didn't. Her father came to visit them that very afternoon. The minute Ned saw the carriage from the Priory turn into the drive, he went running for Nathaniel and Nick, as instructed.

When someone knocked on the front door, Nanny opened it, seeing beyond the man on the steps the Marquess descending from the carriage with the help of a groom. A short, thin man, this lord, and a nasty piece of work from what she'd overheard her mistress saying. But if you were a peer of the realm, she supposed you could be as nasty as you wanted.

He entered without being invited and held out his hat and gloves to her. 'Kindly take me to my daughter. I wish to speak to her alone.'

Oliver, who had been listening from the front parlour, came into the hall. 'My wife prefers me to be involved in any discussions, Lord Iffingham. Thank you, Nanny. I'll take his lordship into the parlour.'

'What I have to say to my daughter is private.'

'I insist on my husband being present,' Ann said from the door of the parlour. Her stomach was quivering with nerves, but she held herself upright and kept reminding herself that she was not in her father's power any longer.

The look the Marquess threw at Oliver was full of hatred as well as disdain. He swept into the parlour, pausing to look round and say scornfully, 'I'm ashamed to see you in such reduced circumstances, daughter.'

'I'm very happy here, Father. A simpler life suits me. Will you take a seat?'

He condescended to sit bolt upright on one of the armchairs so Ann and Oliver went to sit on the sofa together, which made their visitor curl his lip in disgust. 'I cannot countenance such a misalliance, Ann,' he announced. 'I've brought Telling with me and a doctor. They'll do all that's necessary to annul the marriage.'

'I don't want it annulled.'

'You'll do as you're told, for the sake of the family! And you, sir, if you know what's good for you, will stop insisting on this charade of there being a marriage between you and my daughter. Believe me, I have enough influence to make your life a misery if you don't do as I say.'

'My wife and I are quite happy together and neither of us intends to do anything to annul our marriage.' Oliver took hold of Ann's limp hand under the fold of her dress and gave it a quick squeeze and she turned for a moment to smile at him. 'What's more, the marriage has been well and truly consummated, so there is nothing you can do about it.'

'You're very naïve if you think that. My doctor is prepared to swear she's a virgin still, after which it will be quite simple to annul everything.'

'And then what?' Ann demanded.

'You'll marry this man's brother.'

She shuddered. 'I'd kill myself first. You haven't met Walter Dewhurst or you'd not suggest that.'

He looked down his narrow nose at her. 'It isn't necessary to like the person you marry, only to make sure that it is a suitable connection for the family.'

She stood up. 'You couldn't force me say the words of the ceremony.'

'It would be a simple matter to find men willing to swear they'd heard you say them.'

A chill ran through her and she stared at him aghast. He'd do it, too. He cared nothing for any of them.

Smiling, her father stood up. 'I can see that you finally believe me. Come back with me now and end this foolish charade.'

She shook her head. 'No. I'm married to Oliver and I shan't change my mind about that.'

'I'll give you twenty-four hours to think this over, Ann. If you really have been stupid enough to fall in love with this fellow, you'll not want to see him hurt.' He completely ignored Oliver as he walked out, waiting as his host followed him and opened the front door, but not saying thank you for this courtesy.

Nathaniel, who had been listening outside the open window in case he was needed, couldn't believe what he'd heard. He looked at Ned, who was standing beside him, both of them hidden from the carriage and its driver by a large bush. He didn't need to say anything. Ned looked as shocked as Nathaniel felt.

When the Marquess had left, Oliver thanked Nathaniel and Nick for coming across to help out then went back inside the house. Ann was still sitting on the sofa, looking terrified.

'I've been thinking,' he said. 'I believe I'd like to consult my own lawyer about this and perhaps lodge our marriage lines with him for safety.'

Her face brightened a little. 'Yes.' Then she shook her head. 'The railway station will be watched and they won't let you get on a train. They might even take the document from you.'

'This is 1864 and your father is not, I believe, the King of England!'

'He's the Marquess of Iffingham and that's enough for him. No one has ever stopped him doing what he wants since the day he inherited. Anyway, who do you think would come to your aid? The villagers are afraid of him. He's brought some strong men with him and there are no doubt others working on the estate who'll be glad to do whatever he says for payment.'

He went to sit beside her and, as she leaned her head against him, put his arm round her shoulders. 'There has to be a way.' Then he suddenly remembered how he had sometimes avoided his brother. 'There *is*!' He got to his feet and began pacing to and fro as he explained, 'When you're not strong physically, you find other ways of doing things. I used to dress up as a servant to get out of the house and avoid Walter when he was in one of his moods. I could do that, catch a train, travel third-class and then go to see my lawyer.'

She was frowning at him. 'They'll be watching everyone who leaves, I'm sure of it. Every man on his own will be checked.'

'Then I shan't go on my own. Perhaps I'll take Penny and pretend she's my sweetheart.'

Ann pulled a face, 'Penny's a hard worker but she's rather silly.'

'There's no one else in the house. Nanny is too recognisable, Cook's too old and your hair would give you away.'

'I wonder . . .' she said slowly.

'What?'

'About Ginny, Nathaniel's niece?'

'We couldn't ask her. She's carrying a child.'

'Yes, and it shows, so that'd make her a perfect wife for a young labourer.'

They stared at one another then Ann said, 'Send Ned for Nathaniel and we'll ask him what he thinks.'

So for the second time that day Nathaniel walked across the field to Spinneys. When he heard what they wanted, he grew thoughtful. 'It could work, but I'm not sure Ginny should do it. We don't want to do anything to harm the baby.'

'I'll take the greatest care of her,' Oliver promised. 'And I'll pay her for her help – as I intend to pay you, Nathaniel, for what you're doing. Be sure of that.'

In the end Nathaniel went back to the cottage and asked Hannah what she thought. She was unpacking the baskets of fresh food she'd bought at the market and stopped work to consider. 'I think it'd be all right, as long as Mr Oliver is well disguised. I think Ginny would enjoy the outing, actually. She gets a bit restless, stuck in the house all day. Don't forget Nick, though. He'll have to give his consent, too.'

Ginny thought it was a good idea and said she would be happy to help the man they all referred to now as 'Mr Oliver'.

Nick didn't like the idea of Ginny putting herself at risk, so Hannah suggested he go to Preston too, but on his own not with the 'young couple'. That way he'd be able to keep an eye on his betrothed. 'They'd see at a glance that you weren't Mr Oliver, so there's no need for a disguise. And I'll go to Spinneys with you first, Ginny. I want to make sure Mr Oliver's disguise is a good one.'

A young couple boarded the one o'clock train to Preston, the man helping his wife who was clearly expecting a child.

The two men waiting at the station and scrutinising the few people who made journeys barely looked at them, but stopped Nick and asked brusquely who he was and where he was going. Mindful of the need to protect Ginny he didn't tell them to leave him alone, as was his initial reaction, but said he wanted to visit friends in Preston.

The watchers called over the porter, who looked very nervous. 'Do you know this man?'

He nodded.

'Who is he?'

'He's from Blackburn way, staying here with friends.'

'Not related to anyone at Spinneys?'

'Oh, no.' The porter avoided Nick's eyes and when they nodded a dismissal went back to his work with relief. He had not said a word about Mr Dewhurst, whom he had recognised instantly in spite of the disguise, and he guessed this young fellow had something to do with him as well. They'd all had ample demonstration of the Marquess's ruthlessness, seen people not only thrown out of their cottages but hounded out of the village. The porter prayed that wouldn't happen to him, but he couldn't – he simply could not – help men like these two, men who'd boasted of the way they dealt with anyone who upset them. Why, everyone knew Mr Dewhurst wasn't a strong man but he was a kind one and well liked in the village already, as was his wife. As he signalled the train driver to leave, the porter wondered where they were all going.

CHAPTER TWENTY-FOUR

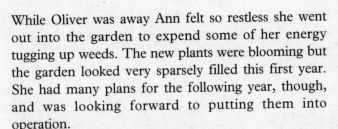

While Oliver was away Ann felt so restless she went out into the garden to expend some of her energy tugging up weeds. The new plants were blooming but the garden looked very sparsely filled this first year. She had many plans for the following year, though, and was looking forward to putting them into operation.

She went round to the back to look at Nathaniel's plants. Some appeared to be dying, but the hardier ones were surviving. She had a chat with Tom, who was pottering around in the kitchen garden, though the poor old fellow could hardly walk now. Afterwards she walked round to the side of the garden away from the lane to sit in the new summerhouse which looked out across the fields. It had only a bare bench, but was already one of her favourite places.

While she was sitting there she heard shouting from the house and jumped up in dismay. What was happening?

Tom appeared in the doorway, panting. 'Your father's sent some men and they've broke into the house to find you.'

She couldn't hold back a whimper of panic, then pressed her hand quickly to her mouth to prevent more escaping. 'What am I to do?' she whispered.

'You could go and hide at the cottage, missus.'

'What if they come after me there? I don't want to bring trouble to Hannah and the boys.'

'Go and ask Hannah what to do, then. She's a rare sensible woman, that one. She's bound to think of something.'

'You'd better stay here and keep out of their way, Tom.'

He nodded and, when she'd gone, sank down on the bench. He wasn't feeling too bright lately. He'd somehow found the strength to run across the garden and warn her, but was now paying for the effort he'd made.

Not finding any sign of Ann in the house, Lord Iffingham's men came out to search the gardens and found Tom slumped on the bench in the summerhouse, only half-conscious. They shook him roughly to wake him up and question him.

'Stop pretending, old man.'

'I'm not pretending. I had a funny turn,' he whined, sagging against the man holding him because his knees had no strength in them. 'What time is it? Must have been lying here a while.'

'Have you seen Lady Ann?'

He looked at them in puzzlement. 'Mrs Dewhurst, you mean.'

They laughed. 'Not for long. Have you – seen her?' More shaking.

'Not since this morning.'

They let him go and stormed off to continue searching.

He collapsed to the ground and it was a while before he could even pull himself on to the bench again.

Ann ran across the field, praying the men wouldn't look in her direction. She burst into the kitchen at the cottage without knocking. 'Oh, Hannah, my father's sent some men to capture me and Oliver isn't here! I don't know what to do.'

'Drat! My Nathaniel's not here, either. He's gone to help fetch another load of slates.' Hannah stood undecided for a minute, then looked at the three boys who had come running in to see what was wrong. 'You're not to say you've seen her here. There are bad men looking for her who'll hurt her.'

'But if they come here, they'll find her,' Gregory protested. 'There's nowhere to hide.'

Hannah set one hand on her hip, studying Ann. 'Not if we disguise her. Eh, it must be the day for disguises! You're about the same height as our Ginny so we'll turn you into her. They'll look at you, but they'll see her.'

Gregory laughed and clapped his hands together. He saw the two other boys edge closer to one another and said warningly, 'You're not to give her away. She's your sister Ginny now, right?'

They nodded, already under his spell and willing to follow his lead.

Very quickly Hannah found a simple print dress of Ginny's and put it on over Ann's finer clothes, pinning the silken skirts up underneath to hide them. She shook her head about the distinctive hair, then snapped her fingers as the solution came to her. 'I know, mob cap! Now where did I put it after I'd washed those walls down?' She found a crumpled cap and pinned Ann's hair carefully out of the way under it, then put a cushion under the front of the dress, adjusting it carefully and standing back to study the effect. 'No, they'd know at once it was only a cushion . . .'

She dived into her bundle of clothes and pulled out a pinafore, tying it round Ginny and nodding in satisfaction. 'That's better. Let's see what the boys say.' She led Ann back into the kitchen and Gregory clapped his hands together in delight.

'She looks a bit like Ginny now.' He patted his stomach and grinned.

'You go and keep watch for anyone coming across the field, boys. And you, Ginny, had better start kneading the bread.'

Ann stared down at the lump of dough. 'I'm afraid I don't know what to do.'

Hannah gave her a quick lesson in kneading dough, watched her start working tentatively on the huge mass in the wooden dough trough that had once belonged to Sarah King. 'Be rough with it. You want to knead it, not stroke it. Yes, that's better.' But she knew this was one batch of bread that wouldn't turn out well. When she was satisfied that Ann had got some sense of a rhythm into her kneading so that she looked right, she said, 'Better rest now and set to work only if they come here. It's hard work, kneading bread.'

'Perhaps they won't come.'

But they did.

Gregory warned them the men were approaching, then Hannah ordered him and the lads to go out and play at the rear of the cottage.

'But we want to watch.'

'It'll look strange you being indoors on a day like this. Do you want to give the game away?'

He slouched out, snatching up his catapult from the shelf by the door and going reluctantly to set up his target.

The men entered the cottage without knocking.

Hannah stared at them in feigned shock. 'Who do you think you are, walking into my house like this?'

'Shut up!' The man in charge nodded to his two companions. 'Search it. This is the first place she'd run to.'

'Ginny' continued kneading the dough and the men gave her the most cursory of glances once they'd seen her jutting belly. They searched the rest of the house very thoroughly, however, ignoring Hannah's protests.

'Who are you?' she demanded as they came back into the kitchen.

'Marquess of Iffingham's men. If you've any complaints about our visit, go and see him.'

They all guffawed. Clearly they were enjoying their moment of power.

'But this cottage doesn't belong to the Marquess of Iffingham.' Just as she was speaking, Nathaniel walked into the house.

Afraid he might give the show away or get into a fight with the men, Hannah felt her heart begin to beat faster. She cast him a quick glance of warning, but he looked at her without expression.

'What are these men doing here?'

'They're the Marquess of Iffingham's men, searching for someone.'

'We're searching for his daughter,' one of them said. 'You wouldn't happen to have seen her, would you?'

'Why should I? And if I had, why should I tell you?'

'Because we could ask you questions in a way you can't refuse to answer.' The man moved forward, fists bunched, grinning in anticipation. 'In fact, I think we'd better do that to be sure.'

Even as he spoke, the builder's two sturdy sons entered the room. 'Ready to start work, Nathaniel lad?' one of them said, as if he hadn't just been listening outside the door.

The three bullies stopped and stared at the men facing them. 'Who are you?'

'None of your business.'

The leader grew red in the face, but the two groups of men were obviously fairly evenly matched and in the end he backed off from a fight. 'Aw, she's not here. Why waste time on such as him?' He jerked his head in Nathaniel's direction. 'If the Marquess wants to question him, he'll have him fetched later.'

As they left, Nathaniel followed them to the door and stood outside it, arms folded, watching them until they re-entered the grounds of Spinneys.

'Nasty pieces of work, them two,' said Sim, the older son. 'I'm not surprised to see Jeb Denny with 'em. He allus were a sly sort, all that family are. You'd better watch out for yourselves, though. We shan't be around to protect you at night.'

Nathaniel looked at them. 'What if I wanted someone around and paid them for their help?'

They looked at one another and shrugged. 'Might be able to find someone, but only after dark. No one would want to be recognised. The Marquess isn't famous for his kindness as a landowner. He'd throw us out of our cottage as soon as blink.'

'I doubt those men will be back tonight. Send anyone who's interested to see me tomorrow evening.' But would there be anyone? Who knew better than Nathaniel how hard it was for tenants to go against a powerful landowner?

He went back into the house to find Hannah still standing where he had left her. Ann was clutching the edge of the table with floury hands, shaking with reaction.

He went across to pat her on the shoulder, forgetting that she was a titled lady, just seeing a young woman who was upset. 'It's all right, love. They've gone now.'

'But for how long?' Ann asked. 'If they dare do this in daylight, what will they try next?'

'I don't know. Is your father a stubborn sort of man?'

'Very.'

'Then he'll likely try something else. We'd best be prepared.'

Hannah watched him wonderingly. Her Nathaniel was telling a noble lady what to do – and the lady was listening with respect.

In Preston Oliver left his two companions to amuse themselves, arranging to meet them behind his lawyer's rooms in time to return to the station and catch the four o'clock train.

Mr Bentley was shocked rigid at the sight of Oliver dressed in a working man's clothing, and even more shocked at what the young man had to tell him. He found it hard to believe at first, but his client had always seemed a steady, sensible fellow and the lawyer could not dismiss what he was saying. 'You say you've brought your marriage lines with you?'

'Yes.'

'That was very sensible. May I suggest you leave them with me? I'll put them in our strongbox at the bank so that no one, absolutely no one, will be able to get them without our permission.'

'And don't believe it if you get written permission from me to give them to anyone else,' Oliver said, feeling like an actor in a melodrama. 'If I want them back, I'll come in person for them.'

'We'd better put that in writing, just in case.' The lawyer got out a piece of paper, chewed the end of his pen and then wrote carefully, calling his clerk in to witness his client's signature.

When they had finished that, Oliver asked, 'Now, is there anything else I can do to protect my wife?'

'Distasteful as it may seem, it might be wise to get a doctor to examine her, to prove that the marriage has indeed been consummated.'

'Like everyone else, the doctor in the village is dependent on the goodwill of the Marquess of Iffingham.'

'Ah. Then perhaps you could bring her to Preston. I know a good man whom I could recommend.'

'I doubt they'd let her leave the village at the moment, and anyway I don't think there's time. Her father gave her twenty-four hours to make up her mind. I'm sure he has some other course of action in mind if she refuses to do what he wants.'

Mr Bentley shook his head, tutting and making little noises of dismay. 'The police?'

'There is only one constable and his family work on the estate.'

'In this day and age! I am shocked, Mr Dewhurst, shocked and dismayed. But you did the right thing coming to me and I shall consult a friend of mine about the situation, if you'll permit? He's a magistrate.' The lawyer raised one eyebrow questioningly and Oliver nodded his agreement. 'If you need further help, let me know and I'll contact him.'

The journey home passed all too quickly. Nick sat in another carriage further back and Ginny again sat next to Oliver.

'I hope everything went well for you today, sir?' she asked shyly.

'As well as could be expected. Did you enjoy your trip?'

'Oh, yes. I haven't had time alone with Nick, not really, for so long. And it was lovely to see such fine shops.' She sighed happily.

When they got back to Spinneys, they found everything in chaos. The men had taken no care in their search and Nanny was still spluttering with indignation about how they'd damaged things. Penny kept bursting into tears and saying she wanted to go home because dear knew what those villains would do next, and Cook was banging the pans around.

'And don't tell me they didn't make this mess on purpose, because they did!' Nanny told her employer, then turned to say sharply to Penny, 'Pull yourself together, girl!'

He was interested in only one thing. 'Where's Ann? Is she all right?'

'Over at the cottage, Tom says. We haven't dared go across to see her.'

All three of them hurried across the field to the cottage, where Oliver found his wife sitting comfortably in the kitchen, a dab of flour on her nose and a ridiculously large apron still tied round her suspiciously broad waist. The room seemed full of people, but he had eyes only for her. 'Are you all right?'

'Yes.' She went to greet him in a little rush.

Hannah was pleased to see them back safely, and also pleased to see that the gentry could love one another just as ordinary people did. Lady Ann was the first person with a title Hannah had ever met but she was a nice lass, all the same.

She smiled across the room at Nathaniel and suggested Oliver stay and join in their discussion. 'If they come again we're all going to be in trouble, not just you, Mr Dewhurst. Those men took a real dislike to my Nathaniel and will be wanting to get at him for standing up to them. Bullies never like that.'

Oliver nodded and sat down at the table. 'I don't know what to do,' he confessed. 'I doubt Ann and I would even be able to leave Beckleton, or I'd take her away within the hour.'

'We should hire some guards,' Nathaniel said, seeing everyone looking at him.

'Will people round here be willing to work for me?' Oliver wondered.

'No. And I don't blame them. They have their families to think about. I thought of going back to Marton, where I used to live, and hiring some of the lads I know there. They're not dependent on that Marquess. What do you think, Mr Oliver? After all, you'll have to pay them.'

'I'll do anything to keep my wife safe.'

Nathaniel nodded then looked at Ann. 'Will your father really keep trying to seize you?'

She nodded. 'Oh, yes. He desperately needs Walter's money. My brother Gerald says he's had some business losses lately.'

'Then I'll have to fetch some additional help. May I ask what the lawyer said, Mr Oliver?'

'He was shocked and couldn't think of anything else I could do, given that the Marquess of Iffingham is a peer of the realm and I've no influence. He did say he'd talk to a friend of his, though I can't see what someone in Preston can do, even if he is a magistrate. But I'm to let them know if anything else happens, and at least our marriage lines are safe now.'

At the Priory, the Marquess of Iffingham glared at his youngest son. 'You know the village better than I do. Where could your sister have been hidden?'

Gerald shook his head. 'I have no idea, sir. I'm sure the parson wouldn't hide her. He's too afraid of you.'

'Not afraid enough or he'd have refused to conduct the ceremony.'

'He said he didn't dare refuse or the Bishop would have created a fuss. As for today, Ann wouldn't have known your men were going to try to capture her so she'd not have had time to get to the village. They even searched the cottage nearby and she definitely wasn't there.' He didn't like the way his father was treating her, but couldn't think what to do about it.

'Well, she escaped and we still don't know how. She could do it again.' The Marquess began to tap the curled fingers of his right hand on the desk, nails making the clicking sound that had always filled Gerald with apprehension. When his father did that, someone was in serious trouble.

'This Walter Dewhurst – you say he's the ruthless sort?'

'Yes. Bit of a rough diamond. Rich as Croesus, but not really a gentleman.'

'Sounds perfect for Ann.'

Gerald hesitated, then decided to intervene. 'She hates him. Surely you could find someone else, sir?'

'When I've finished with her, she'll be glad to take anyone.'

It was best not to comment on that, but Gerald couldn't help feeling sorry for his sister – and less and less inclined to help his father.

'Send for this Walter Dewhurst. I want to see him tonight. In fact, ride across to Marton yourself and bring him back. He can dine with us.'

Gerald blinked at that, but thought it best to do as he was told without further comment.

At Marton Hall he found Walter pacing up and down in the stable yard, looking angry and cracking his whip as he walked. But when he saw who it was, he threw aside the whip and strode to greet Gerald. 'Just the man I wanted to see.'

'M'father wishes to meet you. He's invited you to dine with us.'

'Tonight? I was considering paying my dear brother a visit tonight.'

'Um – better see my father first, I'd say. He's got his own ideas on how to deal with this, and he can turn pretty nasty if you cross him.'

'What does that matter? I can't marry your sister now even if I do get rid of Oliver – she's my brother's wife and the stupid bloody law forbids it, it seems.'

'Ah. Well, Father has that in hand, too. He's brought a doctor from town with him to swear she's still a virgin, and a lawyer to handle the annulment.'

Walter stopped pacing up and down to stare at him, then a nasty smile curved his lips. 'I think I shall get on well with your father.'

Gerald swallowed, liking this less and less. 'You won't, you know. And if you're sensible, you'll not trust him an inch. He's only interested in two things: getting money out of you, and punishing Ann for disobeying him.'

'He can have the money as long as I get what I want.'

Walter's gloating expression added to Gerald's sense of guilt. Dash it, Ann had never hurt anyone in her life, but his father was trying to hurt *her*. He remembered her suddenly as a little girl, always trying to tag along and play with him. Sometimes he'd even let her, but in the past few years hadn't seen much of her. He wished suddenly that they'd had a different father, one he wasn't afraid of, one who cared about his children's happiness.

Walter yelled to a groom, 'Bring the carriage round to the house in half an hour!' then ushered Gerald inside with him. 'I'd better change my clothes. You can ride back with me. We'll send a groom over with your horse.'

As they drove towards the Priory, Walter questioned his friend carefully and got the whole story out of him, including the abortive attempt to kidnap Ann that very day.

'We'll have to get hold of that niece of King's then and find out exactly what happened. If she was at the cottage when they went there, she'll know whether your sister was hiding somewhere or not. I'll make sure she tells us what we want to know.' He would enjoy doing that, as he would enjoy dealing with King once and for all.

'I say, steady on! We can't go round kidnapping people . . .'

'Don't be so soft. If you want something you have to go after it, whatever it takes.' Walter was glad he'd instructed Colin to ride Lord Gerald's horse over to the Priory. He could always rely on his groom to find out exactly what was going on from the servants' gossip.

Tom returned to the cottage at dusk, looking as if he would collapse from the effort of each slow step. Hannah sat him down and asked him what the matter was, he looked so bad.

'I'm on the way out, I reckon, lass,' he said. 'Had a good life, though I wish me and the wife had had childer. But Nathaniel here has kep' me out of the poor-house and looked after me, an' I'll allus be grateful to him.'

'Don't talk like that. You're just a bit run down.'

He raised his hand to pat hers, and even that took a visible effort. 'Don't pretend. I'm ready to go afore I become a burden.'

'Oh, Tom . . .'

'But I could still fancy a piece of your bread, the soft part, and maybe a scrape of jam on it.'

'Of course.' She helped him across to the rocking chair and cut up some of the new bread, which wasn't as light as usual, though Ann hadn't done badly for a beginner. She told him how the bread had been made and he smiled in a tired way.

When she went outside to find Nathaniel, she mentioned that Tom wasn't at all well.

'Do I need to fetch the doctor?'

'No. He's just old and tired. Says he's ready to go.' Tears filled her eyes. 'Oh, Nathaniel, he said such lovely things about you looking after him. It made me feel so proud.'

'Well, I'm proud of you, too, love. Look how you saved Lady Ann today.'

She sniffed and tried to smile at him.

'Eh, it's not like you to weep all over me,' he teased.

'It's been a strange sort of day and I'm exhausted.' She let him guide her to sit on a rough bench he'd cobbled together and they stayed there for a while, hand in hand.

The boys came back, muddy and tired but looking happy. All three stopped to stare at them, then Gregory rolled his eyes and led the way inside, muttering, 'They're doing it *again*.'

'I'll come in a minute to get the tea,' Hannah called.

'Let them wait,' Nathaniel said softly. 'You deserve a rest and I deserve a minute or two with my wife.'

They sat watching the shadows grow longer and listening to the birds calling sleepily.

'We made good progress on the roof today,' he said. 'I'm looking forward to us having our own bedroom, though.'

'If we're allowed to.' She shivered suddenly. 'Did you see those men's faces? They were so brutal and confident. I think they'll be back. Oh, Nathaniel, how can we go against a Marquess?'

'He's only a man, same as us, and it's him who's breaking the law,' he said stoutly. 'Phil and Sim said they'd find us some guards for night-time, but I think I'll have to go across to Marton and bring some others back. I'll maybe do it tomorrow afternoon and come back under cover of darkness, if I can find someone to stay with you. I'm not having my wife and family threatened like this. Nor I don't think Lady Ann deserves it, either.'

'Can her father really have the marriage set aside? She was telling me he'd threatened that.'

'Well, if Mr Oliver's taken his marriage lines to his lawyer, they'll have difficulty saying they don't exist, won't they?'

Across the field Ginny and Nick came into view, strolling arm in arm.

'Those two seem comfortable together,' Hannah said with a smile. It was good to see such happiness amongst all the threats and violence.

'Aye. We'll have the first banns called for them on Sunday. Better send them down to see the parson tomorrow to fix that up, eh?'

'I like a wedding. There's so much hope.'

Nathaniel's stomach rumbled suddenly and he laughed. 'I think we'd better get inside. If I'm hungry, Gregory will be dying of starvation. I can't believe how much that lad's been eating lately.'

'Shall we be safe here tonight?'

'I don't know, love. But it's Lady Ann they want, not us. Still, I'll lock the door and put out some booby traps so we'll know if anyone comes prowling round. It's all I can do till we get some more help.'

They found Tom asleep with the plate nearly slipping off his knee and only half the bread and jam eaten. He didn't stir when they ate their meal, but eventually Nathaniel woke him and helped him outside to relieve himself, then settled him on his mattress in the corner.

'You're a good lad,' the old man said in a thread of a voice. 'You deserve better nor this. An' you've got a wonderful woman there.'

They were allowed to sleep in peace that night, but both Hannah and Nathaniel kept waking up anyway, listening, worrying, wondering what the next day would bring.

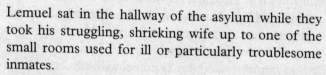

CHAPTER TWENTY-FIVE

Lemuel sat in the hallway of the asylum while they took his struggling, shrieking wife up to one of the small rooms used for ill or particularly troublesome inmates.

Matron came to see him after a while. 'Your wife won't push because she's still refusing to believe she's having the child. Maybe you can have another try at persuading her?'

So he went upstairs to the bare little room where they had Patty tied by the wrists to a bed, something that upset him greatly. She hardly looked like the woman he knew, so wild was her expression and so matted with sweat her hair.

'Patty, love, you must birth the baby . . .'

'Get that man away from me!' She began to scream and thrash around. 'He's evil! So is his mother. Evil!'

He looked numbly at the Matron, not knowing what to do.

'You'd better sit outside the door,' she said. 'Just in case you're needed.'

So he had to listen to the screams and curses from inside the room, tears filling his eyes, both for his wife and for the unborn child.

It was two more hours before Dr Kent arrived. He

had a quick word with Lemuel, went inside to examine the patient and soon came out again. 'I think you'd better go home and leave this to us. It won't be pleasant.'

'Shouldn't I stay?'

'No. There's absolutely nothing you can do and the mere sight of you seems to drive her into a frenzy, Matron says.' He laid a gentle hand on the other man's shoulder. 'This is hurting you badly, I can tell. Go home and get some sleep, then you'll be ready to cope with whatever tomorrow brings.'

So Lemuel walked slowly home, wishing desperately that his mother were here, then growing annoyed with himself for being so soft. But that did no good either because he simply couldn't work out what to do about Patty or little John. Even the coopering was going badly and he couldn't think how to set that to rights, either. He might be a good craftsman, but he was a failure at the business side.

He sat in the kitchen till it grew dark, but no one came for him from the asylum. Eventually his stomach made its needs felt and he lit a lamp and found some stale bread, scraping a smear of butter over it and eating it without even realising that the butter was slightly rancid.

The lamp shed a small pool of light, but the rest of the room was in shadow. Eh, he'd be better going upstairs to his bed, he decided at one point. But he didn't. Wanted to be ready. For what, he didn't dare think.

It was almost dawn when someone knocked on the door. Lemuel woke with a start and rushed to answer it. He found himself facing a solemn-faced Dr Kent. 'Is she all right? Has the baby been born?'

'Can I come in?' The doctor didn't wait for an invitation but guided Lemuel gently back into the room where the lamp was guttering and the fire almost out. 'Let's sit down.'

Lemuel did as he asked and clasped his hands together on the table to hide their trembling. 'Tell me.'

'I'm afraid your wife is dead. The baby too.'

Lemuel couldn't seem to take it in. 'Dead? How can Patty be dead?'

'Many women die in childbirth and she made it more dangerous for herself because she wouldn't do anything we asked. The baby was too long being born and suffocated before we got it out. Your wife haemorrhaged and died soon after.'

Lemuel bowed his head and let the tears fall, silent in his grief as he was in most things. He hadn't loved Patty for some time now, but he felt desperately sad to think of her dying so young and in such a dreadful way.

Dr Kent patted him on the shoulder then went over and began fiddling with the fire, finding some glowing embers and coaxing them into life. The first dawn light filtered in through the windows, seeming to take the colour out of everything.

'Was it a boy or a girl?' Lemuel asked suddenly.

'A girl.'

'Eh, the poor little creature!'

Maurice gave him a few minutes to take it all in before asking, 'What do you want to do about a funeral? Do you have the money for a proper burial?'

Lemuel's head came up and he said quickly, 'Patty's

not having a pauper's burial. I'll go and see Parson this morning. And write to her father.'

The doctor yawned. 'Will you be all right if I leave you now? Only I need to get some sleep. Try to take comfort from the thought that you still have a son to look after. John's a lot better now and we'll bring him back to you as soon as you've made suitable arrangements for looking after him.'

'Yes. Thank you.'

After the door had closed behind the doctor it was a long time before Lemuel moved. What was he going to do now? How could a man look after a small child and earn a living?

Early that same afternoon the Marquess's carriage again drove up to Spinneys.

'He's got a cheek coming here,' Oliver muttered as the sound of it sent them both hurrying across to the window. 'After sending his men to kidnap you yesterday!'

Ann shivered. 'I don't even want to speak to him.'

'Shall I see him for you?'

She shook her head. 'No. That would be cowardly.'

So they sat in the parlour and let Nanny show in the Marquess, as if this were just a normal visit.

When they were all seated her father stared at Ann. 'Well? Have you come to your senses, girl?'

'I haven't changed my mind about my marriage, if that's what you mean, Father. I like being Oliver's wife and the marriage has been consummated so you can't have it annulled.'

'I thought you'd remain stubborn. I should have

forced you to accept one of last season's offers . . . would have done if I'd realised you'd take this ridiculous notion into your head. Marrying a poor man! After this, you'll be reduced to marrying a *nouveau riche* upstart instead, and serve you right.' He turned to look at Oliver, not troubling to hide his scorn. 'Do you really think you can protect her?'

'I can try. Do *you* think you can break up our marriage? After all, we have our marriage lines in a safe place and can produce them for legal scrutiny.'

'I can and shall break up this pitiful mismatch. As if I'd ever accept a man like *you* for my son-in-law! A physical weakling as well as a poor man. It *will* be annulled, and since you'll find it impossible to leave the village, we shall be able to retrieve the marriage lines when we need to. The relevant page has already been removed from the parish records.' He turned back to Ann. 'Someone is likely to be hurt if you persist in this foolishness, you know.'

She stood up. 'I think we've heard enough threats from you, Father. I'd like you to leave now.'

'I'll leave when I'm ready and not before.'

Oliver saw his wife didn't know what to do so offered her his arm. 'Shall we go for a stroll round the gardens, my dear?'

'Yes. That would be lovely.'

They walked out and left the Marquess sitting there.

Coldly angry, he watched them through the window for a moment or two, then rang the bell. Nanny appeared.

'If you care about your master, you'll persuade him to be sensible,' growled the unwelcome visitor.

'I care too much about him to see this marriage to the woman he loves broken up.'

'Love! Such a very vulgar notion. And as for you, old woman, you'll find yourself in the poorhouse when this is over.'

'Better than one of your houses, where everyone is unhappy.'

'How dare you speak to me like that?'

She tossed her head and stared back at him, thinking: Nasty old man he is, Marquess or not. She took care to stay out of reach of his clenched fist as she moved towards the front door, though.

He followed her in a leisurely way, as calm as if he hadn't just threatened to ruin her master's life. Only when he had left did she sag against the wall for a moment. She hadn't thought she'd have the courage to stand up to a lord but she'd dare do anything for Mr Oliver and his Ann. There's going to be more trouble before this is over though, she thought. That man will never allow his daughter to best him.

She went out into the garden to insist her employers come inside at once and not give anyone such an easy opportunity to kidnap Lady Ann again.

Later that afternoon, at the hour set aside by the parson for his more lowly parishioners to consult him, Ginny and Nick walked into the village and arranged to have their banns called for the next three Sundays, then to get married on the Monday morning after that. The parson spoke curtly, hardly even looking at them after one glance at Ginny's stomach, merely checking that they really were entitled to be married in his parish.

When she said where she was living, however, his expression became extremely disapproving.

'You would do better to keep away from Mr Dewhurst,' he cautioned. 'He is a troublemaker.'

'He seems a very kind gentleman to me,' Ginny snapped, annoyed at this criticism of a man who had been so good to her family.

'I need no impudence from you, miss!' he snapped, surprised when she stared back at him defiantly and didn't stammer an apology.

Nick grinned. He'd already found that his beloved was very loyal to those she considered her friends and he liked the way she wasn't afraid to speak up to this starched buffoon.

'Be sure to attend church for the next three Sundays,' the parson said coldly, and showed them the door.

On the way home they stopped beside the river that ran through the village.

'I'd rather walk home that way,' Ginny said wistfully.

Nick put his arm round her. 'Better not. The road will be safer.'

As the road left the village it curved, with only Oliver's house and the cottage still to be passed before it entered the open countryside. The minute the two youngsters were out of sight of the village, three men leaped out of the bushes at them. One clubbed Nick, who fell like a stone, while another seized Ginny, who began to scream for help.

Ned, working near the gates of Spinneys, heard her cries and rushed down the lane, yelling for someone to come and help. The screams were cut off abruptly and he yelled even more loudly, but by the time he got to the road Ginny was gone and there was only Nick, lying groaning on the ground with his forehead bruised and bleeding. Ned couldn't get any sense out of him, so half-carried him towards the house.

They met Oliver in the lane, a shotgun in his hand and a grim expression on his face. 'What's happened?' he demanded.

'I don't know, sir, but Nick went into the village with Ginny and there was no sign of her when I found him, yet it was her screams I heard.'

'Why would they kidnap Ginny?' But after a moment's thought he guessed that Ann's father intended to use the pregnant girl as a bargaining counter. Would the man stop at nothing?

They helped Nick into the house, then Oliver sent Ned to fetch Nathaniel while Nanny tended the poor young man's battered head.

After an initial shriek which made Nanny give her a sharp reprimand, Penny fetched hot water and clean cloths then went running for Nathaniel.

'They hit him hard, sir. He needs to lie down,' Nanny said to her employers.

Nick groaned and muttered, 'Ginny . . . they took Ginny.'

Nathaniel came rushing in, followed by Hannah, and looked at Oliver in dismay as the situation was explained to him. 'You wouldn't think a lord would stoop so low.'

'My father doesn't believe the laws of this land apply to him,' Ann said. 'He'll no doubt send a demand for me to go to the Priory, together with a threat as to what'll happen to your niece if I don't.' She looked at

Oliver, all her love for him showing in her eyes. 'I'll have to go, too. I can't have it on my conscience if she loses the baby.'

Hannah stood by her husband's side, anger searing through her. 'He shouldn't be allowed to get away with it, lord or no lord!'

'That settles it!' Nathaniel's face took on an expression of grim anger and determination few people here had ever seen. 'I'm not only going for help, but tomorrow we'll take the fight to them and rescue Ginny.' He turned to Ann. 'Can you delay going to your father for as long as possible?'

'I don't know.'

'Could you perhaps hide somewhere? Your husband can tell them you're out.'

'They wouldn't believe it. They know we daren't leave the house. I'm sure they'll be keeping watch on all the roads.'

'Well, try to put off going to him until after dark, if you possibly can.' He turned to Oliver. 'Can I borrow your horse, sir?'

'They'll not let you out of the village.'

'They won't see me go. I'll lead it through the woods, not along the bridleway, and then ride for help once I reach open ground. I don't want to bring back the men I'm going for until after dark. They can hide in our cottage till we're ready to surprise his lordship.'

'Take the horse. Ned will help you. You'd better leave Nick here till he regains his senses fully. Don't worry, Nanny will look after him. Do you want to bring the lads here as well, Mrs King?'

Hannah shook her head. Ginny's abduction had

made her feel stubborn as well as angry. 'No. They're not going to frighten me away from my own home. And Phil said he'd find some men to keep guard on the cottage during the night. We'll manage till my husband gets back.'

The builder's sons had arrived as usual to start work that morning, but when Hannah and Nathaniel got back from Spinneys they saw Mr Coxton drive up in his gig, looking very solemn. He didn't offer them his usual cheery greeting.

'What now?' Nathaniel muttered under his breath.

'Whatever it is, we'll face it,' Hannah said.

Mr Coxton beckoned to his sons to come down from the roof, adding, 'And bring all your tools with you!'

The two exchanged puzzled glances, but did as he ordered.

He turned to Nathaniel. 'I'll wait till the lads join us before I explain, if you don't mind.' He fiddled with his coat, buttoning and unbuttoning it till his sons joined him, then took a deep breath. 'I'm sorry, Mr King, more sorry than I can tell you, but I can't let any of my folk work for Mr Dewhurst any more, not if I value my livelihood.'

'What do you mean?'

'Lord Iffingham's land agent came to see me earlier today. Said if we didn't stop working here, we'd never get another job on the estate.'

Both his sons muttered curses under their breath.

Mr Coxton's face was burning with embarrassment and he looked at Nathaniel pleadingly. 'I get most of my work from the estate, you see, so I can't afford to lose it. I delayed coming here as long as I could so the lads could get a bit more work done, but that was all I could do to help you.'

'Well, you three may be interested to know that his noble lordship has had our Ginny kidnapped and will no doubt be making threats against her safety to force his daughter to return to the Priory,' Nathaniel told them.

His voice was so emotionless it didn't sound like his, Hannah thought, watching the shocked expression on the builder's face.

Nathaniel continued to speak, slowly and emphatically. 'Ginny's expecting a child and they've already used violence on her.'

There was dead silence, then Mr Coxton shook his head. 'I'm sickened by that, but I still daren't do anything except obey. He's a powerful man.'

The younger of his sons looked at his father in disgust. 'You're just going to kow-tow to that bloody bully, are you? With that nice lass in danger?'

'I've no choice, lad.'

'Well, I have. Damned if I'll work for a fellow as tries to kidnap honest folk. I can find a job anywhere. You'd better find someone to replace me.'

'Phil, don't be rash . . .'

'Dad, we're not peasants who can't think for ourselves. I've already been disgusted by some of the things I've seen on the estate, including the poor way his lordship maintains those pitiful hovels he houses his workers in. Well, I won't be part of this latest villainy. And what's more,' he turned to Nathaniel, 'I'll come back and help you in any way I can. If you want me, I'll be up on that roof tomorrow morning, no pay asked.'

'Phil!'

'I've had enough of his bloody lordship! He's gone too far. I'm an Englishman and I have a right to my freedom.'

Sim said quietly, 'If I didn't have a wife and two children to support, I'd be with you.'

Phil went to shake Nathaniel's hand. 'I'll drive away now, for Dad's sake, but I'll be back as soon as it's dark to help keep watch. And tomorrow he can tell the land agent I'm no longer working for him. In the meantime I'll be packing my things ready to leave this damned village once this is over.'

'It'll make me feel a little easier, knowing you're there to keep watch on Hannah and the boys tonight. I have to go somewhere and may be late back,' Nathaniel told him.

'I'll bring a stout cudgel with me, too.'

'Do you have a spare one?' Hannah asked.

The men turned to stare at her in surprise.

'It's for me. I don't intend to stand by and let anyone attack me and mine without fighting back.'

Nathaniel let out a crack of laughter, though his expression immediately settled into lines of worry again. 'You're a woman in a million, Hannah love, but I hope you don't have to fight. If anyone dares hurt you, I won't be answerable for my actions.'

Gregory, who had been standing nearby listening in shock, stepped forward to say earnestly, 'I've got my catapult, Dad. I can help too. I'm a crack shot now.'

Hannah put an arm round him and for once he didn't wriggle away. 'Good lad. Always fight back if you can.

You make sure you've plenty of stones handy just in case.'

Nathaniel left a few minutes later, walking across the field to start digging up a young tree at the edge of the copse and re-planting it inside the field for shade. He hoped that would convince any watchers why he was over there. After a few minutes, he moved further in among the trees and when Ned whistled to let him know he was there with the horse, stood his spade against a tree trunk and went to join the young groom.

'There's a message here from Mr Oliver,' Ned said. 'He wants me to deliver a note for him in Preston, as long as I can get away without being seen. I don't like to leave him and the mistress on their own, but he said it was important and one man wouldn't make much difference if it came to a fight. Your Nick's gone back to the cottage now, by the way. And Mr Oliver said if it was all right with you, he'd go across there tonight as well and join the fight if Lady Ann has to go to the Priory. He'll bring his gun. Eh, I wouldn't like to be her, in that nasty devil's power!'

'It's all right with me if he comes across. The more folk there are, the safer my family should be.' But Nathaniel didn't want to leave them for any longer than necessary and was determined to be back before morning. The Marquess wasn't going to get away with kidnapping Ginny.

Ned grinned. 'Here, I'll show you the best way through the copse. I played in these woods many a time when I were a lad. They haven't changed all that much.'

When they got to the edge of the woodland area, he

stopped. 'I don't reckon they'll see you leave the woods here. Go down that path and turn right on to the lane at the end. It'll bring you to the Marton road. Another right turn and then you'll know your way from there. I'm off to catch the train at the next station. Good luck!'

Good luck to us both, thought Nathaniel as he mounted the horse and rode off. He prayed as he rode that Hannah and his son would be all right. His poor little nephews too. The world seemed to have gone mad since his first wife's death.

The ultimatum from the Marquess arrived at Spinneys in the afternoon, delivered by his son. Oliver and Ann had been sure they'd hear from her father before the end of the day and were waiting together.

Ann looked at Gerald scornfully as he stood in her parlour, shifting uneasily from one foot to the other as he offered her an envelope. 'I hope you're proud of your part in this,' she said scathingly, not taking it.

'He *is* our father.'

'If he weren't a Marquess, he'd be a criminal and they'd probably hang him. How is that poor girl?'

'All right, I suppose. I haven't seen her. Um – he says I'm not to mess around, but to make sure you read this and then take you straight back with me.' He pushed the envelope at her.

She struck it from his hand, seeing her chance to delay. 'I'll open it and read it when someone I trust tells me the girl is all right and hasn't lost her baby.'

Gerald opened his mouth then shut it again, looking as if he'd swallowed something that made him feel sick. '*Baby*? She's expecting a baby?'

'Yes. And it shows,' Ann patted her own flat stomach suggestively, 'so they can't pretend they don't realise. For all I know she may be dead now or in the process of losing the baby.'

'Steady on, old girl. Father wouldn't—'

Her voice lashed out like a whip. 'I meant what I said, Gerald! I'll not open or read this letter until someone I trust tells me that girl is all right.'

'He'll go mad. And anyway, who do you trust? Will I do?'

'No. You're on his side. Happy to hurt unborn babies.'

'I am not! I didn't know about that. I never even saw her. I wouldn't . . .' His voice trailed away.

'It'd have made no difference if you had seen her. You'd not have tried to help her. You're weak, Gerald, and I'm ashamed to be your sister.'

He flushed, opened his mouth then shut it again, and stared down at his feet.

Nanny, who'd been unashamedly listening at the door, pushed it open and marched into the room. 'I'll go back with him, Lady Ann love, and send you a note – you can be sure they won't force *me* to write anything I don't want to and Oliver knows my handwriting. What's more, I'll stay with Ginny. She may need looking after.' She turned to Gerald. 'I suppose I can rely on you to see that they don't kill me?'

He gaped at her in shock. 'They're not going to *kill* anyone.'

'They may have killed an unborn child already,' Ann said quietly. 'And I'm afraid they're going to try to kill Oliver. You're part of it, so you'll be as guilty as them.'

He looked at her helplessly. 'I have to do this. You know I do.'

'No, I don't. I think you've *chosen* to do this – as I chose *not* to marry the man Father wanted for me.'

'You'll have to marry him now,' her brother muttered.

She stared at him solemnly. 'I swear to you, Gerald, that I'll kill myself before I'll marry Walter Dewhurst.'

His face went white and he seemed unable to speak or move as he registered the determination on her face, the freckles standing out against her pallor, no hint remaining of the inner beauty that sometimes lit her plain features.

Oliver stepped forward. 'Don't even think of doing that, Ann. They can't change the fact of our marriage. We've taken the necessary steps to make sure of that.'

Gerald looked uneasily from one to the other. 'Don't tell me anything about it!' He turned to the older woman and gestured to the door. 'Come on, Nanny. Let's go and see the girl. I'll get into trouble for doing this, but at least then he won't have to kidnap Ann.'

'You'll still be forcing her to leave her home and husband, though,' Nanny pointed out.

Gerald almost ran to the front door, shouting, 'Hurry up, will you, or I'll not do this!'

'I'll just get my shawl,' she called, then beckoned to Ann and whispered, 'If Walter is at the Priory, I'll put a dot at the end of my name when I sign the letter. If they want me to say something that isn't true, I'll make sure you can't read my signature.'

'Thank you, Nanny. You're a brave woman.'

When they heard the carriage drive away, Oliver

looked at Ann. 'This only delays things. And whatever happens, I want you to promise me you won't kill yourself, my darling girl.'

'I can't promise anything. You don't know my father. He may be planning to kill you.' She flung herself into his arms, weeping. 'I couldn't bear that, Oliver! I love you so.'

They stood for a long time in a close embrace, drawing strength from each other.

Later Oliver went to find Cook and suggested that she stay with friends until these troubles were over. She nodded and went to get her things at once.

He then found Penny and asked her if she thought she could slip home to her father's farm without anyone seeing her.

'I reckon so, sir. Why?'

'I think you'll be safer there. But I want you to tell him why you're there, tell him what the Marquess is doing. The more people who know about this, the harder it'll be to hide the crimes he commits.'

Her mouth fell open in shock. 'You think his men are coming again to get Mrs Dewhurst?'

'They're forcing her to go to the Priory tonight because of Ginny. She won't be here by nightfall. It's me they'll be coming to kill.'

Her reply came in a whisper. 'Kill?'

'I think so.' His voice was steady, no trace of fear showed in his face.

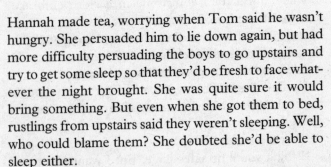

CHAPTER TWENTY-SIX

Hannah made tea, worrying when Tom said he wasn't hungry. She persuaded him to lie down again, but had more difficulty persuading the boys to go upstairs and try to get some sleep so that they'd be fresh to face whatever the night brought. She was quite sure it would bring something. But even when she got them to bed, rustlings from upstairs said they weren't sleeping. Well, who could blame them? She doubted she'd be able to sleep either.

When there was a knock on the door, which was bolted and barred, she went to stand behind it and ask who was there.

'It's me, Phil Coxton.'

Recognising his voice, she opened the door and found him flanked by two other sturdy young men.

'I thought you might need more help than I can give you,' he said, 'so I brought my friends. Is that all right? They're as fed up as I am of working for his lordship. He pays the lowest wages in the district so it'll be no loss to move on.'

'Come in.' She nodded to the two bashful young men. 'Thank you for your help.'

Gregory had nipped downstairs to see what was happening, catapult in one hand, a pebble in the other.

She shooed him back up, ignoring his loud complaints about it not being fair.

'Here's your cudgel, Mrs King.' Phil handed over a stick with a heavy knob of root on the end. 'Keep a tight hold of it if you have to use it. They'll try to rip it out of your hand.'

'I'll hold it very tightly, I promise you. Come and sit down.'

'I think we'll be better keeping watch outside, if you don't mind. I just wanted you to know who your friends are. Shall I put the shutters across the windows for you?'

'Yes, please. Across these windows, anyway. The others still need repairing.'

'I'll join you.' Nick went outside with them.

Hannah went to sit down again, tired but unable to sleep. She couldn't stop wondering where Nathaniel was: if he was starting back yet, if he'd found the help they needed. Keep him safe, she kept praying. Oh, please, keep him safe!

Gerald returned to Spinneys just after dusk, bearing a note from Nanny. He handed it over to his sister in silence, together with his father's original letter.

This time Ann read them both, noting the full stop after Nanny's clearly written signature. 'Ginny's all right,' she said in relief. 'Oh, thank goodness!' She passed the note to Oliver, who nodded.

'Father wasn't pleased about the old lady being involved,' Gerald said, 'so we'd better not delay any longer.'

Oliver moved to stand between Ann and her brother. 'You'll look after her?' he asked Gerald. 'Promise me you won't let them hurt her. She'll have no one but you on her side.'

Gerald looked at him in embarrassment. 'I keep telling you: it's Father who does these things, not me.'

'And we keep telling *you* that you can choose whether you help him or not,' Oliver said. 'Be sure that if anything happens to Ann, I'll kill both him and you, if it's the last thing I ever do, because I'll have nothing left to live for.'

His final words upset Gerald more than anything else either of them had said. He was genuinely fond of his sister, and to add to his guilt at his family's treatment of her there was no mistaking the love she and her husband bore each other. He couldn't help comparing Walter's brutal looks with Oliver's thin, kindly features. 'Father won't hurt her.'

'He'll try to make her marry my brother, a man who made my life a misery from when I was a young child until I left home recently. What sort of life would Ann have with him? He's a bully – and probably worse.' Her hand on his arm made Oliver turn and crush her against him. 'Be careful, my love.' Only because of Ginny and her baby would he have let Ann go to her father without a fight. But he'd find a way to get her back once the girl was free.

Ann nodded, going out into the hall, moving slowly because she was so filled with dread. As soon as she'd got her cloak, Gerald took her arm and hurried her outside.

When they'd gone, Oliver blew out all the lamps and locked up the house. He thought of taking a rifle or revolver with him, but didn't because he knew he couldn't kill another human being. He had never been able to fire at animals, even. As he walked out through the kitchen door, he locked it then looked back once at the dark silent mass of his once happy home before trudging slowly across the field behind. Above him a nearly full moon was shining but clouds kept drifting across it, so that one minute there was bright moonlight shining ahead of him, the next darkness.

Before he got to the Kings' cottage, a burly young man had grabbed him.

'Nay, that's Mr Dewhurst,' another voice whispered.

'I'll take you to the cottage, sir,' Nick said. As soon as they were out of earshot of the others he stopped to ask, 'Is there any news of Ginny?'

'Yes. Nanny went to the Priory to check that she was all right and stayed there to look after her. She sent us a message to say Ginny wasn't hurt – and we had devised a secret code so we'd know it was the truth.'

His companion gulped and stood for a moment with shoulders shaking before sniffing loudly and wiping his arm across his eyes. 'Thank God for that!'

When they arrived at the cottage Oliver had to repeat his news, then Hannah urged him to sit down, worried by how pale he was looking.

'Did you eat anything tonight?' she asked gently.

He looked at her and shook his head. 'I couldn't.'

'Let me get you something.'

'No, thank you.'

'You need to keep your strength up, in case Lady Ann needs you. Just a bowl of pobbies, perhaps?'

'Pobbies?'

'Chunks of bread in hot milk with sugar. Very easy

to eat. I've always given it to my lads when they were sick. It goes down easily.'

He reached out to clasp her hand. 'I don't know what we'd have done without you and Nathaniel. I'm so sorry we've brought these troubles on you.'

She smiled ruefully. 'We had plenty of our own before we met you. There aren't many folk who don't have a few problems in their lives.' She squeezed his hand and said encouragingly, 'You'll eat my pobbies, then?'

'I'll try.'

He managed half a bowl, then pushed it aside and looked at her apologetically. 'I'm sorry. I can't eat any more.'

'That's all right. I made a bigger bowl than usual so that if you ate half, you'd have eaten what I wanted you to.'

He was surprised into laughter.

A voice from the stairs said, 'I'm hungry, Hannah. We all are.'

So she made some more pobbies for the three lads, two of whom barely opened their mouths except to eat and one of whom barely closed his, whether it was full of food or not.

Oliver found the boys' presence very comforting, but most of all it was Hannah who gave him heart and courage. She and her husband were special. Very special indeed. After this was over, he'd make sure they were all right – if he was still alive.

Nathaniel's journey went without a hitch. When he arrived in Marton he went to the inn where lights were still showing and found some of his old friends drinking there. He cut short their exclamations of surprise at seeing him back and explained in a low voice what he wanted and why.

'Eh, I thought folk would have stopped pestering Mr Oliver,' one of the men who'd come to Beckleton with him said. 'And since he's wed now, what can they do about it?'

'The Marquess intends to claim that his daughter's marriage was never consummated.'

They eyed him questioningly, as curious as everyone else.

'It was,' he said shortly. 'I heard her say so myself.'

'Then how can yon lordship claim otherwise?'

'He's acting like it's still his grandfather's day. He's a Marquess so he reckons he can do owt he wants. If we don't stop him, me and Hannah will have to find some-where else to live and I dread to think what'll happen to Lady Ann who's as nice a lass as you could hope to meet, even if she is a ladyship.'

'We've got our own problems here with Walter Dewhurst inheriting,' one said bitterly. 'Maybe we should all emigrate to America and be done with rich folk like them. I've heard tell everyone's equal over there.'

'There are rich folk everywhere. If we were all made equal tonight, some 'ud wake up earlier tomorrow and start getting ahead of the lazy ones. Any road, Walter Dewhurst is in cahoots with the Marquess. He's intending to marry Lady Ann, legal or not, so her brother tells me.'

One man, who'd been threatened with dismissal and

losing his cottage only that day for complaining about increased rents, said recklessly, 'Then I'm with you. This sort of thing wouldn't happen in the city and it's not going to happen in our villages, neither. If we don't stop these rich folk from having things all their own way, I'm moving into Preston. There's work to be had there and no one breathing down your neck. I don't care what I do as long as I put bread on the table and clothes on our backs, though the wife don't want to leave her family.'

Working as quickly as possible, but not as quickly as he'd hoped, Nathaniel gathered together the men he'd expected, plus two others who were furiously angry with their new landlord, and then set off back to Beckleton, travelling openly this time in two carts.

Lord Iffingham scowled at his daughter, who had refused to sit and stood staring accusingly at him. 'So you're here,' he sneered.

'Only because you forced me by an unscrupulous trick.'

'As I shall force you to do everything else I want.'

'No, you won't!'

'Then the girl will suffer for it.'

'But she's expecting a child. . .'

'I know. All the more reason for you to do as I tell you. It'd be a pity if she lost the baby, wouldn't it? You wouldn't like *that* on your conscience.'

Had she ever before realised, Ann wondered, how truly evil her father was?

Gerald, standing to one side in the shadows, looked

quickly at him when he made the threat against Ginny, then down at the carpet.

'Go and bring Dewhurst in to join us,' Lord Iffingham ordered his son, not even turning his head to make sure his order was obeyed.

A short time later Walter sauntered in, smiling to see Ann standing there like a hunted animal at bay.

'Do you still want her?' the Marquess asked.

Walter smiled. 'Oh, yes my lord.'

'Then we'll talk settlements, and when I've received my money she's yours. We won't wait for a ceremony. That'll take too long.' He turned to glance at his daughter before ringing the bell. 'The doctor will examine you now, Ann, and the lawyer will start proceedings tomorrow to have your "marriage" annulled on the grounds of non-consummation.'

'Why even bother to have me examined since we know that's a lie?' she demanded, eyes flashing.

'Oh, we need to do these things properly. Are the women here, Gerald?'

'Yes, Father.'

'Then take your sister upstairs to them and show the doctor up.'

Ann didn't move, so Gerald took her arm. He could feel her trembling, though she wasn't showing fear in any other way. 'I'm sorry,' he whispered.

'You chose to help him,' she said tiredly, dreading the humiliation of what she was about to face.

Two buxom woman were waiting in the bedroom that had once been hers.

'Take your clothes off, please, your ladyship,' one said.

'No!'

She fought them every inch of the way, knowing it was in vain but still determined not to co-operate. She fought the doctor, too, managing to scratch his face.

When he had finished, he looked at her reprovingly. 'You would be wise to do as your father asks, young lady. This violence wasn't necessary.'

'You disgrace your profession,' she said scathingly, seeing a slight flush rise in his cheeks. 'You're a liar as well as venial. You can see perfectly well that I'm no longer a virgin and yet for money—' She broke off, her voice faltering at the enormity of what they were intending to do to her. Then, as he turned away, she grew angry again and yelled at him, 'And what's more, I love my real husband. I always shall.' Through eyes that burned with unshed tears she watched him open the door.

'I shall send up a sleeping draught,' he said. 'You're growing hysterical.'

He didn't even turn back as she continued to yell at him, 'How shall *you* sleep peacefully tonight, though?'

Gerald had been waiting outside. She heard him say to the other man, 'I'll come with you now and bring the sleeping draught back to her.'

Even her brother was working against her. Ann looked at the women, ashamed of her nakedness. 'Am I allowed to get dressed now?'

One of them produced a nightdress. 'He says you can wear this. Nothing else. He doesn't want you escaping.' The other gathered up her clothes and shoes, taking them away.

It seemed a long time till Gerald brought back the

sleeping draught. It took the three of them to force it down her. When they'd finished, Ann lay back tiredly.

'You're disgusting,' she told her brother.

He left the room. Like the doctor, he avoided her eyes.

One of the women looked at her, eyes narrowed in assessment. 'If you climb out of that bed, we'll only put you back into it. You might as well stay put.' When Ann turned away from her and pulled the sheet up to her chin, she went to sit by the fire. 'You'll be asleep in a few minutes, ten at most, then we can get some rest. I never met one as stubborn as you.'

'I'll be next door if you need me. There's a comfortable couch there.' The other woman went out of the room.

Ann stared across at the clock on the mantelpiece, its gilt hands showing clearly in the light of the ornate oil lamp next to it. She waited for the minutes to tick away and the sleeping draught to take effect. When it didn't, she closed her eyes anyway and pretended to be asleep.

Lord Iffingham took Walter to the library. He found that a short time with this boor was more than enough for him and was savagely glad to think Ann would have to live with the creature. It would be a lifelong punishment for her defiance.

It took nearly an hour for him to make Walter realise just how much he would have to pay for the hand of Lady Ann Turner, and it was well past midnight by the time they had come to an agreement.

'Very well,' said his lordship finally. 'I shall get my lawyer to draw up the papers straight away. It will not be necessary to summon your own man of affairs.'

Somehow, Walter didn't dare disagree. This was the only man he'd met since he was fourteen years old whom he truly feared, one who spoke in icy tones and had no compunction at all about treating his own daughter brutally.

'Don't go. There is one more thing to discuss,' his lordship said.

'Oh?'

'Your brother.'

'What about him?'

'It would make things a lot simpler if he were dead.'

Walter sucked in his breath in shock at hearing this put so openly. He'd been thinking along the same lines himself, of course, purely to make sure his wife-to-be had no one left to yearn for, but it wasn't something even he would have thought to discuss openly. 'You can leave that to me.'

'I intend to. However, you may use the men I've brought with me to help catch him, if you wish. They'll do anything for money.'

Walter nodded.

The Marquess rang a bell and gave instructions to have the men waiting at the stables ready to obey Walter's orders. 'You'd better go and see to it, then, had you not?' he told his son-in-law to be.

Outside the library, Walter paused for a moment to draw in a deep breath and kindle his anger against his brother. Then he smiled and made his way down to the cellar. He found the room where the girl was being kept, with the key in the lock on the outside.

'Give me an hour or so,' he said to the man sitting

outside it. 'I'll make sure she doesn't escape while you're away.'

He opened the door and at first saw only Ginny, lying on a makeshift bed and looking as pretty as ever. The mound of her stomach wasn't too big to interfere with his pleasure and he hadn't had a woman for quite a time. When she saw him she gasped in shock and sat bolt upright, letting out a cry of fear.

Then another figure moved out of the shadows and went to stand protectively in front of the girl. Walter laughed. 'Get out of my way, you old hag! I have business with her, not you.'

'I'm not leaving her side.'

He stepped across and grabbed Nanny's arm, yanking her towards the door, exulting in his own strength, enjoying forcing someone to do his will, as he always did.

Ginny was shrieking for help now and holding the old woman's other arm.

'Not now, Walter,' a voice warned from the doorway.

He spun around to see Lord Gerald standing there. 'Why not? It'll only take a short time, the way I'm feeling.'

'Father wants things done quickly and he likes to be obeyed. Besides, you can always have your fun when you've finished the job.'

Walter growled in anger, then went to the cowering girl and lifted her chin. 'I'll be back,' he said, caressing her breast, 'and the more you struggle, the more I'll enjoy it.' He turned towards Gerald, his eyes narrowed. 'I told the fellow on guard to come back in an hour . . .'

Gerald shrugged. 'The women won't get out of here with the door locked, will they?' He followed Walter outside, watched him stride down the corridor, put the key into the lock then after a moment followed him.

Inside the dark cellar Nanny waited for Lady Ann's brother to lock the door but there was no sound of a key turning and, from what that brute had said, there'd be no one outside keeping guard. 'I think he's forgotten to lock the door,' she whispered, trying it and finding that it opened easily. 'Come on, quick! If we can escape from here without being noticed, we'll see if we can find a side door and get out of the house.'

'Can we go back to Nick?' Ginny pleaded.

'Not till we're sure it's safe. There'll be fighting and I intend to keep you and the baby out of harm's way.' Nanny led the way out, turning back to lock the door and remove the key which she slipped into her pocket, smiling to think how puzzled the guard would be when he returned.

Gerald caught up with Walter and accompanied him out to the stables which were well lit by several lanterns in spite of the lateness of the hour. 'Thought you'd like to know the doctor's seen my sister.'

'And? Has she been touched?'

'Of course she has. She's been married for several days.'

'Damn him!'

'What's my father planning now?'

'Now that he's had half my fortune off me, you mean?'

'Yes.'

'He's leaving that to me. But as my brother is an inconvenience to us all, I'm planning to deal with him myself – permanently.'

'Surely you wouldn't do that?'

Walter smiled grimly. 'Oh, but I would. I'll be careful, though, because I've no desire to hang. I'll have men with me to swear he fired first. You coming to join in the fun?'

'Can't. My father's ordered me to stay here.'

Walter gave a mirthless laugh. 'Protecting you?'

Gerald shrugged. 'Who knows why he does anything? But you've seen what he's like. It'd take a braver man than me to disobey him. Would you go against his wishes?'

Walter didn't answer, didn't want to admit that the scrawny old Marquess terrified him. He gave Colin his orders and waited for the other men to join them. They were yawning and complaining about having to do the job in the middle of the night when anyone with any sense was in their bed. They were on foot, but it wasn't far to Spinneys. Walter checked his revolver carefully then started off, letting his horse amble along at a walking pace.

'Funny business, this,' Colin commented. He was the only other man on horseback and was riding close to his master.

'Yes. But it's my brother who'll be the loser, not me.' Walter looked closely at his servant. 'Dear Oliver's going to fire first, as you'll bear witness.'

Colin nodded, but his uneasiness deepened. It was one thing to terrorise poor men who couldn't fight back;

another to murder a rich man's son. He didn't want to be involved in something like that. Dammit, he wished he'd left before now. He dropped back a little, riding behind his master and scowling at the world.

Ann risked another glance at the clock through her eyelashes. Half an hour had passed and she wasn't in the least sleepy. The woman guarding her, however, had come once to check that she was asleep and had now settled herself comfortably in the chair. She was snoring gently, lost to the world. Inch by inch, Ann eased herself to the edge of the bed. When she sat up she waited to see if the woman was only pretending to be asleep, but no, her guard stayed where she was, soft snores coming and going at regular intervals.

Ann looked down at her nightgown, wishing she had proper clothes, but didn't dare waste time trying to find some. Noiseless on her bare feet, she made her way across the room, knowing exactly how to open the door of her former bedroom without making a noise. When she closed it behind her she stood perfectly still, listening.

The whole house was silent.

She went down the servants' stairs. No one else was around. Those not on duty would probably be in bed. She heard distant voices as she crept along the nearby corridor and paused only to snatch a shawl off the hook by the door. It was a grey, matted old thing which the maids used when they had to go outside on rainy days to use the privy. She hugged it to her, feeling better to have something to cover the fine cambric of the nightgown because even though it was nearly summer it was quite cool at this hour. She slipped out into the night, breathing a sigh of relief as no one noticed her go.

First she intended to find Oliver, then to get him to go into Preston with her before her father found out she'd escaped. She'd walk there if she had to! Their lawyer would help them find a doctor to prove that their marriage had been consummated, and after that they must go far away. She was too tired tonight to think where, but there must be somewhere her father couldn't reach them. Walter Dewhurst too. He would never be able to marry her but she was still afraid of him.

One thought warmed her: Gerald must have helped her because he was the one who'd brought up the so-called sleeping draught. She owed him a great deal for this chance of freedom and hoped for his sake her father didn't find out what he'd done.

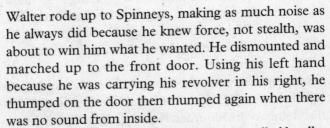

CHAPTER TWENTY-SEVEN

Walter rode up to Spinneys, making as much noise as he always did because he knew force, not stealth, was about to win him what he wanted. He dismounted and marched up to the front door. Using his left hand because he was carrying his revolver in his right, he thumped on the door then thumped again when there was no sound from inside.

For the benefit of the men with him, he called loudly, 'Come out, you coward. I know you're in there. Come out and answer for what you've done to that innocent girl.'

Colin rolled his eyes. It sounded like a very bad stage play of the sort for which his master had a weakness. What did the nobs call them? Oh, yes, melodramas. He hid a smile as he watched the gang the Marquess had provided shuffle their feet. They didn't care what his master was saying, wanted only to earn their money.

When there was no answer Walter went to the parlour window and peered inside. There was no sign of a light and he smiled to think of his brother woken up at this hour and cowering in his bed. 'Break the windows and get us in!' he ordered, standing back while one of the men smashed the window then kicked or knocked away the broken glass round its edges and climbed inside.

As Walter climbed through after him the damned moon went behind the clouds so he ordered, 'Find me a light, Colin!'

The two men with him fumbled their way to the kitchen where they found a couple of lamps standing ready. Colin lit them with a spill which he poked into the embers of the range.

'The kitchen fire's almost out,' he told his master as he brought one of the lamps back. 'I doubt anyone's in the house.'

'Nonsense! My brother will be hiding somewhere. He always used to hide from me at home. I found him sometimes, but mostly I just left him to rot, knowing he'd be damned uncomfortable. He must have passed some very cold nights while I slept comfortably in his bed.' He chuckled at the memories then led the search, stationing his men at strategic points so that no one could sneak past.

It took a while before Walter was satisfied his brother wasn't concealed anywhere in the house. 'We'll go over to the cottage then,' he decided. 'The Marquess suggested Oliver might try to hide there.' And even if he wasn't there, Nathaniel King lived in at the cottage and Walter would enjoy a short diversion. He intended to get that insolent fellow right out of the district one way or the other, and if he could send him off impoverished, all his possessions destroyed, so much the better. Maybe he'd even burn down the cottage tonight. Yes, that might be fun. Oliver owned it after all, so it wouldn't matter. You could lose everything in a fire, even your life.

Looking at him sideways as they walked across to the cottage, Colin wondered what his master was grinning at. Planning something nasty, no doubt. He himself was feeling more and more worried. Walter was indulging himself in any violent act he fancied now that his father wasn't around to keep him in check. With a sigh the groom looked up at the sky, wondering when it would start to grow light. He hated fumbling around in the dark like this. Wished he wasn't involved in this whole sorry mess.

When lights appeared at Spinneys, going from window to window, the watchers knew people were searching there. Phil came to the door to tell those inside what was happening and Hannah woke with a start from an uneasy slumber at the kitchen table.

'I reckon they'll come here next, Mrs King,' he said. 'Are you sure you don't want to take the little lads and get as far away as you can? They'd not find you if you hid in the woods.'

Something inside her wouldn't give in so easily. 'We're not leaving our home.' She poked her head into the bedroom and called, 'Boys! Time to wake up.'

Andrew let out a little whimper of fear.

'Chin up,' Gregory told him, for once needing no urging to get out of bed quickly. 'We're going to beat them.' When the others were ready, he organised his small troop. 'Andrew, you be ready to pass me more pebbles when I tell you. Edwin, you can have your own catapult ready, but don't fire unless I say.'

He suggested that he and his cousins hide near the privy and fire their catapults at the invaders from there, but his stepmother refused to let them out of the cottage.

It wasn't fair. He was going to miss all the fun!

The moon was low in the sky now, still shining fitfully. As the gang crossed the field towards the cottage clouds raced across it, so that at one moment their path was well-lit and the next plunged into darkness. When they drew near, Walter told his men to fan out and not let anyone escape.

Suddenly one of them yelled and there was the sound of a scuffle, then, 'Damn! He got away!'

'They've got guards posted!' a second man called.

'And we're not letting you into the cottage,' another voice replied from the darkness, recognisably local by the accent.

'You can't stop us. There are more of us than you.' Walter didn't know that, but it never hurt to make your opponent feel at a disadvantage. He stopped and took aim, firing blindly towards the cottage, hoping the sound of the gunshot would make the people inside more afraid. He loved that sound and the feeling of power a gun gave you.

His gang of men gradually closed in on the cottage, driving the defenders back but finding it difficult to pin them down in the darkness.

The moon stayed behind the clouds for longer this time and Walter cursed it because he was looking forward to shooting someone. But he could see no clear targets, only dark shapes heaving to and fro as they fought. Well, there were only two men he really wanted to see in his sights and he could wait for them.

'Leave the lads to it, sir,' Colin said from beside him. 'Much safer to use fists than guns. You don't really want to kill anyone, surely, whatever the Marquess says?'

'Oh, but I do. My bloody brother and King.'

Walter's voice was gloating, and his eyes were gleaming as if he was looking forward to a treat. In fact, he looked so out of control that Colin shivered and wished yet again that he wasn't here tonight.

When she slipped outside through the kitchen door, Ann heard the sound of shooting from the direction of Nathaniel's cottage. There were one or two men moving about the grounds too as if checking that everything was all right at the Priory. Once she narrowly missed being seen, and decided she'd better hide until things grew quieter. Pulling the shawl closer round her shoulders, shivering, she turned on to a little-used path that led to her grandmother's grotto, an artificial cave whose walls were covered in shells. Her bare feet were hurting and she was sure one was bleeding where she'd stubbed her big toe against a sharp-edged stone, but she pressed on.

When she got to the grotto she felt her way inside, sinking down onto one of the benches and listening desperately for sounds of pursuit. It felt eerie with only the sound of water dripping here and there into the little pools that had been created. She hated the stifling darkness, for no moonlight penetrated beyond the entrance, and it was cold, so very cold. But she had to stay hidden for a while and was sure no one would find her here.

Inevitably her thoughts turned to her husband. If

Walter had killed Oliver, she didn't know what she'd do. *Please don't let him die!* she prayed again and again.

Twice she crept outside and along to the end of the path that led to the grotto, but there were still men moving about and lights showing in the stable area. What was going on?

The third time she ventured out there was only the yard light showing in the stables and, though she listened carefully, no sound of people moving about the grounds. She decided to make her way home, thankful she knew the gardens so well and could use small paths that kept her hidden.

When she got to Spinneys she walked round it, keeping to the shadows and checking that no one was watching for her. There was enough moonlight to show the gaping, broken windows of the parlour but no sign of life. She was used to the noises of the night, had often stood by her bedroom window at the Priory and listened to them with pleasure. Now she used that knowledge to stay very still and check that no one else was disturbing the small animals which came out with the stars. At length it seemed to her that the night creatures were getting on with the business of finding food or mates undisturbed, so she decided to risk going inside her home.

To her relief the kitchen door was open and she didn't have to try to climb inside the house through the broken windows at the front. Making her way through the dark building, moving and listening carefully, she checked for signs of a body, using only the moonlight to guide her and praying with all her heart that she wouldn't find Oliver dead. But although the furniture had been thrown around, she saw no sign of him in the main areas. Please let him have escaped, she prayed, and please let me escape too.

Once she thought she heard a sound and stood still, her heart pounding with fear. But no other sounds followed it so she started moving again.

In her bedroom she flung on some clothes and shoes, then went downstairs again.

She froze as a shot rang out from the direction of the cottage. Her heart began to pound and she hurried out of the house. Once she got to the end of the garden she could hear cries and shouts, see dark figures moving about in the field, but couldn't make out what was really happening. She looked up at the sky, wishing dawn would come. Surely it couldn't be far away? She seemed to have been shrouded in darkness for such a long time.

But she had to know if Oliver was safe, so she began to creep forward.

Some distance from the cottage on the other side of the wood, Nathaniel also heard the shot which seemed to shatter the peace of the night. At this hour, it could mean only one thing.

'They must be attacking the house or cottage!' he called to his companions. 'See how fast you can get those horses pulling the carts, lads. I'm going ahead.' Cutting across the fields, he urged his mount to go faster, knowing the poor horse was exhausted, but so desperate to get back and protect his wife and son that he pressed on anyway.

Only, he didn't have a gun and clearly someone else did.

*   *   *

The defenders backed towards the cottage, bleeding and bruised. 'Dammit, there are more of them than I'd expected,' panted Phil. 'Do you think you could get away, Bert, and bring help?'

'Will anyone from the village come?'

'They have to. Look, our farm's closest. My brother will come to our aid and Dad too, I reckon, if you tell 'em we're in danger.'

Bert seized his opportunity and flung down his cudgel, yelling, 'I've had enough!'

The attackers were taken by surprise and he was off towards the back of the field before they could stop him.

Walter laughed. 'Let the coward go! One less to deal with.' He raised his voice. 'Not long now, little brother! And this time I'll settle your hash once and for all.'

Inside the cottage Oliver looked at Hannah. 'It's me he wants. If I promise to go out to him, he may agree to leave the rest of you alone.'

'I wouldn't trust him. And anyway, I wouldn't buy my life at the price of yours.'

Even as she was speaking, the three remaining defenders burst through the door and slammed it shut, barring it carefully. Phil went to the house side of the kitchen and inspected the door there. When he found it opened inwards, he asked, 'Got a hammer, Mrs King?'

She opened it again and held up the lamp to show him a row of tools set out neatly in a line against the wall of the corridor by Nathaniel. She felt like sobbing at the sight of those tools. He was so careful with his possessions. Would he ever use these again?

Phil pushed her gently back into the kitchen, bringing the tools he needed and some planks that were lying around. He nailed a couple of short ones across the inner door to hold it shut. 'That'll keep 'em from coming in that way for a while, mebbe, and the shutters will protect the windows.' He could see how anxious Hannah was, so added, 'I've sent Bert to ask my father for help. Let's pray it comes quickly. We won't be able to delay 'em for long.'

Someone thumped on the outer door. 'Surrender if you value your lives!' Walter called. 'It's my brother I want, not the rest of you.'

'Don't listen to him,' Hannah said quietly.

'But they've got Ann. If they threaten to hurt her . . .' Oliver let the words trail away, unable to put his worst fears into words.

'Her father wants her alive so that he can marry her to your brother. The one thing you can count on is that she won't be killed, whatever they threaten.' Hannah looked at him with compassion. 'You can't give in to him, Oliver.'

'My brother always manages to win, by fair means or foul,' he said despondently, then took a deep breath and squared his shoulders. 'You're right, though. I shouldn't despair. Not yet.'

There was the sound of an axe whacking into the outer door and a panel splintered.

'Get ready,' said Hannah. 'They'll break it down soon.' She hefted the cudgel in her hand, trying to get used to the weight of it. She wasn't going to stand and weep, she was going to fight, because she had something worth fighting for in Nathaniel and her new family.

Outside the cottage Walter was fretting at the delay, eager to finish off his stupid brother and claim Lady Ann for his own.

No one heard the horse approaching. Its rider dismounted quietly and turned it loose, sure he could get closer on foot from here on without being noticed. Finding a slight hollow close to the cottage, he lay flat in it to assess the situation.

When the kitchen door burst open, the defenders made a rush outwards, taking the attackers by surprise for a moment or two. Hannah thumped one man across the head before he realised she meant to join in the fight, then she turned to face another coming up behind her.

'You'll not take *me* by surprise, you bitch!' he growled.

She was looking outwards across the field and suddenly saw her husband creeping up behind her new opponent. Joy filled her. Nathaniel was back! Surely, surely, he'd brought some other men to help? She feinted with the cudgel to keep her attacker's attention and stepped back quickly as Nathaniel reached the unsuspecting man, swung him round and punched him.

For a while longer they held the villains at bay, but there were more men attacking than defending and in spite of their valiant efforts it was clear they were going to be defeated. During a pause where no one was attacking him directly Nathaniel stood in front of Hannah, panting and bleeding profusely from a cut on the cheek, and saw Walter corner Oliver by the garden wall. He tensed and took a quick step forward.

'As if you could defeat us!' Walter mocked his

brother. 'Though you certainly tried. Such a pity you got shot in the mêlée!' He raised his gun and aimed it at his brother.

'There are too many witnesses who can swear you killed him in cold blood!' Nathaniel called, deliberately drawing Walter's attention away from Oliver, who was facing his brother without flinching or pleading for mercy.

Walter let his gun drop slightly. 'I might know *you* would try to interfere, King!' He smiled in anticipation. 'I think I'll deal with you first.'

'Don't do it, Walter,' Oliver begged. 'It's me you want.'

'Oh, you'll get your turn.'

Just as Walter was raising his gun to shoot Nathaniel, a pebble hit him on the temple and the shot went wide.

Nathaniel seized the opportunity to pull Hannah to the ground and lie down in front of her.

With a yelp of pain Walter swung round to see who had hit him and saw Gregory standing near the house with his catapult at the ready for another shot.

'You're not killing my father!' the lad shouted.

'I'll kill whom I please,' Walter shouted back. 'Might is right.' He threw a gloating smile sideways at Nathaniel then aimed his gun at the boy.

'*No!*' Nathaniel scrambled to his feet and launched into a desperate run, yelling, 'Get back, Gregory!' But there was no way to reach Walter in time to prevent him from firing.

Tom had also come out of the cottage and was standing next to the lad. He threw himself in front of Gregory just as the shot rang out. Blood spurted from the old man's chest and he crumpled without a sound.

Hannah rushed to kneel by Tom, but there was enough moonlight for her to see that he was dying. You couldn't mistake that look. She didn't even think about Walter or the danger she was in, her whole attention focused on the old man.

'I saved him, didn't I?' Tom whispered as she cradled him against her. 'I saved your lad.'

'You were wonderful. See, he's here beside me, safe and well.'

A look of immense satisfaction came over Tom's face as he breathed his last in her arms. She kissed his brow and laid him gently on the ground, tears running down her cheeks as she turned to Gregory and said, 'Never forget that a brave man gave his life for you.'

Fortunately for them all, Walter seemed transfixed by what he had done, staring at the old man and his bloody chest. Suddenly he threw back his head and began to laugh.

Colin was sure then that his master had run completely mad. He'd been holding back for a while. Now he turned and ran towards the edge of the field intending to find his own horse and escape.

Drawn by the shot and Tom's death, the men on both sides had abandoned their struggles. They were muttering to one another, clearly uneasy about what they had witnessed.

Walter turned to them and yelled, 'Shut up! It was an accident.'

'That were no accident,' one called.

'I'm not doing no killing,' another said, taking a step backwards.

'Shut up, I said!'

Nathaniel launched himself at Walter while his attention was distracted and the two men began a desperate struggle for possession of the gun. Walter yelled for his men to come and help him, but no one did.

Oliver glanced across at his home and saw a figure come creeping through the gate in the wall of Spinneys, a figure he'd recognise anywhere. Abandoning caution, he ran across to sweep his wife into his arms. 'Are you all right? Tell me you're all right?'

'I'm fine, Oliver. What's happening?'

He put his free arm around her shoulders, keeping a wary eye on his brother. 'Walter wants to kill me and Nathaniel. I think he's gone mad because he tried to shoot Gregory first. The old man who helps in the garden stepped in front of the lad and took the bullet instead. He's dead. How does Walter think he'll get away with it?'

He turned to look back at the two figures still locked in their struggle. The other combatants had forgotten their own animosity in the expectation of seeing a good fight with a pair of well-matched opponents, though a couple of them were still lying on the ground and one was leaning against the cottage wall as if too dizzy to stand. By unspoken agreement the others formed a rough circle round the fighters, some shouting with approval when blows were landed.

'Nathaniel's fighting Walter and if my brother wins, we shall be in trouble.' But like the other spectators, Oliver couldn't tear himself away.

By the cottage, Hannah watched her husband's life-or-death struggle, her heart pounding with anxiety.

'My dad will win, won't he?' Gregory asked suddenly.

'Yes, of course,' she said automatically, though she was by no means sure.

At last, after a desperate struggle, Nathaniel managed to knock Walter's gun out of his hand, but although that removed one danger, they were still so well matched physically that neither man seemed able to overcome the other.

'Colin! To me!' Walter yelled suddenly.

But no one came.

'One of you men, help me!' he panted as he dodged another punch.

No one made any effort to obey him.

Nathaniel said nothing, saving his breath.

The sun hadn't yet risen but there was enough chill grey light to watch them by. The circle of spectators bulged and moved as the onlookers tried to stay clear of the fighters. The two combatants were exchanging occasional punches, grunting as blows fell, but chiefly struggling for supremacy. Each of them was panting hard now.

'He's run mad, that Walter Dewhurst has,' one of Lord Iffingham's men whispered to another. 'No one can get away with killing people in cold blood.'

'I'm not staying here to be hanged for what *he* did,' his companion muttered.

But still they couldn't tear themselves away from the fight.

In a surprise move Walter managed to grab Nathaniel by the throat, squeezing with all his strength. As his opponent struggled for breath and tried desperately to dislodge his hands, Walter kneed him hard in the crotch. Nathaniel doubled up in pain and fell to the ground.

Walter stepped back, looking round for Colin and not finding him. 'Well, you cowards,' he yelled at the men who'd come with him, 'what are you waiting for? We can finish them off now.'

'I'm not murdering anyone,' one man shouted back. 'Let alone a woman and a lad. You've gone mad!'

'I'll show you who's mad!' Walter roared. He looked round for his revolver, pounced on it and picked it up. They all scattered before him.

Hannah pulled Gregory round the corner of the cottage. She longed to go to her husband who was still on the ground, gasping for breath, still incapacitated by the low blow, but she knew if she tried that would only give Walter another target.

Oliver and Ann sprinted for the shelter of the cottage wall.

Laughing, Walter turned back towards Nathaniel, who was still rolling round in agony, raised the revolver and aimed it.

'Stop in the name of the law!' a new voice called from across the field. It held the note of authority.

Walter swung round, expecting to see the Marquess but finding instead two gentlemen he didn't know coming towards them on foot. The strangers were accompanied by several police constables, with Ned bringing up the rear.

'Who the hell are you?' Walter demanded.

'I'm Mr Oliver Dewhurst's lawyer,' one of the gentlemen said.

'My name's Thornton and I'm a magistrate from

Preston,' the other told him. 'You're under arrest for murder, Walter Dewhurst. This officer,' he indicated the local constable, 'saw you shoot an old man in cold blood. You'll stand trial for that.'

Walter laughed wildly and turned to look for his brother, forgetting Nathaniel but still hoping to take Oliver's life before anyone stopped him. As the constables raced towards him, he realised his brother wasn't anywhere to be seen and turned back to Nathaniel, only to find that his other opponent had vanished as well.

'Damn you all!' he shouted. Facing the two gentlemen again, he laughed as he put the revolver to his own temple and pulled the trigger.

The shot echoed across the field and everyone fell silent, watching as Walter's heavy body keeled over to lie very still on the ground in an ungainly sprawl of limbs and arms.

'Cover his head up!' shouted the magistrate. 'There are ladies present.'

Gulping audibly, the local constable stepped forward and used his pocket handkerchief to drape the shattered remains of Walter Dewhurst's head.

'Now, perhaps someone would explain exactly what has been happening here?' the magistrate shouted.

The group of attackers, who'd stood frozen in shock like everyone else by Walter's actions, suddenly took to their heels and the police officers jolted into pursuit, Ned joining in enthusiastically.

Hannah gave Gregory a quick hug then they both hurried across the garden to Nathaniel, who had crawled to shelter behind the remnants of the low wall.

'He was too tricky for me,' he wheezed, still in pain. 'He was quite mad.'

'Is he dead?'

Hannah shuddered. 'Yes, thank God.'

'And Tom?'

'Dead too, but oh, Nathaniel, he was so proud of having helped and he died happy.' Suddenly she burst into tears and could only hold her husband and sob because it seemed impossible that this dreadful night really was over, that they were safe now.

He managed to smile at Gregory over her shaking shoulders and the boy gave him a wavering smile in return. Then Nathaniel turned back to comfort Hannah, his wonderful, brave lass.

Two carts came jolting across the field and reinforcements tumbled out of them.

'Ah, bugger it,' a voice said. 'We're too late for the fun.'

'Quiet, please! Is Mr Oliver Dewhurst here?' the magistrate called.

Oliver stepped forward, his arm around his wife's shoulders.

'Your man delivered your letter and I brought help,' the lawyer told him.

Amazed that he'd made such a difference to the outcome, Oliver managed a faint smile. 'Perhaps we should all return to my house once you've secured our attackers?' But before he did anything else, he went across to Nathaniel and Hannah. 'I don't know how we'd have managed without you two. You undoubtedly saved my life between you, and to say I'm grateful is not nearly thanks enough.'

'What exactly is going on here?'

Oliver swung round as the Marquess of Iffingham strolled across the field to join them with an air of disdain.

'You know damn' well what's going on, you villain!' Oliver shouted, feeling anger well up in him.

The Marquess didn't even look in his son-in-law's direction. 'I heard the sound of shots nearby so came out to investigate.'

Gerald stepped out from behind him and introduced himself to the magistrate, then startled everyone by saying, 'My father was involved in planning this attack, as I can bear witness. He kidnapped my sister and another young woman, and hired the men who helped Walter Dewhurst. Many people in the village must have seen two of the men arrive in his company. And it was he who suggested Walter should kill his brother. I heard him.'

'He's lying!' the Marquess snapped, then growled in a low voice, 'Pull yourself together, Gerald! Think of the family.'

'I think I *have* pulled myself together, for the first time in years,' his son retorted. 'And what sort of family kills innocent people and breaks up happy marriages? Not the sort I want to belong to.'

Ann came to stand next to him. 'My brother isn't lying. My father did kidnap me, but Gerald helped me to escape tonight. Gerald, what about Ginny? Is she all right?'

He smiled at her. 'I think so. I accidentally forgot to lock the cellar where my father was keeping her, so I dare say that redoubtable old nurse of Oliver's will have taken her somewhere safe until the fighting's over.'

Nick pushed to the front of the crowd. 'Do you know where?'

'We're here,' Nanny's voice called from the wood at the far end of the field. 'And Ginny's all right.'

Nick set off towards them at a run.

'I think the principals should retire to your house, Mr Dewhurst,' the magistrate advised. 'I for one wish to know exactly what happened here.'

'I shall leave you to your enquiries then.' The Marquess turned away as if there was no question of himself being called to account and found himself facing a wall of men, the battered young villagers who'd helped guard Hannah and others who were strangers he didn't even recognise. He ignored the latter and spoke to the group he did know. 'If you value your jobs and homes, you'd be wise to stop meddling in matters which don't concern you.'

'They do concern us!' someone yelled. 'And we're not having you treat folk so badly any more.'

'You tried to have Mr Oliver murdered,' another called.

'An' you're a stingy bastard, too,' a third added, raising a few barks of laughter.

'I should be obliged, my lord, if you'd accompany us,' the magistrate said frostily.

'Certainly not!'

'Then I'm afraid we shall have to compel you.' He nodded to the constables.

Two of them moved forward and for the first time in his life the Marquess found himself being treated as an ordinary man. He tried in vain to free himself from their grasp.

'He'll get off if it comes to a trial,' Oliver predicted. 'He's rich enough and well-connected enough to hire the best lawyers, and will no doubt concoct a story to explain all this.'

The magistrate overheard him. 'I hope to prove you wrong there, young man. You won't change your mind about giving evidence to incriminate him, I trust?'

'Of course not.'

Thornton turned to the group of bystanders. 'I'd appreciate your continued assistance as we have so many prisoners.'

'We won't let 'em escape, your worship,' one man called.

The main protagonists left them and made their way towards Spinneys, all weary but knowing they had to explain exactly what had happened if justice were to be done.

Nick and Ginny joined them there, arms round each other's waist, and Nanny, seeing so many notables in her master's house, went straight to the kitchen to start a fire and make some nice hot tea. She needed a cup herself if no one else did.

When two young men from Marton peeped through the doorway, remembering their last visit and the refreshments they'd been offered there, she beckoned them inside and set them to work. With their help, she soon got a fire blazing and the big kettle moved over the hottest part of the hob. Other men came to join them till she found herself with a kitchen full of helpers.

One of them grinned suddenly. 'I've just realised, we won't have Walter Dewhurst as landlord at Marton any more.'

'He's a bit too dead for that,' another agreed.

'Who will we have, then?' a third asked.

'Well, Mr Oliver's the only Dewhurst left now, isn't he?' the first one said. 'Not that I've ever had much to do with him. Quiet sort of chap. He'll inherit, won't he?'

'I hope so. Nathaniel King thought well enough of him to fight for him, which says summat about him, as far as I'm concerned.'

'Mr Oliver's as good a master as anyone could want,' Nanny said, her voice thick with tears suddenly.

One of the men patted her awkwardly on the shoulder then another pointed out that the kettle was boiling and she pulled herself together, making up for her momentary weakness by speaking especially sharply as she gave orders for getting the tea things ready.

It was fully light before Nathaniel and Hannah were able to take the boys home to the cottage, leaving Ginny and Nick to follow at their own pace. Even Gregory was yawning and hardly said a word. Apart from the broken door, it all looked very normal. Tom's body had been taken away.

'Bed,' Hannah said firmly as they went inside.

There was a knock on the door and with a muttered, 'What next?' Nathaniel went to open it a crack, ready for anything. But he relaxed and opened it wider, holding a low-voiced conversation with whoever it was.

'They've taken Tom to lie in the church,' he said when he came back.

'That was a kind thought.'

'We'll give him a good funeral and a place in the churchyard. No pauper's grave for him after what he did for us.'

'He'd like that.' Tears filled Hannah's eyes again. 'Oh, Nathaniel, I thought you and Gregory were both going to be killed! If Tom hadn't stepped forward like that . . .'

He pulled her into his arms. 'It's all right now, lass. It's over.'

She clung to him. 'I can't believe what the past few months have been like.'

'All the troubles led you to me and for that at least I'm thankful.' He looked at her and, regardless of the audience, said firmly, 'I do love you, you know.'

'I love you, too.'

Gregory rolled his eyes at the other boys, who grinned back at him.

'If I weren't so tired . . .' Nathaniel whispered.

Hannah smiled, then became aware of their audience. 'Bed!' she repeated loudly. 'You three can sleep with us in the bedroom and we'll leave Nick and Ginny in here.' When they didn't move, she added, 'Even you can't say you're hungry after all the bread and jam you ate at Spinneys, Gregory King! I'm coming in there in five minutes and if you aren't asleep . . .'

He sighed loudly but led the way into the next room, stifling a yawn. Andrew paused at the door to throw Nathaniel and Hannah a shy smile then disappeared after the others.

'Maybe tomorrow we can move the boys into their own room?' Nathaniel said.

'Definitely.'

The glances they exchanged promised much.

Soon silence reigned in spite of the bright sunshine outside, and those in the bedroom didn't stir until well into the afternoon. Gregory was the first to get up and went into the kitchen looking for food. Hannah slipped out of bed to join him, staring in surprise at the covered dishes on the table. 'Where did these come from?'

'Neighbours brought them,' Ginny said. 'Wasn't it kind of them? We never had neighbours coming into the house at home. My stepfather didn't like it.' She blinked back a tear as this reminded her of her mother and Nick gave her a quick hug.

Nathaniel came out of the bedroom next, stretching and yawning, his hair rumpled and happiness shining in his face as he looked round at his family.

His nephews came out to stand beside him and when he ruffled their hair, they didn't flinch, just gave him more of those tentative smiles. 'It's good to have neighbours again, to be settled somewhere,' he said. 'But it's best of all to have a family to love. And that's what we are now, a family.'

Which brought tears to Hannah's eyes and made Ginny sob, but their smiles were soon back in place as they all sat down to eat a meal together with no shadows threatening their peace.

CHAPTER TWENTY-EIGHT

June

Ginny and Nick's wedding took place on the first Monday in June. The church was full of people from the village, there out of sheer curiosity. In the front to one side sat the family, and on the opposite side Mr and Mrs Oliver Dewhurst, both looking radiantly happy.

Next to his sister sat Lord Gerald, who was now running the estate while his father languished in prison awaiting trial. Her brother seemed, Ann thought, looking sideways at him, both taller and older since that dreadful night. Their eyes met and she smiled at him.

'All's well that ends well,' Gerald said quietly.

'It won't really end until the trials are over and sentences passed.'

'Whether he's convicted or not, our father's shattered by being held in prison. He looks years older. I think he's lost his venom now whatever the outcome may be. He is nearly seventy, after all.'

She shuddered. 'I hope I never have to see him again as long as I live.'

'Strangely, he expressed the same sentiments about you.'

'Yet *you* go and see him?'

'Well, it's fallen to me to hold the family together. Mother's not a scrap of use and the others say they'll have nothing more to do with him. I know he's a villain, but I can't just abandon him.'

The parson stepped forward, frowning round, though not daring to shush such august guests. When they were all silent, he gestured to the bride and groom to step forward. He made the ceremony as brief as he could, annoyed by all this fuss over two common youngsters who had pre-empted the sacred rite because of their lust for one another, and clearly didn't deserve to be happy.

When he'd grudgingly pronounced them man and wife, he led them quickly through to sign the register. Everyone else left the church, some villagers lingering outside for a few minutes, wanting to offer the newly-weds good wishes for the future. When that was done, the young couple led the way towards Spinneys, everyone having elected to walk to and from the church on such a beautiful sunny day.

As Hannah turned to follow the newly-weds she saw a figure come down the village street from the direction of the railway station and tugged at Nathaniel's arm to make him stop. 'I think that's . . . yes, it is!' She let go of him and began running down the street to fling her arms round the thin young man standing hesitantly there, a little child in his arms.

'Lemuel! What a lovely surprise!'

'I need to see you, Mam. I seem to have come at an awkward time, though.'

'It's never the wrong time for me to see my son,' she said firmly.

Nathaniel held out his arms. 'Come to me, little Johnny! I'm your new grandad.'

To Lemuel's surprise, his son gurgled with pleasure and let the stranger take him. When his mother linked her arm in his, he began to relax. Just to be with her made him feel better.

'Is it all over now?' she asked gently, knowing what had happened from his letters.

'Yes, Patty's buried – and her mother, too, next to her, because the poor old thing died a few days later. I've got Mrs Perry from the village coming in to help with John, but . . .' he hesitated. 'I wanted to talk to you. About the business. Only this is clearly not a good time and . . .'

But as usual his mother surprised him. 'You don't like running a business, do you, love?'

'No.' He stared down, walking a few more steps before looking at her, shame in his face. 'And I'm no good at it, either. I've had an offer to buy it and I've accepted it. I don't know what I'm going to do now, apart from raise my son, or even where I'm going to live.'

Nathaniel had been listening to them and intervened to say, 'We'll talk about that after the wedding feast. But it's clear to me you should come and live near us, lad, unless there's a good reason for you to stay in Hetton. Families should stick together.'

Lemuel blinked at him, overwhelmed by this warm offer and the kindness behind it from a man he barely knew.

'Come and join us for the wedding feast, then we'll talk afterwards,' Hannah urged, drawing him forward.

Lemuel still hesitated. 'They won't want me. I'm a stranger.'

'Of course they will. You're my son.'

During the wedding breakfast which had been provided at Spinneys she kept an eye on him, making sure he wasn't left standing alone, because apart from the fact that he'd always been shy with strangers, she could see he was in a very emotional state of mind. And he was so thin! She's have to feed him up.

As for little Johnny, Nanny soon found a way to take him off them and look after him, which made both her and the child very happy.

After the feasting was over and people started leaving, Oliver came up to Hannah and Nathaniel. 'Will you stay behind for a few minutes? We want to ask you something.'

So they sent Lemuel across to the cottage with the boys, because Ginny and Nick had gone off to spend a night or two in Preston, a wedding present from the Dewhursts.

'Come and sit down,' Ann said. 'It all went very well, didn't it?'

Hannah beamed at her. 'Yes. It's been a lovely day. And thank you so much for having the wedding feast here.'

'It was our pleasure. How nice that your son turned up today as well.'

'Yes. He's selling the cooperage. Poor Lemuel's no good at managing a business.'

'You two would be good at it, though,' Oliver commented.

Nathaniel looked at him in surprise. It seemed to him that both the Dewhursts had been brimming with suppressed excitement for days. 'Oh?'

'We have a proposition for you,' Oliver said. 'My lawyer has hurried things through and it's official now that I shall inherit Marton Hall and estate.' He pulled a wry face. 'I'm not sure how happy I am about going back to live there, but there's no one else. The good news is that Jack Lexham has agreed to act as my land agent again.'

'He's a grand chap,' Nathaniel agreed.

'But he says the work is too heavy for a man his age and he wants an assistant. He and I thought we'd offer the job to you, Nathaniel.'

Hannah had never seen her husband so lost for words. Ann smiled across at her sympathetically and they all waited patiently for Nathaniel to pull himself together.

'But I know nothing about the job.'

'You will by the time Jack's trained you. He thinks you'll do well, says you're a natural leader and good with figures. Well, we've seen your leadership skills for ourselves.'

Nathaniel looked at Hannah. 'What do you think, love?'

'I think we'll do whatever will make you happiest.'

'We're not taking no for an answer,' Ann said cheerfully, 'so you might as well say yes straight away.'

He smiled at her. 'Oh, might I? And if I do, what can I expect?'

'You'll receive an annual salary of two hundred guineas, plus a house and garden,' Oliver said.

'A house big enough for all your family,' Ann added.

'What about your son, Mrs King?' Oliver asked. 'I gather he's at a loose end now. Do you think he'd like to work with the estate carpenter? I've a lot of plans for improving my tenants' living conditions and will need more craftsmen.'

It was Hannah's turn to be speechless, then she tried to express her feelings. 'It's as though everything we've ever dreamed of has come true – and more.' Then it came to her. 'Why, these are real threepenny dreams!' And then she had to explain what she meant, everyone voting it a lovely idea.

Later she and Nathaniel walked across to the cottage hand in hand, not saying anything, not needing to. They found Lemuel and the boys waiting for them and explained what Mr Dewhurst had wanted.

'Hurrah!' Gregory shouted at once. 'I can go back to my old school in Marton. You'll like it there, you two.'

As his cousins nodded uncertainly, Hannah wondered how long it'd take to build up some confidence in them. But if anyone could do it, her Nathaniel could.

Only when the children had been sent to bed did Lemuel pull something out of his pocket. 'I thought you'd like to read this in private, Mum. It's from our Malachi.' He put the letter into her hand, bent to kiss her cheek and whispered, 'You're the best mother ever.' He then left them alone because he and his son were sleeping at Spinneys in the next bedroom to Nanny Parkin.

She unfolded the letter and read it, tears of joy in her eyes as she learned how much Malachi loved living in Australia. Then with a gulp she flung her arms round Nathaniel's neck and wept on his shoulder.

'Nay, then! Nay, then!' he said when the tears had

lasted for a long time. 'We've had enough crying.'

With a sound that was half-sob, half-laugh, she drew back a little. 'I don't think I've ever been so happy in my whole life.'

'Well, no one would guess it from the way you've been weeping all over me.'

'It's just too much happiness to take in at once.'

'I'll have to see that your life stays that way, then you'll get used to it.'

'Oh, Nathaniel, I don't expect miracles.'

'I do, now that I've met you.'

In the bedroom they no longer shared with his parents, Gregory whispered to the others, 'It's gone silent out there. I bet they're kissing and cuddling again. Ugh!'

'I like to see them doing it,' Edwin said.

'I bet you'll grow up as soppy as them!'

They gave each other mock punches, rolling round laughing until Nathaniel opened the door and yelled at them to shut up and go to sleep. When he'd closed it, he held out his arms to Hannah. 'Come to bed now, my lass.'

They settled down in their own bedroom which was shabby but with the roof finally fixed at least.

Cradling her face in his hands, he kissed her deeply and lovingly, then began to caress her.

She had thought she would be too tired to love him, but found she was responding to his lightest touch and soon began her own shy exploration of his body – not an old man's body, slack with years of over-eating like her first husband's had been, but a firm, vigorous body.

With Nathaniel, lovemaking soared to the heights of

ecstasy and they both cried out in joy before relaxing into a final tired embrace.

Afterwards, with a muttered, 'I love you,' he slipped into a deep sleep.

Hannah lay awake for a while longer, still warm and happy from her husband's embraces and from the joys that seemed to have been heaped on her head today. No dream that she'd ever allowed herself could have lived up to what she had now.

And maybe, if life was good to her and Nathaniel, she'd see Malachi again one day. People did travel to Australia for visits, she knew. In fact, that would be her new dream from now on. It was a sixpenny dream, she admitted to herself with a wry smile, but if Nathaniel did well as a land agent, surely they'd be able to afford it one day when the lads had grown up?

Anna Jacobs is always delighted to hear from readers and can be contacted:

BY MAIL

PO Box 628
Mandurah
Western Australia 6210

If you'd like a reply, please enclose a self-addressed, business size envelope, stamped (from inside Australia), or an international reply coupon (from outside Australia).

VIA THE INTERNET

Anna has her own web domain, with details of her books and excerpts from them. She invites you to visit it at http://www.annajacobs.com

Anna can be contacted by email at
anna@annajacobs.com

If you'd like to receive email news about Anna and her books every month or two, you are cordially invited to join her free announcements list. Just email her and ask to be added to the list, or follow the link from her web page.